## IRISH CHAIN

"A terrific whodunit! The dialogue is intelligent and witty, the characters intensely human, and the tantalizing puzzle keeps the pages turning."

—Jean Hager,
author of *The Redbird's Cry* and *Blooming Murder*

"A blue-ribbon cozy . . . This well-textured sequel to *Fool's Puzzle* . . . intricately blends social history and modern mystery."
—*Publishers Weekly*

## FOOL'S PUZZLE

*Nominated for an Agatha Award for Best First Mystery*

"Characters come to full three-dimensional life, and her plot is satisfyingly complex."
—*The Clarion-Ledger* (Jackson, Mississippi)

"Breezy, humorous dialogue of the first order."
—*Chicago Sun-Times*

"I loved *Fool's Puzzle*. . . . [Earlene Fowler] made me laugh out loud on one page and brought tears to my eyes the next. . . . I can't wait to read more."
—Edgar Award–winning author Margaret Maron

*Berkley Prime Crime Books by Earlene Fowler*

FOOL'S PUZZLE
IRISH CHAIN
KANSAS TROUBLES
GOOSE IN THE POND
DOVE IN THE WINDOW
MARINER'S COMPASS
SEVEN SISTERS
ARKANSAS TRAVELER
STEPS TO THE ALTAR
SUNSHINE AND SHADOW
BROKEN DISHES

# GOOSE IN THE POND

EARLENE FOWLER

BERKLEY PRIME CRIME, NEW YORK

This is a work of fiction. Names, characters, places, and incidents are either the product of the authors' imagination or are used fictitiously, and any resemblance to actual persons, living or dead, business establishments, events, or locales is entirely coincidental.

GOOSE IN THE POND

A Berkley Prime Crime Book / published by arrangement with the author

PRINTING HISTORY
Berkley Prime Crime hardcover edition / May 1997
Berkley Prime Crime mass-market edition / March 1998


For information address: The Berkley Publishing Group,
a division of Penguin Putnam Inc.,
375 Hudson Street, New York, New York 10014.

The Penguin Putnam Inc. World Wide Web site address is
http://www.penguinputnam.com

ISBN: 0-425-16239-7

Berkley Prime Crime Books are published
by The Berkley Publishing Group,
a division of Penguin Putnam Inc.
375 Hudson Street, New York, New York 10014.


PRINTED IN THE UNITED STATES OF AMERICA

15 14 13

*For Allen*
*your love sustains me*

# *ACKNOWLEDGMENTS*

Always my thanks to:

The Father, Son, and Holy Spirit—Isaiah 53:5; Deborah Schneider—an agent with grace and class; Judith Palais—editor extraordinaire—can I call you Wonder Woman, can I?; Christine Hill—bookseller and my first friend in San Luis Obispo—for feeding me, housing me, comforting me, and making me laugh—and to her family, Jim, Kate, and Adam Hill, for welcoming me into their lives; Joy Fitzhugh—rancher, good friend, and rebel general in the War of the West—for sharing with me her life, her home, and her delicious homemade jerky; Abbott and Lorna Fitzhugh—for their kindness and wonderful stories; Karen Gray—dear friend, expert quilter, and the best dang deputy district attorney in San Luis Obispo (or anywhere)—for opening her home and her heart—and to David Gray, her husband, who always kept smiling when dead bodies were discussed (in detail) over dinner; Jim Gardiner, Chief of Police, San Luis Obispo—for good-naturedly answering my sometimes convoluted questions, and to Elaine Gardiner—for her hospitality and friendship, and giving me the real scoop on being a chief's wife; the fine folks at the San Luis Obispo Police Department, District Attorney's Office, and County Sheriff's Department; for moral support and patient endurance of my whining—Ginger Matthews, Jo-Ann Mapson, and Doris Land; Debra Jackson, my sister—for generously creating quilt squares on demand; my TLC group—for their prayers and friendship—Stu Anthony, John Catlett, Kay & Marvin Foster, Marguerite & Lorin Zechiel, Steve Zinner; my husband, Allen—'cause I wouldn't have nothin' if I didn't have you.

## GOOSE IN THE POND

***Like many old quilt patterns, Goose in the Pond was probably inspired by nature, giving us a hint at the playful and creative imaginations of early quilt designers. Seen as far back as the early 1800s and made from a combination of tiny squares, triangles, and strip blocks, it emulates the ripples created by a goose swimming across a body of water. Any colors and fabric may be chosen for this pattern, as Goose in the Pond, like a beloved folktale, lends itself well to individual interpretation. Thought to have originated in Massachusetts, it is also known throughout different parts of the country as Toad in the Puddle, Young Man's Fancy, Mexican Block, Patchwork Fantasy, Bachelor's Puzzle, Unique Nine Patch, and Scrap Bag.***

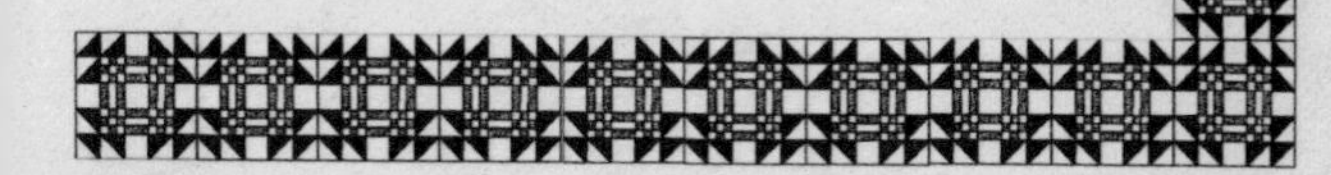

# 1

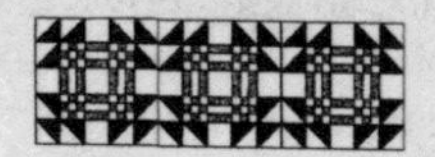

"I HATE THIS," I said, my breath coming in short, painful bursts. "It's unnatural."

"You'll learn to love it," Gabe said, his baritone voice encouraging.

I frowned up at him. "God never intended the human body to endure agony like this. I don't care what you say—this is *not* fun."

"We have all the right equipment for it." He reached over and patted my backside. "Yours is cute, and we want to keep it that way."

I swatted at his hand. "Watch it, Chief Ortiz, or I'll have one of your men arrest you for lewd and lascivious behavior."

Laughing, he sprinted ahead, then turned around to face me, jogging backward. After a mile and a half, he'd barely broken a sweat. Above us, a swirl of salty early-morning wind rattled the tops of the peeling eucalyptus. Pine trees scented the air with a sharp, lung-cleansing scent. "Benni, sweetheart, you're getting close to middle age. Your heart and other significant parts of your body need the aerobic exercise."

"I'm *not* middle-aged. I plan on living until I'm a hundred, so I won't be middle-aged for fifteen years. Besides, I'm riding three times a week now that I'm helping Grace down at the stables. That's aerobic exercise.''

He gave a derisive laugh. ''Sure, for the horse.''

I slowed to a walk, looking down at the obscenely white hundred-twenty-dollar Adidas he'd talked me into buying. The bright orange stripes glowed in the pale California sunshine. For that much money, they should have come equipped with tiny oxygen tanks. I leaned against a sycamore carved with a heart and the words JULIO LOVES HIMSELF and held my aching side. ''I can't go any farther. Please, let me die in peace.''

He trotted up beside me. ''Quit whining and turn around.''

I obliged and instinctively arched toward his hands as they kneaded my neck and shoulders, groaning out loud at the pleasurable feel of his strong fingers pressing deep into my muscles. He bent down and ran his bristly mustache down my damp neck, tickling it lightly with his tongue.

''Don't tempt me like that in public, *querida,*'' he whispered. ''I'm used to hearing those sounds when I've got you flat on your back and naked.''

''You arrogant—'' I clenched my fist, turned, and aimed for his stomach. He saw it coming and tightened his muscles. Those days at the gym were obviously helping. It was like hitting a concrete block.

''Ow,'' I said, shaking my hand. ''Do you realize you think about sex way too much for a *middle-aged* man?''

His blue-gray eyes, a startling anomaly against his tanned olive skin, sparkled with amusement. ''I'm telling you, it's the vitamin E. Not to mention how attractive you look in those shorts. I'm going around the park one more time. Want to join me?''

I glanced down the gravel trail we'd just run around Laguna Lake, one of the major attractions of San Celina's Central Park. ''No, thanks. I think I'll walk back to the car and get some money to buy duck food.''

He checked his watch. ''See you in about fifteen

minutes.'' He took off down the trail at an easy jog.

I watched him until he disappeared into the heavily wooded park. After almost seven months of marriage, the sight of his lean, powerful body could still make my heart beat faster. But he had lost ten pounds in the last month, and it showed on his six-foot frame, narrowing his face and causing his already prominent cheekbones to sharpen. Though I tried not to show it, I was worried. His mood had been light and cheerful lately. Too light and cheerful. Four weeks ago, his best friend, Aaron Davidson, San Celina's former chief of police and Gabe's first partner when he was a rookie cop, died from liver cancer. It was the Sunday before Labor Day weekend. We had just visited him at the hospice before attending a barbecue at my dad's ranch. Later that evening, Aaron died, his wife, Rachel, dozing at his side. Gabe accepted his friend's death with quiet dignity and no fuss, helping Rachel with the funeral arrangements and giving a eulogy at the service that left most of the congregation, including a bunch of tough, cynical cops, in tears. He had taken care of all the millions of irritating but necessary details that arise when someone dies. Esther, Aaron's daughter and only child, told me they would have never made it through those first few weeks without Gabe's calm, gentle strength. What no one knew but me was that he'd never taken the time to grieve himself. And still hadn't. And that worried me.

I peered out over the Laguna Lake. The waterline was higher than usual this year due to the heavy spring rains that flooded most of California. The Central Coast had taken a particularly harsh beating. In North County, many of the small tourist-supported towns had experienced massive damage in their trendy art galleries, restaurants, and vineyards. Half the cattle roads on Daddy's ranch had washed away, and Gabe and I had spent most of our spare weekends helping clear them with his Kubota tractor. Luckily San Celina's new library resided safely on a high bluff overlooking the lake. Morning sun glinted off its dark tinted windows, causing a ripply reflection in the brown muddy water. The gray, prisonlike structure continued to win all sorts of architectural awards, but even a year after its completion, people still grumbled and complained about its land-scarring ugliness. Behind it rose the late September hills of San Celina, mountains of butterscotch gold marching all the way to the Pacific Ocean five miles away. I glanced back at the library. It was closed on Sundays, and the park was still relatively empty. Gabe and I had passed only two other people on our jog around the lake—an elderly man and woman walking a basset hound. But in the parking lot there were now three more cars parked next to Gabe's sky-blue 1968 Corvette. I smiled at the license plate frame I'd had made at the mall for our six-month anniversary. GABE AND BENNI—IN LOVE FOREVER. With a good-natured shake of his head, he'd attached it to his car. Apparently he'd taken quite a bit of ribbing about it from his officers at the police department.

"So I'm crazy about my wife. Sue me," he'd told them, according to his new secretary, Maggie, who kept me informed on all the office scuttlebutt.

After a long drink of bottled water, I stole a handful of parking-meter quarters from his glove compartment and purchased some veterinarian-approved duck chow from the dispensers the city had recently installed. The humane society and local wildlife lovers, concerned for the wild bird population's long-term health, were attempting to discourage people from feeding them processed bread and junk food. The blue-and-white Wonder bread wrappers floating in the marshy grasses of the lake testified to the fact that they hadn't quite persuaded everyone yet.

I stuck the pellets into the pocket of my zip-up sweatshirt and headed down to the lake, where I was enthusiastically greeted by a contingent of local waterfowl. The speckled brown ducks, white geese, and nervy seagulls were old hands at being fed by sentimental human beings and assumed that any person walking near the lakeshore was automatically a soft touch. As I tossed bird feed out to them they crowded around my feet, nudging each other aside like jealous schoolchildren. My thoughts drifted back to Gabe and how both our lives had radically changed in the last year.

It had been a little over a year and a half since my first husband and childhood sweetheart, Jack, was killed in a senseless car accident involving too much liquor and a split second of young, foolish judgment. A lot had happened in my life since Jack died—losing the ranch we owned with his brother, moving to San Celina and making the transition from being an "aggie" to a "townie," landing the job as curator to the Josiah Sinclair Folk Art Museum and Artist's Co-op, meeting Gabe in the circumstances surrounding a murder at the museum, falling in love, and getting married after knowing each other barely three months.

"You've certainly lived life this last year like it's going out of style," my Gramma Dove said yesterday when I was out at my father's ranch helping her put up a batch of peaches. Though technically she is my paternal grandmother, she treats me more like a not-quite-bright-or-especially-responsible youngest daughter. That's because my own mother died twenty-nine years ago when I was six years old and Dove moved out from Arkansas to help her oldest son, Ben, my father, raise me. Lugging my thirteen-year-old uncle Arnie, the youngest of her six children, her fabric and yarn collection, her favorite Visalia saddle, and her almost complete set of Erle Stanley Gardner books, she took charge of the Ramsey Ranch household and has, with cast iron claws, ruled the roost ever since.

"Well, Gabe's been through a lot more than me," I said, screwing the lid on the twenty-first jar of peach preserves.

"That's the gospel truth," she said, pouring me a glass of sweetened iced tea. "Comin' here thinking he was just going to stay a few months and ending up taking the police chief's job, all them murders, and then marrying you, which, Lord knows, would be life changing enough for any man—''

''Hey, just a minute—'' I protested.

She ignored me and kept going. ''Then there was that nasty business in Kansas with his friend and now Aaron passin' on. And didn't you say he hadn't heard from his boy in a while? Heavens, by now a lesser man would have hightailed it to the hills to howl and lick his wounds.''

''He is under a lot of stress,'' I agreed. ''And not hearing from Sam for five weeks hasn't made it any easier.'' Gabe had finally grown used to the idea that his eighteen-year-old son, Sam, had dropped out of UC Santa Barbara and was working in a surfboard shop on Maui while trying to find the perfect wave. They'd even managed an amicable phone conversation or two in the last month. Then, when Gabe called the shop to break the news about Aaron, some clerk said Sam had quit six days before, and no one knew where he was. Gabe had discreetly used his law-enforcement connections, but so far there was no sign of Sam. ''Gabe won't talk about it, but I know he's worried.''

''Kids,'' Dove said, shaking her head and spooning more cooked peaches into a Mason jar. ''Dang little heartbreakers. Every last one of them. Ought to line 'em all up when they're twelve and smack 'em with a wet rope just for the heartache they're gonna give you.''

''Please, spare me the dramatics,'' I said wryly.

''Ain't nothin' dramatic about it. I've spent over fifty-five years of my life worrying about one youngun or another. I'm seventy-six years old and I deserve a break.'' She was referring to my uncle Arnie from Montana, who'd moved in on Daddy and her four months ago because his wife had finally kicked his lazy butt out. He and my father argued like two polecats tied at the tail, and Dove was getting fit to send them both to Alaska. Permanently.

A brazen peck at the toe of my Adidas brought me back from my musing. A green-necked mallard gave a brassy quack and ruffled his neat wing feathers. He'd pushed ahead of all the dull brown girl mallards and was demanding more than his fair share.

"Men," I said, throwing him the last of my food just because of his noisy persistence. "You're all so pushy." He honked again, and I showed him my empty hands. "That's all, buddy." He gave me a disgusted look and waddled away.

The sky flushed a salmon pink, and the sun peeked through the dense trees, warming the chilly air a few degrees. I dug around in my sweatshirt pocket for a rubber band and pulled my curly shoulder-length hair into a high ponytail. While I picked my way along the marshy shoreline, my mind drifted over the other problems facing me this week.

The folk-art museum was hosting the first San Celina Storytelling Festival in connection with our latest exhibits—a display of story quilts designed by California quilters and in our newly remodeled upstairs gallery, a collection of Pueblo storytelling dolls on loan from Constance Sinclair, great-granddaughter of our museum's namesake as well as our temperamental and very rich benefactress. It was a joint effort with the San Celina Storytellers Guild. We were all keeping our fingers crossed and hoping it would show a profit and consequently turn into an annual event. Storytellers from as far away as Reno, Nevada, and Yuma, Arizona, were registered for the festival, which started this Friday night at six o'clock.

We obtained permission from the city to turn the large empty pasture next to the museum into a temporary campground so the visiting storytellers didn't have to spend much for accommodations. Our shoestring budget had been augmented by a community arts grant from San Celina County, advertising and booth space sold to local merchants, and a generous sum from Constance Sinclair herself, who had recently taken a fancy to the art of storytelling thanks to the influence of her niece, Jillian. I'd arranged for portable restrooms, trash removal, booths for the artists to sell their crafts, and volunteer docents to give tours of the exhibits.

The three-day event was turning out to be the biggest project the museum and co-op had ever attempted. Everything had run smoothly . . . so far. The co-op board and the board of the Storytellers Guild had gotten along as well as you could expect from a bunch of temperamental artists. It helped that some of the storytellers were also co-op members. They were the ones I unabashedly begged to serve on the festival committee.

A loud quacking distracted me again. From my shoreline perch, I peered toward the sound into the brush and reeds hugging the shore. It was the high, frantic call of a bird in trouble. Just last week, Gabe and I had to free a seagull's wing from a plastic six-pack carrier left by some littering idiot. I moved through the tall grasses toward the panicked screeching, my shoes making soggy depressions in the soil. The sounds seemed to radiate from an undergrowth of trees drooping over the water. A thick forest of cattails rustled. Water splashed and fluttered; brown wings flashed. I glimpsed a movement of something white and blue in the algae-covered water. Someone had dumped a load of trash that had trapped a helpless bird. Unfortunately the whole mess was just far enough into the lake to be out of my reach.

I made a disgusted sound and glanced at my new Adidas. Removing them and wading into the cold ankle-deep water was one option, but I'd be risking more than expensive jogging shoes. People were also known to throw away beer cans, broken bottles, and other objects dangerous to bare feet. I looked around for a stick. After a few seconds of searching, I found one that appeared long enough and stretched out as far as possible. I was at least a foot short. The squawking grew more frantic. There seemed to be no choice but to brave the lake. The first step was the worst; freezing water rushed into my shoes and instantly soaked my socks. Mud swirled around my ankles like milk in black coffee. A mental picture flashed through my mind of Gabe's irritated expression when he saw my once pristine shoes. He'd think I did it on purpose to avoid jogging. The idea certainly had merit. It *was* possible I might not get around to replacing them for a very long time.

The small female mallard's wing was trapped by a piece of white cloth snared in the underbrush and covered with swamp grasses. I prodded the pile until the duck sprang free and swam away quacking indignantly. Idle curiosity caused me to poke around a bit more. Then I felt my stomach drop.

A hand floated up from the mound.

I moved closer and used my stick to push away the brush covering the body. It moved gently in the murky water; a strand of blond hair trailed out like dark yellow seaweed. A leg clad in red-striped tights appeared. The edge of a long blue dress covered with a once white apron clung like glue to the lifeless form. My stomach seesawed again.

I knew who it was.

A scream rose instinctively from my diaphragm. I stifled it by sticking my fist in front of my mouth and slowly backed out of the water.

When I touched solid ground, I scrambled up through the trees toward the trail. When I reached the trail, I broke into a flat-out run for the parking lot. The rhythmic *squish, squish* of my soaked shoes matched the pounding of my heart. *Find Gabe,* I repeated silently over and over. *Stay calm. Find Gabe.*

*Oh, Lord,* I prayed. *Oh, no.*

I knew who it was.

The ruffled apron, the striped stockings, the long blond

hair usually worn in a bun and covered with a pouffy blue-and-white hat. It had to be Nora Cooper, the library's weekly storyteller and the older sister of a college friend, Nick Cooper, who was also the library's head reference librarian. Nick and Nora Cooper. Their mother had been a great fan of the old mystery series featuring the urbane detecting couple and their dog, Asta. Her enthusiasm had doomed her two children to a lifetime of lame jokes.

Nora Cooper. I'd become better acquainted with her in the last few months since planning the storytelling festival. Who would want to kill her? She was a tiny, even-tempered woman who loved children and adored her storytelling job at the library. She'd been one of the first people who'd volunteered to be on the festival committee, and that alone made me immediately view her with goodwill. She was a dedicated worker who wasn't afraid to push up her sleeves and do the most menial jobs—ones I often got stuck with because the artists always seemed to have some project they absolutely needed to finish. She and I single-handedly typed and affixed two thousand address labels to the bright pink festival brochures. I'd come to appreciate her amusing and often piercingly accurate observations of artists, children, library patrons, and the various members of the library staff itself. She was scheduled to appear twice at the festival this weekend. Her specialty was nursery rhymes, and she'd worked up a popular act that included songs, participatory dancing, and puppets she'd designed and sewn herself. She always dressed up in the same costume, one that fit her theme perfectly.

Who in the world would want to kill sweet little Nora Cooper?

For cryin' out loud, who would want to kill Mother Goose?

# 2

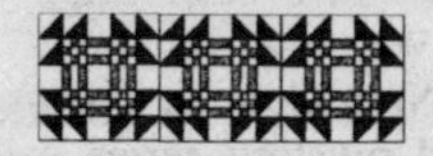

MORE TIME HAD passed than I realized, because when I reached the car, Gabe had already returned. He'd been waylaid by two attractive young women in their late twenties wearing ovary-squeezing spandex shorts and matching sport bra tops. The taller one said something and playfully shook a fuchsia nail at him, tossing her tawny mane of hair. He gifted her with an amused smile, then tilted his head and drank deeply from a dripping liter of Evian water. The two women stared at his sweat-shiny body as if he was the last cream puff in the bakery and they'd been dieting for six months.

"Excuse me," I said, pushing through the middle of them. A strong waft of musky perfume almost gagged me. "Gabe, we need to talk." I kept my voice genial and smiled, trying to keep the panic off my face. I knew this was something he would want kept quiet until he got backup. I shifted from one foot to another, my shoes making a gross sucking sound. They all looked down at my wet, stained Adidas. The lion-haired woman's top lip curled up slightly in disgust.

"Hi, Mrs. Ortiz," said the shorter one, an auburn-haired woman with thick, sexy eyebrows. "We were just telling the chief about the underwear bandit in our apartment complex. He sneaks into our laundry room—"

"That's great," I said, still smiling. "Make a report, and I'm sure he'll get one of his detectives right on it." I grabbed his forearm in a steel grip. "Gabe, we *need* to talk."

The short woman looked at her friend and raised her eyebrows. The friend giggled in response. Then she turned back to Gabe. "See you at work tomorrow, Chief Ortiz." She smiled with all her shiny white caps and waggled her fingers at him before sashaying away.

"Jealous, Ms. Harper?" Gabe teased. "The redheaded one is our new records clerk. I think the other one works for the mayor."

"Gabe." *Take a deep breath,* I told myself. Gold stars sparked at the corners of my eyes. "Gabe—" My voice choked.

His face sobered. "Sweetheart, what is it? Are you okay?" He grabbed my shoulders and scanned me up and down. "Did someone—"

"I'm fine. It's just that . . . there's a . . ." I swallowed hard. "A body."

"What?" His face turned to granite and immediately went into what I call his Sergeant Friday look. "Where?"

"She's over here." I broke away and started back toward the lake when he caught me by the upper arm.

"Wait, let me get my cellular. I can call the station while we walk." In a low voice he snapped orders into the compact phone as he followed me through the marshy brush. When we reached the scene, I pointed to Nora's partly submerged form. The sun had moved out from behind the jagged early-morning clouds and was brighter now, glistening on the greenish film that coated the gently moving water. Other than that, nothing had changed since I'd been here ten minutes before. Of course, what did I expect? Nothing was going to change for Nora ever again.

He flipped the tiny black phone closed. "Backup will be

here in a few minutes." He pulled me to him in a quick, warm hug. "Are you okay?"

"Yes," I said, shuddering slightly in his embrace.

He tilted my face up with his hand and peered worriedly into my eyes. "I'm sorry you had to see this, but you're going to have to hang tough a little longer. Tell me what you saw and everything you did."

I told him about the trapped duck and how much of the debris I'd poked away with my stick. Before I could tell him I thought it was Nora Cooper, the library's storyteller, a couple of patrol officers pushed through the trees. The first one to reach us was Miguel Aragon, my best friend Elvia's second-to-youngest brother. At twenty-four years old, with a forty-four-inch chest and a loaded 9mm automatic on his hip, it was hard to believe Elvia and I had, as young teenagers, dressed him up one Halloween as a teapot and taken him trick-or-treating. His rendition of "I'm a little teapot, short and stout" sung in the heart-melting soprano of a five-year-old netted us a lot of full-sized Hershey Bars and a few silver dollars.

"What's up, Chief?" he asked, using his artificially deep, professional cop's voice. He nodded at me. "Benni."

I lifted up a hand. "Hey, Miguel."

"Drowning, possible homicide," Gabe answered in his clipped, unemotional cop's voice. "We need to get some tape strung here. Take it all the way to the top of the trail. I don't want anyone getting close to the scene. You and Williams need to keep the spectators back. Johnson and Rodriguez will be here in a few minutes to assist. Careful where you walk."

"Yes, sir." He turned and spoke to his partner, a freckle-faced kid who didn't even look old enough to buy cigarettes.

"Stand over there," Gabe said to me, pointing to a flat piece of ground. "I'm going to try to locate the point of entry and look for footprints." He swore softly in Spanish as he surveyed the dense woods. "This is going to be practically impossible."

Within the next hour, the small area became bumper-to-bumper with crime-scene personnel. On the trail above us, a large group of gawkers had formed. It was close to ten o'clock now and people had started arriving at the park for after-breakfast walks or to claim a spot for noontime picnics. The *San Celina Tribune* had obviously heard about the murder. A bleary-eyed reporter was already harassing the cops for a statement. The somewhat more liberal *Central Coast Freedom Press* had also sent a reporter, a young man who looked as if he should be working on Cal Poly's college newspaper. A fresh-faced female reporter in a navy power suit from our local TV station KCSC and her camera person was ready for whenever they could maneuver Gabe into giving an official statement. He was going to look real cute on the local evening news dressed in his faded black running shorts and gray San Celina Feed and Grain "Give Your Bull the Best" tank top. The reporters jockeyed for position behind the yellow crime-scene tape, reminding me of Dove's Rhode Island Reds when she fed them every morning.

Gabe walked over and rested a warm hand on my neck. "I'm going to be here awhile. Go on home and get out of those wet shoes."

"There's one more thing," I said. "I think I know who it is."

"What?" He frowned in annoyance. "Why didn't you tell me this before?" His tone was accusatory. Holding back information from each other had been a problem between us since the beginning of our relationship, and although we'd both gotten a bit more open, there was still an occasional trickle of distrust. On both sides.

"I was getting ready to tell you when Miguel got here," I said, exasperated. "Since then, you've been just a *little* preoccupied."

Instantly contrite, he ran his hand over his face. "I'm sorry, it's just . . ." His voice trailed off, and he gestured at the busy crime scene.

"I know." I laid a hand on his forearm. As much as the old-time residents, he hated how violent crime on the Central Coast was becoming a more frequent occurrence. That was one of the reasons the city council had implored him to accept the job of chief of police last February. San Celina needed the experience of someone who'd dealt with homicide and other violent crimes on a daily basis, as Gabe had during his twenty years with the LAPD.

"So, who is she?" he asked.

"If it's who I think it is, her name is . . . was Nora Hudson . . . uh . . . Cooper."

"Hudson or Cooper?"

"She goes by Cooper now, though I'm not sure if it's official. She's getting a divorce and she mentioned changing back to her maiden name."

"You know her?"

"She works as a storyteller at the library. She dresses like Mother Goose. That's her . . . well, theme, I guess you'd call it."

"That explains the odd-looking clothes. Anything else?"

"I've known her since college. She's a couple of years older than me. Actually, I know her brother better."

"Who's he?"

"Nick Cooper. He's head reference librarian."

He raised his dark eyebrows. "Nick and Nora?"

"Yeah, pretty hokey. Their mother loved old mysteries apparently."

"Do you know her parents' address?"

"They're dead. It's only her and Nick. He lives over by your old house on Houston Street. I don't know the exact number. He's in the phone book, though." I felt a stab in my heart. "Who's going to tell him?"

"Probably Jim, once he gets here and I can give him the

particulars.'' Captain Jim Cleary was Gabe's right-hand man. He was an even-tempered black man in his late fifties whose easygoing personality was the perfect counterbalance to Gabe's sometimes fiery temper and stubborn perfectionism. A couple of months ago Jim organized a weekly basketball match between the young patrol officers and older, higher-ranked officers with the loser having to spring for pizza and beer at Angelo's Big Top Pizza downtown. Invariably the senior officers lost, which boosted the morale of the patrol officers immensely. That small activity had gone a long way toward establishing a stress-relieving camaraderie within the ranks. Jim was subtly teaching Gabe that strong leadership and a sense of humor were not mutually exclusive.

''What's her ex-husband's name?'' Gabe asked. ''Does he live around here?''

I looked down at the ground. This was already getting complicated. ''Roy Hudson. He's a member of the co-op and the Storytellers Guild. He lives with my friend Grace.''

''Grace?''

''Grace Winters. She owns the stables where I ride.''

Gabe's face looked thoughtful.

''What?'' I asked.

He shook his head as if it were nothing. ''Why don't you go on home? I'll pass your story on to the detectives. You can come down to the station tomorrow and give an official statement.''

''Okay,'' I said, glad to get away. ''What time will you be done?''

''I have no idea. I'll try to keep you posted.''

''Want me to bring you some other clothes?''

He looked down at his outfit and gave me a rueful smile. ''Why don't you drop them down at the station? That's where I'll be heading after this.''

''I'll bring you some lunch, too.''

"Great. Don't talk to the reporters and be careful driving home."

"Yes, sir, Chief Ortiz," I said, backing away from him. "Is it me or the Corvette you're worried about?"

His mustache twitched in a half smile.

"Jerk," I mouthed.

I ducked under the yellow tape and was instantly pounced upon by a reporter from the *San Celina Tribune*. The yuppie reporter who accosted me was intent on one thing—furthering his career by scooping the *Central Coast Freedom Press*. He wore a brownish tweed jacket and black Levi's. His blond hair stood up in wet-looking spikes revealing a clean pink scalp.

"Mrs. Ortiz, it's rumored you found the body. Can you tell us what happened? Do you know who the victim is? How were they killed?" His photographer, a tall, big-shouldered woman wearing ragged overalls and a red tank top, aimed her lens at my face.

"Ms. Harper, and no comment," I said automatically. Then I added in the interest of good public relations, "Sorry."

"Is the victim male or female? Was there any mutilation? Do you think it's the work of a serial killer?"

"Excuse me." I pushed past him. When he realized he wasn't going to get anything from me, he scurried back to the edge of the crime scene, where he was kept at bay by a couple of burly San Celina police officers.

During the drive home I thought about Nora, wondering who would kill her. Could it possibly be a random crime? The thought sent ice crystals through my veins. Serial killers hadn't touched the Central Coast yet, and I hoped they never would. It seemed unlikely, though the alternative was just as frightening—being murdered by someone she knew. That instantly brought to my mind her soon-to-be-ex-husband, Roy Hudson. He would likely be first on Gabe's list of suspects, and that troubled me. Roy, though a bit of a redneck at times, was basically a nice guy. He was also one of the best farriers in the county. More importantly, I'd grown fond of Grace while riding at her stable these last few months. Though her and Roy living together and united against Nora, whom I also liked, was certainly not a situation I approved of, when I was with each of them, I kept my opinions to myself. Since all three were involved with the storytelling festival, I'd attempted to keep their paths from crossing too often.

I wondered how soon Nick would be notified. Should I call him or drop by? What *was* the proper thing to do when a friend's family member is murdered and you're the person who found the body?

At home, Mr. Treton, my iron-spined, elderly neighbor, was clipping the hedge separating his two-story gray and blue Victorian house from my Spanish-style bungalow. I'd rented the neat, two-bedroom house when I moved off the Harper Ranch into town. It was perfect for one person, with square little rooms and a newly remodeled terra-cotta-and-white Southwestern tile kitchen. After Gabe and I married, he just sort of moved in his clothes and books, gradually mingling our possessions. Unfortunately he'd not planned on getting married when he came to San Celina and had paid for a year's lease on a woodframe house over by Cal Poly. It had a huge garage and a yard full of mature shade trees; we'd discussed living there, but my house was closer to our jobs and homier, with all my quilts and mismatched antiques, so we nonverbally seemed to have decided on it. The lease on his house was up at the end of September, and he still had some things he hadn't moved yet, though I'd subtly nagged him about getting to it. One thing that was still there was his stereo and a good part of his extensive collection of Southern jazz and blues CDs. I suspected there was a deeper motivation than laziness that kept him from moving everything he owned into my . . . our house.

I carefully steered the Corvette into the narrow driveway.

My own vehicle, a red 1977 one-ton Chevy pickup with HARPER'S HEREFORDS in chipped lettering on the doors, sat out on the street, having lost the honored driveway spot to the Corvette. Inside our minuscule one-car garage reigned the real star of our vehicular family, the newly restored blue 1950 Chevy pickup that Gabe's father had owned and we'd had shipped back from Kansas two months ago.

"Hey, Mr. Treton," I said, climbing out of the car. "Hedges are looking good."

He grunted and continued trimming with his beat-up hand clippers. No newfangled, fancy electric ones for Mr. Treton. "Just another way the electric company's trying to rip off honest Americans," he'd grouse. He was a thirty-year army man who believed insubordination from anyone, including plant life, needed to be promptly nipped in the bud.

"Talked to your grandmother lately?" he asked, his clippers never stopping their *clop, clop, clop.*

"Not since yesterday," I said, smiling good-naturedly. He knew Dove checked up on me almost every day. She used to say it was because I needed watching over since I was living alone in the city and didn't have the sense God gave a duck. Now that I had the personal protection of the chief of police, she said she had to make sure, in the interest of public safety, that I wasn't driving Gabe too crazy. "Do you need something?"

"All out of honey," he grumbled. He'd grown addicted to Dove's fresh clover honey when she used it to bribe him into giving her reports on my daily activities. She didn't require his detecting services any longer, but Mr. Treton still craved the honey.

"I'll swipe you a couple of jars next time I go out to the ranch," I promised. He nodded his thanks and attacked a rebellious mock orange tree.

Inside the house I kicked off my ruined shoes and peeled off my wet socks, gave them a satisfied smirk and padded across the room where the answering machine winked its red insect eye. A well-known and mostly well-loved voice brayed out, practically melting the wax in my left ear.

"Where are y'all?" Dove asked. "Benni Harper, it's seven o'clock in the morning, and you haven't gotten up this early since you left the ranch. If you're there and occupied, call me when you're through. And you take it easy now. Gabe's ticker isn't as young as yours."

I snickered and didn't rewind the tape so Gabe could hear Dove's comment on his sexual endurance. Only my grandmother would have nerve enough to tease him that way. Glancing into the bedroom where the sheets and thin blanket were shoved in a tangled heap at the foot of the king-sized bed, I had to say she knew us better than we'd probably like to admit.

I went into the kitchen and grabbed a Coke before returning her call. With everything that had just happened, I suspected it would be a long and detailed conversation. Back in the living room, I picked up the cordless phone and settled down on the brown tweedy sofa, but before I could dial, it rang.

"Benni, help," a panicked voice wailed. "She's back."

"No one here by that name," I said, and hung up.

# 3

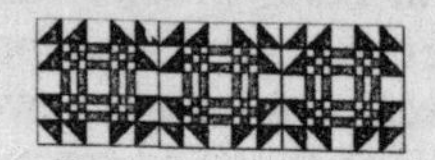

SECONDS LATER, THE phone shrilled again. I waited three rings before reluctantly picking it up, knowing without a doubt that trouble lurked at the end of this line.

"Very amusing, young lady," Dove said. "If you were still living within spittin' distance of me, I'd be taking you out behind the barn with a hickory switch."

"Have to catch me first," I said smugly.

"Don't think I can't."

An arrow of panic shot through me. "She's not here already?"

"No, thank the Lord. We pick her up at the airport tomorrow. She says she's done left W.W. for good." She paused for emphasis. "Again."

"She" was Dove's only sister and only sibling, Garnet Louann Wilcox. She and Dove, though they loved each other to pieces, got along about as well as two porcupines in a gunnysack. W.W. (pronounced in the way that only Southerners can—Dubya, Dubya) was, or rather is, Garnet's husband, William Wiley Wilcox. They'd been married fifty-three years, all of which time, Uncle W.W. was *the* plumbing contractor of choice in the Sugartree, Arkansas, area, about fifty miles north of Little Rock. After fifty-five years, he'd finally retired to live out his dream, designing and building custom-made yard fountains. According to

Dove, who, much to her dismay, was getting semiweekly updates, Aunt Garnet and Uncle W.W. were having difficulty getting used to being around each other all day. It sounded like the pressure had finally gotten to both of them and Aunt Garnet decided to take a powder. Except for her only child, Jake, in Pine Bluff, whose wife, Neba Jean, had absolutely forbid Garnet to ever cross the threshold of their mahogany-paneled three-story split-level house again, poor Aunt Garnet had nowhere else to flee. Her only other close relative was her granddaughter and Jake and Neba Jean's only child, my cousin Rita. Last we all heard, Rita was traveling the rodeo circuit in an old Winnebago with her bull-riding husband, Myron "Skeeter" Gluck.

"What are you going to do?" I asked.

"You know, we're so busy with this remodeling and what with the house all torn up, I was thinking—"

"Not a chance, Dove," I interrupted. "Gabe and I are still newlyweds. And I've got the storytelling festival this weekend and now there's this murder that Gabe has to worry about . . . and since when are you all remodeling?"

"I've been considering it," she said defensively. "Now's as good a time as any to start. What murder?"

We temporarily shelved the subject of Aunt Garnet while I told Dove about Nora Cooper and my morning's gruesome discovery.

"Her mama made the best apple pan dowdy," Dove said, tsking under her breath. "This would've tore her heart to pieces."

"I guess I should go visit Nick. We only see each other occasionally now, but we were good friends in college."

"Take some banana bread," Dove advised. "Or a fruit pie."

"Okay, I'll drop by the bakery."

Her pointed silence admonished me. Dove didn't approve of anything bought in a bakery, especially if you were taking it as a token of sympathy. "Your generation," she was always harping at me. "Y'all are too lazy to pick your own teeth."

I ignored the disapproving vibes floating over the phone lines and asked what Daddy and Uncle Arnie thought about Garnet's visit.

"When they heard about it they lit out of here like two fresh-branded calves. Haven't seen 'em since. And now that we're back on *that* subject—"

"Gotta go," I said. "I need to buy that pie. Call you later." I hung up while she was still sputtering, knowing I'd pay big time for that little bit of bravado. In our family there were two sets of rules—the Ten Commandments and Dove's Rules of Order. I had just broken one of the biggies—cutting her off when she was in the middle of cajoling you to do something. When she didn't call me right back, I knew I was really going to get it, that she was plotting big time. That meant I'd never see it coming.

After a quick shower and change into clean Wranglers, a plain white T-shirt, and my old brown Ropers, I grabbed up Levi's and a pale yellow polo shirt for Gabe. I pointed the pickup toward Blind Harry's Bookstore and Coffeehouse in downtown San Celina. My best friend, Elvia Aragon, manager and head *honcha* of the bookstore, would most likely be there, even though Sunday was technically her day off. She'd kill me if I didn't tell her about my morning's activities before she heard it on the news. Grimacing at my poor choice of mental words, I maneuvered for a precious parking space in our already congested downtown shopping area. The influx of people moving into San Celina County and shopping downtown had been great for the merchants, but heck on the local residents, who were accustomed to finding a parking space on the first try. I pumped my last quarter into the meter, attempting to be a model, law-abiding citizen now that I was the police chief's wife.

Blind Harry's Bookstore resided a block away in part of

a two-story brick row building that once held the offices of San Celina Trust and Savings, an institution that bit the dust during the 1929 stock crash. Until six years ago, it had been a bookstore called simply San Celina Books and Stationery. Then Cameron McGarry, a mysterious Scottish man who owned casinos in Reno, a cattle ranch in Wyoming, and oil wells in Oklahoma, acquired it during a drive through town. He bought it as a whimsical tax write-off and hired my friend Elvia as the manager for peanuts, probably feeling very smug and politically correct for accommodating two minorities in one fell swoop. It warmed my heart to watch her blow his socks off. Under her fair but somewhat military-style management, she built Blind Harry's into the most popular and profitable bookstore/coffeehouse between Los Angeles and San Francisco. Her success story had been written up twice in the *L.A. Times,* once in the *San Francisco Chronicle,* and in numerous Latino newspapers.

The basement coffeehouse, lined with floor-to-ceiling bookshelves packed with used books free for the borrowing, was crowded for a Sunday. The antique mantel clock on the Hemingway shelf had both hands lifted in surrender, reminding me of my promise to bring Gabe lunch. I ordered an avocado, Jack cheese, and alfalfa sprout on cracked wheat bread and scanned the chattering crowd for Elvia. She sat in a back corner at one of the round oak tables, her dark head bent over three-inch thick sheaves of computer printouts. Though she had a beautiful office upstairs complete with French Country antique furniture, all the latest computer equipment, and soundproofing, she still preferred to do much of her paperwork downstairs in the coffeehouse. She claimed the noisy conversations relaxed her, that complete silence was too distracting after all those years living with six brothers.

''No rest for the wicked, huh?'' I flopped down on one of the oak ladder-back chairs she'd purchased for a song when they refurnished the new library. The only way you could tell it was her day off was she wasn't wearing one of her many Chanel-Armani-Donna Karan power suits. Instead she wore black leggings, Italian leather flats, and a flowing café au lait silk blouse that probably cost more than my truck's new clutch.

"*Hermana gringa,* you have no idea. What's up? I thought you and *tu esposo el chota* were out building lung capacity this morning."

"I'll have you know I jogged a whole mile and a half."

"And?" Her liquid voice held a hint of laughter.

"Is it too late for an annulment?" I asked with a dramatic groan.

She pointed a French-manicured nail at me. "I warned you about getting hitched up with a Latino man. They want to run your life like they're five-star generals and you're a buck private with no chance of advancement. Not to mention he's a cop. And a cop in management."

"Ah, he's not that bad," I said, grinning. "Besides, I never could resist being sweet-talked in Spanish."

"Tramp," she said, taking a sip of her iced cappuccino. "You just married him for the great sex."

"Shh," I said, putting my finger over my lips. "He thinks I married him for his fascinating personality and government pension."

She rolled her luminous black eyes, and we were both giggling when José, Blind Harry's cook, brought over my order and told Elvia briefly that they were running low again on almond-flavored Tortani syrup.

"Double the order next time," she told him, then raised her eyebrows at me. "What's with the food to go?"

I stopped laughing, suddenly feeling guilty for making jokes after having discovered only hours earlier the body of someone I'd known and liked. But as Gabe once said, people joked automatically to protect themselves. Especially those who saw man's inhumanity to man on a regular basis.

"If cops didn't," he'd told me, "they wouldn't last a year. That's why you hear so much grotesque humor at crime scenes. If any of us contemplated emotionally at the moment what really happened and how it could happen to us or to someone we love, we'd end up eating our guts or our guns." His blue-gray eyes turned dark with sadness. "Some cops lose that ability to disengage, and that's what they do. Too many."

Elvia's face instantly sobered. "Benni, what's wrong?"

I hugged myself, running my hands up and down my upper arms, trying to smooth out the gooseflesh. "You remember Nora Cooper, don't you?"

Her brows furrowed in concentration, smoothing out when they placed the name. "Nick Cooper's older sister. He works at the library, right?"

"Head reference librarian. Nora works there, too."

"What about her?"

"She's dead."

"That's too bad. Was she sick?"

"No, she drowned. It might be murder." I grabbed her cappuccino and took a large gulp. She could tell I was upset so she didn't harp like she normally would about me drinking out of her glass. I set the glass mug down, my hand shaking slightly. "I found her body."

Elvia pushed her computer printouts aside and leaned closer. "Tell me what happened." Her shiny black hair caught the overhead light and flashed. It reminded me of Nora's lifeless strands floating in the water. I closed my eyes for a moment.

"Benni," Elvia said softly. "Do you want to go up to my office?"

"No," I said, opening my eyes. "I'm fine."

Remembering my single quarter's worth of parking time, I gave her the condensed version. I finished her drink as I talked, and suddenly realized when I was through that I was ravenously hungry and deliriously happy to be alive.

Survivor's guilt pricked at my conscience, that small relieved voice whispering, "Aren't you glad *you* weren't the one who died?"

"Would you like another one?" she asked. She held up the glass mug and motioned at the counter clerk to bring us two more.

"I can't stay long," I said. "This is Gabe's lunch. He hates eating the food they order when they're working on an investigation. It's always pizza or hamburgers or some junk food. And I'm bringing him a change of clothes."

"How's he taking it?"

I rested my chin in my palm and sighed. "Like he does everything, stoically, *professionally*. He really doesn't need this right now."

"And exactly when does a person *need* a murder investigation in their life?" she asked ironically.

"You know what I mean."

"Yes, I'm sorry. I don't mean to be facetious." She and I had discussed my worries about Gabe, the strain he'd been under the last few months with his friend's death in Kansas and now Aaron's death and how he never spoke of either of them. She viewed his quiet reticence with more dispassion than me. Not only because he wasn't her husband, but because she was accustomed to the Latino male's way of handling emotion.

"He's reacting exactly how any of my brothers or my dad would," she assured me. "He'll come around eventually or work it out in his own way."

"He seemed a little more open when we got back from Kansas, then Aaron died, and he's . . . well, he's not exactly depressed. It's just like it never happened. I don't think holding things in necessarily works them out. I think people need to talk about their feelings."

"That's your Southern background. All you people *do* is talk. But does it really help? You all are just as crazy as the rest of us."

I gave her a weak smile. ''Sometimes crazier.''

She wrinkled her nose delicately, reminding me of a fussy, purebred cat. ''Well, I didn't want to actually say it—''

''You know as well as I do talking about things is healthier, but I guess you're right. He'll come around in his own time. I know when Jack died I didn't want people poking at me to do things.'' I sipped the iced coffee drink the clerk set in front of me. ''On the other hand, sometimes it was what I needed, you and Dove pushing me back into life before I thought I wanted to go. A person isn't always their own best judge of what they need.''

''Go feed him,'' she said, pushing the white sack toward me. ''Mama says if you can't do anything else for a man, you can always feed him.''

I laughed and stood up. ''I love your mama. I need to visit her soon.''

''This week,'' she said firmly. ''She's been complaining about not seeing you enough. Are you going to visit Nick?''

''Yeah, I'm going to drop by the bakery and get a pie.''

''Give him my condolences. I'll send some flowers.'' She gathered up her computer printouts and stood up. ''I'd better do it now before I forget.''

''I'll call you later and let you know what happened.''

I took my cappuccino over to the counter and asked the clerk to pour it into a paper cup and added a just-baked apple turnover to Gabe's lunch. As the clerk added it to my tab I heard my name called out over the buzz of the crowd. Peter Grant stood up and waved at me. I grabbed my sack and maneuvered my way through the noisy room to his table.

Peter and I had known each other most of our lives. His parents once owned one of the largest almond orchards in North County. We met in 4-H and had shared lots of Cokes and baskets of greasy chili fries at the MidState fair while hanging out waiting for our animals to be judged. In college, we took a different route. My major had been American history with a minor in agriculture. His was environmental studies, emphasis on the radical. When his family was forced to sell the orchard after a few bad years and move to San Francisco, Peter remained on the Central Coast. He managed the small mountain sports store he'd worked at since college, taught mountain climbing on the side, and fought passionately for the rights of spotted owls, redwoods, and gray wolves. An avid rock and mountain climber, at thirty-seven he very rarely wore anything but shorts, T-shirts, and hiking boots. He had that yuppie outdoorsy look that, had he been taller, could have made him a lot of money posing for Eddie Bauer catalogs—a trim, muscled body, healthy brown hair, clear brown eyes, skin tanned a glowing ocher. Today he wore a pale tan T-shirt depicting a house with a red circle and slash painted over it and the words SAVE OUR OPEN LANDS. He was at the forefront of the fight for zero development and a permanent greenbelt surrounding San Celina. He'd recently added storytelling to his hobbies, and naturally his stories had a strong environmental emphasis. The troubled look distorting his even features told me he'd heard about Nora.

He wasn't alone at the table. Next to him sat Ashley Stanhill, another local storyteller and current president of the San Celina Storytellers Guild. Ash and I had worked closely together promoting the storytelling festival. A traditional Southern storyteller, he could tantalize an audience with his smooth-as-Black-Velvet Mississippi accent and sinfully sensual smile. He'd only lived on the Central Coast a little over a year, but according to the co-op's warp-speed grapevine had already managed to break more than a few female hearts. There was nothing particularly special about him—medium height, russet hair, deep blue eyes. You'd never look twice at him when he walked down the street except for thinking that maybe he bore a passing resemblance to the actor Dennis Quaid. But when he turned his attention on you, it was like you were the most perfect specimen of woman God had ever created. I'd been to one of his storytelling sessions, and though the children were held rapt by his silky-voiced performance, the women were absolutely mesmerized.

Peter gestured to the chair across from him. Ash nodded solemnly and sipped his espresso, his blue eyes observant as a cougar's.

"I suppose you both heard," I said, sitting down, then added quickly, "I can't stay long. I'm taking lunch over to Gabe at the station."

"Did you really find her body?" Peter asked, his normally calm face mobile with agitation. A faint sheen of perspiration coated his cheeks.

"Unfortunately, yes," I said with a sigh.

"We've called an emergency meeting of the festival committee. We're going to meet at the museum." He glanced at his black diver's watch. "I told them two o'clock. I wasn't sure how long it would take me to reach you. I tried calling, but no one answered."

"You must have just missed me. I have an answering machine."

He waved his hand irritably. "I refuse to give in to the control the industrial complex is gaining over our lives through the addiction to useless environmentally destructive machinery."

I shrugged. I understood what he meant, but with that attitude he was going to miss a lot of messages.

"Old Pete here wishes we'd go back to sendin' smoke signals with a bonfire and a blanket," Ash said, giving me a conspiratorial wink. "More environmentally responsible. At least until the EPA shut it down."

"Shut up, Ash," Peter snapped. "This is a disaster. Our guild's first storytelling festival, and it has to be overshadowed by Nora Cooper."

I leaned back in my chair, shocked. I thought he was upset because of Nora's murder when apparently it was only the festival he was worried about.

"Let's talk about it at the meeting," I said sharply. "We can also discuss how we all might give some support to her brother, Nick."

His face flushed slightly, and he looked down at his blunt rope-callused hands, avoiding my gaze. "I didn't mean it the way it sounded."

"Good, because it sounded pretty heartless," I said. "See you at two."

There was a space free in front of the police station, a tan stucco building with a gurgling beige-and-blue tile fountain that local college students occasionally filled with detergent. If you exchanged the plain San Celina Police lettering for the word PODIATRY, no one would even bat an eyelash. Since it was Sunday, I knew the lobby door would be locked, so I walked around back to the maintenance yard and pressed the red buzzer. A young officer with greenish-blond hair and a bad cold opened the gate and informed me that Gabe was in his office.

The oak door to Gabe's office was closed. I stood for a moment and studied the brass plaque that had replaced Aaron's only a few months ago: GABRIEL ORTIZ—CHIEF OF POLICE. Its permanent look wrapped around my heart like a flannel quilt. Removing Aaron's name from the door had been a big step for Gabe. I was glad he did it before his best friend died. It would have been a lot harder now.

Gabe was leaning back in his black leather executive chair talking on the phone. He rested the bottoms of his running shoes on the edge of the glossy oak desk in a less-than-professional position, especially in his cotton running shorts. I set the white paper sack and his clothes on the desk in front of him and waved hello before settling down in one of his padded office chairs. He gave me a welcoming smile and continued to talk on the phone. Or rather listen.

Whoever it was on the line was chattering like a hysterical parakeet, and Gabe answered with an occasional "Yes, I understand. No, sir. Yes, sir, I certainly will." He swung around and stared at the picture on the wall behind him, another gift from me. It was a black-and-white framed poster of Albert Einstein sitting in a wing chair, his fingers threaded loosely in his lap, giving the photographer a slightly bemused look. Printed above his feathery white hair was a quote that made Gabe throw back his head and laugh when he read it—GRAVITATION CANNOT BE HELD RESPONSIBLE FOR PEOPLE FALLING IN LOVE.

He swung back around and hung up the phone, giving it a dark scowl.

"Who was that?" I asked, pushing the lunch bag toward him. "Here, eat. What do you want to drink?" I went across the room to his small oak-paneled refrigerator. The choices were limited. "Looks like it's water, grape soda, or water." I made a face. Welch's grape soda. There were some things about this man I'd *never* understand.

He stood up and stretched. "Give me a Welch's. I know I need to restock. The Neighborhood Watch commanders cleaned me out yesterday."

I handed him a frosty purple can. "Who was flapping their gums at you over the phone?"

"The mayor, who else?" He popped the lid and sat back down. "He's upset about this murder, of course. He's up for reelection next year and he wants to run on a get-tough-on-crime platform." He unwrapped his sandwich, a weary expression on his face. "That means my life is going to be miserable for the next year. And right before he called, the city manager called and gave me his nickel's worth. They both want this murder solved as quickly as possible."

I perched on the edge of his desk. "That's certainly an obvious sentiment. I think everyone would like it solved fast. Did she drown?"

"No. The medical examiner's first assessment was that

she was killed somewhere else and dumped in the lake."

"Why does he think that?" I leaned over and picked a slice of cheese off his sandwich.

"The rope ligature marks around her neck are a slight hint."

"You mean like rope burns? She was strangled by a rope?"

"Very good, Detective Harper. Now, thanks for lunch, but don't you have something you need to attend to? Maybe planning a gourmet dinner for your hardworking husband?"

I reached over and snagged a slice of avocado. "I'm guessing that's your not very subtle way of telling me I'm asking too many questions. And Chief Ortiz, the only gourmet dinner you'll be getting this week is the one you're holding in your hands. I'm up to my ears in storytellers and artists, not to mention I got a phone call from Dove this afternoon."

"And?"

"You'll never guess who's back in town." I reached for his sandwich again. He held it away from my grasp.

"If this is all I'm getting, then I'm not sharing. Who's back in town?"

"Aunt Garnet. Or at least she will be as of tomorrow. She and Uncle W.W. are on the outs. Dove's having a hissy fit over it. Aunt Garnet's visit, that is, not their marriage woes."

"The infamous Aunt Garnet," Gabe said, chewing thoughtfully. He took a long drink from his grape soda, then grinned at me. "Well, they're *your* family. I'd help, but as you can see I'm going to be extraordinarily busy the next few days. Sorry." He set his can down on his desk blotter, not looking the least bit remorseful.

"Don't act so smug," I warned, slipping down off his desk. "If Dove has her way, Aunt Garnet will be staying with us. And believe me, if you think Dove meddles—"

He reached over and pulled me between his legs. "*Querida,* I have complete confidence in your ability to maneuver around your grandmother. Now give me a kiss and run along like a good girl. I've got work to do."

I bent down and kissed him, nipping him sharply on his bottom lip.

"Ow!" he said, jerking back. "That hurt."

"Then don't talk so condescending to me, Friday, or the next time I'll draw blood."

He laughed and ran his hands over my hips. "What makes you think that's a turnoff?"

"You're a real sicko, Chief." I gave him a real kiss that time. A slow, lingering one. "What time will you be home?" I eventually asked.

He rubbed the back of his neck. "Who knows? You know how these things go. As soon as I get changed, Jim and I are going to head over to the sheriff's crime lab and wait for some test results. Looks like it might be a long day. What do you have planned?"

"There's an emergency meeting of the festival committee at the museum at two o'clock. I ran into two of them when I dropped by Blind Harry's. They're very upset about Nora's murder."

His face grew sharp and questioning. "What are their names?"

"Peter Grant and Ash Stanhill."

"That first one sounds familiar."

"He's very active in environmental rights here in San Celina. You've probably seen his name in the newspaper. He and his friends would love for all the ranchers and farmers to just donate all our land to the public trust. Of course, I don't know what he expects us to do for a living or where in the world he and his vegetarian friends would get their broccoli and salad greens, not to mention the leather for their Birkenstocks—"

He interrupted me. "Did they know Nora Cooper well?"

"Peter did. We all went to Cal Poly together. She was a few years older than us. I don't know if Ash knew her well but I could casually ask—"

Gabe stood up and rested his hands firmly on my shoulders, squeezing them in warning. "No."

Before I could answer, a knock sounded on the door. "Come in," Gabe called out.

The door opened, and Jim Cleary's head appeared. "Am I interrupting anything?" He gave us a wide, white smile.

"Nope, Benni was just leaving," Gabe said evenly. He kissed the top of my head. "See you tonight. Stay out of trouble, *niña*."

I rolled my eyes at Jim. "You promised me that you'd have that arrogant macho stuff trained out of him by now."

Jim stepped into the room. He was wearing dark slacks, a pure white dress shirt, and a conservative striped tie. He was head deacon at St. Stephen's Baptist Church over near the lake where Nora was killed, and from the looks of his attire, he'd been called straight out of church services. He held up his hands. "I never made any promises. You know there are some cases that even fasting and prayer won't help—only a miracle straight from the Good Lord Himself." He gave me a broad wink.

"Amen, Brother Cleary," I replied.

"You get in here," Gabe said good-naturedly to Jim, then pointed at me. "And you beat it."

It was one o'clock when I left the police station, and I decided to make a quick pit stop at home to use the bathroom and scrounge in the refrigerator for a bite to eat. Standing in front of the refrigerator, I was chugalugging a can of Coke and trying to remember just how old that enchilada from Pepe's was when the doorbell rang. I tossed the aluminum tray in the sink, not entirely certain whether those green specks were peppers, and answered the door. I stared up into a darkly tanned, high-cheekboned male face wearing a dazzling smile that would have buckled my knees had I been fifteen years younger.

"Hi, Mom," he said. "What's for dinner?"

# 4

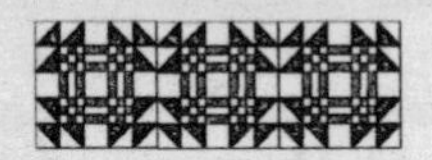

I WAS SPEECHLESS.

He tilted his head and lifted one dark brown eyebrow in question. His friendly, open expression reminded me of a sweet-natured Irish setter we'd had on the ranch when I was a girl. Reddie was a terrible ranch dog with the bad habits of sucking eggs and chasing calves, but he had a perpetually happy spirit that could make even the grumpiest ranch hand crack a smile.

"This is the Ortiz residence, isn't it?" he asked, his smooth young face turning slightly worried. He scratched his cropped brown hair and looked down at the envelope in his hand. He flashed his brilliant smile again. "You're Benni, aren't you? I'm Sam Ortiz, your stepson."

"Uh, yes," I finally managed to say. My mind started darting in a million directions. Gabe's son? Here? Now? This was all he needed. Aaron's death, Nora's murder, his errant son showing up on his doorstep. The bright yellow duffel bag sitting at his feet was huge, as if it contained all his worldly possessions. A surfboard in a lime-green nylon cover leaned against it. I glanced behind him. No vehicle except the Corvette in the driveway. How did he get here? How long did he plan to stay?

His eyes flicked over my shoulder into the house. "Can I come in?"

"Oh, yes, of course. Come on in. It's great to finally meet you." I held out my hand, and he enveloped it with a large cool hand that felt so much like Gabe's it startled me.

We stood in the middle of the living room without speaking for a minute or so. My mind was still speeding a hundred miles an hour. Sam took my disorientation in stride and quietly inspected his surroundings while I tried subtly to study him. He was dressed in the loose, faded jeans common to his age group and a bright turquoise Hawaiian-patterned T-shirt that complemented his glowing burnt-sienna tan and muscled biceps. Gabe's first wife, Lydia, was a full-blooded Mexican-American, and Sam had inherited her chocolate-colored eyes and a skin tone darker and more coppery brown than Gabe's. He was taller than Gabe by an inch or so, and except for his well-developed arms, still had the slim boniness of a late-adolescent male. When he and his muscles matured, he was going to be a very striking, formidable-looking man. Like his father.

"Do I have mustard on my chin?" he finally asked, still smiling.

I shook my head and felt my neck turn warm. Apparently I'd been as subtle as a clown. "I'm sorry. You don't look much like your pictures, and we weren't really expecting you. . . ." I gave him an apologetic look. "I'm usually much better with surprises. It's been a rough morning. Your dad's going to be just thrilled—"

He interrupted me with a cheerful laugh. "Benni . . . can I call you that? I was kidding about the mom part. You're way too young to be my mom."

I smiled at his shameless compliment. He'd certainly learned better than his father that a little charm can go a long way in easing an awkward situation.

"I know my dad, Benni, and thrilled he *won't* be. That's okay. I'm his only kid, and he's stuck with me." He fiddled with the small gold hoop in one ear. I could already hear

Gabe grumbling about *that*. "I hate to bother you, but could I have a glass of water?"

"Oh, sure," I said. "Do you want something else? We have Cokes and orange juice, and I'm not sure what else."

His eyes brightened. "Got any grape soda?"

I groaned. "Forget the blood tests. You *are* Gabe's son."

In the kitchen I filled a glass with ice while trying to decide what course of action would be most prudent. Call Gabe? Let him walk in on Sam without warning? Take off for the hills while there was still time? I glanced at my watch. It was twenty minutes until two. If I left now I'd just make it to the museum in time. The meeting shouldn't last longer than an hour or so and most likely Gabe wouldn't come home until later tonight. I could be at the door to meet him before he even saw Sam. I couldn't imagine how I was going to break it to him short of "Guess who's coming to dinner?"

I walked back into the living room carrying the purple soda. Sam was studying the wedding portrait Gabe and I had taken in Las Vegas. It hung on the wall next to Sam's formal high-school graduation photograph, back when he was earring-free and a year and a half younger. That pudgy young man didn't look at all like this handsome, lean-faced surf bum standing in my living room. He turned around when he heard me walk in.

"I can't believe you trapped my dad. Ever since I was eleven, when he and Mom got divorced, he never dated a woman longer than a month or two. What did you do, cast a spell on him?"

"Here." I shoved the glass into his hand. "Why is it everyone always assumes that *I* trapped *him*? Doesn't it ever occur to anyone that it might be the other way around? Believe me, he's no garage-sale Rembrandt." I felt myself flush again. *Good job, Benni. Very mature. You've known this boy exactly three minutes and you're already trashing his dad.*

"Hmm, the dove has talons." He took a long drag off his drink. "I see now why you attracted him."

I glared at him. He responded with a wide innocent smile. It wouldn't have worked except for the purple mustache staining his upper lip. I burst out laughing. Why should I hold it against this kid just because his father and I had such transparent pathologies?

"I bet you drove your parents crazy as a child."

"Past tense?" he answered, sitting the glass on the table. "So, where is my dad anyway? Don't tell me he's working on a Sunday?"

I picked up my purse. "Unfortunately he is. There was a homicide this morning down at Laguna Lake. He probably won't be home until late and he'll be pretty upset." I hesitated, then said, "Sam, your father tried to call you a few weeks ago—"

Sam lifted his hands in entreaty. "I know, I know, I should have left a number. But I was all bummed out 'cause my girlfriend broke up with me. I went to stay with a friend who had a house on Kauai. His phone was disconnected, and like I said, I was so bummed out 'cause of this chick—"

"Sam, he was trying to call because of Aaron."

Sam's face grew still. His throat rippled with a tiny convulsion. "He died, didn't he?"

I nodded. "I'm sorry. Rachel was with him. And your dad and Esther saw him just hours before. The funeral was three weeks ago."

Tears pooled in Sam's dark eyes, and I was amazed to see one slowly roll down his cheek. "Aaron was a good guy. He taught me how to dive when no one else could." He impatiently swiped at his cheek. "I never thought he'd . . . how's Dad taking it?"

"I'm not sure," I said honestly.

"In other words, Mr. Tough-Guy-Show-No-Emotion. Right?" A tinge of bitterness etched his words.

I didn't answer. He obviously knew his father's personality, but *I* didn't know Sam well enough yet to discuss Gabe with him.

"What about my mom? She and Rachel were good friends at one time. Before the divorce."

"She couldn't come to the funeral. She apparently couldn't get an important court date changed since Aaron wasn't an immediate family member." I touched his forearm. "Sam, I have an emergency meeting I have to attend. Are you going to be okay?"

He shrugged, feigning coolness though a faint sheen of water still coated his eyes. "Yeah, sure. I saw him the last time I was here. And it doesn't much matter about the funeral. I don't really believe in them and I'm sure dad handled it perfectly, like he does everything. He didn't need *me*."

I didn't contradict his statement, though I wasn't sure of its accuracy. Maybe Sam was just what Gabe had needed. At any rate, this whole father-son thing was beyond my area of expertise and was something that, like it or not, Gabe was going to have to deal with. I gestured down the hallway. "The guest room is on the right. You can put your stuff in there. Feel free to eat whatever you like. I'll pick up some groceries after my meeting. Like I said, I don't know when Gabe's going to be home, and he won't be in the best mood when he does."

"Worry not, *madrastra*. I can handle my dad." He flopped down on Gabe's new cordovan leather recliner, pushed himself all the way back, and crossed his feet. He wore faded blue Vans with no socks. "Don't forget, I've had a lot more practice than you." He grinned up at me.

I smiled back. *Madrastra*—stepmom. Elvia's youngest brother, Ramon, called her that whenever she tried to mother him. A term of endearment if said in the right way. It didn't take long for this kid to winnow his way into a person's heart. I could only hope his irrepressible charm and the love I knew Gabe felt for him would outweigh his transgressions.

"I'll see you in a couple of hours, then," I said.

"I'll hold down the fort," he called back, his voice as confident and easy as if he'd known me forever.

Five vehicles were in the museum's gravel parking lot when I arrived. That meant almost everyone was there. I sat in my truck for a moment and swept my eyes over the museum's buildings. They looked spit and polished and ready for a party. The terra-cotta roof of the two-story Spanish hacienda looked especially nice since we'd cleaned all the tiles and replaced the broken ones. The bougainvillea bush hugging the top of the long wooden porch bloomed in a fiery spray of red-and-orange leaves. Thanks to a group cleanup day, there wasn't a shrub or bush untrimmed or a wilted petal in any of the oak-barrel planters filled with wildflowers. I reminded myself to buy film for the museum's camera and take a picture of the buildings while they were looking so great. These days, I was feeling pretty smug because I'd finally found an assistant who could keep the museum grounds looking this perfect even if acquiring him had been none of my doing. He had been recommended to me by one of our quilters, Evangeline Boudreaux.

"D-Daddy might well be seventy, but he can outwork you and me, yes, ma'am," she'd told me about her father in her French-tinged south-Louisiana accent. "And he sure could use someplace to go every day."

"D-Daddy?" I said, laughing. "Is that his real name?"

"Oh, his given name is Michel, but everyone's called him D-Daddy for as long as I can remember. He's one tough old rooster and a real hard worker. He'll be fixing stuff before you even knew you wanted it fixed."

So three months ago, her father, D-Daddy Boudreaux, started his second career as my new assistant, and the museum and I were both the winners. No equipment ever stayed broken longer than a day, and except for the heavy lifting, which the men in the co-op took over, D-Daddy ran the museum with the no-nonsense vigor of someone who'd commanded a commercial fishing boat for thirty-nine years. I always teased him that he was after my job.

"Now, now," he'd say, shaking his favorite Sears Craftsman hammer at me. "Don't nobody can take your place, no. You just go on now and take care them artists. Let D-Daddy do what he do best."

As I stepped up on the porch D-Daddy came out of the museum's double Spanish doors. He ran his palm carefully over his thick white wavy hair. That hair, according to Evangeline, was his one area of pure vanity.

"He spends more money on hair products than Dolly Parton," she said, poking absently at her own wavy black hair.

D-Daddy's dark eyes widened with pleasure when he saw me. "*Ange!*" he said. "*Comment ça va?* A tragedy, no? Nora was such a sweet girl."

"I'm fine, D-Daddy," I said, smiling at the nickname he gave me the first time we met—angel. He'd said my hazel eyes and unruly reddish-blond curls reminded him of the pictures of angels in his *grandmère*'s old family Bible. "It is sad. But Gabe's working on it now. If anyone can find her killer, you know he will."

His dark brown eyes sparkled mischievously. "With a little help from his *ange gardien,* eh?" He hitched up his gray work pants and followed me into the museum. The storytelling quilts were all hung, and by the looks of it, he'd been polishing the framed histories of each exhibitor.

I laughed and shook my head. "No way. I don't need a divine revelation telling this guardian angel to stay out of it. Believe me, he'll be in no mood for anyone stepping out of line, especially now." I told him about Sam's unexpected appearance.

He picked up a clean white cloth and bottle of Windex.

''It's a hard road, father and son. But is good for the chief. He too shut down, that one.'' He clucked disapprovingly, sprayed glass cleaner on the cloth, and ran it along the top of a frame.

''No argument from me on that front,'' I said. ''Is everyone here?''

''Out back. They be already fightin' like cats and dogs. You best get in there before there don't be no storytellers to be tellin' the stories come Friday.'' He pointed upstairs where the new exhibit area displayed Constance Sinclair's prized collection of Pueblo storytelling dolls. ''I'll be up the stairs cleaning. Anyone get outta line, you just holler, and D-Daddy come runnin'.''

''Thanks, but I think I can handle this group.''

''I'll come runnin','' he repeated. He took his job as my assistant very seriously, fancying himself a bit of a bodyguard.

I walked under the ivy-and-honeysuckle-covered trellis that connected the museum and the hacienda's old stables, now the artists' studios. The sun had emerged from behind the checkered clouds, and I could feel its heat filtering through the thick ivy canopy. It matched the hot words that assaulted my ears before I even opened the studio doors.

''How would you like this fist shoved down your throat?'' It was the voice of Roy Hudson, Nora's future ex-husband, as the song goes, and an aspiring cowboy poet. A thought occurred to me. Would he be legally considered a widower now?

I stepped into the large airy workroom. Only one of the group sitting in the circle of folding chairs acknowledged my presence. Evangeline gave me a tremulous smile. I slipped into the folding chair next to her.

''What's going on?'' I asked in a low voice.

Her gray eyes slanted down with concern. She whispered, ''Ash just said to Grace that the timing of Nora's death and the advertisement for Zar's services in today's newspaper seemed an awful big coincidence. Then he asked her what she was doing Sunday morning."

"Well, it looks like we're off to a ripping start," I said with a tired sigh. Zar was Roy's prize-winning Thoroughbred stud; at least he was if possession really did constitute nine tenths of the law. The horse was part of the divorce settlement that Nora and Roy couldn't agree upon. Though Roy offered to pay her half Zar's original cost, Nora insisted Zar was worth ten times that amount in future earnings and wanted the higher amount, which, of course, Roy didn't have. They'd been haggling about it for almost a year. Grace had kept me apprised of the whole story as we exercised horses together at the stables she owned off Laguna Valley Road.

"Calm down, Roy Rogers," Ash drawled. "I was just tuggin' your choke chain. Don't get your leather panties all in a bunch."

Roy jumped up from his chair and started toward Ash, but was stopped when Grace threw her body directly in front of him and held him back. Her small, square hands splayed across his chest.

"Roy, honey, let it go," she said. "He's just trying to get your goat, and you're letting him do it." She was a short, stout woman with arms as muscled as a ditch digger's from years of wrangling horses. Her abundant red hair belonged on a storybook princess—curly as corkscrew noodles and full of light. It seemed at odds with her square, solid body and strict mouth. She was wearing faded Wranglers and a new blue plaid shirt.

Roy, a lean man with tough, stringy muscles, straightened the corduroy Gator Ropes cap on his shaggy brown hair and allowed Grace to coax him back to his chair. But he continued to glare at Ash with narrowed eyes. Grace unconsciously stroked his forearm much in the same way a person might try to calm an agitated animal.

"Let's get started," I said, pretending I hadn't noticed

the altercation. ''I'm sure we all agree Nora's death is a horrible tragedy. I was thinking that in her honor we might think of something that we could commemorate her memory with at the festival. Any ideas?'' I pulled a notebook out of my purse and surveyed the committee members.

Evangeline's face visibly relaxed. In the six months I'd known her, I'd noticed that conflict of any type made her nervous. Many times I'd seen her walk out of the co-op studios when there was even the slightest hint of it. She was a tall woman with broad shoulders and long slender legs, but she had the grace of someone who'd come into her size gradually. She possessed the most pleasing voice I'd ever heard, clear, warm, and melodic, with a laughing quality that compelled you to move in close. Perfect traits for a storyteller.

''Perhaps we could dedicate part of the program to her,'' I suggested when no one answered. ''Maybe the children's storytelling competition?'' I looked around and tried to gauge their reactions. Roy wore a disgusted expression. Grace was attempting to look neutral, but the deep lines between her eyes gave her true feelings away. Peter and Ash both looked as if they didn't care one way or the other.

''There's a few members missing,'' I continued, ''but we've got enough to vote.'' Behind us the front doors swung open.

''Have I missed anything important?'' Jillian Sinclair asked. Behind her was Dolores Ayala, whose specialty was Mexican folktales and colorful, hand-painted folktale pottery.

''Sorry I'm late,'' Dolores said. ''It was busy down at the restaurant.''

''Hi, Dolores, Jillian,'' I said. ''We were just discussing what we should do to honor Nora Cooper at the festival this weekend. Why don't you both take a seat, and we'll continue?''

Only two seats were free, one next to Ash and one on

the other side of Evangeline. Dolores and Jillian reached the seat next to Ash simultaneously, and for a split second they stared at each other. Jillian pursed her bright coral lips and calmly sat down. Dolores turned and crossed the circle, her face blank, but her eyes flashing angrily. She dropped down next to Evangeline. Ash leaned over and patted Jillian's silk-trousered knee with a familiarity that seemed to confirm what we'd all speculated—even the sophisticated Jillian Sinclair had at some time fallen for Ash's line.

In the next hour we finally agreed on sending flowers to Nora's funeral, whenever that might be, and giving a short testimonial in the opening ceremonies rather than during the children's storytelling competition.

"Children see and hear enough violence," Evangeline wisely pointed out. "I think we should honor Nora, but not at the expense of the children."

As the meeting broke up, Ash and Dolores huddled in a corner discussing, I assumed, their tandem-storytelling performance and workshop at the festival. Though her specialty was Latin-American folktales and she did have a performance scheduled in both Spanish and English on Saturday, she and Ash had worked up an act using local San Celina history. Dolores's face was animated as she showed Ash a book she pulled from her old green backpack.

"Aren't they just the cutest thing since the Captain and Tennille," Jillian commented, walking up beside me. A strong cloud of expensive perfume filled the air around me like tule fog.

I shrugged, not sure how she meant the remark.

She touched my hand lightly, her nails tickling my skin. "I'm sorry, I didn't mean that the way it sounded. That old green animal strikes again. She's very pretty. And talented." She grimaced in a delicate, practiced way. "And young."

Her honesty disarmed me, and I smiled. "Yes, she is. But you're no wilting violet yourself."

''Thanks,'' she said, smoothing back a strand of platinum chin-length hair. ''I turned forty this year, and I'm feeling a bit left behind.'' She was thin as a marsh reed with tiny features and a skittishness about her, like a finely bred horse. She was a lot like her aunt Constance—intense, perfectionistic, high-energy. But she differed in one significant way. She wasn't a snob. Although a trust fund made her wealthy enough to buy us all out twenty times over, she was a hard worker and didn't ''hold airs,'' as Dove would say. She had been the director of the library for the last three years, a job she was given because of familial connections. But detractors had to reluctantly admit, she was highly qualified for the job, with impeccable credentials from USC and experience at libraries in San Francisco and Sacramento. She apparently ran the place with the grace of a born diplomat and, according to Nick, was the most completely fair boss he'd ever worked under.

''Have you talked to Nick yet?'' I asked, drawing her attention away from Dolores and Ash, who were laughing softly at some shared joke.

She scratched a corner of her glossy mouth with a polished nail. ''Just briefly on the phone. I'm dropping by his house after this. He's going to need time off, and that's certainly going to wreak havoc on the budget. But never mind, that's my problem. Have you been to see him?''

''No, I'm going to try and get by there today. I know he and Nora were very close.''

''The only ones left in their family,'' Jillian said softly. Then I remembered that her whole family—mother, father, and brother—had been killed in a plane crash when she was ten. She came to live with Constance, her mother's only sister, who'd never had children of her own. With five years' difference in our ages, Jillian and I never ran in the same crowds, but she, according to my uncle Arnie, had been popular in school with both sexes. To add tragedy upon tragedy, Jillian's husband, a talented architect who had helped design the new library, had left her a few months ago for a younger woman he'd met at some marathon in Hawaii. "Sent her a 'Dear Jane' telegram from Honolulu," Nick had told me. "Quit his job the same way."

"At least Nick has all of us," I said to Jillian.

She gave her hair a minute toss, as if mentally shaking off her personal troubles, and smiled. "That's right, and we're going to be there for him. After I see him I need to start thinking about what I'm going to say to my employees Monday morning. Is there anything you can tell me about the progress of the investigation?"

"Sorry. They've just got started. I'm sure Gabe will talk to you if you give him a call. He'll let you know what you can say."

"I'll call him from my car. I really want my employees to feel safe . . . to *be* safe. Whatever I have to do to achieve that, I will." She tucked her tiny leather clutch under her arm. Casting one last surreptitious glance at Dolores and Ash's lowered heads, she straightened her spine and pushed through the studio door.

I watched her walk out, an old country-western song coming to mind. Looking for love in all the wrong places . . . who would have ever thought a corny line like that could ring so true?

"So, has the Empress of San Celina got everything under control?" Dolores said behind me.

I turned around and faced her, surprise on my face. "Actually, she's very concerned about Nick. And about the rest of her employees."

Dolores shrugged. "I suppose." She still wore the frilly white Mexican blouse that was part of her uniform at her parents' restaurant downtown, but she'd replaced the full colorful cotton skirt with faded Levi's. Her waist-length black hair was pulled back in a braid tied with a red ribbon. Right at this moment her smooth brown cheeks were flushed a rosy cinnamon. I hoped it wasn't just because of Ash's attention. According to Nick, who hired Dolores as a part-time library clerk in the reference department, she came from a very traditional Mexican family—the youngest of eight children—and a dalliance with a Southern lothario spouting a line as lethal as the smoothest Kentucky bourbon would no doubt only bring her heartache.

"How's the tandem-storytelling project going?" I asked.

"Great! I'm learning so much from Ash about voice and style and structure. No one can set a mood like him, and his memorization techniques . . . well, what can I say. He's just . . . great!" I felt my heart sink. That glow wasn't from learning storytelling techniques, and I suspected that he was indeed setting a mood—and she was falling right down the rabbit hole for it. I glanced over at him. He was talking to Peter but he must have sensed my scrutiny. He looked up and gave me an amused smile, as if he knew we were discussing him and enjoyed it. I turned back to Dolores, who was pulling out the Historical Society's book of San Celina pioneer tales.

I finally broke away, using the excuse of company at home. "I'll see you at the final meeting Wednesday evening," I told her.

On the way through the museum I ran into Evangeline and D-Daddy deep in conversation. I glided past them, raising my hand in good-bye.

"Benni, wait," Evangeline called. She said one last thing to her father and met me at the front door. She laid a tentative hand on my shoulder. As big as she was, her touch was as gentle as a butterfly landing. "You did a good job refereeing in there," she said. "Nora's . . . well, this whole thing has everyone just a little shaky. But I just wanted to tell you I appreciated how you handled everyone."

"Thanks," I said, giving her a rueful smile. "I hope things will be a bit more calmed down by Friday night."

"Does Gabe have any idea who might have killed her?"

"Not the last time I talked to him. They're probably doing the autopsy as we speak. They'll know a lot more after that."

She gave a small shudder and brushed a dark curl out of her eyes. "Murder's such a drastic thing."

"Yes," I agreed, though I thought the word *drastic* was an unusual choice. Tragic, horrible, even frightening seemed more appropriate. "I guess someone would have to really be angry to take another human being's life."

"Or—"

"Evangeline, *chère,* come here," D-Daddy called.

"The captain calls," she said, smiling. "Let me know if there's anything I can do to help."

As I walked out to my truck I wondered what she was about to say about murder before D-Daddy interrupted her. Did she know something about Nora's life that might shed some light on who killed her? Evangeline, though joining the co-op only six months before, had become something of a surrogate mother and confidante to many of the artists. I'd even bent her sympathetic ear a time or two when the clashing personalities of the artists had irritated me beyond my ability to keep silent. She had a way of encouraging your most intimate confidences just by the way she concentrated on your every word with her dark consoling eyes.

At the grocery store I walked up and down the aisles trying to figure out what kind of food to feed an eighteen-year-old boy, particularly one I'd only talked to for a couple of minutes. I settled on the basics of boxed granola-style cereal, orange juice, milk, vegetables and fruits, cheese, chicken, spaghetti, and for myself, just to get through an evening promising to be emotional, a box of Ding Dongs. Most of the time Sam would have to fend for himself, or Gabe would have to take him out, because I was busy almost every night through Sunday. Not that it was different from my usual way. Food was something that Gabe and I, along with finances and housing, hadn't quite worked out in our marriage, though we'd been living together for over seven months. At this point it had been catch-as-catch-can on meals, with the local restaurants profiting. Our finances had settled into a comfortable pattern of him paying the rent and utilities and his own personal bills and me paying my personal bills as well as things like insurance, household repairs, and what food we do keep around the house. But we'd never talked about any long-range plans. It all seemed to stem from him still having that house over by Nick's. Somehow, I felt, when he was forced to mingle all his possessions with mine, we'd have to face up to the fact that we were indeed and most certainly forever-and-ever-amen legally hitched and we would be compelled to come up with some sort of team plan.

I climbed out of the truck and was, as Dove would say, trying to juggle a lazy man's load of three bags of groceries and my purse when a patrol car pulled up behind me. Gabe stepped out and gave the driver a wave of thanks. My heart quickened to a rate that would have set off five-star alarms if it had been hooked to a monitor.

*Please,* I thought, *don't let Sam walk out right this minute.*

Gabe trotted over and grabbed two of the slipping bags. "What's this?" he asked, his voice pleased. "Did my wife actually listen to my pleas for a home-cooked meal?" He peered down into one of the bags. "Fresh asparagus? Chicken breasts? Mushrooms? Was I dropped off at the right house?"

"Gabe, honey, before we go in—"

His head popped up, his expression frozen for a split second. "What's wrong?" he demanded. "What have you done?"

"What do you mean what have I done?" I shifted the third bag in front of me for protection. "What makes you think I've done anything?"

"For the duration of our relationship you have at times

called me Ortiz or Chief or Friday or Gabe, as well as a few things I'd just as soon not remember or repeat. Once, in the deepest throes of passion, I think you might have even whispered 'baby' in my ear. But you have *never, ever* called me anything that remotely resembled a loving endearment like honey.'' He set the brown bags on the hood of the truck. ''I repeat, what have you done?''

I set my bag next to the other two. ''I really resent the fact that you assume that I've—'' Before I could finish, I heard the front door open. My heart landed with what I swore was an audible thud to the bottoms of my well-worn boots.

In horror then surprise, I watched Gabe's face go from suspicious to confused. His slate-blue eyes widened, and a quirky smile tugged underneath his mustache. I let out my held breath. Maybe this reunion wasn't going to be as emotional as I thought.

He let out a low wolf whistle.

''Who in the heck is that?'' he asked.

# 5

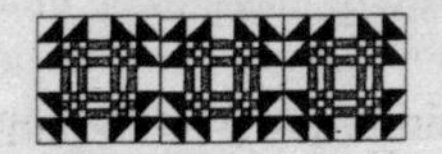

I SWUNG AROUND, my heart pounding. If that kid wasn't Sam, then *who* was he? Then I let out a loud groan.

"Hi, y'all," said the vision in a minuscule denim skirt and tight pink angora sweater. "What's for supper?"

I slumped against the truck, Sam temporarily forgotten.

"Well?" Gabe said, his eyes glued to her as she took the three porch steps, as the song goes, one hip at a time. Her bright pink cowboy boots with RIDE 'EM COWBOY in carmine red leather across the shaft, reached the bottoms of her very shapely knees.

"Rita," I said, groaning again.

Gabe nodded his head, impressed. "Ah, the infamous cousin Rita."

I punched his arm. "You can shove your eyes back in your head now." Though I couldn't blame him. Rita always had that effect on men. If you compared our vital statistics—five feet almost one inches, reddish-blond hair, hazel eyes, and a hundred and five some-odd pounds—we could be sisters. Except hers is packaged a lot more glittery than mine. Sort of like the difference between Las Vegas and Cheyenne.

She had played a significant offstage role in the crime where Gabe and I met a little less than a year ago. She was a witness and possible suspect, and I hid her whereabouts from the law—that is, Gabe—while trying to find the murderer. He heard a lot about her during the investigation, but before they met, she ran off with Skeeter Gluck, bullrider ordinaire.

"My new cousin-in-law," Rita purred, shimmying up to Gabe. She held out one Pinch Me Pink–nailed hand while fluffing her starched Reba McEntire curls with the other. "I'm just tickled to finally meet you. A real-life police chief. Tell me, is it true what all my girlfriends say about cops?"

He grinned. "Depends on what they're saying."

Her shameless once-over down the length of him made it clear that her girlfriends weren't talking about their ability to fill out crime reports.

"What are *you* doing here?" I asked, my voice not a little ungracious. Then our other guest popped into my mind. I turned back to Gabe. "Gabe, there's something else—"

The front door opened again. We all turned and watched Sam step out on the front porch.

"Hi, Dad," he said, his face as calm and casual as if he'd just seen his father ten minutes before. "Catch any bad guys today?"

Gabe's face shifted into that blank, absolutely still expression that always reminded me of those dogs who don't give any warning before they bite. His eyes turned from an amused blue gray to hard flint. Even Rita had the good sense to step back and clamp her mouth shut. He looked down at me and asked in a frosty voice, "How long has he been here?"

"A couple of hours, but—"

He strode past me toward his son. I held my breath, not sure what he would do when he reached the front porch. Without a word, he walked right by Sam, through the front door, and slammed it behind him.

"My, my," Rita said. "I bet if I'd've touched him right

then, he'd've just burned my little fingertips right to the bone.'' Her thin eyebrows shot up. ''Repressed passion. I like that in a man.''

Ignoring her, I walked over to Sam. His big hand rested on the adobe arch, a blank expression similar to Gabe's on his face. He'd gotten what I think he wanted, surprising his father, but I wasn't sure the result was what he'd anticipated.

''Sam,'' I said. ''You and Rita put the groceries away. I'll talk to your father and see if we can't get this straightened out.'' Though how I was going to do that was a mystery to me.

Sam gave a sharp sarcastic laugh. ''Don't sweat it, Benni. Believe me, he's happiest when he's pissed at me.''

''Sam, that's not true.''

He ignored my reply and went out to the truck. He picked up the bags, making a low comment to Rita that caused her to erupt with a squeaky giggle.

Inside, I stood in front of our closed bedroom door for a moment, thinking, *This is all I need this week,* then chided myself for being so self-centered. This had to be tough on Gabe. Maybe I made the wrong decision in not calling him immediately about Sam, but the scenario hadn't worked out quite the way I planned. Who would have ever expected Rita to show up? Why *was* she here, and what in the world was I going to do with her? Well, that little problem was going to have to wait. I straightened my shoulders and opened the door.

Gabe stood next to the bedroom window looking out at the yellow rosebushes along the side fence. His hands were relaxed at his side, but the stiffness of his posture said his anger was still in full bloom. He turned and faced me. ''How long has he been here?'' he asked again.

''Only a couple of hours—''

''Why didn't you call me? I don't appreciate—''

I held up my hand to silence him. ''I made the decision

not to call because I figured it would be even harder if you heard it over the phone. I was certain I'd get home first and catch you before you saw him."

His bottom lip disappeared under his mustache. "I don't appreciate being humiliated by my own wife in my own home in front of strangers."

"No one was trying to humiliate you, Gabe. And Rita is, unfortunately, not a stranger, but a relative. Believe me, I had no idea she was here. I still have to find out the story behind *that*. But let's get back to the real issue here, and that's you and Sam."

"There's no issue. He's here because his money ran out."

"That may be so," I said carefully. "We honestly didn't talk long enough for me to find out. I had to go to a meeting about the storytelling festival right after he showed up. But I'm sure—"

"He won't be staying long. He made his bed and he can sleep in it."

I went over and slipped my arms around his waist. His body was stiff and unyielding. "Gabe, why don't you just hear him out? He *is* your son."

He pulled away from my embrace and started for the door. "He can stay for a couple of days, and that's it. I'm sick of bailing him out because he's too irresponsible to stick to any plans. He claims he's a man. Well, men don't expect other people to take care of them."

I followed him into the living room, not knowing exactly how to answer. The room was empty. A brown paper grocery sack with writing on it was propped on the pine coffee table.

*Rita and I walked downtown to get dinner. See you later. Sam.*

I let out my breath in a long sigh. Confrontation temporarily averted. Though normally not a procrastinator, I was thankful this male butting of heads was delayed. The thought of Gabe's eighteen-year-old son spending a cozy evening with my twenty-two-year-old I-never-met-a-man-I-couldn't-help-but-seduce cousin Rita was not my fondest wish, but I had to trust Sam. His virtue was certainly the least of my problems at this point.

Gabe set the note down without commenting.

"Why don't you take a hot shower, and I'll fix dinner," I coaxed him. "Everything will look better once you've eaten."

He grunted what I assumed to be an agreement and pulled his polo shirt over his head. As he showered I whipped up a chicken, wild rice, and mushroom casserole. It was on the table thirty minutes later when he came into the kitchen, wet-haired and subdued. After resisting my attempts at light conversation, I left him to his silence and turned my thoughts to how I was going to organize the sleeping arrangements in our two-bedroom house. Then I moved on to worrying about the upcoming festival. The storytellers would start arriving on Thursday, and though I was certain I'd anticipated every problem or potential problem, I mentally went over everything one more time, looking for breaks in the fence.

"Good dinner. Thanks," Gabe said, standing up. "Leave the dishes, and I'll do them tomorrow before my run. I think I'm going to watch TV in bed. You want to lock up?"

"Sure. I've still got my opening speech for the festival to work on. I'll stay up until the kids come home." I gave him a teasing smile.

His face sobered. "I guess you should give him a key. I don't want either of us having to wait up every night just so we can lock up after him."

"Good idea," I said, feeling more optimistic. Though his voice sounded chilly, at least he wasn't suggesting we lock Sam out. Of course, that still didn't take care of the problem of Rita. There was no way I was giving her a key to my house—I'd been down that potholed road before when I first moved into this house and she'd lived with me for a few months at the urging of my family and against my better judgment. Skeeter, before he acquired the position of Rita's next of kin, had been a surprise guest one morning when I staggered into my kitchen wearing only a T-shirt and a pair of Jack's hunting socks. A very short T-shirt. My cousin-in-law, who bears a striking resemblance to the country singer Dwight Yoakam, saw more of me the first minute we met than Gabe saw until our wedding night.

I dug out the spare key from a kitchen drawer and set it on the coffee table. Then I settled down on the sofa, pillows propped behind my head, and picked up the file containing my half-finished speech. Television music filtered through the closed bedroom door. I could make out the cheery opening score of *The Rockford Files,* one of Gabe's favorite programs. He watched the reruns on cable whenever he could, even though he'd seen all the episodes a dozen times. Their familiarity and the good-natured personality of Jim Rockford never failed to relax him.

I turned back to the blank tablet in front of me and chewed on the tip of my pencil. When it was decided we'd put on this festival, Elvia, as usual, provided me with more than enough literature on the art and practice of storytelling. Though I'd seen the occasional puppet show at San Celina's Thursday-night farmers' market downtown and heard various children's-book authors read their works at Blind Harry's Bookstore, I had never seen a professional storyteller until I accompanied Constance and Jillian to a storytelling festival in Santa Barbara eight months ago. The scope and beauty of this art form had charmed me. And like most folk art, I was again surprised at the completely separate world in which the storytellers lived and worked. Like quilters and wood-carvers and weavers and dozens of other folk artists, the storytelling community had its own kings and queens, rivalries and intrigues, magazines and conventions, rules and traditions.

That was something that constantly amazed me about people—how they formed little universes around a common interest. As a museum curator and not an actual participant in any of the arts I presented to the public, I often felt like an outsider, albeit a welcome one. I sometimes envied the artist's all-consuming obsession. But despite my lack of esprit de corps with the artists, I appreciated the glimpse into mini-societies closed to most people.

I looked over the notes I'd gleaned from the four books Elvia found for me and one I'd borrowed from the library. I had decided to open my welcome speech with a short history of storytelling and my own personal definition of the art.

*Storytelling is a form of oral artistry whose sole purpose is to preserve and communicate ideas, images, experiences, and emotions common to all people.*

Oral artistry. I liked the sound of that. Painting a picture with the spoken word.

*We are all characters in the stories of our individual lives, making choices and living with the results of those choices. Consciously and unconsciously we pattern those choices after someone we admire and want to be like, and often that someone is first shown to us in a story.*

I thought about the many people who'd read or told stories to me throughout my life—public school teachers, Sunday school teachers, aunts and uncles, my father and Dove. Much of who I am was formed by the stories passed on to me or, as storytellers liked to emphasize, through me. Because, as many of them pointed out, stories were a living thing and like an unplayed symphony, useless until heard.

I picked up my pencil and added, *Telling a story is a way of moving closer to another human being. It is a shar-*

*ing of the heart and soul and intellect. It says you and I, we're alike in this one particular thing.*

I had started making notes on how during the Middle Ages troubadours and minstrels were often the only means of relaying information from one community to another when the front door opened. A gust of cool evening air rushed into the living room, bringing Rita and Sam with it. Heads close together, they laughed loudly at a shared joke.

"Hey, you guys," I said, putting a finger over my lips. If Gabe had fallen asleep, the last thing I wanted was him waking up to the happy sounds of his capricious son and my cousin Rita.

"Sorry," Sam said, grinning at me and untangling Rita's arm from his. "So, *madrastra,* is *mi padre* safely locked away, or should I sleep with one eye open tonight?" A loud giggle erupted from Rita. I shot her a fierce look.

I tightened my lips, irritated for the first time at his carefree manner. Didn't he understand how upset his father was?

"I need to get to bed," I said. "We need to discuss the sleeping arrangements because there is only one guest room."

"It's got a queen-size bed," Sam piped up, his dark eyes dancing.

"Which only one of you will occupy. Rita, you can sleep in the guest room, and I'll make up the sofa for Sam."

"Why does she get the bed?" Sam whined. "I was here first."

"Because I said so." There was a very good reason for my decision. Though I didn't relish the idea of Gabe having to walk past his sleeping son on his way to work the next morning, I had lived with Rita and knew what sort of Frederick's of Hollywood outfits she slept in. I gave Rita a stern look. "It's too late to go into it now, but tomorrow we're going to talk."

"Yes, ma'am," she said, rolling her eyes. She blew a

kiss to Sam. ''See you tomorrow, surfer boy.'' He gave her a goofy smile.

After everyone was situated, I took a shower, standing under the stream until the water ran cool. Gabe lay asleep on the bed in front of the flickering television set. An old *Laverne & Shirley* was playing. I gently pried the controller out of his hand and clicked it off.

''I was watching that,'' he mumbled, his eyes still closed.

''You hate *Laverne & Shirley*,'' I said, pulling off my thick cotton-velour robe and crawling under the sheets next to him. His body was already warm with sleep, and I cuddled up next to him.

''I like Lenny and Squiggy,'' he said, pulling me closer and nuzzling my neck. ''I love the smell of you fresh from the shower.''

''Gabe,'' I protested in a harsh whisper.

''What?'' He ran a hand down my thigh.

''It's late.''

He glanced at the bedside clock radio. ''It's only eleven o'clock.''

''I'm tired.'' He nibbled on my neck, and I gave a soft laugh.

He rolled over on top of me. ''Relax, I'll do all the work.''

I pushed on his chest, still laughing. ''There are *people* in the house.''

He looked down at me with smoky blue eyes and smiled slowly. ''Then, *querida*,'' he said, his voice dropping down to a faint whisper, ''we must be very . . .'' He brushed his lips lightly across mine, his hands busy elsewhere. ''Very . . .'' He kissed me harder, knowing just the right maneuvers to melt my last ounce of resolve. ''Quiet.''

''You know way too much about me,'' I said as he pulled my T-shirt over my head.

Afterward, as I rested my head on his chest, my mind

drowsily traveling from one irrelevant subject to another, he brought up our houseguests.

"So what's your cousin's sob story?" he asked, his fingers catching in my tangled hair.

I opened my eyes and studied the small cleft in his chin. "I have no idea. I haven't had the opportunity to ask, but I bet I know the answer. My guess is she caught old Skeeter fertilizing a stray heifer or two. I don't know what she was thinking, hooking up with a rodeo bum like him."

He chuckled and rubbed his face in my hair, inhaling deeply. "Let me see now, Skeeter is the one who's seen you naked, right?"

I sat up and smacked him with my feather pillow. "I was wearing a T-shirt. And that's an incident I'd just as soon forget, thank you very much."

"I think I deserve equal ocular access to *his* wife," he teased.

"Like they say, Friday, don't wish for something. You might get it."

"Intriguing thought."

"Just don't think about it too much." Knowing this was as good a mood as I was likely to see him in for the next few days, I said, "We need to talk about Sam."

He frowned and, avoiding my eyes, punched his pillow into shape. "Nothing to talk about. He can stay a couple of days then move on."

"He's your son. How can you—"

"I'm perfectly aware of who he is, and since you don't know anything about *my son,* I'd prefer you let me handle it."

"Well, excuse me for caring." I shoved my pillow back in place and turned away from him.

"*Querida,*" he said, his voice tired. "I don't mean to sound harsh. I just need to handle this my way. It's more complicated than it looks. Can you try and understand that?"

I turned over on my back and stared at the ceiling. He leaned over and started kissing me softly along my hairline. "Sweetheart, please—"

"What did they find out down at the lab?" I asked, changing the subject.

He sat up and leaned against the pine headboard, staring at the blank television screen across the room. "The autopsy didn't give us any surprises. She was strangled with some kind of rope and dumped in the lake. She'd been dead approximately eight to ten hours, which means she was killed the night before around eleven o'clock or so. Other than that, there are no leads yet."

I pulled our quilt over my shoulders and shivered. "Who told Nick?" It hit me right then that I'd never called or gone by. Sam's sudden appearance, the fight among the storytellers, then Rita's arrival had pushed everyone's problems but my own clear out of my head. I kicked myself mentally and promised myself that I'd go see him first thing tomorrow.

"Jim. The guy was upset, as you can imagine, but he was able to answer Jim's questions pretty coherently and he voluntarily gave us a key to her apartment."

"Did you find anything that might give a clue to her killer?"

He shrugged. "I dropped by when the detective team I assigned to her case was going through her things. It's hard to say. We weren't surprised to find that someone had been there before us. The place was a mess. There's nothing worse than searching a place that's already been trashed. We took her computer down to the station, but all her floppy disks were missing. Someone obviously thought there was something on them that might point to their identity. That's my guess anyway."

"She made her own puppets," I said, sadness weighting my heart. "They were beautiful. I wonder what will happen to them."

"That's up to her heir, which appears to be her brother."

"So you have no leads at all?"

"Not unless she's got a million-dollar insurance policy and her brother is the beneficiary."

"Nick would never kill Nora! They were very close."

Gabe reached over and gave my head a condescending pat.

"He wouldn't," I repeated stubbornly, though with less conviction. The longer I was exposed to police work, the less sure I was becoming of my fellow human beings' basic goodness. But I steadfastly refused to become as cynical as Gabe. *Someone* in this relationship needed a positive outlook.

"Come here," Gabe said, pulling me over and tucking me under his arm. "Our bed is not the place I want to discuss my work. Tell me how the meeting with the storytellers went."

"It was almost a free-for-all when I arrived." I nuzzled my cheek on his chest hair.

"Why?"

I told him about the argument between Roy and Ash. "I think there's more history to that fight than the comment about Zar's stud fees."

"Why do you say that?"

"Well, knowing Ash's reputation, it occurred to me that he might have had a fling at one time with Grace. She and Roy have broke up a few times in the last year, and Grace has enough of a vindictive streak to do something like that if for no other reason than to irritate Roy."

"Refresh my memory. Grace is . . . ?"

"The woman Roy is living with now. She owns the stables off Laguna Valley Road. You know, behind the redwood Methodist church. It's where I've been riding the last couple of months."

"I take it Roy and Nora's divorce wasn't an amicable parting."

"Not by any stretch of the imagination. Nora divorced him because he was cheating on her with Grace while their eight-year-old son was dying. You really can't blame her. That is pretty low."

"So for revenge, Nora was holding up the divorce proceedings because of the property settlement of some horse."

"Zar's more than just some horse. Grace says he's worth twenty-five thousand dollars. Maybe more."

Gabe whistled under his breath. "People have been killed for less."

I scratched his stomach lightly. "I just can't picture it, though. Roy might be a hothead, but he'd held off this long, and Grace told me last week he and Nora were getting close to an agreement. That's why they were advertising Zar's services in the paper. She said they had agreed to split the stud fees until the final details of ownership were worked out."

"So what about this Ash? With a name like that, it is a good thing he was never a cop."

"It's short for Ashley. Ashley Stanhill. He owns that new restaurant on the corner of Alvarez and Elm, near the Art Center. Eudora's Front Porch. He's from Mississippi. He's got a gorgeous accent and that kind of cockiness that a woman wants to hate, but somehow just can't 'cause it's so incredibly blatant. He seduces women simply by being so audacious."

"Oh, really?"

I pulled on his chest hair. "Not me, you jerk. *Other* women."

"Ow," he said, grabbing my hand and pressing it to his chest. "You're really into inflicting pain today. So, tell me more about the environmental guy you mentioned this afternoon. The political one."

"Peter Grant. I've known him since I was a kid. We were in 4-H together. His parents owned one of the biggest almond orchards in the state. They sold it and moved to San Francisco and he stayed. He's one of those guys who's never gotten married, lives for his hobbies and his causes."

"Which are?"

"In a nutshell? Mountain climbing, scuba diving, zero growth, owls, redwoods and wolves, and whatever new animal or cause is the current political poster child. He's president of the GreenLand Conservancy."

"The group that's trying to buy up land around San Celina and make a permanent greenbelt? I understand to a degree what they want. I'd hate to see San Celina turn into another Orange County."

"Yeah, but the problem always comes back to private ownership. It's real easy for people like Peter to say the land shouldn't be owned when it's not *his* land being legislated. I wonder how generous he'd be if his parents still owned that almond orchard. If ag people and environmentalists don't find a way to work together somehow, the ranchers and farmers will have to sell out to whoever can buy the land just to pay their inheritance or income taxes. And developers are the only people with that kind of money. I just wish he'd realize we all have the same goals, keeping San Celina from turning into one big suburb."

"It's a volatile situation, no doubt about it, but so far both sides have just flung words. So, who else was there?"

"Jillian Sinclair."

"Constance Sinclair's niece."

"Right. And there was Evangeline Boudreaux and Dolores Ayala."

"Did they know Nora well?"

"Well, Jillian was her boss at the library. I think Dolores and Nora were passing acquaintances. Nora and Evangeline have left together quite a few times, so I assume they'd struck up a friendship. Evangeline's the type that everyone confides in, so I wouldn't be surprised if Nora was telling her all the juicy details about her and Roy's divorce."

"That's everyone who was there?"

"Well, D-Daddy was on the grounds, but not actually at the meeting."

Gabe slid down and tucked the quilt around us, signaling he wanted to go to sleep. I poked him in the side. "Wait a minute, I think I've just been had."

Without opening his eyes, he gave a lazy smile. "And if I wasn't so tired, I'd have you again."

"I thought you didn't want to bring your job to our bed. That was a low-level interrogation, Friday."

"Now, you're always wanting to help me with my investigations. It would be even more helpful if you would write all these people's names down so I can give them to my detectives. Anything else you want to add about any of them? You probably have a better handle on the relationships among these people than my detectives could get."

"Me? You're actually consulting *me* on a case? Someone call the newspapers. Someone call the television stations. Someone call the pope. A miracle has occurred in San Celina. Gabriel Ortiz is actually *asking* his wife if she has an opinion about a case. Why, it's unbelievable. It's—"

"Pipe down," he said good-naturedly. "And answer the question."

"Honestly, Nora was a nice person. Though a bit sharp-tongued at times, she was never mean. I can't imagine why anyone would kill her."

"I know you like this Grace and Roy, sweetheart, but don't be surprised if it turns out to be one of them. Most homicides involve money or sex, and *they* hit the bell on both accounts."

"I don't even want to think about that."

"Well, just remember, no questions," he reminded, yawning. "That's my job."

"You know, with how involved I am with all these people, this time I think I'll listen to you."

"That'll be the day," he replied.

The next morning, as usual, he was up before me. I lifted my head from where it was jammed into my pillow and watched him through slitted eyes as he pulled on shorts and a sweatshirt. The man's discipline was phenomenal and sometimes more than a little irritating.

"Your turn to put on the coffee," I mumbled.

"I do believe it's your turn this week, but since you were so good last night, I'll give you this one." He bent over and tied his jogging shoes.

I struggled up and rubbed my crusty eyes. "Are you saying that if I *wasn't* good I'd be fixing my own coffee?"

He grinned. "Now, don't put words in my mouth."

"Chauvinist," I said halfheartedly.

"Just think of it as conditioned reflex. Like Pavlov's dogs."

"That's not a very accurate analogy."

"It's as good as I can do on an empty stomach. I'll jog by Stern's Bakery and get some fresh bagels," he said, unperturbed by my grumpiness. I was relieved to see he was starting out in a good mood, though how long that would last was debatable. He and Sam still hadn't actually talked yet.

"Then I'll make the coffee," I said. "I need to get up anyway. I have a million things to do today."

He left the room, and I grabbed my robe. In the living room I was surprised to find him standing motionless, staring down at his sleeping son. His expression broke my heart—a combination of raw longing and deep anger.

He turned when he heard me. His face recomposed itself into his blank, no-one's-going-to-touch-me look. "I'll be back in a half hour," he said in a normal tone. "Don't have time for a full run."

I held my finger to my lips and pointed at the kitchen.

"Don't worry," he said, his voice flat. "Sam sleeps like a log. Always has, ever since he was a baby." Only the strange light in his eyes revealed the emotion watching his sleeping child stirred in him.

While he was gone I made coffee and sliced tomatoes and Swiss cheese to eat with the bagels. As I worked I plotted my day. First, go see Nick. Last night must have been horrible for him, and I wondered if any of his friends had come to stay with him. I had just poured my first cup of coffee when a bleary-eyed Sam wandered into the kitchen. He wore a pair of baggy purple-and-black shorts and a stretched-out sweatshirt faded an odd grayish blue.

''Is Dad gone?'' he asked, pouring himself a cup of coffee.

''He's jogging,'' I said. ''He should be back in about a half hour.''

''Maybe I should split, then,'' he said, holding his mug with both hands and shivering slightly.

''Sit down,'' I said, pointing to a dining chair. ''You're not going anywhere. You and Gabe are going to have to come to some kind of truce. You two may not be able to solve every problem you've accumulated in the last eighteen years, but you can at least be civil.''

''So tell *him* that.''

''I intend to.''

He smiled over his mug. ''Wow, I bet you and Dad really tie it on sometimes. He hates anyone telling him what to do.''

''So I've noticed.'' I set cream and sugar down in front of him.

''I drink it black.''

''Just like your father.''

He scowled and took a long gulp.

We were on our second cups when Gabe walked into the kitchen.

He glanced quickly at Sam before laying the white bag in front of me.

"There's a dozen in there," he said, pouring himself a cup of coffee.

"I'm starved," Sam said, sitting down at the table. I set out bowls, granola cereal, milk, orange juice, and bananas. "I'm toasting my bagel," I said, my eyes darting between the two silent men. "Anyone else?"

They both grunted affirmative, glanced at each other, then back down into their bowls. After a few minutes of attempting conversation, I finally gave up and decided the slurping of milk and crunch of bagels were the only sounds I was likely to hear from these two this morning. By the time everyone was finished, I'd made up my mind that I was not going to come home after a stressful day at the museum to this unresolved standoff.

I licked my spoon, then slammed it down on the table. Both heads snapped up and stared at me. "Listen up, boys. I will not put up with this childish game of each of you waiting to knock the stick off the shoulder of the other. I know you can't resolve all your problems in one visit, but you can be pleasant to each other for as long as Sam is here." I turned and faced my stepson. His dark brown eyes were wary. "First you, Sam. Just how long do you intend to stay?"

His tanned face grew stubborn. I immediately nipped that attitude in the bud. "Now don't go all juvenile on me. You want to be treated like an adult, so that's exactly what I'm doing. An adult who visits has a set time in mind. We need to know what yours is."

"I don't know," he said, shrugging. "A week, I guess." He shot his father a fierce look. "Maybe I should just leave today."

Gabe threw his napkin down on the table and stood up. "Run away when things don't work out like you want. Why doesn't that surprise me? That's always been what you do best."

Sam jumped up, his face twitching with anger. "Well, I

guess you were right, Benni,'' he said, though his eyes never left Gabe's face. ''I *am* just like my father.'' His right hand beat a nervous drum pattern on his thigh.

I took a deep breath and intervened. ''Look, why don't you two deal with all that old baggage later? Right now why don't we just agree that Sam is going to stay a week and see how it goes? Frankly, he's my new stepson, and I'd like to get to know him. How about we try that? Just a week?''

I suspected that Sam didn't have anywhere else to go and was probably short on money and I also suspected that Gabe didn't really want him to leave. What they needed was just a little time to get used to each other again. At least that's what I was hoping. When I was growing up on the ranch and the men in our family got to growling and snapping at each other, Dove would just send them packing off to different parts of the ranch to work until they could stand being around each other again. Of course, that was easier done on a two-thousand-acre cattle ranch than in a small two-bedroom house in a medium-size college town.

''Well, guys, how about it?'' I looked at the vein in my husband's left temple and the set of his jaw, gauges I'd learned to monitor for clues to his emotional temperature. His jaw seemed just a little less rigid than it had minutes ago. ''Gabe?''

''A week,'' he said, and strode out of the room.

Sam shook his head and picked up his almost empty glass of orange juice, concentrating on swirling the liquid around and around. ''I should just leave,'' he said, his voice sad now that Gabe had left.

''No,'' I said, picking up the cereal box and closing the flap. ''I meant what I said. I would like to get to know you. Give your dad some time. He'll come around.'' I made my voice light and positive.

He picked up the carton of milk and carried it over to the refrigerator. ''I think I know him better than you, Benni.

He'd probably be happy if he never saw me again."

"I *know* that's not true." I stopped wiping the table and looked up at him. "Look, just let him get used to you being here and see what happens."

He shrugged. "Whatever. To be honest, unless I go down to my mom's in L.A., I don't have anywhere else to go and about ten bucks to get there." He said the last part with his head down, not meeting my eyes.

Just as I thought. I opened the cupboard and pulled out a red Folger's coffee can where I kept some household money. I counted eighty-nine dollars and some change. I held the bills out to him.

"I can't take your money," he said, his face coloring. "That's not why I said that."

"I know. But it comes with two strings attached."

He eyed the money longingly. "What?"

"One, call your mother and let her know you're here and all right."

He nodded. "And the second?"

"Be patient with your dad and try not to bite when he makes sarcastic remarks. Heaven knows, I understand how hard that is. But he's going through a rough time with what happened in Kansas and with Aaron. I think he really needs you right now and just doesn't want to admit it."

Sam shook his head dubiously. "I think you're wrong but I need the money." He took the bills and slipped them into the pockets of his shorts. "I'll pay you back."

"Maybe I am," I agreed. "But let's give it a try anyway. And consider the money a late graduation present."

"So," he said, his face relaxing. "What's there to do in this town? What are you going to do today?"

"As you probably saw last night, downtown's a nice place to hang out. Lots of boutiques and coffeehouses. Pick up the *Freedom Press*. It has an entertainment section that tells what's going on in town. As for me, I'm going to go visit a friend of mine this morning and then go to the folk-art museum and finish getting the grounds set up for the storytelling festival this weekend.'' I smiled at him encouragingly. ''We can always use more volunteers. Why don't you come by the museum this afternoon? I'll give you the two-bit tour.''

''Maybe I will,'' he said. ''But the problem is, I'm pretty much hoofing it. How's your rapid-transit system around here?''

''Lousy,'' I said, thinking for a moment. I took the spare key to my old truck from a kitchen drawer. ''You can drive my truck, and I'll drive your grandpa's old truck.''

''The restored one?'' Sam's eyes lit up. ''Wow, Dad told me about it over the phone. That was so cool of Otis. Why can't I drive that?''

'''Cause your dad isn't quite ready for that yet,'' I said wryly. ''He's not going to be thrilled about me driving it, but it's the only way we can get you some wheels.''

''Maybe I can talk him into it,'' he said, his eyes still dreamy.

''Maybe,'' I humored him, thinking, *Not in this lifetime, sonny boy.*

I was thankful Sam was in the bathroom when Gabe came into the living room dressed for work. I straightened his tie and informed him of our plans.

''Be careful,'' he said. ''Maybe I should drive Dad's truck.''

''Okay, but then I drive the Corvette.''

I watched his face struggle with the choices. ''I guess I'll take the Corvette. You're not going anyplace off-road, are you?''

''Oh, go catch some bad guys,'' I said, kissing him and pushing him toward the door.

I dressed quickly in jeans, a sleeveless denim shirt, and boots. With a quick brush of hair and teeth, I was ready for my visit with Nick. All I had to do was stop by the bakery and buy a pie. When I walked back into the kitchen,

Sam was loading both last night's and this morning's dishes in the dishwasher. A package of chicken breasts lay on the counter.

"Thanks," I said. "What are you doing with the chicken?"

He smiled at me. "I'm not a complete scrounge, *madrastra.*" He took a long glass pan from the bottom cupboard. "I thought I'd marinate some chicken breasts in this great teriaki-ginger sauce I learned in Hawaii. We can broil them for dinner. Maybe steam some vegetables and rice to go with it."

I unsuccessfully hid my surprise. "You cook?"

He wiped his wet hands on his sweatshirt. "I worked for a few months as a chef's helper in a hotel restaurant in Haleiwa. I mostly just cut up vegetables, but I learned a few things watching the chef."

"Well, anyone who cooks around here is more than welcome."

After picking up a fresh cherry pie at the bakery, I drove to Nick's house. He lived near the college on a cul-de-sac that ended at one of Cal Poly's pastures. The street had become more familiar to me in the last few months because Gabe's leased house was at the end of the same street. Nick's house sat above the pavement, perched over his two-car garage. A red Harley-Davidson Sportster was parked in front of the garage doors, a black helmet resting in the bushes as if he'd flung it there when he dismounted. I picked it up and balanced it carefully on the leather motorcycle seat. A steep set of white wooden stairs led to an intricately carved front door with a stained-glass porthole window. An overgrown ash tree in his tiny front yard canopied the deep front porch.

He answered the door on my third knock. He looked thinner than the last time I saw him a week ago, though I knew that was just an illusion. Death, it seemed to me, did that to survivors, seemed to shrink them for a time, as if a part of them physically left when the person they loved did. His shaggy auburn hair was slightly greasy at the crown, and the whites of his blue eyes were faintly yellow and webbed with red lines. He wore a pair of dark jeans, a gray athletic shirt, and scuffed black motorcycle boots.

"Nick, I'm so sorry," I said. We did an awkward dance for a moment as I tried to hug him while balancing the pink box holding the pie.

"Come on in," he said, taking the box from my hands.

I followed him into his shaded living room. With the greenish sunlight dappling the room and the large picture window peering over his neighbors' rooftops, it felt like we were in a tree house. He pushed aside a pile of newspapers on the leather sofa to give me a place to sit. Crumpled fast-food containers and empty beer bottles littered the glass coffee table. He sat across from me in a plaid chair, cradling the pink bakery box in his lap.

"Thanks for the cake," he finally said.

"It's a pie, and you're welcome."

We sat uncomfortably silent for a moment. He set the box down next to him and picked up a worn acoustic guitar propped next to the white brick fireplace. "What's Gabe found out so far?" he asked, running his fingers along the edge of the instrument.

"Not much," I said. "But he's got everyone he can spare working on it." I hugged my bare upper arms. For some reason, though the temperature had already started climbing toward the high eighties, his house felt like a refrigerator. "They'll find who did this, Nick."

He squinted at me, his light eyes cynical. "I'm glad you have so much confidence in our boys in blue. Too bad they couldn't be there when someone decided to kill her."

I didn't answer. His remark was unfair, but I also knew from experience that during those first few days after such a shock, a person can't always be held responsible for what they say. I picked up a pillow needlepointed with the figure of a soaring eagle and pretended to study the stitchwork. "Do you need help planning the service?" I asked gently.

He rubbed a hand over his face. "Man, I'm sorry, Benni. I sound like an ungrateful ass. I know Gabe's doing his best. I'm just so angry at whoever did this, I can't see straight." He thrummed his fingers down the strings of the guitar, then stopped their sound with the flat of his hand. "Truthfully, I don't know what to do and I don't even know who to ask."

"I can ask Gabe when they will release her," I offered.

"You know it was just me and her. This is all my responsibility now, and with the two of us she was always the one—" His voice broke. "She would be the one to find out these things."

"I know, but she had friends. You have friends. We'll help you."

"Thanks," he mumbled, staring out the huge picture window into the ash tree's thick foliage. I followed his gaze. Through the leaves, the sloping umber hills of San Celina seemed to undulate before our eyes. "I hope they found something in her apartment." He looked back at me. "And I hope they're looking real close at Roy and his horsey girlfriend. They had more reason to want her dead than anyone."

Again I didn't answer. One of the problems with living in the same small town your entire life was sometimes your loyalties got intertwined and complicated. Although Roy annoyed me sometimes with his smart-ass personality, he was basically a good guy. And I liked Grace. I liked her a lot. I didn't want to believe either of them would kill Nora.

"I'll call you as soon as I find out about when they'll release Nora," I said, standing up. "Is there anything else I can do? Do you have enough food? Want me to go grocery shopping for you?"

His face softened, and he gave a quiet laugh. For the first time since I walked in, he looked more like the kindhearted guy I'd known for years. The guy who would spend an hour helping a schoolchild find all the right reference materials for an overdue report on California missions or help a frightened senior citizen research a list of medicines prescribed to them by a doctor too busy to explain the side effects. "I'm eating fine," he said, pointing to the coffee table full of fast food wrappers. "You remind me of Nora. She was always concerned I wasn't eating enough."

"You loved each other very much," I said.

His eyes teared up. "Yes."

"We're doing a special tribute to her at the storytelling festival," I said. "Maybe you'd like to come see it."

"Is Roy going to be there?"

"There's nothing I can do about that, Nick. He's in the program."

"Then I'll pass. But thanks for thinking of her."

"Nick, when the detectives talked to you, did they ask who—"

He broke in. "I think I know what you're going to ask. I told them that the only person I knew who could possibly want her dead was Roy Hudson and that woman he left my sister for. They are the only ones who could benefit from her death, and frankly, any man who could screw around on his wife when his son is dying is capable of anything in my book."

At the door, he studied me for a long minute before speaking. "I was the last one to see her."

"What?"

"Gabe didn't tell you?"

I shook my head, not wanting to go into detail about how little Gabe told me about his work.

"I left her at the library at six o'clock. She knew the lockdown procedure and she had some stuff she said she wanted to work on in the computer lab. It was really against the rules, but Jillian's pretty relaxed about that kind of stuff. We'd done it lots of times. We were supposed to have breakfast together the next morning.'' His voice cracked again. ''If I'd only stayed. If I'd—''

''Nick, don't beat yourself up. There's no way you could have known.'' The path he was walking down was one way too familiar to me. That overwhelming, but entirely false feeling that somehow, if we'd just done things differently, we could have changed fate and prevented the tragedy. ''I'm so sorry,'' I said again.

He just nodded and closed the door behind me without answering.

On the drive to the folk-art museum I castigated myself for even bringing up the investigation. Some friend I was. But Grace was my friend, too, and I didn't want her and Roy to be hurt by this either. We'd become pretty close in the few months we'd exercised, trained, and doctored her horses together. Going to the stables three or four times a week eased somewhat my homesickness for daily ranch life. Our small rented house didn't allow pets, so playing with Grace's dogs and helping with her animals had become a welcomed respite to this new life in town that deep down I couldn't believe was permanent.

I pulled into the museum parking lot and parked in my habitual spot under a huge oak tree whose dark gray trunk was crisscrossed with tree scars professing various undying loves and the nineties equivalent of ''Kilroy was here.'' The parking lot was jammed with vehicles, and there was a corresponding amount of frantic activity in the neighboring field. The barbed-wire fencing normally separating the pasture from our parking lot had been temporarily removed, so I walked straight into the field, waving at different local merchants as they decorated their booths for the festival. In the center of the field D-Daddy was supervising a group of boisterous college boys unloading hay bales from a new Ford pickup.

We were providing three storytelling areas—the main one in the center under a rented canopy, which would have a plain wood backdrop and hay bales for seating, and two smaller areas, both under large, leafy oak trees. They would also have hay bales for seating, but the storytellers themselves would have to provide any backdrop—imaginative or otherwise. All of them were far enough from each other so one storyteller's voice wouldn't overshadow another. The workshops would be held at staggered times in the main room of the co-op studios.

"To the left," D-Daddy yelled. "Left!" Three young men pushed the backdrop up. One kid wearing a peach-colored bowling shirt with *WORLEY'S ELECTRICAL SUPPLY* embroidered on back ran around and caught the teetering wall. They steadied it with long two-by-fours while trying to figure out how to add another brace to make it steady. "*C'est ça,*" D-Daddy said. "That's it."

"Everything's looking great," I said, walking up to him.

He pulled out a dark blue bandanna and wiped his perspiring face. "Told them boys in the wood shop two braces weren't near enough. Guess they'll listen next time. Everything's close to done, you bet."

"Gee, D-Daddy, what do you need me for?"

"To give light to the heavens, *ange,*" he said, giving me a toothy smile and gesturing skyward. His thick white pompadour glistened in the sunlight.

One of the kids struggling with the backdrop snorted loudly. D-Daddy snapped his long fingers and told him to get cracking or there'd be no lunch for him come noon.

Inside the museum I walked through the exhibit, thankful again for D-Daddy's unexpected presence in my life. The story quilts were all hung evenly and properly with the wooden clip hangers the woodworkers had recently made. On the other side of one of the freestanding walls in the main exhibit hall, I heard a voice singing softly "*Jolie blonde,* you steal my heart away" in that sweet lilting tempo common to Cajun music. I peeked around and found Evangeline standing on a footstool making a few finishing stitches on her already-hung story quilt. Though I hadn't made a sound on the museum's speckled commercial carpet, she must have sensed my presence. She spun around quick as a sparrow, her face icy with panic, small embroidery scissors held point outward.

I held up my hands. "I surrender."

She laughed uneasily. "Benni, you startled me." She hopped down off the folding stool, her wide cheekbones flushed with tiny rosebuds.

"Sorry," I said. "What are you doing?"

She glanced over her shoulder, then gave me a rueful smile. "You know quilters. We just can't ever really finish anything." She laughed. "Or maybe I should say *fabric artists.*"

I laughed at her emphasis. There'd been a constant though good-natured rivalry between the traditional quilters, who preferred utilizing historic patterns and reworking them in creative ways, and the avant-garde quilters, who believed in free-form expression, tended to avoid traditional piecing, and insisted on being called fabric artists rather than quilters. This exhibit celebrated both groups, as storytelling quilts used both techniques. But even looking at the displayed quilts, you could guess each quilter's preference. Evangeline, being a natural peacemaker, moved effortlessly between the two groups, her gentle sense of humor keeping the conflict light and playful.

"It's marvelous," I said, scanning her story quilt—*Cajun Days and Nights.* I'd just typed up her explanation about the creation of the quilt yesterday and, as I had with each quilt, studied it closely after transcribing her words from my tape recorder. She'd chosen to present her story in an easy, entertaining way that would draw the spectator into the quilt. It unfolded in rows like a comic strip—every other square was a traditional pieced pattern—Little Schoolhouse, Ocean Waves, Streak of Lightning, Crosses and Losses—contrasting with the intricate appliquéd story squares showing some aspect of Cajun life—a swing in a drooping cypress tree, an old bearded man in a small pirogue fishing in a swamp, a woman rocking her baby while her husband lies sleeping under a quilt, a flock of orange-legged cranes hiding among some marsh reeds, a ramshackle building with a sign advertising SMALL ACCORDIONS, BOUDIN, HOT LINKS, USED TIRES, RUBBER BOOTS—CHEEP. There were sixteen squares in all. The colors were as bright and eye-catching as a circus poster.

"I just had to add some beading to this woman's dress," she said. "I really need to learn to let go, I guess. I've got four commissioned quilts I simply have to get finished."

"That's what you get for being so talented," I said.

She stepped down off the ladder. "I really want to finish them on time so people will keep commissioning me. The sooner I quit working at Eudora's, the happier D-Daddy will be." She worked part-time at Ash's coffeehouse/restaurant, and her father wasn't real pleased with it. He and Ash had tangled more than a few times since we'd started planning this festival. I'd never figured out just what the problem between them was. I'd heard rumors that when Evangeline first came to town, she and Ash had a short fling, but I didn't put much stock in it. Rumors of Ash's conquests had to far outweigh the true number of women he'd actually slept with. And Evangeline, gentle spirit notwithstanding, didn't impress me as being anyone's fool. She and D-Daddy were very close, though, and I assumed she just wanted to quit at Eudora's to make him happy. He told me once they didn't need her money, his Social Security and savings could support them, but I was sure Evangeline wasn't the type of woman to live off anyone—even her father.

"So, what's up with my lover?" she asked, her dark eyes twinkling with humor. It had become a running joke between us about her name and Gabe's. I'd completely forgotten, until she mentioned it one day, about those ill-fated

Acadian lovers of Longfellow's narrative poem, Gabriel and Evangeline.

"He's probably in another meeting chomping at the bit," I said. "The thing he hates most about being chief is that everyone else gets to do the fieldwork and he has to sit and listen to politicians strategize and complain."

"Poor Gabe," she said.

"And it's only going to get worse, what with Nora's death." I nodded toward the co-op studios. "How's everyone doing?" I'd come to rely on Evangeline to keep me informed on the general emotional tenor of the artists.

"Everyone's buzzing, of course. It's such a sad thing. Nora was only a few weeks older than me." Her face became as pale as unbleached muslin. She touched a hand to her stomach. "It makes me sick to even think about it."

I nodded and changed the subject. "How's your story for the festival coming along?" Evangeline's specialty was, naturally, Cajun folktales, and a few days ago she'd given me a performance of the Gabriel and Evangeline story she'd modified. She'd turned it into a comedy—making Gabriel and Evangeline fat and sassy Hampshire pigs (with her humble apologies to Gabe and his cohorts) separated on the way to the slaughterhouse. Unlike Longfellow's lovers, their tale ended happily, with them wallowing in a cool Louisiana mud puddle, grunting as the sun set behind a weathered gum tree. By the end of the story, she'd had me giggling like a little kid.

"I'm as ready as I'll ever be," she said. "I'm nervous, of course, but once I can look into people's faces, I'm fine." She rubbed her palms down the sides of her faded gingham shirt. "How's things in the North Forty?"

"With D-Daddy in charge? You have to ask?"

She laughed. "You're right. What do you have planned today?"

I gestured around the room. "Everything's done here, thanks to your dad, so I guess I'll just go to my office, have a cup of coffee, and contemplate the cosmos.'' And Gabe and Sam, I thought, then took a deep breath. And Rita. I'd almost forgotten about *her*.

''Why the sigh?'' Evangeline asked, her eyebrows curving inward in concern.

I waved my hand. ''Nothing, just some unexpected company. I'll fill you in later. Want a cup of coffee?''

''No, thanks. I have to get changed and get to work.''

''Don't forget the last board meeting Wednesday night at Angelo's,'' I said. ''The pizza's on me.''

''Seven o'clock, right? I never miss a free meal.''

After a quick raid on the never-empty coffeepot in the co-op's small kitchen, I walked past the wood shop into my windowless office. The now familiar scent of wood shavings, hot glue, and wet leather calmed my agitated soul almost as much as the comforting ranch smells of my childhood. I set my mug down on my desk and surveyed my very full ''in'' box. I had things to do, there was no doubt about it, but I was nervous and antsy, as I always was before a big museum function, and I knew I'd probably be better off tackling my paperwork next week when the festival was over.

I propped my feet up on my desk and stared at the double-framed pictures of my husband. One showed him sober-faced and perfectly groomed in a dark suit posing for his official chief-of-police portrait. The other was a snapshot I took one afternoon last summer when he was washing his dad's old Chevy truck, right after it arrived from Kansas. He wore a pair of shredded Levi's cutoffs, and his thick black hair was at the shaggy stage just before he gets a haircut. Soapsuds dotted his dark chest hair, and his face beamed with pure adolescent pride and joy. It was my favorite picture of him.

A sharp tap on my door startled me out of my daydreaming.

"You busy?" Peter Grant asked. Without waiting for an answer, he sat down in one of my metal office chairs. He wore a dark green T-shirt today stating GO CLIMB A ROCK and he was scowling.

"What's wrong?" I asked, setting my coffee cup down.

"What isn't?"

"Okay," I said, keeping my voice neutral. This sounded serious. "I guess we're playing twenty questions. Is it something to do with the festival?"

"It's Roy."

"What about him?"

"One of the stories he's going to tell on Saturday trashes environmentalists. Stop him."

I contemplated him for a moment. We were treading on delicate ground here. I didn't know what the content of Roy's story was, though I'd certainly find out, but one storyteller demanding another storyteller change his story was asking a lot.

"How exactly does he do that?"

He shifted uncomfortably in his seat. "I haven't actually heard the story, but someone said he trashes them."

"Who?"

He shook his head. "I don't want to get anyone else involved."

"Okay, I'll look into it. If there's anything that I think is demeaning to anyone, I'll certainly discuss it with him, but there's no law—"

"Not good enough. I demand he be stopped. I think the ranchers have paid him to make me look foolish and push their own agenda."

"I'm sure that's not true, Peter. As for what's in his story, we've got a small thing called the First Amendment going here. Unless there's something I find unsuitable for a family crowd in his story, I can't really tell him what to say any more than I could ask you to change your stories."

His tanned face drew into a sneer. "Why should I have expected anything different from *you?*"

I bit back my response, refusing to rise to his baiting. "Look, this festival is not supposed to be about pushing political agendas. The whole point of storytelling is to bring people together, consider someone else's point of view. Why can't you and Roy work this out between yourselves?"

"I knew you'd wimp out," he said with a bitter laugh. "What's wrong? Afraid I might sway some people in my direction?"

"I believe people have the right to hear *both* sides and make up their own minds. I just find one thing funny about you, Peter."

"What's that?"

"You're so free and easy about wanting what I own to be publicly administrated, I wonder how you'd feel if the shoe were on the other foot."

"I'd think about the common good."

"Oh, really? Let's see, you own a home, right? And if I remember correctly, it has a pool."

He looked at me suspiciously. "So?"

"You use that pool, what, two or three times a week? I think when you're not using it, it should be available for the common good. I think you should open it up to all the people who don't have the financial means of owning a pool. And if anybody accidentally hurts themselves while playing in your pool, they should have the right to sue you. It is, after all, your responsibility."

"That's ridiculous. It's not the same thing."

"Why? Because someone owns five hundred acres and you own a quarter acre? Isn't the common good what we're talking about here?"

He pointed a finger at me. "I'm warning you, Benni. If Roy does anything that makes me or my friends look bad, he'll be sorry."

"Don't threaten me, Peter. I have the authority to pull you out of the festival and I won't hesitate to use it if I think there's going to be trouble." I smiled sweetly at him. "All for the common good, of course."

His face flushed a deep red, and he stormed through the door, almost knocking D-Daddy down in the process.

"What his problem?" D-Daddy asked, vertical worry lines folding over his white eyebrows. He looked at my face and said, "That man bother you, *chère*? You say the word—" He held a fist up in front of him.

I covered his big-knuckled hand with mine. "It's nothing. Peter and I have been trying to push each other out of the pen since we were calves."

D-Daddy shook his head dubiously, but didn't press it.

"How's it looking out there?" I asked, changing the subject.

"By Friday it'll be perfect, I guarantee."

"I've never doubted that for one moment."

"Evangeline here?"

"She left for work about a half hour ago."

His good-natured expression turned sour. "She don't need to work there, no. I'll take care of her."

"I'm not getting in the middle of that fight," I said. "I'm going to go to lunch in a little bit. Want me to bring you back something?"

"No, Evangeline make me lunch today. In the icebox."

"Well, man the battle stations while I'm gone. I think I'll drop by the stables for a little while, too. I'll be back around four."

I puttered around the office for a few minutes after D-Daddy left, trying to decide what I felt like eating. The argument with Peter had left me restless. I had enough to worry about without the stress of a possible fight between environmentalists and aggies at the festival. I wondered what Gabe was doing. I wondered what Sam was doing. I wondered if they'd run into each other in town and what would happen if they did. I wondered why in the world I was letting it bother me. As I was leaving, the phone rang, and another worry jumped to the front of the list.

"There's no food in this house," Rita whined.

"Get a job," I said, and started to hang up. I quickly amended my statement. "But not in San Celina."

"I ran into Gabe this morning," she said, her voice carrying that smug tone I knew too well.

"How?" I asked, seeing as when I walked him to his car this morning, she wasn't even up yet.

"He forgot his briefcase. We ran into each other when I was coming out of the shower."

I groaned inwardly and asked, "Oh, geez, were you dressed?"

"For pity's sake, Benni, of course I was. What kind of trailer trash do you think I am?"

I took the fifth on that one.

# 6

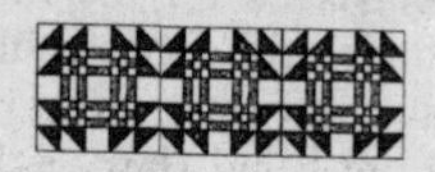

"I'M STARVING," she said. "Want to go to lunch? I'll tell you all about Skeeter—that no-good, double-dealing bull jockey."

"Gee, I'd love to, but—"

"Please, Benni." A small sniffle came over the line. "I don't have anyone else to talk to." Another sniffle. Louder this time. Then she brought out the big guns. "You're *family*."

I curled my toes in frustration and gave in. "How about meeting me at Blind Harry's in a half hour? You can walk there from the house."

"Walk?" she squealed. I jerked the phone away from my ear. "Can't you pick me up?"

"No," I said firmly, determined at least to have a modicum of control. "It's only about a half mile. You did it fine last night."

"I wasn't alone last night. Walking is so boring."

"It's great for stress."

"I'll tell you what'll relieve my stress," she snapped. "A quick divorce. That lyin' son—"

"Rita, hold that thought for Blind Harry's."

"Not there," she said peevishly. "That Mexican friend of yours, Elena What's-her-name, always gives me sour looks. I can't enjoy my lunch if someone's glaring at me the whole time.''

''It's *Elvia,*'' I corrected for the millionth time. But I caught her not so subtle drift. Elvia couldn't abide Rita and made no bones about showing it. ''Okay, there's a new cafe around the corner from Blind Harry's. It's called Eudora's Front Porch. It's on the corner of Alvarez and Elm. You'll like it. The menu reads like one of Aunt Garnet's Sunday dinners.''

Since I was driving, I reached Eudora's in five minutes, which gave me time to relax before being bombarded with Rita's marital woes. Ash had done an incredible job in carving a niche for Eudora's in a town already close to the saturation point with restaurants and coffeehouses. He'd taken an old two-story Victorian house and transformed it into a popular meeting place for local musicians and artists as well as attracting a large clientele for his authentic Southern menu. The house was painted a pale butter yellow with white trim, the wraparound porch crowded with white wicker furniture. Inside the spacious house, the living room, now the main dining room, was filled with artfully mismatched antique chairs and resin-coated oak tables. On the walls were framed copies of all of Eudora Welty's book covers and black-and-white prints from her photo essay of Depression-era Mississippi. In the center of each table were glazed widemouth pots made by one of his regular customers. Inside the pots were small tablets and freshly sharpened pencils. ''We don't ever want a brilliant idea or image to go unrecorded,'' Ash was fond of saying. To the right was a coffee bar where drinks and food could be ordered. At the end of the bar sat an antique brass cash register that made that satisfying *brriing* when it swallowed your money, making you feel as if business was still being conducted, sans computers, in a civilized person-to-person way. Elvia told me that Ash had talked three very prestigious citizens into investing in Eudora's on the strength of his personality alone. One of them was Constance Sinclair herself. Recalling how Jillian looked at Ash, it wasn't hard to guess how he'd accomplished getting Constance's money.

Each of the three main rooms was named for a famous Mississippian. As was expected, the writers and storytellers claimed the Bill Faulkner room, the musicians occupied the Elvis Aaron room, and the visual artists and photographers the Marie Hull room. I ordered an Italian cream soda and told them I would wait for my lunch companion in the Elvis room. I preferred this small but airy back room not because it was usually filled with musicians, as pleasant as their impromptu harmonica and guitar concerts could be, but because it looked out over Ash's colorful backyard garden of roses, peonies, impatiens, and geraniums.

I grabbed an abandoned *Freedom Press* newspaper, and like everyone else in San Celina, after scanning the front page of the weekly paper—this week a story about whether coyotes were friends or predators—I compulsively turned to page five to see who the Tattler had skewered this time. The anonymously written column the paper had been running for eight or nine months now and had become the hot topic among hometown folks. The columnist respected no boundaries about whom he attacked—politicians, longtime residents, merchants, local artists, community activists, conservatives, liberals. The Tattler was a nonpartisan gossipmonger. No names were ever mentioned, so thus far the *Freedom Press* had avoided any lawsuits. More than any column in the newspaper it garnered angry and virulent letters to the editor. Everyone compulsively read and discussed it with the sick obsession of freeway gawkers at a bloody car wreck. This week the Tattler was attacking a local garden club's benefit dinner/dance to raise money for the planting of a community rose garden in front of the county courthouse honoring their longtime president, a local society matron whose husband was a popular divorce attorney and gentleman rancher.

The Tattler wrote: *How inspired and blessed the homeless will be when they gaze upon the splendor of a perfect Sterling Silver Beauty as they dig through the trash bins for their morning meals.* Then he went on to chastise a local liberal bookstore for refusing to carry Rush Limbaugh books and then turned around and lambasted Rush for writing such ridiculous claptrap to begin with.

After a quick scan of Elvia's book review of a storytelling book on special this week at Blind Harry's, I set the paper down. My eyes rested on the pale peach roses in Ash's garden, and I mentally ran over my day's schedule. Listen to Rita and find out her plans, sign my statement at the police station, go to the stable, then back to museum to see how things were faring. Then home and a continuation of last night's standoff. Remembering Gabe's request for the festival committee members' names, I pulled one of the small tablets from the pot in front of me and jotted them down. Peter Grant. Gabe had obviously remembered him and had one of the detectives get in touch with him this morning. Roy Hudson, Grace Winter, Evangeline Boudreaux, Ashley Stanhill, Dolores Ayala, Jillian Sinclair. I scratched my cheek with the tip of the eraser then added Michel ''D-Daddy'' Boudreaux, though he certainly wasn't a suspect. D-Daddy, for all his blustering, wouldn't hurt a fly, I was sure of it.

So who else could want her dead? Except for her storytelling friends, I knew Nora had always been a bit of a loner and that it had gotten worse since her son died a year ago. He'd been in a coma for months after a car hit him while he was riding home from school on his bicycle. Her life, according to Nick, had become a vigil of sitting day after day next to her son's bed—sometimes twelve and fourteen hours at a time. Gradually her few friends dropped away, Roy left her, and so when her son finally died, she had no one except Nick left in her life.

Maybe it was someone she worked with at the library. I thought about the two children's librarians, whom I knew casually. Both appeared to be normal, middle-aged women with husbands, children, and mortgages. Maybe a clerk or a page she aggravated? I couldn't imagine any of the employees I'd seen at the library putting a rope around Nora's neck, squeezing the life out of her, then dragging the body down to the lake. It took an awful lot of determination . . . and hate to drive a person to those measures. Then again, as I'd slowly learned over the last few years, perhaps everyone was capable of murder if put in the right circumstances. The why. That was always the most frightening, yet intriguing part of a murder, and as Gabe said, the unknowable part. He'd often said to me we can know the physical circumstances that lead up to and cause one human to take the life of another, but what we can never know is why this particular time, under these particular circumstances, the abused woman finally decides to fight back and kill her abuser, the younger brother who has suffered his older brother's taunting insults for years decides to stab him, the robber decides that *this time* he'll kill the convenience-store clerk for a bottle of wine and two packs of Camels.

"Be careful now, darlin'." Ash's smooth voice startled me. Before I could move away, his thumb brushed over the space between my eyebrows. "Concentratin' like you are is going to put some ugly ole frown lines between those pretty little hazel eyes of yours." He sat down in the padded mahogany chair across from me and crossed his legs. He wore tasseled leather loafers, a sand-colored silk shirt, and khaki wool slacks in a baggy forties style reminiscent of Clark Gable and Jimmy Stewart. A strand of hair fell rakishly across one amused blue eye, and I resisted the urge to reach over and brush it back. As obvious as his cocky posturing was, there was something about him that made a woman want to experience that intimate this-is-between-you-and-me half smile he bestowed like a coveted Mardi Gras doubloon on whoever struck his fancy. Guys like him made me want to chew glass, especially when I felt the magnetic pull to react like every other woman.

"I'm waiting for my cousin," I said. "She's from Arkansas, so I thought she'd enjoy the food here."

He nodded. "Try the Brunswick Stew. It's my grandmama's recipe. And there's Mississippi mud pie on the dessert menu today." He flashed me a white smile.

"Sounds good." I rubbed my thumb over the notebook in front of me.

"What brilliant thoughts are we recording today?" he asked, snatching the notebook from under my hand.

"Nothing important," I said, grabbing for it a second too late.

He just grinned and flipped it open. I watched his face as he read the list. Thank goodness I hadn't gone with my first inclination and listed reasons I thought each person could be guilty next to their names. His face slowly turned serious. He tossed the tablet on the table.

"What's the list for?" he asked.

"Nothing," I said, shrugging, trying to appear nonchalant. "I'm just making notes for—" My mind went blank. I carefully ripped the pages out of the notebook trying to come up with something. Survival brain cells kicked in. "My opening speech Friday night. I'm going to thank all the people who served on the festival committee." I was saved from further explanation by the lovely sound of Rita's whiny drawl.

"Lordy, I'm about ready to melt clean away," she complained, tip-tapping across the glossy wood floor wearing tiny white shorts, a matching cropped tank top with a red sequin heart over her right breast, and strappy backless sandals. "Thank heavens for that sweet ole gentleman next door who was kindly enough to give me a lift."

"Mr. Treton?" I asked, amazed. "You talked Mr. Treton into giving you a ride?" My neighbor, as diligent as he was about watching over my place when I wasn't there, never did *anything* out of the kindness of his heart. As always, I'd underestimated the power of Rita's hormonal persuasion.

Ash jumped up and held out his chair. "Please, darlin', take my seat and let me get you a cool drink." He called out to a busboy cleaning off a table. "Jimmie, fetch us a couple of iced teas." He turned to Rita. "Sweetened or unsweetened?"

"Why, sweetened, of course," she said, tossing her big, curly hair and bestowing her most adoring smile on him. He threw one back at her as he grabbed a chair from another table, flipped it around, and straddled it, his eyes never leaving Rita's face. *Oh, geez,* I thought. Now I knew why Ash irritated me so much, he was a male version of Rita. I watched, amazed, as the two of them threw each other flirting glances like cards in a poker game—I'll see your wink and raise you a cute little ole flick of a tongue.

Their games continued through the meal, which Ash insisted was on the house just as he insisted on joining us. As I ate my Brunswick stew and picked at my corn bread, I tuned out their voices, and though I tried to fight it, my thoughts drifted back to the puzzle of Nora Cooper's death. I glanced at Ash and wondered if he and Nora had ever been an item. I couldn't imagine it. She didn't seem to be his type. Then again, anything that had the XX chromosome seemed to be his type.

Ash walked us out and brazenly kissed Rita's hand before helping her up into the passenger side of my truck. I gunned the engine in an attempt to drown out her annoying giggle.

"Thank you for a lovely lunch, ladies," Ash said. "We must do it again sometime." He stuck his head through Rita's open window and called to me over the engine's roar. ''See you at the meeting Wednesday night.'' He looked up at Rita, his eyes speaking volumes. ''And, darlin', I'll be seeing more of you later.''

''Absolutely,'' she said.

''What does he mean by that?'' I asked as we drove down Lopez Street. It was two o'clock, and downtown was already crowded with students and shoppers. A long red-and-white banner advertising the San Celina Storytelling Festival stretched out over the busy street and flapped in the breeze. I waited patiently while ahead of me an electric blue Nissan pickup truck double-parked so six teenagers could scramble out of the bed.

''We have a date!'' she practically crowed. She sat back against the bench seat and sighed contentedly. ''I'm really starting to feel better, Benni. Thanks for being there for me.''

I flexed my fingers on the steering wheel. ''Rita, what about Skeeter? You know, your *husband.* The one you promised to love, honor, and cherish.''

She flipped the sunshade down, searching for a mirror, slapping it back up when she didn't find one. She pushed her bright pink bottom lip out in a pout. ''That two-timing jerk. As far as I'm concerned, we aren't married anymore. For all I care, his next bull can gore him in his precious coconuts.''

''I think I better warn you. Ash is not known around these parts for being, shall we say, particular or consistent in his female companionship.''

She turned wide eyes on me. ''Benni, you aren't my mother.''

''Fine, just don't come crying to me when he tosses you aside like a used tissue.''

''Have I ever?''

Considering that was exactly why she was now sleeping in my guest room, I almost let her have it. Instead, I decided to fight back with an even dirtier weapon.

"Guess who's flying in today?" I asked, making my voice as chipper as a flight attendant's.

"I haven't the foggiest." She opened her little white purse and rummaged around, pulling out a plastic tube of lipstick. She twisted it open and inspected the tip.

"Aunt Garnet."

The lipstick froze halfway up to her lips. "Oh, shit."

Aunt Garnet tended to inspire that feeling in many people.

"Does she know I'm here?" Rita asked, her voice desperate.

"Not yet," I said cheerfully. "But you know the grapevine in this town."

She quickly retouched her lips and threw the gold tube back in her purse. "She's going to pitch a fit when she hears about me and Skeeter. Lordy, I hate it when that woman is right. I'll never hear the end of it."

"Just thought I'd warn you. Where would you like to be dropped off? I've got a million things to do today, so I don't have time to goof off."

"Don't take me back to your house. I 'bout dropped dead of boredom there." She glanced out the window. "Just leave me off anywhere. I'll shop around. Maybe I'll buy a new outfit for my date with Ash tonight."

"If you're interested, Sam's cooking dinner tonight."

"He's such a sweet boy," she said, twisting a finger around a reddish-blond curl. I idled the truck in front of the new Gap store.

"Emphasis on the boy part. He's Gabe's son, Rita. Lay off, okay?"

She feigned a shocked look and opened the truck door. "Benni, I'm just crushed. You know I'd never do anything to hurt your new little family."

Why didn't her reassurance make me feel better?

It was only after she was waving me a cheery good-bye

that I realized she'd escaped before I could ask her about her long-term plans.

At the police station, Maggie, Gabe's secretary, informed me he was in a meeting with the city manager but would be finished in a half hour.

"The Grand Poohbah left orders for you to give your official statement to Detective Ryan and then wait for him." Her smile was warm and generous as she stuck a yellow pencil in her dark upswept hair. In her tailored plum business suit and leather pumps, a sedate twin of Natalie Cole, you'd never guess she was a better cowboy than most of the hands Daddy had ever hired. What's more, she was one of the few people who wasn't rattled by Gabe's stern manner. She treated him like a sweet, rather slow younger brother even though he was twenty years her senior. Surprisingly, he not only tolerated it, but also seemed to like her assertive control over his schedule.

After agreeing to be recorded, I followed Detective Ryan, a large-bellied man with a prickly broom of a mustache, into the windowless, tan interrogation room and gave my version of discovering Nora's body.

"Any leads yet?" I asked playfully when he turned off the recorder.

He shifted uncomfortably in his chair, torn between not wanting to offend either the boss's wife or the boss.

"That's okay," I said, rescuing him. "I'll ask Gabe."

"Thanks," he said gratefully, and escorted me back to Maggie's desk.

"Give it to me," she said to the detective, holding out her hand for the cassette. "It'll take forever for one of the clerks to type it, and there's no need for Benni to make two trips." She slipped the cassette into her Dictaphone machine. "His Royal Highness is free now," she said to me, slipping on the headphones. "I'll transcribe this while you two lovebirds coo in there, and it'll be ready for you to sign when you're through."

I smiled. "You know, Maggie, with your efficiency, you're going to be giving the King Ranch a run for their money someday." Her goal, one we'd talked about many times, was to utilize her degree in ranch management and buy her own ranch using her great-grandfather's cattle brand.

She grinned back at me. "Honey, you can hang your hat on that one."

Gabe stood next to his window, hands in his pockets, looking out at the maintenance yard. He turned around and smiled when he saw me.

"You're a sight for sore eyes," he said, coming across the room and pulling me into a bear hug.

"How are things going?" I asked.

"Lousy," he said, nuzzling the top of my head. "Have you seen the *Tribune* today?"

"No," I confessed, pulling away and looking up at him. "I picked up the *Freedom Press* when I was having lunch with Rita, but I only read Elvia's book review and the Tattler's column."

He gave a disgusted "hmmph" and sat down in his chair. "That column is nothing but cheap, yellow journalism. I don't know why you read it."

I shrugged. "Curiosity, I suppose. Just like everyone else."

"And as long as people keep reading it, that junk will keep being printed."

"I gave my statement," I said, changing the subject because he obviously was feeling grumpy, and a gossip column in a local paper wasn't the cause. "Maggie's typing it up now."

"Good."

I opened my purse and pulled out the sheets of paper from the tablet at Eudora's. "And here's those names you asked for last night."

He read down the list quickly. "Thanks. I'll give them

to Jim at the update meeting this afternoon."

"Any leads?"

He looked back down at the list in his hand. "Anything else you want to tell me about these people?"

I didn't answer for a moment, letting him know his attempt at avoiding my question didn't work. "Peter Grant and I had an argument today."

He looked up at me, his face intent. "Really? What about?"

"Same old thing. Private property rights and the common good. And I guess there's some trouble between him and Roy. I think they're both going to try and turn this festival into a political battleground, but they'll have to go through me to do it. I'll toss both their butts out without thinking twice."

Gabe leaned back in his chair, his mustache twitching in amusement. "I have no doubt about that. Should I beef up security Friday night?"

"Nah, I can handle it. They won't backtalk me too much. Everyone knows I have high connections in local law enforcement."

"Not to mention a very protective husband."

"Now, an update from the home front." I spent the next twenty minutes telling him about my lunch with Rita. By the end of my story, I actually had him smiling.

Maggie knocked and opened the door. "All done, kids."

I signed the statement, and Gabe walked me out to the parking lot. "We'll talk more about your storytellers tonight," he said. "Just don't go asking them any questions, okay? That's my job."

I made a cross over my heart and held up three fingers.

"I know for a fact you were never a Girl Scout," he said. He leaned against his dad's truck and stroked the fender. "How's it running?"

"Fine. And don't worry." I poked him in the chest. "I'm

taking very good care of it. Are you going to make it home for dinner?''

His eyes lit up. ''Are you cooking again?''

''No, but there will be a home-cooked meal waiting for you.''

''Your cousin Rita?'' he asked dubiously.

I laughed out loud. ''That was a joke, wasn't it? Actually your son is cooking us dinner. I think he's trying to say he's sorry. Think you can make it home by six o'clock?''

He turned and inspected an imaginary spot on the truck's fender. ''Depends on what's happening with the Cooper case.''

I didn't press it, though I was itching to. ''Well, don't work too hard.'' I stood on tiptoe and kissed him lightly. He pulled me close in a tight hug, then turned back toward the station. After a few steps, he stopped and turned around. The wind softly ruffled the top of his black hair. In his gray Brooks Brothers suit he appeared the consummate professional, but I saw through it to a lanky, pain-racked sixteen-year-old boy whose father died before he could teach his son all he needed to know about being a father.

''Be careful,'' he said, his face still. ''I mean it.''

''Yes, sir,'' I said solemnly, giving him a small salute, then mouthed the words *I love you.*

*''Yo tambien, querida.''*

A short while later I felt a surge of anticipation when I turned right at the redwood Methodist church and drove down the gravel driveway to Grace's stables. Less than fifteen minutes away from both my house and the museum on a back road that eventually led to Montana de Oro State Park and Morro Bay, it had, over the last five or six months, become my semisecret place of retreat. Though I tried to make it out to the Ramsey Ranch at least once a week, I missed the satisfying routine of caring for animals on a daily basis, working in a garden, and living far enough away from civilization that when you sat on your front porch at night, the screeching you heard came from an owl and not your teenage neighbor's tires taking a fast corner.

The road forked at the end, one gravel road leading to her house and the other to the stables. The house was a square, neat two-story with white trim, gray shingles, and an old chimney. Across the front was a white picket fence laced with pink and yellow tea roses, and to the left grew a hundred-year-old oak tree under which sat a wrought-iron patio set. Pockets, her gray tabby cat, sat in the middle of the glass-topped table and licked one white paw.

I drove directly to the stables, knowing that was where Grace would likely be this time of day. Two large arenas flanked a wooden breezeway barn that housed approximately thirty horses. Grace's boarding and training operation was small but exclusive, and as a rancher I teased her quite a bit about the pampering the spoiled city horses received.

"Some of them dress better than I do," I'd said, watching her peel a pink paisley blanket and hood off a glossy Morgan owned by a society woman in town who rode dressage. "Daddy'd bust a gut laughing if he saw the outfits some of these horses wear."

"And they eat better than all of us," she'd replied.

I parked in front of the closest arena. Because school was still in session, only one person was riding this early in the afternoon. By three-thirty, the place would be packed with schoolgirls in skintight breeches and expensive riding boots braiding their horses' manes, discussing the next competition, and giggling over Grace's new seventeen-year-old stable hand, Kyle.

I rested my arms on the metal railing and watched Jillian Sinclair take her huge bay, Flirtatious Fred, through his paces. From inside the barn, I heard Michelle Wright telling all the guys within hearing range that if they wanted her heart they'd have to "take it like a man. . . ."

Grace's high, reedy soprano echoed out of the building as she sang along. Above me, eucalyptus leaves whispered in the warm breeze.

"What do you think?" Jillian asked, riding up to me. She pulled off her helmet and shook out her pale hair. I reached up and ran my hand down the bay's soft cheek.

"Lookin' good," I said. "You have a competition coming up?"

"This Sunday in Santa Barbara. I'm going to have to miss the last few hours of the festival on Saturday night because I want to get him down there early to settle in." She patted the horse's neck. "He's going to do me proud this time, no doubt about it." She swung down, locked the irons in place, and walked Fred over to the gate. I followed and unlatched it from my side.

"Thanks." She led the horse over to a tie bar, pulled off the expensive English saddle, and tossed it over the fence. "Hot walker for you today, sweetie," she said, kissing the horse's forehead. "I don't have time to work all that energy out of you." She pulled off the bridle and handed it to me, haltered Fred, and tied him to the bar. She hefted the saddle and walked toward the tack room in the front of the barn.

"How was it this morning at the library?" I asked inside the large tack room. She threw the saddle over a wooden saddle rack and pulled off her expensive leather gloves.

"People are edgy, of course. I tried to reassure everyone as best I could, but there wasn't much I could say. According to Gabe, there aren't many leads. But I assume you know that." She tossed the gloves on top of a small refrigerator and pulled out a bottle of mineral water. "Want one?" Her thin white shirt was glued to her body with perspiration.

I shook my head no and hung the bridle on a free hook.

"If there were any leads, he probably wouldn't tell me anyway, right?" She took a quick sip from the mineral water and held the dripping bottle to her forehead.

''Probably not,'' I agreed. ''Even I have trouble prying information out of him about cases.''

''Well, I soothed everyone and told them they didn't have anything to worry about, but that they should use the buddy system when walking to their cars, especially the ones who work late on Tuesdays and Thursdays.''

''Good idea anytime, actually.''

''Yes, it probably is.'' She looked at me curiously. ''Did you go to see Nick?''

''This morning. I don't think he's doing very well.''

She nodded in agreement and set her water down on a table crowded with equine medicines and grooming products. ''I thought the same thing when I went by yesterday. I told him to take as much time off as he needs. He and Nora were so close, and now he's all alone.'' She bit the inside of her cheek. ''I know how he feels.''

''Yes, he and Nora—''

''Benni! I thought I heard your voice,'' Grace interrupted, stepping into the tack room. ''Hey, Jillian. What are you two yapping about?''

Jillian and I glanced at each other guiltily. She picked up her water and took another quick sip. I picked at a hangnail on my thumb.

Grace's freckled face scanned both our faces, then scowled. ''As if I didn't know. I can't tell you how sick I am of hearing about Nora Cooper. When she was alive, I couldn't go ten minutes without hearing Nora this, Nora that. I guess it's not going to be any different now that she's dead.'' She grabbed a large plastic feed bucket full of grain and stomped out.

''Well,'' Jillian said after a few uncomfortable minutes, ''I guess she's made her position clear.'' She tucked a loose section of her thin white blouse into her khaki breeches. ''Someone should mention to her that it doesn't look very good, her going on like that about someone just murdered.

Especially since she's living with the deceased's soon-to-be ex-husband."

I smiled wanly, getting her point. "And that someone would be me?"

Jillian gave an apologetic shrug. "You do seem to be her only friend."

"I'll try and talk to her. I don't want her making things tougher on herself than necessary."

"She probably is one of the more obvious suspects, isn't she?"

My mouth opened in surprise. "Jillian, I can't believe you said that."

She tossed her empty water bottle in the small waste-basket. "I bet I'm not the only one who's thinking it. Don't you think that Gabe has her high on his list of suspects?"

"You know I can't talk about that."

Her sharp, tiny features wrinkled in chagrin. "I know. Please, forgive me for my speculations. I guess I've got a bit of the Tattler's blood in me. Maybe that's why that column is so addictive." She gave my shoulder a quick pat as she walked out. "Call me if you hear anything."

"Bye," I called after her. Her flippant accusation of Grace irritated me, though what she said was true. But her admission about liking the Tattler's column neutralized my anger somewhat. I was just as guilty as her. I actually looked forward to reading the gossip column every week, which was starting to really prick at my conscience. What was it in us human beings that caused us to enjoy reading or hearing about the mortification of other people?

I found Grace at the wash racks scraping water off a sorrel Arabian with a white blaze on his forehead. I stood to the side and watched her for a moment without speaking.

"Miz Jillian all through playing horsewoman?" Grace finally asked.

"I don't know," I said, leaning against the metal post of the rack. "Look, we weren't talking about you, Grace, but we were talking about Nora's murder. I don't know how else to say this, but you're going to have to get used to that over the next few weeks. You know we don't have many murders here in San Celina, so it's bound to be big news."

She flicked the water off the scraping blade and continued to run it down the horse's flank. He shook his head, spraying water in my direction. "I know, it's just that I'm already tired of the weird looks people are giving me." She wiped the back of a wet hand across her forehead. Sun-bleached ringlets of copper and gold had escaped from her braided hair and feathered her oval face. "When I stopped off at the feed supply this morning to pick up my order, the two girls behind the registers actually whispered 'that's her' behind my back when I was looking at some new halters. I feel like I'm wearing a big scarlet *A*."

"I'm sorry."

She threw the scraper into a nearby bucket and untied the Arabian. "I know a lot of this is my own fault. Shoot, I'm living with her husband. I slept with him when their son was dying. She was holding up their divorce so we couldn't be together. Honestly, if I was looking for a suspect in this, the first one I'd pick would be me."

"Or Roy," I said, then regretted it.

She looked at me blankly. "Yes, I guess he would be just as obvious as me. But he didn't do it. And neither did I." She led the horse toward the hot walker, where Fred was already meandering in a circle. "We are each other's alibis that night. Did Gabe tell you that?"

"He doesn't talk about his cases at home, you know that." She and I had discussed our men's lack of communication many times over glasses of lemonade and bags of Doritos in her large country kitchen. She clipped the Arabian to the walker and gave him an affectionate pat on the haunch. Then she turned and faced me. "I know you never approved of my relationship with Roy, but I appreciate the fact that you never preached at me."

I smiled. "Except once or twice."

She smiled back. "Everyone is entitled to an opinion, and I do respect yours. I'm not proud of the way he and I got together, but that's water under the bridge now." Her face sobered. "I just want you to know that I didn't have anything to do with Nora's death, but I'm not sorry she's dead. She wasn't as sweet and innocent as she led everyone to believe."

I didn't answer, not knowing quite what to say. Grace's stories about Nora were colored with the prejudice of a woman in love with a man in the midst of a bitter divorce. How much could I believe?

"I didn't kill her," Grace repeated. "And Roy didn't either. You believe me, don't you?" Her face tensed as she waited for my reply.

"Of course I do," I said, flinching inwardly at the tiny lie. Did I think she killed Nora? Though she was quiet and easygoing most of the time, I'd seen Grace lose her temper before. It was as quick and volatile as an illegal firecracker and just about as predictable. Once Roy had to physically hold her back when she took a pitchfork and went after a teenage boy who'd jerked the mouth of one of her horses so hard it broke skin. If Roy hadn't caught her, I have no idea what would have happened. Could that protective instinct toward her animals carry over to her lover? Though I hated admitting it, both she and Roy had the motive, means, and opportunity to kill Nora. They both had bad tempers, a reason to want Nora dead, access to ropes. . . .

She looked past me to the thick oak groves that bordered her property. "Thanks for the lie, but like I said, I'd suspect me, too."

There didn't seem to be anything else to say. I toed the ground with my boot tip. "Need any help today?" I asked, changing the subject.

''Thanks, I've got things pretty much under control. Want to have a ride? Tony can always use the exercise.''

I glanced at my watch. It was close to three-thirty, and in the next half hour the arenas, small rings, and hot walkers would be as crowded as rush-hour traffic in Orange County. ''I'll take a rain check. I'm really just avoiding work, but I needed a quick animal fix.''

She grinned. ''Then stick around. I'm giving the Three Amigos a flea bath this afternoon. They're about ready to drive me nuts.''

I automatically scratched the back of my neck at the thought. ''No, thanks, I don't miss them that much.'' As if on cue, Dos, the second of her three male Kelpies named Uno, Dos, and Tres nudged my leg, wanting to be petted. I bent down and vigorously scrubbed behind one upright brown ear. He smiled his little dingo smile. ''You shameless old beggar, I'm going to take you home with me.'' He yelped in answer, blinking his golden eyes.

''Please, take them all,'' Grace said.

''After their flea dip,'' I answered.

''Coward.''

''We sold three of your wreaths over the weekend,'' I told her as she walked me out to Gabe's truck. As a sideline, Grace made bay leaf wreaths out of leaves she gathered off the Ramsey Ranch. Decorated with dried native flowers and cleverly laced thin satin ribbon, they'd become a popular gift item in the museum's gift shop.

''Great, we need the money. Roy's doing okay now that he's got regular customers, but that can change in a heartbeat.'' She bit down on the corner of her lip, her face worried.

I hadn't even thought about Roy's connection with the murder affecting his farrier business. Horse people were particular and fickle about who took care of their babies. There were quite a few good farriers practicing their trade in San Celina County, so Roy did have something to worry about. I touched Grace's hand. "I'm sure Gabe will find who did this fast, and things can get back to normal."

"Whatever *that* is," she said, then laughed uneasily. She ran her hand down the old Chevy's shiny blue fender. "Why're you driving this old thing? Or more accurately, why is Gabe letting you drive it?"

"That's right, we haven't had time to talk about *my* problems. You aren't going to believe it." I quickly told her about Sam and Rita's spontaneous arrivals and the aftermath. "And I won't even go into my great-aunt Garnet's marital problems," I added.

"I'll stick to being a murder suspect, thank you, ma'am," she said. "Less stressful. With this storytelling festival coming up, sounds like you've really got your hands full."

"No kidding." Her mention of the festival reminded me of Peter's complaint about Roy's story. "Have you heard Roy's story for the festival?"

"Only about a hundred times. Why?"

I explained about Peter's objection.

"For cryin' out loud," she said. "There's not a thing wrong with the story Roy's telling. It's all about a cow-camp cook and his rock-hard biscuits. There's not an environmentalist within a hundred miles of it."

"What do you think this is all about, then?"

"Roy's probably just making up stuff to irritate Peter. You know how Roy feels about those open-space people. They've tangled before at city council meetings."

"Roy wouldn't do anything to cause a ruckus at the festival, would he?"

"Like what?"

"Like tell this story that he's been teasing Peter with."

She shook her head. "No way. That would only make Roy look bad. He's just starting to make a name for himself and he wouldn't do anything to screw that up. I'm telling you, he's just poking at Peter. If Peter was smart, he'd just ignore him."

I sighed and gave Dos one last scratch behind the ears. "I hope you're right." He arched under my petting, then took off after a squirrel that darted across the gravel driveway and sped around the corner of the barn.

"Trust me, Benni."

I gave her a crooked smile. "Why do those words always evoke fear and trepidation in my heart?"

"Girlfriend, you are getting as cynical as that husband of yours. See you tomorrow?"

I opened the truck door. "I'm not sure. My days are pretty full this week. But you'll be at the final committee meeting Wednesday night at Angelo's, won't you? Remember, I'm paying for the pizza."

"With my best boots on." She grabbed my arm before I climbed into the truck's cab. "Benni?"

I turned and looked at her in question.

"I know this is asking a lot." Her nostrils flared slightly, and she took a deep breath. "If you find out anything, could you let me know? I mean, this looks real bad for me and Roy, and I'm not asking you to break any laws, but you talk to so many people, and if you hear anything, could you . . . you know, just clue me in? As a friend?"

Feeling emotionally torn, I struggled for an honest answer. "I'll try," I finally said. "But Gabe's not telling me much. He's trying to keep me out of it."

She looked up at me with pale green eyes as translucent as opals. "I know. I guess I was just trying to find out if this was going to affect our friendship."

"Not if I can help it," I said, and meant it.

"Thanks. I have a feeling I'm going to need all the friends I can get." She let out a low whistle, and Uno and Tres appeared from behind the house. "Where's your pesky brother at?" she asked them.

I watched her in my rearview mirror as she walked back

to the barn, the two perky-eared dogs bouncing around her feet. It occurred to me that I never asked her if any detectives had questioned her and Roy. They must have, recalling her remark about being each other's alibis. That was almost as good as no alibi when both of them had very good reasons to want Nora dead.

*Stop it,* I told myself. *She's your friend, and the least you can do is believe she's innocent until it's proven otherwise.* One thing I knew for sure, if they were guilty, I sure didn't want to be the one to discover it.

It was almost four o'clock when I reached the museum. There was less activity going on, though a few people still milled about with hammers and saws. D-Daddy's old Toyota station wagon was gone, so I safely assumed that he'd completed all the things on my work list for today. He wouldn't have left otherwise. In the studios, a couple of quilters had a double-sized story quilt spread out on a wide worktable and were discussing it in low tones.

"What's happening?" I asked, walking over and peering down at the intricate quilt. It was the *We Are All God's Children* quilt that was a joint co-op project and was being raffled off at the festival, the proceeds going to our local hospital children's wing, which had taken severe cuts with the last city budget. Twelve squares showed scenes of family life from twelve different cultures that thrived in San Celina County. The Latino square showed a Christmas Eve celebration that included a Santa Claus piñata and a colorful Mexican crèche scene on the fireplace mantel. The square, which I'd designed and quilted, was adapted from an old photograph of Elvia's family.

"We're checking it over one last time," said Meg, a thin woman who was partial to long, baggy cotton dresses and musk perfume. Her specialty was modern quilts based on paintings by women artists.

"Looks perfect to me," I said.

She and the other lady chuckled. "You know quilts are

never perfect or finished," Meg said. "Just abandoned."

I smiled at the comment I'd heard so many times from artists. "Well, I've bought twenty-five dollars' worth of raffle tickets, so I'm hoping it comes home with me. I have the perfect spot for it in my living room."

"Good luck," Meg said, laying tissue paper across the top of it and rolling it up. "I can't think of a better home for it."

After checking with the security guard we'd hired for the week to make sure he knew the proper way to lock up after the last artist left, I headed home, wondering what interesting scene awaited me tonight.

Ash's new Mustang convertible was arrogantly parked in the driveway, blocking the garage. He and Rita emerged when I was halfway across the lawn. She wore a pink lace dress that would have made a good doily and matching four-inch heels.

I scowled at him, hoping I conveyed my mental disapproval of him dating my cousin who was still a married woman. He answered with a smooth, knowing smile.

"Don't wait up," Rita called over her shoulder, climbing into his car. "I've still got my key. And you got a message from Dove."

"What?" I stuttered, watching the silver sports car back out of the driveway and resisting the temptation to throw something at it. Who would have ever expected her to keep a key after all this time? And what did Dove want? I found Sam in the kitchen tossing a salad in a large glass bowl and singing. The table was set for three. A basket of whole-wheat dinner rolls sat in the center of the pine dining table.

"Rita won't be joining us," Sam said, setting the salad on the table. It was a green salad using romaine lettuce, radishes, cherry tomatoes, and Parmesan cheese. He pointed at the salad. "It doesn't exactly go with the chicken, but it's all you had."

"Looks wonderful," I said.

''I called Dad's office,'' he said, turning back to the oven and pulling out the chicken. A heavenly aroma of garlic and ginger filled the room. ''According to Maggie, he left about ten minutes ago.'' He opened a pot on the stove and poked at the rice, then checked the vegetables he was steaming.

I picked up a roll and tore off a bite. ''The station's only a mile away. He should be here any minute.''

Sam set the food on the table, and we tried to make light conversation and not watch the cow-shaped kitchen clock. After thirty minutes it became pretty clear that he wasn't going to show up.

''Maybe he got called back to the station,'' I said. ''That happens sometimes.''

He gave me a cynical look. ''Right. Well, enjoy it.''

Before I could answer, he was out of the kitchen, and I heard the front door slam. I looked at all the food spread out in front of me. Resigned, I picked up the salad tongs and served myself. I was in the middle of my second helping of the ginger-garlic chicken when I remembered that Rita said Dove left a message. I chewed my chicken thoughtfully, wondering if she was trying to pawn Garnet off on me. She obviously knew by now that Rita was here as well as Sam and that I didn't have any spare bed space.

After putting away the leftovers, I reluctantly checked the answering machine. To say she'd left me a message was an understatement. My answering machine looked like a Vegas slot machine that hit the big one.

''Honeybun, I need to talk to you. Please give your grandmother a call.'' *Monday—one P.M.,* the automated voice informed me.

''Benni, I need to talk to you right away.'' *Monday—1:37 P.M.*

''Benni, call me NOW.'' *Monday—3:14 P.M.*

''Young lady, if you don't get on the phone right now and call me, you'll be sorry.'' *Monday—3:51 P.M.*

''You've had it.'' *Monday—4:28 P.M.*

I glanced at my watch. It was seven o'clock. I knew that her first day with Aunt Garnet was always the hardest. Maybe things had settled down by now. Maybe they were getting along for a change.

Then again, maybe I'd better leave the house for a little while.

# 7

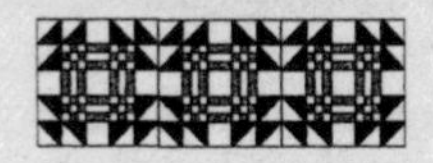

DOWNTOWN WAS MORE crowded than usual for a Monday night. I finally gave up trying to find street parking and settled for a space on the top of the new four-story municipal parking garage. The air was pungent with the smell of coffee and cinnamon and car exhaust. Gangs of students bunched in front of every open coffeehouse and cafe. School had only been in session for about a month, and everyone was still in an insouciant summer mood. The frantic days of finals and term papers were a distant, unreal worry.

In front of Blind Harry's, San Celina's most infamous homeless person, the Datebook Bum, sat on the curb next to his huge canvas bag of junk. His tangled gray head was bent over a maroon leather business diary as he furiously wrote mysterious messages to himself. He was a lovable if sometimes cranky man who, like many longtime homeless, appeared ageless. His dirt-encrusted face and clothing-layered body could be anywhere from thirty to seventy. He'd stubbornly refused any help—only staying in the local homeless shelter when the weather was particularly harsh. No one had ever found out his name or whether he had any family. About six months ago, in exasperation, Elvia, who sent food out to him a couple of times a week, asked him if there was *anything* she could do for him. He shyly pointed to Blind Harry's window display showing the latest in business books and products and asked her in a gentle, cultured voice for the maroon leather business appointment book. With the compulsion humans have for naming things, we'd taken to calling him the Datebook Bum, and in his eyes Elvia was the queen of San Celina. I dropped a dollar bill and all my change into his red coffee can. He looked up briefly and nodded.

I contemplated going into Blind Harry's and perusing the new-book section, but I had a stack of books at home I hadn't even started yet, so I continued walking down the crowded street all the way to the neon-lighted Art Deco Fremont Theater, where they were doing a Gene Autry Monday-night film series. I studied the old cowboy-movie posters, concluding that a movie wasn't what I was in the mood for either. I finally ended up down at a small coffee-house off the main drag called Coffee To Go Go. They had an outside patio with plastic chairs and glass-topped tables nature had decorated with red-and-yellow leaves from the surrounding maple trees. There was a raised concrete platform in one corner for musicians to ply their trade when the mood struck them. Some wonderful impromptu concerts were held there, especially on summer nights when the moon and stars lit it bright as the Grand Ole Opry stage. I sat down in the almost empty patio and waited for my cafe mocha to cool. It was quiet enough for me to hear the silvery rushing of San Celina Creek, which flowed next to the patio right through the center of San Celina. Across the creek, the mission's outside lights flickered on as dusk started to lengthen the shadows of the buildings and bring a cool heaviness to the air. The falling sun turned the church's pale adobe walls to a soft amber. I leaned my head back and closed my eyes for what seemed just a second. When I opened them again, it was almost dark. Somewhere a guitar played a hauntingly familiar blues riff that seemed to coil sensuously through the myrtle and pine trees hanging over the creek.

I threw my cold coffee away and followed the music, taking the wooden bridge over the creek. I found its source on the wide steps of the mission. Nick Cooper sat alone, playing his beat-up guitar.

"Hey," I said, sitting down beside him. "You don't have a hat out. Where am I suppose to put my money?"

He shook his head slowly and kept playing. "Free concert tonight, folks. I'll share these blues with anyone."

After the song was over, he laid the guitar aside and stared out over the creek. "Gabe called me and said they might be able to release Nora's body next week and that he'd speed it up as much as possible." He nodded slightly. "Thanks for taking care of that."

"No problem," I said, stretching out my legs. "How're you doing?"

He shrugged. "Not so good. I can't sleep. I've been living off coffee and glazed doughnuts. I feel like I'm walking through a fog." His sharp laugh seemed to bounce off the shadowed walls of the mission. "Other than that, I'm on top of the world."

I slipped my arm around his shoulders. "Let me buy you dinner."

"Thanks anyway, but I'm not hungry."

"I know food has no taste right now, but you need to eat."

"Yes, Mom," he said, giving me a slight smile.

I slapped his back playfully and laughed. "You know, I *am* beginning to sound like someone's mother, but I have a good excuse. Let me tell you what's going on at my house." Hoping to take his mind off his sorrow for a moment, I told him about Gabe and Sam and Rita and Dove and Aunt Garnet and Uncle W.W. By the end of my story, we were both laughing.

"It sounds a lot funnier when I tell it to you," I said.

"You're lucky to have such a large, caring family."

"We are large, I'll give you that."

"I'm thinking about leaving San Celina," he blurted out.

I pulled my knees up and rested my chin on them, staring out at the dark trees shadowing the creek. "I felt the same way after Jack died. Everywhere I went, something reminded me of him. But I think you shouldn't make that decision for a while. Everything's too raw right now."

He ran his plastic pick softly over the guitar strings. "Actually, I'm just wishing. Gabe pulled the old don't-leave-town-without-reporting-to-us bit on me. He was nice about it, though."

"I don't think he really suspects you. Why should he?"

Nick held the guitar pick up and studied it as if it were some rare artifact. His hands were soft and white and long-fingered. "The land I'm going to inherit. I'm surprised he hasn't told you about it."

"What land?"

"The land that Nora owned. A little bit of dirt that's causing a lot of ruckus with Peter and his friends."

"Which one?"

"Bonita Peak and the land surrounding it." He ran the guitar pick along the edge of his jaw. The rasp of his whiskers against the plastic sounded loud in the quiet evening air.

"Nora owns Bonita Peak? Since when? How did she get it?" Bonita Peak, next to Laguna Lake, where I'd found Nora's body, was a popular hiking spot for locals. Covered with oak trees, monkey flowers, wild raspberries, and Indian paintbrush, it held a lot of personal memories for me as well as a lot of other San Celinans. From the peak you could survey the town of San Celina, watch the sun glint off Morro Rock as it protruded stark and black from the gray Pacific Ocean, while turkey vultures gracefully cruised air currents. The absentee owner had, for as long as I could remember, allowed public access. But in the last few months, something changed. A fencing crew had come in from Santa Barbara, strung barbed-wire fencing all around the bottom of the hill, and posted large "No Trespassing" signs. Local hikers, mountain bikers, and rock climbers had been attempting to find out what was going on. So far, all they'd gotten was a lot of double-talk from some L.A. law firm. Somehow one of them discovered that an expensive housing development complete with private golf course was being considered, with the peak being open only to the owners of the half-million-dollar homes.

"Since about three months ago. And she got it the same way I did," he said, shrugging. "Someone died, and she inherited it."

"What?"

"Let me tell you something right off that not many people know. Nora and I weren't technically full siblings."

"You weren't?"

"My father raised Nora from the time she was two years old, but her biological father owned an oil company. Our mother was his secretary for a couple of years. He was married, of course, so when she got pregnant, he paid her off, and she came up here and eventually married my dad. Nora never even knew until after mom died and we found the adoption papers."

"That must have been such a shock."

He leaned back on his elbows and stretched out his legs. "It was, but she handled it pretty well. After the initial discovery, we never talked about it again. As far as I'm concerned, she is . . ." He paused. "Was my sister. Period. Then a few months ago Nora got a letter from a law firm in Los Angeles telling her that her biological father had died and left her some land. Apparently he felt guilty in his old age. It turned out to be Bonita Peak and the land surrounding it."

I gave a low whistle. "That land's worth a fortune."

"You bet, and she was determined to sell. The rumors

about that housing development are true. The papers were being drawn up this week."

"Why would she sell Bonita Peak to a developer? She grew up here. She knew how much it means to the people of San Celina."

He sat up. Anger shadowed the planes of his face. "It was the only thing in our life that we ever really disagreed on. All our lives we depended on each other. Dad died when I was only eleven and Nora thirteen, and that's when Mom started drinking. We had to grow up real fast and somehow we sensed early that fighting against each other would only make things harder. I was so happy when she inherited that land because I thought she felt the same way I did about it. But Nora went crazy after Joey died. She got it in her head if the hospital had only had the right trauma equipment and staff, Joey wouldn't have lapsed into that coma . . . that he'd still be alive today."

"Would it have made a difference?"

"Who knows? General Hospital had taken a lot of cuts in the last few years. You know they closed their trauma unit down five years ago. The closest one is in Santa Barbara now. The doctors won't say, of course. All they'll say is it never hurts to have the type of personnel and equipment trauma units provide. Who's to say if they'd had all the latest equipment that Joey wouldn't still have died? But when she inherited the land and the developer told her how much he was willing to pay for it, she decided to sell it and donate a big chunk of money toward revitalizing the emergency room at General Hospital and some to an AIDS hospice for children down in L.A. She got involved with this group of parents who lost children, and went down there to tell stories to the children four or five times. She said that it helped her to see that there were worse ways for Joey to have died."

"Both are good causes."

He turned troubled eyes on me. "I know. But I understand what the GreenLand Conservancy is saying. If we develop all our open land, we'll end up looking like Los Angeles or San Jose—all concrete and shopping malls. What kind of legacy is that for the next generation?''

"I guess none of that matters when your child is dying."

"I guess not." He drew in a deep breath. "I don't know what to do now that I'll have the responsibility of the land. Either way I'm going to look like a jerk. Nora had already told the hospital and AIDS hospice they could expect big donations. And now that the decision is mine, I'm not so sure that Peter and my beliefs are the right ones. Even if one child's life was saved because of the equipment that money could buy . . ." He cradled his head in his hands.

"You don't have to make a decision right away, do you?"

He shook his head. "No, but everyone's pulling at me. The lawyers are going to try and rush this through probate so I can make my decision. There's no way I can afford the taxes, so I'll either have to sell it or donate it to the conservancy." He stood up and slung his guitar over his shoulder. "I can't talk about this anymore. If you hear anything, let me know."

"Sure," I said, watching him walk down the mission steps toward the bridge.

I started walking myself, my thoughts a confused jumble. The words *common good* kept repeating in my head. Both things in this situation were for the common good. So which one was more worthy? Deep in my gut the thought of Bonita Peak being turned into an upper-middle-class housing project made me sick. But what about the suffering of people still alive? If I knew the money went toward saving the lives of accident victims or making the last days of children with AIDS easier, would I be able to overcome my distaste over seeing more of San Celina's pristine open land turned into stucco houses? And what about my stand on personal-property rights? Didn't Nora have the right to make that decision? Wouldn't I give up the ranch, even everything I owned, to save Gabe's or Dove's or Daddy's life? I loved our land, but I loved the people in my life more. Personal rights versus common good. Where does one draw the line?

A small practical voice added, *That certainly adds more people to the list of who would want Nora dead.* How far was Peter willing to go to make sure Bonita Peak was saved? I was pretty sure that Nick would be an easy person to sway in the conservancy's direction, especially when he was feeling this vulnerable. And though I hated to admit it, it certainly made Nick's position as a suspect more viable—at least in the police's eyes. After what happened to us in Kansas, I'd come to learn a fine line separated love and hate and how very easy it was to slip, just a split second, over that line. And a split second is all it takes to kill someone.

Before I realized it I found myself in front of Eudora's. A cup of strong coffee was what I needed right now. There were more immediate problems waiting for me on my own personal home front.

It was a busy night at the cafe. Monday evening was officially "group" night, when local writing, music, and artists' groups received half off all coffee drinks in an effort to persuade them to hold their meetings at Eudora's. Though many groups steadfastly continued to meet at Blind Harry's, the basement coffeehouse could only hold so many, and Eudora's had successfully acquired the overflow.

From the Elvis room came the raucous sound of bongos, harmonicas, and a cheery fiddle, much too upbeat for my present mood, so I took my cup of plain old coffee into the quieter though just as crowded Faulkner room. In one corner a group of senior citizens were energetically critiquing someone's tongue-in-cheek poem, "Ode to a Grecian Goat."

Finding no unoccupied tables, I started back out when

someone called my name. The pushy tone made me shut my eyes briefly and wonder if I could successfully ignore it, claiming the noise had made it impossible to hear.

"Harper, I know you hear me," the scratchy voice called. "Get over here. I want to talk to you."

I reluctantly turned around. He was sitting in a small corner table surveying the crowded room like a self-satisfied potentate of a small but powerful nation. To the world "he" was William Henry Hedges, owner, publisher, and paper-clip counter at the *Central Coast Freedom Press*. To me, he was plain old Will Henry, acquaintance and general irritant since sixth grade.

In school, all the way through our junior year of college, when he transferred to UC Berkeley, Will Henry had been thin as a metal fence post, with elbows and knees as knobby as a old cow's. He'd sprawl in the back of classrooms, his feral smile in place, and make fun of whoever didn't believe the way he did at that particular moment. Radical when it was chic, he'd softened both physically and politically as he'd aged. Back in the seventies, his clothing preference ran to musty-smelling Mexican serapes, bell-bottomed jeans covered with peace signs, and those thick tire-tread-soled sandals. Now he carried a tight potbelly that hung slightly over his artificially faded jeans and had replaced his serape with a tweedy jacket. He wore expensive Birkenstock sandals, and though his hair was still long, I knew for a fact it was regularly cut and styled by Elvia's brother Miguel's girlfriend at the mall. A gold dagger-shaped earring glinted from one ear. Still wild enough to shock a few old grandmas.

With his sandaled foot, he pushed out the chair across from him and gestured for me to take a seat.

"Always the consummate gentleman," I said. "What do you want?"

He frowned and pushed the chair with his foot again. "Shit, Harper, sit down for a minute and quit gawking at me like I just French-kissed your grandma. There's something I need to tell you."

"With a gracious invitation like that, how can I resist?" I remained standing and sipped my coffee. "Will Henry, I'm busy. So what is it?"

He stood up and pulled the chair out, running his tongue nervously over his wide-gapped teeth. "Benni, just give me a minute, okay?" He bent closer and whispered, "I have some information for Gabe, but I don't want to go in to the station."

That got my attention, just as he knew it would. I sat on the edge of the chair, setting my drink and purse on the table. "What information?"

"You want anything? A cappuccino? A muffin? It's on me."

"Just tell me what you want to tell Gabe."

He sat back in his chair and folded his hands across his hard little belly, his wolfish expression returning. "Who shoved a branding iron up your butt, Harper? Why are you treating me like this? I haven't trashed ranchers in months. And didn't I do that article pointing out to all the veg-heads how many animal products they used without even knowing it?"

I felt the back of my teeth tighten. He knew why he rubbed me the wrong way, but I wasn't about to get into it with him here at Eudora's. We'd been on the outs ever since he wrote about the methamphetamine lab that had been found on Daddy's best friend's ranch last year. It had been booby-trapped, and the trip wire the horse stumbled over caused one of their ranch hands to be thrown and shatter his collarbone. The horse had broken his leg and had to be shot. Not to mention that after the police busted the lab, the cleanup was the financial and legal responsibility of the landowners. Living on the edge like most ranchers did these days, it almost drove them into bankruptcy. Will Henry's paper only moaned about how much tax dollars the bust cost and complained that if all drugs were legalized, then things like this wouldn't happen. Not one word about the victimization of the innocent rancher.

"If you don't spit it out in the next minute, I'm outta here."

"Okay, okay," he said, sitting forward. The gray in his shaggy hair appeared yellow in the pale cafe lighting. "You have to promise that I won't be dragged into this."

I frowned. "You know I can't promise that. Maybe you should be talking to Gabe if it's that serious."

"I just don't want people to get the wrong idea. I don't want my reputation ruined."

"What reputation? Will Henry, everyone thinks you're a mouthy jerk who'll do anything to sell newspapers."

His soft cheeks pulled in at my comment, and for a moment I regretted my words. I didn't like deliberately hurting someone's feelings, but there was something about Will Henry that made me want to bite before I was bitten.

"People think I'm a jerk?" he said, his voice a bit sad.

"Please," I said, sighing deeply. "I'm tired. Could you just tell me what it is you want to tell Gabe?"

"I want to go on record that it wasn't my idea . . . entirely. The concept was mine, but she did it."

I felt like throwing my coffee at him. "Quit talking in circles."

He leaned forward and whispered, "Nora was the Tattler."

"What?"

"I said—"

"I heard what you said. I'm just . . . shocked. She wrote all that hateful stuff? How . . . why . . . ?"

"I edited it, but she gathered the information and wrote the column. That woman was incredible. Between working at the library and all the festivals and other things she was involved with, she knew more dirt about people in this town than the priests down at St. Celine's Catholic Church."

"What possessed you to even start a column like the Tattler?"

"We came up with the idea one evening when she was dropping off her art column. We were drinking tequila and talking about how phony people were, how politicians and public officials were such liars. It started out by being something where we could right some wrongs, hold people responsible for their actions, you know? But with a sense of humor. Sort of a Doonesbury kind of thing. Then she really got into it and started getting juicy stuff on lots of people besides politicians and government people, and, I don't know, it just sort of snowballed into seeing how far we could push the envelope."

"But why would she do that?" I turned accusing eyes on him. "Why would you?"

"Shit, I don't know why she did it. Maybe after all the pain she'd been through she just wanted to inflict a little of her own. A lot of people weren't very kind when her kid was dying. She did have scruples. She'd never let anything bad be said about nurses. She said they were the only ones who stuck by her while her kid was sick. But I did it for the pure and simple reason it sold papers. Circulation tripled when we started the column. Advertisers were willing to pay anything just to get on the same page as the Tattler. I was close to bankruptcy when we started running the Tattler, and we're making a profit now. A good profit."

"That's disgusting," I said.

He shrugged. "That's business."

"What about principles?"

"Principles are a lie perpetuated by the bourgeois in an attempt to keep the proletariat from getting ahead."

I stood up and picked up my coffee. "That's pretty ironic coming from a successful member of the merchant class himself. Tell me, when was the last time you actually had to get up off your fat butt and work manual labor to bring in the beans? I'll let Gabe know what you told me. What happens after that is up to him."

"Question for you, Miss Smart-Ass Harper," he said. "How many times have *you* missed reading the Tattler?" He gave me a close-lipped smile.

I whipped around and strode out of the room, glad my hair had grown long enough to hide the red I was certain colored my neck as well as my face. He was right. I wasn't any better than Nora and him. The readers of trash are just as responsible as the writers. A column like that could have died a quick death if we'd all protested it when it came out by not reading and discussing it as much as we did. Why *was* that so hard to do?

On the drive home I mulled over the information I'd received from Nick and Will Henry. I was a bit annoyed at Gabe for not telling me about Nora owning the disputed land. What would it have hurt for him to tell me that? With so much at stake, that put a whole new spin on things and opened the murder suspect list to a much larger group of people. The fact that she was the Tattler increased it even more. I'd forgotten to ask Will Henry if anyone else knew that Nora was the Tattler, but I assumed that no one did. The identity of the columnist had been a popular coffeehouse topic since the column started. Everyone had assumed that Will Henry himself wrote the column—it had the sort of sarcastic tone he was known for—but he'd sworn up and down that he wasn't the author. Now I, for one, knew that was true. I also couldn't help but wonder what was in this week's column. I wished I'd kept my cool long enough to ask Will Henry.

When I arrived home, it was obvious that more than the discussion of Nora's secret identity was on the activity chart tonight. Parked behind Gabe's Corvette was one of the brown Ramsey Ranch trucks. I looked in my rearview mirror as I pulled in front of the house in time to see my red pickup pull in behind me. Sam waved cheerily from behind the wheel while Rita stretched her head out the window to gaze in the side mirror and poke at her hair. She left with Ash and returned with my stepson. I'm not sure I wanted to know the story behind that. I laid my head on the steering wheel, wondering briefly just who was being delivered by the Ramsey truck, what new things Gabe and his son could fight about tonight, when in the world Rita would leave, and just for a second, how long it would take me to drive to Atlanta, Georgia.

# 8

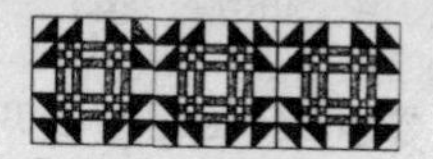

"SHE CHEATS!" DOVE was saying indignantly when I walked in the living room. I'd left Sam and Rita to wander in on their own, hoping I'd have a few minutes to put out one fire before another started. And this fire was a big one. The last time Dove was this mad was when she caught a group of hunters tramping around our land without permission. Lucky for us, this time she didn't have a loaded shotgun in her hands. Gabe, his tie undone and a bottle of Coke in his hand, listened with a combined expression of sympathy and panic. His face brightened when he saw me.

"My own sister," Dove sputtered. "A Christian woman. President of the Women's Missionary Union. I'm here to tell you I'm downright shocked. I confronted her, just like the Bible says to, and what does she do? She denies it! Lying! She adds lying to cheating. Lord have mercy. My sister the liar and cheat." Dove paced back and forth in front of the sofa, her normally pale complexion pink as a hothouse rose.

"I'm sure she didn't realize—" Gabe started.

"The heck she didn't!" Dove spun around and shook her finger at me. "I'm staying here until she apologizes or goes home. I'll tell you what's going to freeze over before I ever play dominoes with *that* woman again."

"Dominoes?" I squeaked. "That's what this is about?"

Dove crossed her arms over her ample chest. "I always knew she was the one in the family who got Uncle Hooter's weak genes. He was a gambler and a womanizer till the day they planted his no-good carcass in the ground."

"What did Aunt Garnet actually do?" I asked.

Dove enunciated her words carefully, as if she were talking to a very slow child. "She . . . cheated." She gave a disgusted "hmmph." "And for matchsticks. For heaven's sake, what in the world did she care about winning a stack of matchsticks? What in the heck did she think she'd do with them, build the biggest bonfire in Sugartree? She's going senile, that's got to be the answer. That, or she's as crazy as I always knew she was."

I looked over at Gabe, who by this time wasn't holding back the grin that had started in his eyes and worked down to his mouth. I gave him a hard look. This might be funny to him, but apparently he had missed the part where Dove said she was staying here until Garnet apologized. There was one thing he didn't realize about Dove and her sister—neither one of them apologized. Ever. For anything. Before I could answer, Sam and Rita came in.

"Who's crazy?" Sam asked. He looked over at Dove with interest, flashing his most endearing smile. "Not this lovely lady, I'm sure."

Dove smiled back at Sam. "You must be Gabe's son. I heard you was here visiting. My, you are a fine-looking young man."

He bowed slightly. "Thank you, ma'am. I owe everything I am to my gracious and beautiful mother and upright and hardworking father."

Dove looked at me and winked. "He's certainly the little charmer, isn't he?" She glanced over at Rita. "What in heaven's name are you doing here? That nasty ole cowboy finally get fed up with you?"

Rita tossed her head and sniffed daintily. "I left *him*. As a matter of fact, Ash took me to see a lawyer today who told me it was definitely a case of irresponsible differences.''

''He got that right,'' Dove said with a harsh cackle. Gabe turned his head, trying to hold back his laughter. I didn't even try to stifle the laugh gurgling up from my chest. You had to love Rita. Sometimes she could drive a post into the ground with one swing.

Rita turned and glared at me. ''It's not funny. I wish everyone would realize I'm in real pain here.'' She pushed past us and ran to the guest bedroom, slamming the door behind her.

''I'll go talk to her,'' Dove said, picking up her large flowered suitcase. ''We're going to be bunking together anyway, so I may as well get her feathers smoothed down.''

''Wait a minute, we need to talk about this thing between you and Garnet. What exactly—''

Dove patted my shoulder as she passed me. ''It's gettin' late, honeybun, and I'm tired. Breakfast is at seven-thirty.''

Before I could protest, she disappeared into the guest room. I looked at Gabe, who was still grinning.

''You won't be so happy when there's no hot water for your shower.''

He laughed. ''I'll use the showers at the station.''

''Speaking of showers,'' Sam said, not looking at his father. ''I think I'll take one right now.'' He breezed past us and claimed the bathroom. Gabe stared after him a moment before turning to me.

''Alone at last,'' he said, downing the rest of his Coke. ''Is there anything to eat? And where have you been? You usually leave a note.''

''And you usually call,'' I answered, snatching the empty Coke bottle out of his hand and heading for the kitchen.

He followed after me. ''Sorry, we got so involved . . . why are you mad?''

I tossed the bottle in the trash and started putting dishes in the dishwasher. ''Sam cooked you dinner. We waited, and you never showed up. That short and sweet enough for you, Friday?"

"Look, I just wasn't ready—"

"To be decent to your son," I finished.

"No," he replied. He paused for a moment, and I could tell he was picking his words very deliberately. "Benni, I'm really sorry you have to be caught in the middle of this thing between me and Sam. As I told you before, there's a lot about him you don't know. It's not your fault. Everyone falls in love with him. *At first.* You think I haven't been taken in a million times by that smile of his? Lydia and I both have, especially after the divorce. She and I have discussed this many times, and we both agree that *we* caused a lot of his manipulating personality. Hopefully it's not too late to try and correct some of our mistakes. I want him to become a self-sufficient adult who doesn't try to just get by scamming off friends and family."

I looked down at the ground guiltily.

He groaned softly and took my hands in his. "You gave him money, didn't you?"

"He didn't ask," I said defensively. "I offered."

He squeezed my hands, his face sad. "Sweetheart, he never asks. That's how good he is. *That's* what I want to try and change before it's too late. I want him to become a responsible member of society, not a leech."

"At the cost of your relationship?"

"Even at the cost of that. My responsibility as a parent to raise a child who can fit into our society is more important than having a child who thinks I'm the most wonderful person in the world."

Can't you have both? I wanted to ask but held back. Who was I to ask that question? I'd never even had children. He pulled me into his arms.

"I'm sorry," I mumbled into his chest. "I just wish it was better between you two. You never know when . . ." I trailed off. His arms tightened around me, and I felt him rub his face across the top of my head. I knew we were both thinking about Aaron and I worried again about Gabe essentially ignoring the fact that his best friend had just died. Was his anger at Sam a reaction to that? I knew that was how some people reacted to death—push away everyone you care about with the irrational thought process that if you don't get close to anyone, then you can't be hurt when they're taken away. "Gabe—" I started.

He let go of me and opened the refrigerator. "Can we discuss this another time? I'm hungry and tired and would honestly rather talk about anything but my problems with Sam."

"Okay," I said, watching him take out the leftover chicken and rice. "While you eat, I have some stuff to tell you about Nora's case." I filled him in on what I learned from both Nick and Will Henry. "So, why didn't you tell me Nora inherited Bonita Peak and the land surrounding it?"

"I only found out about it this morning. You and I haven't really had a chance to talk, have we?" He scooped chicken and rice onto his plate, then put it in the microwave.

I considered his answer, still not satisfied. "Were you going to tell me?"

He hesitated just a moment too long.

"Gabe! Don't you think that's something I should know? I am working with these people."

"That's exactly my problem. I'm going to ask you just to trust me on this. I'll tell you as much as I think you need to know to be safe."

"At first I thought you were right, that it would be better if I didn't know anything. But I've changed my mind. I think now that the more I know, the safer I'll be."

"I don't agree," he said, taking the steaming food over to the table.

"Why not?"

"The more you know, the chances are greater you might accidentally, verbally or nonverbally, let something out, and that could put you or others in danger." He sat down and started eating. "I think we both agree that you do not possess the most poker face in the world."

"I resent that. I can keep a secret just as well as you."

"If you were hurt in any way because of my job, I'd never forgive myself. Aside from that, I also took an oath when I became a police officer. I am entrusted with public safety, and that requires me to make the decisions I think most prudent at the time. Sometimes I err on the side of caution, but that's just how I am." His eyes softened. "I know this has been hard for you, being thrown into being a cop's wife without knowing what it would be like. But you can't compare our relationship to what you had with Jack. He might have told you everything, but running a family ranch is vastly different than policing a city."

I didn't answer for a moment. He was right; I was used to a different type of relationship, one where there weren't any secrets, professional or personal. And logically what he said about public safety and his responsibility made sense. So why did it still make me so mad?

"Look," he said. "Haven't I been a little better about being open about my feelings and talking to you about my job?"

"On some things," I admitted reluctantly. "But I wasn't involved with those cases."

"My point exactly. *Querida,* give me a break." He reached over and stroked my cheek with the back of his fingers. "I'm doing the best I can."

"I know." I grabbed his hand, suddenly tired of all these conflicting emotions. Right here, right now, I loved him, and he loved me. Let the rest take care of itself.

Later in bed, my troubling thoughts kept me wide awake, staring at the strips of moonlight painting the ceiling. "Gabe, are you asleep?"

"Mmm," he replied.

"We didn't talk about what Will Henry told me. About Nora being the Tattler. Did you know that?"

"Um-hm," he said.

"You did? How?"

"Informant."

"An informant? Where? At the *Freedom Press*?"

"Yes."

"Gabe, were you—" I stopped myself from asking if he was going to tell me. It was too late to get into another argument. An informant at the paper—was it somebody I knew? I fell into a fitful sleep, all the suspects twirling around in my dreams in a tiny colorful cyclone.

Singing woke me the next morning. Something about a pretty woman walking down a street.

"Gabe," I moaned, folding my pillow over my ear. "You forgot to turn off the alarm."

The voice became louder. The tangy scent of Aramis aftershave tingled in my nose. Pretty woman . . . he sang into the pillow.

I opened my eyes and stared into his. "What are *you* so cheerful about this morning?"

He straightened up and started tying his tie. "It's a beautiful day and I'm happy to be waking up with the woman I love at my side."

"Seriously."

"Seriously, there's every reason I shouldn't be in a good mood with what's waiting for me at the office, but I am." He leaned over and kissed my nose. "Take advantage of it."

"Okay, who's the informant at the *Freedom Press*?"

He checked his tie in our full-length mirror, then turned to me. "Sorry, next question."

I stuck my tongue out at him.

He just grinned and said, "You'd better get moving. It's seven-thirty."

"I don't have to be at the museum until ten."

At that moment the scent of bacon frying and the clatter of pans filtered through our bedroom door. I groaned and fell back into the pillows. "Dove. I forgot about her. I can't believe this is happening to me."

"I'd give you some sympathy, but I'm fresh out." He pulled his suit coat out of the closet. "See you in five minutes."

I pulled on jeans and a sweatshirt and made tracks for the kitchen. Dove was serving up grits when I sat down.

"You're late," she said, peering up at my plastic kitchen clock.

"That clock's five minutes fast," I mumbled, looking around the pine kitchen table. Sam and Rita's chairs were empty. "Where's the rest of the crew?" I dished up some grits, doctored them with salt and butter, and reached for the scrambled eggs.

Dove laid a plate of crisp bacon in front of me and a bowl of oatmeal with fresh strawberries in front of Gabe. "Rita get up before ten o'clock?" Dove waved her metal spatula in the direction of the guest room. "She's just like her mother. Those Caldicotts always did think God made the sun raise and fall just so they'd know when to get up and go shopping."

Gabe looked at me and winked. "Where's Sam?" I asked. Gabe's face turned sober as he picked up one of Dove's huge baking-powder biscuits. He passed the plate to me.

"Left early," Dove said, sitting down next to Gabe, a big smile on her face. "Said he had to catch the early waves down by Morro Rock. Apparently he heard through the grapevine that all the chicks surf the north side of the rock." She cackled. "My, he's a nice young man. Helped me pound out the dough for my biscuits early this morning. Has a marvelous singing voice. I'm going to try to get him to join the church choir."

"He won't be here long enough for that," Gabe said succinctly.

Dove raised her eyebrows and didn't comment. "What're you doing today, honeybun?"

I bit into a thickly buttered biscuit and chewed before answering. "Going to clean up some last details about the festival. Give the museum one last going over. And I'm having lunch with Elvia and her mom."

"How is Sofia? That heart spell must have 'bout scared her to pieces."

"Doing great, Elvia says. Doctor says it was just stress. Elvia and the brothers are thinking about buying her a treadmill, but they're sure she won't use it. Rafael and Brenda just got back from Hawaii and brought her some fresh pineapple, so she's making *atole*."

Gabe's eyes brightened. "My grandmother used to make that whenever we visited her in Mexico. Bring me some, okay?"

"Sure." I turned back to Dove. "Now, about you and Garnet . . ."

Dove picked up her plate and stood up. "I don't want to discuss that scarlet woman. *If* she has the nerve to call, just tell her I said Matthew 7:23." She tossed her plate in the sink. "I cooked, y'all can clean up. I have a Historical Society meeting this morning." She stomped out of the room.

Gabe looked at me in confusion. "Got a Bible handy?"

I sighed. "I don't need one. She and Garnet have bandied that verse back and forth for as long as I can remember: 'Then I will tell them plainly, I never knew you. Away from me, you evildoers.' "

Gabe gave a delighted laugh and started clearing the table. "That's great."

"Yeah, well, let's see how funny you think it is when Dove is still here two weeks from now."

He gave me a serious look as he stacked dishes in the

dishwasher. "Two weeks from now this house better be occupied by only two people."

"Gee," I replied. "I wonder where we're going to live."

When I arrived at the museum, it became immediately apparent that tempers and nerves were running short. Nora's murder had added a ribbon of tension to the festivities. Inside the museum our head docent, Mildred Posner, was training a group of five senior citizens.

"Here's our illustrious leader now," Mildred said. "I was just telling them about the first murder you solved during the antique-quilt exhibit last November." Dark eyes sparkled mischievously behind her thick glasses.

"Mildred," I said, "that's *not* supposed to be a part of the tour."

"I know, but you have to admit it gives the place ambience."

"Not the kind we're trying to achieve." Laughter rippled through the small group. I answered with a perfunctory smile. I didn't want to discourage anyone who wanted to get involved, but to them the murders here were just another piece of gossip, a sort of urban ghost story, but to me they were a very real and sometimes still frightening memory.

"What are you teaching them today?" I asked, changing the subject.

She perused her note cards. "We've gone through the history of the adobe and of the Sinclair family. I was just going to start the tour of the storytelling quilts. I read all the histories last night."

"Mind if I follow along?"

"Not at all. You can tell me if I get anything wrong."

The first quilt was made by a woman in Morro Bay who had been married for fifty-three years to a captain of a commercial fishing boat. *Waiting for Henry* was its name. Incorporating the traditional quilt pattern Ocean Waves and using a mixture of hand-dyed multicolored fabric with touches of nautical fun prints, she created a Grandma Moses–style scene of a man out on a wildly tossing ocean hauling in nets, while on a high bluff in a blue-and-white saltbox house his wife stands leaning against a silver widow's walk looking out to sea. Around her shoulders was a bright patchwork quilt embroidered with tiny little fish.

The typed card next to the quilt read, "I spent many hours 'waiting for Henry' and worrying every day about whether the sea would give him back to me. Quilting was a real blessing and comfort to me during those stormy days and nights. And fish, which have supported Henry and me all our married life and sent our two kids through college, always seem to sneak their way into my quilts, whether I intend them to be there or not. The fisherman's nets are actually strings from the nets my husband used before retiring—thank the Lord—three years ago."

I followed Mildred through the tour of thirty quilts in the display and was still delighted by each quilt even though I'd studied them closely myself before interviewing the quilter and recording her story. Most of the quilts followed a common style in story quilts—capturing a moment in the artist's life and freezing it much like a photograph. There were quilts that told of summer days at the beach or mountains, a favorite pair of shiny black tap shoes, a great-grandfather's smelly pipe, a devastating flood that killed a family's three hundred chickens. Tiny moments of people's lives recreated, using myriad pieces of fabric, leather, buttons, and beads.

One especially delightful entry was by a black woman about her grandmother, a native of Tennessee. The title of the quilt was *My Grandmama's Flags.* Bordered by a Peace and Plenty pattern, the center was an array of colorful flags from all the states where her grandmother had family. In the center was a tiny woman with skin the color of milk chocolate sitting in a porch swing underneath a flagpole displaying the American flag. Behind her head, like a huge halo, was an array of smiling faces ranging in color from creamy coffee to rich mahogany.

"My grandmama collects flags from wherever she has family. We were taught from the time we were young children that the first thing we had to do if we moved out of Tennessee was to send her a flag of the state or country we lived in. She has a flagpole in front of her small cabin in Tennessee and whenever one of her children or grandchildren came to visit her or on their birthdays, they can always know that their flag will be waving over her log cabin. She taught all of her kids and grandkids how to quilt. Out of fifty-seven of us, thirty-five are still quilters, including my father. This quilt is my salute to a very special lady, who at eighty-eight still cooks all day every Saturday to make meals to take to the 'old people' at the retirement home."

When we reached Evangeline's quilt, though, even after seeing so many intricate and touching quilts, it elicited an amazed murmuring from the docents-in-training. Evangline's details of Cajun life and the intricate needlework in each of the twelve squares gave her quilt a quality not unlike a painting by one of the masters. It could be rediscovered again and again, as each time you viewed it, another detail revealed itself.

After the group moved on to a bold surrealistic quilt incorporating and celebrating the stylistic features and Native American themes of the Canadian artist M. Emily Carr, I lingered in front of Evangeline's quilt. The Cajun culture had always fascinated me. It brought back wonderful memories of a summer trip with Dove when I was ten and visited an old school friend of hers in Houma, Louisiana. We went to a Cajun dance called a *fais do do* in a concrete-block VFW building, where I learned to eat crawfish and danced with an old Cajun man whose face was as wrinkled as used tinfoil. Because of his perfect timing and ability to dance with two partners, he had the ladies lined up waiting for their turn, toes anxiously tapping.

I studied each of her squares, admiring the details, and paused for a long time to study the Cajun dance-scene block that reminded me so much of the one in my childhood memories. I remember Dove's friend Doris telling me to *ferme ta bouche*—shut your mouth—about going to the dance when we returned to Aunt Garnet's. Aunt Garnet was an old-fashioned Hardshell Baptist and thought any kind of dancing the pure work of the devil.

I strained on my tiptoes to see the top three squares—a bayou scene that showed a pelican in which, if you looked closely in his white chiffon beak, you could see tiny handmade fabric fish. The middle square held a row of babies lying on a quilt-covered bed while the grown-ups danced at the *fais do do*. I'd heard Evangline talk about this square when she was making it. If you undid their tiny diapers, you could tell whether they were boy babies or girl babies. That was the kind of playful detail that made Evangeline's work so special. In the upper right square a woman held a baby in a blue flannel blanket as her husband napped in a brass bed covered with a finely stitched miniature crazy quilt. Staring at it, the overhead track lighting caused my eye to catch a glint of something. Too far away for me to see closely, I grabbed the rickety wooden stool from behind the gift-shop counter and carried it over to the quilt. The glint, I could see at closer inspection, came from a small glass bead Evangeline had sewn right underneath the woman's dark brown eyes. That puzzled me. Did it represent a tear? What was she crying about? Was something wrong with her baby? I opened the tiny flannel blanket held closed by a strip of Velcro and found . . . nothing. Nothing? Where was the baby? That wasn't a detail Evangeline would leave out. Before I could inspect the square any closer, a gruff voice startled me.

"Benni, what you doing?"

Grabbing the adobe wall for support, I turned and faced D-Daddy. The severe expression on his weathered face reminded me that he once captained a fishing boat full of rough, sea-hardened deckhands.

"Nothing," I said, climbing down from the teetering stool. "There . . . I thought I saw a loose thread in one of Evangeline's squares. I took care of it." I startled myself with the quickness of my lie. What instinct kept me from revealing the real reason I was inspecting the quilt?

He gave me an odd look and took the stool from my hands. "Better be careful, *ange,*" he said. His black eyes held tiny pinpoints of light.

"What?"

He held the stool up and jiggled the loose legs. "These chairs, they aren't too steady, no. You could fall and hurt yourself. I'd better take this out the back and glue it."

"Okay, thanks." Following him to the studios, I wondered if this twinge of foreboding I felt was real or just a figment of my sometimes overactive imagination. D-Daddy didn't seem happy I was inspecting his daughter's quilt so closely, and that made me wonder why. I'd learned one thing about story quilts as I'd talked to the quilters and fabric artists as they made and discussed them these last few months. They were often like personal journals and used to either celebrate some wonderful memory or sometimes purge a bad one. I wanted to take another look at Evangline's quilt, only now I would have to be more discreet about it.

At eleven-thirty, Elvia called.

"Mama's serving lunch at noon," she said "Pick me up, okay?"

"Sure. What's she making?"

"White enchiladas."

"I'm on my way."

On the drive over, my thoughts compulsively turned back to all the tiny connections and ambiguities that surrounded Nora and her murder. What did we know so far? That Nora owned Bonita Peak and was going to sell it to developers.

That made Peter a more than likely suspect, and he had plenty of access to ropes through the mountain climbing store where he worked. Both Roy and Grace had grudges against her and also had access to ropes. *Oh, for cryin' out loud, Benni,* I said to myself. *Everyone in San Celina County has access to ropes.* Then there was the new development of her being the Tattler. If someone besides Will Henry knew her identity, it was possible other people knew it, too. Would they kill her over a nasty piece of gossip? I thought back over the last few months of the Tattler's column. Was there anything there bad enough to kill someone over? Not that I could remember. It would have to be something so terrible it would ruin someone's life. It all felt like a game of Scrabble when you get your letter tiles and, no matter which way you arrange them, can't make any words. If you just had a few vowels—

Elvia was waiting for me in front of Blind Harry's. "Mama's really looking forward to seeing you," she said, climbing into the truck.

"I'm looking forward to seeing her, too. Not to mention her *atole*. Gabe asked me to sneak him some."

"We'd better get some while we can. The brothers and their *familias* are coming over tonight. That's the equivalent of a swarm of locusts."

The house where Elvia grew up was in an older section of San Celina where the houses were as individual as the people who lived there, many of them, like the Aragons, for more than forty years. Her parents' neat yellow-and-white woodframe house sat on a huge corner lot that was the envy of the neighborhood. Flowering beds of red and pink impatiens and dozens of blooming rosebushes surrounded the house. They received almost as much loving care from Elvia's mom as her fourteen grandchildren. Two huge walnut trees thick with leaves shaded the green lawn, trunk sections slick as glass from the decades of children who'd shimmied up and down them like little spider monkeys. I'd spent many cool and comfortable hours perched on one of the tree's massive branches, reading or giggling with Elvia as we threw green walnuts on her protesting brothers below us. The house itself always reminded me of a patchwork quilt, with rooms tacked on like bright happy squares, making it bigger as each new baby came into the family.

Inside Señora Aragon's red and yellow kitchen, the smoky smells of hand-burned chilies and simmering pinto beans flooded me with warm memories of rainy afternoons after school sitting at the round maple dining table doing math homework with Elvia, waiting for Dove to pick me up. Elvia hugged her mom and set a basket of fresh strawberries on the table.

"*Chiquita,*" Señora Aragon said, taking my face in her plump, brown hands and kissing my cheek. "You look *bueno*. The *señor,* he is treating you right?" She searched my face with inquisitive eyes.

"Yes," I said, smiling. "He's a pain sometimes, but he's treating me fine. He'd have to answer to you and Dove otherwise."

She clicked her tongue. "*Sí,* he is a pain. He is a man, no?" She pointed at the strawberries and said to Elvia, "*M'hija,* put these over on the counter and help Benni set the table. The enchiladas are ready."

We spread the red-and-white plastic tablecloth over the table and helped Señora Aragon set out the creamy white enchiladas, Spanish rice, pinto beans, and hot flour tortillas. After answering Señora Aragon's questions about the health of my family and how my job was going, I fell into silence and listened to her and Elvia discuss the latest family gossip, which was, by sheer virtue of its size, quite detailed and extensive. As their conversation gradually fell into the half-Spanish, half-English they felt comfortable speaking around me, I let my mind wander, remembering the happy hours I'd spent in this kitchen and anticipating the sweet-tasting *atole* I was going to eat in the next few minutes. A familiar name caused me to mentally rejoin the conversation.

"Juanita Ayala," Señora Aragon was saying.

"Ayala?" I repeated. "Is she related to Dolores Ayala? The Ayalas who own the Celina Cantina Restaurant on Marsh Street?"

Elvia nodded. "Her mother. Mama was just telling me about talking to Señora Ayala after mass on Sunday. Apparently they almost lost the restaurant a while back. They were damaged heavily during that horrible rain last winter because their roof was bad, and they never completely recouped their losses." Elvia shook her head, her thick-lashed eyes narrowing in disapproval. "They only carried the minimum insurance and didn't keep it current. Really stupid move, business-wise. Insurance is the *one* thing I never scrimp on."

"Don't be so hard on them, *m'hija,*" her mother said. "They lose so much money when Roberto was in hospital with his kidneys." She stood up and picked up my empty plate. "Sometimes the times are harder than the money you save for them." Her voice held a gentle reproof.

"I know, Mama," she said. "I'm not saying anything against them, but it wasn't a smart business move."

Señora Aragon stacked my plate on Elvia's and said to me, her eyes dancing with amusement, "Not everyone is as smart as *mi hija la patrona,* eh, *chiquita*?"

"I'd venture to say no one," I answered, laughing as I dodged Elvia's swatting hand.

As Señora Aragon dished up the vanilla-scented puddinglike *atole,* making sure I got plenty of pineapple chunks just like when I was a girl, I asked, "You said almost, Mama Aragon. Did they get a loan or something?"

"She tells me only that the Virgin Mary answered her prayers, and they got some money from heaven." She rolled her eyes skyward as if checking to see if any bills would come floating down and bless her. She shrugged and handed me a ceramic bowl of the dessert. "When mass was over, we lit some candles like we *always* do." She purposely avoided looking at her daughter. Elvia let out an irritable breath. Her mother had been lighting candles in an attempt to get her daughter married since Elvia turned eighteen. "She whispered to me—for the Sinclairs."

"The Sinclairs?" I said, puzzled. "Did they loan them the money?"

Señora Aragon set a bowl in front of Elvia and gestured for us to start eating. "No loan," she said, wiping her hands on her faded cotton apron. "She says they owe no one. She lit a candle for that, too. To thank God."

I thought about that as I finished my dessert and helped clear the table. Brushing away our offer to do the dishes, Señora Aragon walked with us out to the truck and handed me a Tupperware bowl full of *atole*. "Tell Gabriel he has not been to see me in a long time and I am keeping count. Next time, he only gets *atole* if he comes to get it."

"I'll tell him," I said, kissing her cheek. "He's just been very busy these last few days. I guess Elvia probably told you his son is visiting."

She nodded and smoothed back a strand of gray hair that had the nerve to sneak out of her tight bun. "It is good for a man to know his son better."

Elvia hugged her mom and reminded her what the doctor said, to sit down and rest once in a while.

"Ah," Señora Aragon replied, swatting irritably at the air around her. "Plenty of time to rest when I die."

"Why would the Sinclairs give the Ayalas money?" I asked the minute Elvia closed the truck door.

"This is the most uncomfortable vehicle I've ever ridden in," she complained, strapping the seat belt around her waist. "You know, Gabe makes a good salary. Why don't you get rid of that old Harper pickup of yours and buy yourself a new car?''

''If I had a new car, I'd be having to cart Sam around everywhere because I wouldn't let him drive it, and Gabe wouldn't let him drive this truck or the Corvette.'' I shifted into third with a jerk. I still had a bit of a problem with gears on the steering column. ''This is a classic, Elvia. You of all people should appreciate that.'' She owned a perfectly restored 1959 Austin-Healey with the original upholstery.

''I feel like a farmhand riding in this,'' she complained.

''Don't be a snob. We both come from a long line of farmhands. Why do you think the Sinclairs would give the Ayalas money?''

''I have no idea. They certainly run in different social circles. Maybe Constance just likes the restaurant and doesn't want it to close.''

''Then I could picture them loaning the Ayalas money, but *giving* it to them? Remember, this is Constance Sinclair we're talking about. She's been very generous with the folk-art museum, but it is named after her grandfather. I don't think she's ever given any money where it wasn't made very clear and public that she was the donor. She likes praise and gratitude. In great quantities and very openly.''

''Maybe Jillian gave them the money and Constance doesn't know about it. Jillian's pretty well heeled herself, I hear.''

''Maybe, but that would be even weirder.'' I pulled in front of Blind Harry's and idled in front.

''Why?''

''Let's just say there is no love lost between Dolores and Jillian. They both want Ash Stanhill's head in their trophy case.''

''Or whatever,'' Elvia said, pulling out her purse and reapplying a layer of crimson lipstick. ''I can't abide that man. And it's not jealousy because his restaurant is doing so well.'' She twisted the gold tube closed. ''Do you know he's refused to join the downtown merchants' association? Said he doesn't have time to sit around with a bunch of small-timers discussing trash cans and washing sidewalks. Cretin.''

''Ask around about the Ayalas, okay? Just to ease my curiosity.''

She gave me a doubtful look. ''Whenever you talk like that, I know you're headed for trouble. Does Gabe know about this?''

''There's nothing for him to know. I'm just curious, that's all.''

She climbed out of my double-parked truck, giving a severe schoolmarm look at the car honking behind me. ''I don't like it. Whenever you use the word *curious,* I always end up having to visit you in the hospital.''

Since it was past three o'clock, I dropped by the museum one last time to check on things, gave a few final orders, and headed home. I was pleased to find the house empty, but assumed that by suppertime the others would be wandering in, so I put on a chicken to bake and then checked the answering machine.

The first message was from Gabe. ''I'll be home by six. Love you.''

The second was from Dove. ''I'll be home for supper, honeybun. I'm starved. Spent the day cataloging farm utensils at the Historical Society.''

The third was from Sam. ''Don't wait up. Bye.''

Great. Gabe was going to love that one.

The last message was in a strong, Arkansas twang. ''Micah 6:12.'' The click of the slammed receiver echoed across the empty room.

The Old Testament not being my strong suit, I pulled out my Bible and looked it up. This verse was a new one in Dove and Garnet's battle of the memory verses.

"Her rich men are violent; her people are liars and their tongues speak deceitfully."

*Oh, that'll get a rise out of Dove,* I thought, setting the leather Bible back down on the coffee table. Her people are liars . . . was Aunt Garnet calling me a liar, too? Geez, I didn't want to be included in this biblical Hatfield and McCoy feud.

I sliced unpeeled potatoes and laid them in a long casserole dish, covered them with garlic pepper, drizzled butter and chopped red onions, and parked them next to the chicken in the oven. I was washing fresh green beans when Gabe walked into the kitchen.

"Smells good," he said, nuzzling the back of my neck. "And the food does, too."

I turned around and kissed him. "Have a good day?"

"Not really, but I don't want to talk about it."

He pulled off his jacket and rolled up the sleeves of his white shirt. "Need some help?" I purposely stayed away from the topic of Nora's murder while we finished washing the green beans and put them in the steamer. As he set the table I told him about my lunch with Elvia and her mom. Not certain yet whether it meant anything, I left out the part about the Sinclairs saving the Ayalas' restaurant.

"Did Señora Aragon send any *atole*?" he asked hopefully.

"Yes, but next time she says you have to come get it yourself."

Dove walked in just as Gabe was carving the chicken. Rita came in a few minutes later.

"We can get started. Sam has other plans," I said, ignoring Gabe's scowl. Make up your mind, I wanted to snap. Do you want him here or not?

After supper, I casually mentioned to Dove that she had a message on the answering machine.

"From who?" she asked, her blue eyes flashing.

I shrugged. "They didn't leave a name."

As she listened to the message her cheeks turned pink. "That . . . that . . ." she sputtered. "Of all the nerve." She glared at all of us, then fled to the guest room, slamming the door behind her. Rita rolled her eyes and took her iced tea out on the front porch.

Gabe looked at me, confused. "What in the world does that Bible verse say?"

I smiled. "Oh, it's not so much what it says, although that's going to make her mad, too. It's where it's from. They've had this battle of verses before, but they'd always stuck to the New Testament, which both of them have practically memorized. By giving a verse from the Old Testament, she's making Dove actually look it up, which gives Garnet the upper hand. That means Dove will have to find a suitable rejoinder from the Old Testament so Garnet will have to look it up. It's a whole new spin on their old game." I groaned and flopped down on the couch. "This could go on for decades."

He shook his head and laughed. "Your family is certifiably nuts."

"Tell me a new story, Chief."

He glanced around the empty living room. "If I've learned nothing else these last few days, it's that I'd better take a shower when the bathroom is free." He started unbuttoning his shirt. "Then I have some reports to read."

I joined Rita out on the porch swing. Dusk had begun to fall, cool and silky, bringing the ocean breezes and the clean smell of Mr. Treton's freshly mowed lawn. We swung silently for a few moments, the squeak of the swing imitating the late summer crickets.

"You doin' okay?" I asked. She'd been unusually quiet during supper.

She shrugged, then drew her knees up to her chest and rested her small, pointy chin on them. Across the street, three knobby-kneed boys in baggy shorts tossed a Nerf football back and forth, calling out plays as they wrestled each other to the ground.

"How did your date with Ash go?"

"All right," she said. "We went and heard a blues band. Then we had dinner at his restaurant, but something came up and he had to leave. So I called here, and Sam came and got me."

We didn't speak for a few more minutes. "So what did the lawyer say?" I finally asked.

I heard a small sniffle. "I can get a divorce anytime. Daddy said he'd wire me the money. All I had to do was ask." Another small sniffle.

For the first time since she arrived, I felt sorry for her. "Rita, is that what you want?"

"I want him to never have screwed around on me," she said bitterly. "I want—" She started crying softly. "Shoot, Benni, I still love him. What a stupid fool, huh? The guy's a lyin' cheat, and I still love him."

"You're not a stupid fool," I said, putting my arm around her. "The problem is we can't always choose who we fall in love with. I don't know what to tell you, though. This is something only you can decide."

"The lawyer said I should think about it for a few weeks."

"He's right." A part of me panicked. "Uh, are you going to be heading on back to Arkansas soon? I bet your mom really misses you."

She stood up and stretched. "Haven't really thought about it. I'm here to tell you, though, Mama's about the last person I feel like seeing now." She tugged down her tiny denim shorts. "Well, I'm beat. I'll talk to you tomorrow."

I sat on the porch for a long time afterward, enjoying the solitude and the falling dusk. The streetlight at the end of the street flickered on, and the boys across the street went inside. I stared up into the black sky, the stars sprinkled across it like a dusting of confectioner's sugar, and thought of Rita and Skeeter, Roy and Nora and Grace, of Jillian and Dolores and Ash, of Dove and Garnet, me and Gabe, of the betrayals, big and small, we enact on people we loved or claimed to love or once loved. I rubbed my arms briskly and sat up. It was getting late, and my thoughts were getting depressing.

I was opening the screen door when the red Harper truck pulled up in front of the house. Sam popped out, grabbed his surfboard from the bed, and started across the lawn. I sat down on the steps and waited for him.

"Hi," he said, propping his surfboard on the porch and sitting down next to me. "How was your day?"

"Busy. How were the waves?" I smiled teasingly and bumped his shoulder with mine. "And the chicks?" He smelled clean and slightly salty.

He grinned. "Dove squealed on me, huh? It was great. But that's not all I did today."

"What other kind of mischief did you get into?"

"I got a job." His face glowed with pride, like a five-year-old showing his first finger painting.

"A job? Where?"

"At Eudora's. I'm working the counter four nights a week. I started tonight. I hope it's okay, but I used your name as a reference. I was going to ask you first, but I saw the 'Help Wanted' sign and just went for it."

"No, that's fine."

"Mr. Stanhill said you and he were old friends. When I told him who I was, he said he'd give me a try. I mean, if you can't trust the police chief's son, I guess you can't trust anyone. That's what he said, anyway." He tightened his bottom lip. "I don't know how Dad's going to take it, but I want to pay you that money back and I need to save some so . . ." He left it open.

"I'll tell him. I'm sure he'll be happy for you." Actually, I didn't know how he would feel. I don't think he intended on Sam setting up shop here in San Celina, and then there was the question of where he would live. I rubbed my forehead.

''No, he won't. He'd be happy to see me split,'' Sam said, standing up, his voice cool. ''You can tell him I will as soon as I save some money. Until then, just let him know I'm looking for another place to crash.''

''Don't worry about that. We'll figure something out that everyone can live with.''

''Just tell him, okay?''

As he started up the steps a paperback book fell out of his sweatshirt pocket. I picked it up and glanced at it before handing it back to him.

''Pascal?'' I commented. ''Is that your father's book?'' Gabe had been doggedly working on a master's thesis in philosophy since I met him. His books and notes were scattered around the house like confetti.

He glanced over his shoulder furtively, as if expecting Gabe to storm out of the house and demand the book back. ''I just saw it lying around. Is he looking for it?''

''No, he's too busy with Nora's murder to be working on his thesis right now. He probably doesn't even miss it.'' I looked at him thoughtfully. ''Are you finding it interesting?''

He lifted one shoulder in an indifferent shrug. I felt like hugging him. I knew exactly what he was doing because I'd done it myself: trying to find a clue to Gabe's personality in the underlined passages of his schoolbooks. I wish I could tell him that it was futile, that his father was more complex than that, that those underlined passages were only vague hints about who he was.

''I think I'll go to bed now,'' I said. ''Congratulations on the job. And don't worry about repaying the money. I told you it's a gift.''

''I'll pay it back,'' he said, his voice firm and unyielding. ''I'm *not* a flake, no matter what my dad says.'' He touched my arm lightly when I brushed past him on the porch. "Thanks, *madrastra*. Thanks for being cool about all this."

"You're welcome, stepson."

In our bedroom, Gabe was propped up against our pine headboard, reading a thick file. He peered at me over his gold wire-rim glasses.

"Was that Sam?" he asked.

"Yes." I undressed, pulled on a clean T-shirt from his dresser drawer, and crawled into bed.

He went back to reading his files. I picked up an oral-history book Elvia had just given me on rodeo cowgirls in the first part of the century. Without looking up from his files, Gabe asked, "Is he okay?"

I laid the book down. "Gabe, he's just fine, which you'd know if you'd gone out to see him."

His head didn't move. "We'd just start arguing again."

I sighed and scooted under the covers. "Yes, you're probably right. If it'll make you feel any better, he got a job today and is planning on not only paying me back, but saving money so he can leave. He told me to tell you he'd find another place to live as soon as he could."

A muscle in Gabe's jaw twitched. "I'll believe *that* when I see it."

I punched my feather pillow irritably. "You're impossible."

"So you've told me once or twice." He flashed a smile that could rival Sam's on the devastation meter. "Kiss me good night anyway?"

I bared my teeth at him, and he laughed. His lightheartedness made me feel a little more hopeful. Maybe there was a chance for him and Sam to reconcile yet.

"Anything new on Nora's case?" I asked after we'd turned out the light.

"Benni—"

"I know, I know, not my business. So what else is going on among the criminal element of San Celina? What about that underwear bandit those two bimbos were telling you about Sunday?''

''Caught him with the goods, so to speak. A security guard at Mountain Meadows Apartments saw a man behaving suspiciously in the laundry room and called us. Once we got him down to the station, he confessed to all the thefts.''

''What was he doing that tipped the security guard off?''

Gabe's soft laughter filled our small bedroom. ''Had his jeans off and was pulling on a pair of Victoria's Secret lace panties he swiped from the dryer. In a very attractive shade of teal blue, I'm told.''

''That's gross,'' I moaned.

''You asked. Oh, one more thing you might be interested in. As a matter of fact, I brought you something.''

''What?''

''You know that homeless guy who sits out in front of Blind Harry's all the time? The one Elvia feeds?''

''Sure, we call him the Datebook Bum. What about him?''

''Found him dead in a storm drain over by the Von's grocery store on Ryman Avenue. I brought you his diary. Thought you and Elvia might like to look through it.''

I felt my throat constrict. ''How did he die?''

''They'll do a quickie autopsy tomorrow. Probably some infection or pneumonia, like it usually is with street people. We didn't find any identification. We'll try running his prints through the FBI, but most likely he'll be buried as a John Doe.'' He shifted next to me. ''We went through the canvas bag we found with him. Nothing but junk. Neat junk, but just junk. He was clean. No needles or drug paraphernalia.''

''He's been around here a couple of years,'' I said. ''He just showed up one day. We tried to help him, but he never wanted—'' My voice cracked; tears started flowing before

I could stop them. "What about his family? What if they're looking for him?"

"*Querida,* don't cry." He pulled me to him. "We'll do our best to find them, but you know a lot of these homeless people don't even have families."

"Oh, Gabe, that's even sadder."

He hugged me tightly. "I should have waited until tomorrow to tell you. I didn't realize it was going to upset you like this."

"I'm okay. It's just all the emotional stuff that's happened the last few days. I guess this was just the icing on the cake. You know, even as irritating as our families can be, we're lucky to have them."

"I suppose," he said, his voice neutral in the darkness.

# 9

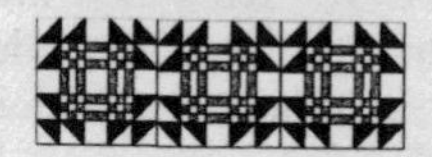

FOR A CHANGE, I beat everyone getting dressed. While Gabe was still shaving, I was pulling on my denim jacket.

"The homeless man's business diary is in my briefcase," he said when I kissed him good-bye.

"Do you need it back?" I asked.

"No, we'll probably just toss the rest of his stuff. I flipped through it. He was apparently a pretty sharp guy at one time. Very organized."

"I won't be home for dinner tonight," I said. "Have a final meeting at Angelo's with the festival committee. I'm treating them to pizza in hopes of bringing a little harmony to the group."

He looked at me with concern, his face half-covered with shaving cream. "Are you all right?"

I kissed the clean side of his face. It was slightly wet and soapy tasting. "I'm fine. Just got a little emotional last night. It's so easy to see the homeless as an ambiguous social issue. It's different when it's someone you know. I wish now I'd tried a little harder to find out more about him. Maybe I could have helped him better."

He turned back to the mirror and ran the blade under his chin. "*Querida,* sometimes people just can't let others get too close. Maybe you helped him the most by letting him be who he wanted to be."

"I suppose," I said, not certain whether he was talking about the homeless man or himself.

As I wandered through the house picking up things I'd need today, I discovered Dove on the sofa perusing her large-print Bible for a suitable comeback to Garnet, Sam in the kitchen scrambling eggs, and Rita, I assumed, still lingering in bed. I found the maroon datebook and stuffed it in my purse.

"I won't be home for dinner," I called to Dove. She nodded and licked her finger, flipping rapidly through her Bible. She paused at a passage, then jotted something on a tablet.

The early-morning air was brisk and refreshing; the sky as bright as a new dime. I picked up the *San Celina Tribune,* unfolding the paper and pulling out the lifestyle section. There was a major write-up on the storytelling festival I wanted to read. I'd leave the rest for Gabe to peruse while he ate breakfast. When I saw the front-page headline, I froze.

MURDERED STORYTELLER NAMED AS TATTLER

I quickly scanned the article. "An unnamed source tells the *Tribune* . . . " The article went on to question how long the police had known this information and what else they were hiding from the public.

I rushed into the house, where Gabe was already on the phone, his freshly shaven face steely with anger. Apparently someone had just called and informed him about the article.

"Find out," he demanded. "I'll be there in a half hour."

He turned and saw me standing there holding the newspaper.

"I guess you heard," I said, handing it to him.

He glanced over the story. "This screws up everything.

That was the first solid lead we've had, and now that it's public, we're back to where we started.''

''Who do you think told the newspaper?''

''I don't know,'' he said grimly, taking the towel draped around his shoulders and wiping his neck clean of shaving cream. A tiny spot of congealed blood dotted his chin. ''But I'm going to find out.''

The phone rang again, and I hightailed it out of there. His day was going to be a stressful one, no doubt about it. I fervently hoped Sam was working late tonight.

I drove to McDonald's and bought a large coffee, an Egg McMuffin, and another newspaper. I read every word of the article twice. As usual, the *Tribune* wasn't kind in its assessment of how the police were handling the investigation. They even took a few potshots at their rival, the *Freedom Press,* too. Not that Will Henry would mind. It would only help him sell more newspapers. On the way to Grace's stables for the early-morning ride I'd been promising myself for the last few days, I wondered how this would affect the festival and whether it would help or hinder the police in their investigation. It could drive the killer underground or make him nervous enough to slip up and reveal himself. Or *her*self, I reminded myself. I shouldn't make generalities. It all came back to words again—how they can build up or tear down, make things easier or harder for people, cause wars or negotiate peace. The power of words to help or heal.

At the stables Jillian's silver Jaguar and Roy's old pickup were the only vehicles in the gravel parking lot. Roy was repairing one of the wooden jumps in the front arena, so I assumed Jillian was working Fred in the back one. I opened the gate and walked through the dusty arena.

''Hi,'' I said. ''Where's Grace?''

He stood up, slipped his pine-handled hammer back in his tool belt and squinted at me. A trickle of sweat dripped off his narrow nose. ''Went to pick up an order at the feed store. She knew you was comin', though. Said Tony needs to be taken out if you feel like it.''

''Sure. Me and Tony are old buddies.'' I ran my hand down the white-painted jumping post. ''What happened?''

''Some smart-ass kids messin' around. I spend more time around here repairing things than anything, but those little brats are our biggest business. I'm trying to get caught up 'cause I'm hitting the road for a few weeks.''

''Got some rodeo gigs lined up?'' His specialty act, performed with an Appaloosa he'd trained himself, included fancy roping tricks à la Montie Montana.

''Yeah. A couple of them are running cowboy poetry performances along with the rodeo. I'm hoping to make a few extra bucks and sell some books.'' Recently, with the financial help of Grace, he'd self-published a book of his cowboy poetry and sold it whenever and wherever he could. He hacked and spit. ''Providing I'm allowed to leave town, that is. Nora's murder has really screwed things up.''

I looked at his sun-webbed face, half-shaded by his straw cowboy hat. Did he feel *any* sorrow over Nora's death, or had the bitterness gone so deep and hard that he truly didn't care?

When I didn't answer, he said, ''I know you think I'm a real asshole.''

I shrugged. That's exactly what I thought, but wasn't about to say it.

He pushed his hat back and rocked on the heels of his cracked leather boots. ''Look, I'm sorry she's dead. I never wanted anything like that to happen. Shit, when things were good between us, they were really good. Then the accident happened, and everything changed—'' His voice shook on the last word. ''We just couldn't make it, and I hope they catch the garbage who killed her, but I've got to go on with my life.''

I still didn't reply. I wanted to understand both sides, but it was hard to forget how he cheated on her when their son was dying, when she needed him the most. Disloyalty was tops on the list of things I despised.

He looked at me with glazed eyes. "You know, when Joey was dying, I felt so mad, so *useless,* all I wanted to do was kill something. I was raised by my pa that a man takes care of his family, that he goes after whoever messes with them. But who was I going to go after? After the accident all we could do was watch him die. Little by little, he went farther and farther away from us. Every minute of the day was taken up watching him die. It took nine months. And she couldn't think or talk about anything else. So many people were good to us . . . to her. She belonged to this group, had other mothers to talk to. I didn't have anyone. She was lost to me from the day the doctors told us Joey would probably never come out of the coma. I was shoeing for Grace at the time, and she listened to me. The thing between me and Grace just happened. We didn't plan it. It just happened."

I knew this story, having heard Grace's version. Though deep in my gut I abhorred the act of adultery, and I instinctively drifted in the direction of feeling more sympathy for Nora, I couldn't deny that Roy's pain from his son's death ran deep and sincere.

But all that had happened a year ago, and a lot of bitterness had overshadowed the sadness they both felt over Joey's death. I knew from Grace that Roy and Nora had not only fought over Zar's ownership, but also the money from a trust fund that had been set up for Joey from donations and from an insurance policy they'd taken out on him when he was born. Roy, anxious to get his breeding herd started, fought her for every penny.

"I told him to just let it be," Grace had told me after he'd interrupted one of our kitchen-table talks with an angry diatribe about Nora. "That we'd save the money on our own. But I think he's just so angry, he has to take it out on something . . . or someone."

I stared down at Roy's rough, strong hands. Had he finally gotten angry enough to kill? I shook my head slightly, trying to dislodge the thought. "Don't forget our final meeting and pizza at Angelo's tonight."

"What time are we all supposed to be there?"

"Seven. Remember, this is the last meeting before the festival, so any concerns you have need to be taken care of tonight 'cause it's going to be crazy starting tomorrow."

"Everything's jim-dandy with me." He settled his hat on his head and checked the post he'd just fixed by giving it a firm shake.

"Including your story?"

He grinned slowly. "Mr. Greenpeep still all a-twitter? Grace said she told you I was just razzin' him."

"Try and cool it with Peter during the festival, okay? I don't care what kind of personal problems you two have, I just don't want any shenanigans at the festival."

"Shenanigans?" He laughed and spit again.

"I mean it, Roy. I'll throw you out of the festival right in the middle of your story. And that's a promise."

He swept off his hat and bowed. "Yes, ma'am, Madam Chairman. This cowboy will be on his best behavior, or you can kick my sorry butt out."

"Don't kid yourself. I will."

"Would I kid the police chief's wife?" He turned and picked up his toolbox. "See you tonight."

As I watched him walk away it occurred to me that he never mentioned the newspaper article. I couldn't help wondering if he'd suspected that Nora was the Tattler. Being married as long as they had, I knew from my own experience that there were little patterns of speech, certain words that, if he was paying attention, might have tipped him off. On the other hand, maybe he didn't even read the column.

I saddled up Tony, a three-year-old sorrel quarter horse, and headed toward the path behind Grace's house that followed San Celina Creek. I rode for about an hour, enjoying the rhythmic creaking of the saddle leather, the soft hum of bees darting around the orange California poppies, and the smell of the wild onion and goldenrod. Tony's smooth gait relaxed me, and I let my mind drift, idly identifying wildflowers from knowledge gained during my 4-H days—copper red and orange blazing stars, hairy prickly poppies, tall, prideful prince's plume. About a half mile from the stable, I stopped under a blue oak tree next to the creek and dismounted, letting Tony graze for a few minutes. I was leaning up against the tree trunk, tossing ripe acorns into the creek, when Jillian rode up.

"Just the lady I needed to speak to," she said. She stayed mounted on Fred, and from my place on the ground his eighteen hands made him appear as enormous as the Trojan horse. He blew wet air and shook his head.

She patted his huge neck. "I have something for you and the museum down at the library."

"Really, what?"

"Money."

I smiled up at her. "With humble apologies to Julie Andrews, I believe I like that a whole lot better than whiskers on kittens. Who's giving it to us, and what do we have to do for it?"

"Some friend of Aunt Constance's who collects quilts," she said. "It's only two hundred dollars, but money's money."

"I don't care if it's twenty bucks, I'll take it." I reached up and fondled Fred's velvety muzzle. "Guess you'll miss the after-hours storytelling session Saturday night." Copying the Santa Barbara festival, we'd elected to have an adult storytelling hour featuring stories too scary or mature for kids.

"Unfortunately, yes. My event is at nine o'clock Sunday morning, and I want both of us to be rested for it." Fred startled when a bumblebee swung past his head. I jumped backward as she calmly brought him under control.

"How's things settling down at the library?" I asked.

She absently combed Fred's glossy mane with her fingers. "Everyone's still talking about it, but we're basically back to normal."

"Did you read this morning's *Tribune*?"

She frowned deeply and moved both reins to her left hand. "Yes, and I think it's rapidly sinking to the depths of the *Freedom Press*. Why can't they just leave the poor woman alone? I feel so bad for Nick. This will devastate him."

"Were you surprised? I sure was."

She continued combing Fred's hair, her eyes sympathetic. "You know, not much surprises me anymore. I liked Nora, but it was obvious she was a troubled person."

I didn't answer because I felt sort of foolish. It hadn't been obvious to me. I'd found her pleasant and completely easy to talk to once I pushed all Grace's prejudiced comments to the back of my mind. But then again, maybe I'd have felt differently had I known she was the Tattler. I tried to remember what all we talked about as we were labeling and folding festival brochures. I hoped it wasn't anything she could use to embarrass Gabe. Not that I had to worry about it now.

She rode past me and called over her shoulder, "If I'm not there, just ask my secretary to give you the check. It's under my crystal dolphin paperweight. See you tonight."

I watched her move through the tall grass until she crossed the creek and rode up into a stand of oak trees. She appeared small and defenseless atop such a large animal, but I knew that was only an illusion. She was an expert horsewoman and, more importantly, hated to lose. I had no doubt she'd take first place in her event on Sunday.

After grooming Tony and putting him on the hot walker, I told Grace's stable hand, Kyle, to let Grace know exactly what I'd done with Tony. Roy's specially equipped farrier truck was gone, so I assumed he was out on a job. I decided to drop by the museum one more time on the chance that there might be more fires between the artists that needed tamping out. Though I loved the special festivals and programs we put on four or five times a year at the museum, I dreaded the inevitable clashes between the co-op members. The whispered topic of the day was, of course, the news of Nora's secret job.

I spent the next few hours putting the finishing touches on my opening speech interspersed with people drifting into my office, asking me if I'd heard and giving me their two cents on Nora Cooper's motivation. A story had started circulating about her being killed because of the last column she wrote. If they found the column, they'd find the killer. As intriguing as that speculation was, it was exactly that. We'd most likely never know what was in that column since all her computer disks were missing. That, apparently, was one piece of information that the *Tribune* didn't know. More than one person tried to pry out of me what the police had found when they searched her place, but I was determined that no one was going to find out anything by looking at *my* face. To avoid more questions, I left for the library to pick up the check.

Once there, I headed straight for Nick's office, purposely ignoring the library employees' questioning faces. He sat at a computer typing words and symbols I assumed somehow correlated with the books on the shelves.

"Hey, guy, how're you doing?" I sank down into the office chair next to his cluttered desk. He punched a few more keys, then swung his chair around to face me. His eyes were still red-rimmed, but the whites seemed a little clearer today.

"Okay, I guess. I'm letting my staff work the front desk for a few days while I hide in here." He ran his hand over his face. "That newspaper article has everyone gawking at me like I'm a sideshow freak."

"Did you know?" I asked, then instantly regretted it. "I'm sorry, that's really none of my business."

"It's all right." He leaned back in his chair. "I think I suspected, but she never came right out and said. I knew she wrote that art column for the *Freedom Press* and that she and Will Henry were pretty tight. I guess I was sort of hoping all the time she spent there was just the beginning of a romance or something. She needed something to get her mind off Joey's death and getting revenge on Roy and Grace. We argued about it a lot, her getting on with her life. It seems like the last six months that's all we did was argue. But she would never listen to me. I was just her little brother. She was acting crazy in so many ways, wandering around Central Park after dark, following Roy and his girlfriend until they called the cops on her, hanging out in bars over by the interstate." Bitterness flickered in his eyes. "What could I do? All I wanted was for her to be happy. But it seemed like she was doing everything she could to avoid it, like it was some penance she had to pay."

I chewed on my bottom lip for a moment. "Maybe we can't help people in that kind of pain. Maybe the best thing to do is just be there when they need us." *Good advice,* I told myself. *Why does it sound so logical and easy when you're giving it to someone else?*

"And what if they never need anyone? Are we supposed to just sit there and let them destroy themselves without even trying to help?"

"I don't know," I answered honestly, thinking how similar all our human problems were. "I guess it's just one of those things you have to play by ear."

He turned back to the computer, studying the numbers and letters as if the answer could be there somewhere in all that brightly lit information. "If you find out anything more, will you let me know?"

I paused, not wanting to make a promise that might prove impossible to keep. "If I can."

I went by Jillian's office, but she apparently hadn't gotten back from her lunch break yet. Her secretary, an auburn-haired girl with frizzy bangs and Ben Franklin eyeglasses, led me into Jillian's neat, bleached-pine office.

The phone buzzed, and her secretary, gesturing toward Jillian's desk, scurried out to answer it.

I walked over to the sliding-glass window and gazed out at the new patron's patio and garden that overlooked Central Park. It was the library's final construction project, and Jillian had personally thrown a T.G.I.O.—"Thank Goodness It's Over"—after-hours party for the employees and other people who'd suffered during the construction. We'd eaten catered shrimp puffs, egg rolls, and chocolate fondue while strolling through the authentic English-style garden. The patio off Jillian's office that led to the garden had been decorated with hundreds of pink and black balloons and blooming rose trees. Jillian looked gorgeous that night in a sparkly silver dress and her aunt's ruby earrings. A trooper to the end, you never would have guessed she'd received a "Dear Jane" telegram that very day. Her tale of romantic misfortune spread with grass-fire speed as things always did in San Celina. But according to Nick, she never missed a day of work or ever let on she was hurt. She'd never even put away his picture, he'd said. Then he had added, "I think she's still hoping he'll come back."

More forgiving than I'd be, I thought, picking up the glass dolphin. The check for the folk-art museum was right where she said it would be. When I turned to leave, my eye caught the silver frame that displayed her husband's picture. I picked it up and studied it closely. He was indeed handsome, breathtakingly so, sitting on his polo pony, his blond hair shiny with damp curls, his grin self-assured and white as chalk dust. Around the eyes, he reminded me a little of Ash Stanhill.

"Find the check?" Jillian said, startling me. She was dressed in an tawny brown linen suit with a short skirt that showed off her slender legs. A gold horse-shaped pin decorated one wide lapel.

I set the photograph down, my face tingling with shame. "Yes, thanks."

She walked briskly around her whitewashed pine desk. "Good. I'm sure you can use it."

"Yes, we can," I stammered, still horribly embarrassed. She sensed my discomfort and gave me a serene smile.

"I don't mind you looking at my husband's picture, Benni."

"He's very handsome," I said.

"Yes, he is." She ran her fingers over the top of the frame. "For a long time, I thought he'd come back. I know everyone laughs at me behind my back. I know how this town works, but sometimes it's hard to let go of the past. Even when it wasn't that great, at least it was familiar."

I nodded. It was an insight that had never occurred to me, missing a troubling past simply because it was familiar. But losing as much as she did, so young, I could almost see how familiarity and consistency could be as important to her as love and loyalty was to me.

She sat down in her pale leather executive chair and started shuffling papers. "It's Angelo's at seven tonight, right?"

"Yes, and hopefully this meeting will be a bit calmer than the last."

"Don't place too large a bet on that one," she said with a small laugh.

I was halfway out the door when she called me back.

Her small features pinched into a troubled look. "Benni, I . . . I have something I need to tell you. Could you close the door, please?"

I did as she asked, waiting expectantly.

Her deep blue eyes looked directly into mine. "There's something I failed to inform the detectives when they questioned me."

Though I knew the judicious thing would be to tell her to contact the detectives, I compulsively asked, "What?"

"On Saturday I told them the last people to leave were Nick, Nora, and Dolores." She touched a finger to her mouth nervously. "Nick has keys and knows the lockup procedure. When I left, he was looking something up in *Books in Print* for Dolores, a book she needed for her storytelling performance this weekend."

"Where was Nora?"

"I saw her through the window as I was doing the traditional last walk through the library. She was in the children's computer room working on something."

"Did you tell the detectives all this?"

"Yes."

"Then what . . . ?"

"I came back." She gave a jittery laugh. "I'd forgotten my briefcase and I came in the employee entrance, through Technical Processing. I was going to dash up the back stairs and pick it up. That's when I heard them."

"Who?"

"Nick and Nora. They were fighting. He was really yelling at her. I was shocked. I'd never heard him even raise his voice before."

"What were they fighting about?"

She shrugged. "I didn't stick around to find out. I was so horribly embarrassed that I just left my briefcase. At the bottom of the stairs, I bumped into Dolores. She heard them, too. You can ask her. We both mumbled something inane and went to our respective cars."

"Do you think she told the police?"

"I have no idea, but that's why I thought I'd better tell someone. If she did, I didn't want it to look like I was covering up anything."

I looked at her pointedly. "Except you were."

Her cheeks flushed shell pink. "Yes, I suppose I was. It's just that I *know* Nick wouldn't kill his sister and I didn't want him suffering any more than he already has.''

''I agree with you about Nick, but the police need to know everything possible about what happened the last few hours of Nora's life even if it seems irrelevant.'' Which, I thought, this was anything but.

''Could you tell Gabe for me?'' she asked.

''Yes, but you know you'll be getting another visit from a detective. They'll probably want to corroborate your story with Dolores's.''

''I know. Everything I told you was the truth. She'll verify that.'' Her voice trembled slightly. ''Benni, I held back this information because I really care about Nick. When I first took over the library, he was one of the few people who had an open mind about me and didn't assume I was just window dressing placed here by my aunt. Please make Gabe understand that. It wasn't my intention to break the law or make the investigation more difficult.''

''He'll understand, I'm sure.'' Sure, and I'm going to be voted the next Miss Rodeo America.

I ate lunch at a new Mexican restaurant near the library where the owners didn't know me. It was a relief to eat my chile relleños in peace without having to talk about Nora's murder and answer the awkward question—just what *is* your husband going to do about it? Not to mention the somewhat embarrassing fact that everyone assumed I knew more than I did. That's why I ended up with confidences like Jillian's. Though there had to be some advantages to being the police chief's wife, I'd yet to discover them.

Rooting around in my purse for something to read while I ate, I came across the maroon datebook I'd taken out of Gabe's briefcase this morning. I idly flipped through the daily calendar part, sampling a piece of cramped writing here and there. Gabe was right, the Datebook Bum must have been an intelligent man. I went back to January 1 and started reading. The entries were short, to the point, and meticulously kept. They recorded everything from what he ate at the Mission Food Bank that day (January 27—"Baked chicken breast, mashed potatoes, and corn this evening. Ate all but two bites of corn. Chicken overdone.") to whom he spoke to (February 9—"Ms. Aragon from Blind Harry's said good morning. She wore her yellow suit today. Donna at San Celina Creamery gave me a vanilla cone. Turned down offer of sprinkles.") to what junk he collected ("Deck of playing cards minus red diamond queen and ace of spades—table outside of Art Center; Six cans—three Coke, two Pepsi, one Dr Pepper—garbage bin outside Angler Sporting Goods; five ballpoint pens, two working, three not, plastic bag outside Bryant's Business Supply"). This went on for pages and pages.

After reading through three months of entries, I began to perceive a pattern. Like a milkman he'd established a regular route in a roughly two-mile radius. It began and ended at Blind Harry's but took in at least fifty other stops including a health food store where the homeless could get free vitamins, St. Celine's Catholic Church, where good people provided afternoon coffee and doughnuts in the recreation hall, the local YMCA that allowed free showers on Mondays and Thursdays. He even made a once-a-week trip to the library, where he recorded which magazines he read, what this week's story hour was about, which library employee acknowledged him ("Nick in Reference said good morning. Offered me coffee. I declined. He wore a new red polo shirt"), and what was in the library's huge trash bin outside ("Ingram's shipment came in today. Half a tuna sandwich in white paper bag. Too much mayo and walnuts").

I pushed the datebook aside while I finished my lunch and thought about the mysterious, secret world of the homeless. How they observed the rest of us as we went about our daily activities never realizing our every move and word was being scrutinized. I'd read through March and hadn't seen my name mentioned yet. I would definitely have to flip through it tonight when I had time and see if I'd come under his astute powers of observation.

Back at the museum, I buckled down and worked on cleaning up the last few details of the festival. At five o'clock, I told the few artists left in the co-op buildings I was leaving and reminded them to lock up after themselves. Before closing up the museum, I took one last quiet walk through the quilt exhibit. Nine o'clock tomorrow the doors would officially open, with our first tour scheduled for nine-thirty. We'd have crowds for the next three days during the festival, so I knew this would be my last chance to really absorb the quilts.

I roamed through the exhibit randomly, standing for a long time in front of my favorites, amazed, as always, how each time you look at a story quilt, more details, more parts of the "story," pop out at you. When I reached Evangeline's, I remembered my promise to myself to look at that one square up close. Something in me whispered that there was more there than could be seen on a quick first look. And the fact that the woman was holding a blanket that at first glance appeared to be a baby, but wasn't, certainly intrigued me. I stood on a stool and unfolded the miniature blanket again. It was, as before, empty. I studied the picture closely, trying to discern what the wide dark eyes of the mother were trying to convey, what the bead of a teardrop represented, why the man was sleeping while his wife cried and walked the floor with her empty bundle.

The tiny crazy quilt the man slept under was incredibly intricate and not any bigger than a Fig Newton. It was a separate piece, appliquéd onto the bed with only the back of the man's head showing. For some reason, I had the strongest urge to see what was under that quilt.

I dug through my purse and found my Swiss army knife and with its compact scissors carefully snipped at the delicate stitching along the edge of the blanket and slowly lifted it up. Involuntarily, I held my breath, not knowing what I'd find.

There was nothing there.

Staring at the plain muslin fabric, I let out my breath and laughed at my own silliness. What was I expecting to find?

*You're really getting a sick way of looking at things,* I told myself. Just because one time the clue was in the quilt doesn't make it automatic. I looked in dismay at my handiwork. Though it wasn't obvious when you stood in front of it because the square was on the highest row, if anyone studied it carefully, the side I'd snipped would be obvious. I'd have to take the whole blanket off and restitch it to make it look right. Even then Evangeline might notice. But she'd certainly notice if I left it the way it was. I glanced at my watch. I was fifteen minutes late already for the meeting at Angelo's, so I couldn't resew the blanket now. I'd have to swing by here afterward and repair it before the exhibit opened tomorrow.

On the way out, I told the security guard that I would be back to finish up some work, so not to worry when he saw my truck later on tonight.

Angelo's Big Top Pizza was wall-to-wall students, office workers, and noisy kids by the time I arrived. Knowing that Wednesday night was popular ever since Angelo started his "All-you-can-eat-pizza-and-spaghetti-feed" to attract more weekday business, I'd reserved the small back room they normally used for birthday parties. When I arrived, Roy was busy playing a pinball machine with Grace cheering him on, while the rest of the group had already finished two pitchers of beer and was starting a third.

"I called the order in from the museum," I said, flopping down on the redwood bench next to Jillian. "Hope four large pizzas are enough. I ordered two thin, two thick crusts. Pepperoni, sausage, vegetarian, and black olive."

"Sounds good," Ash said. "Want a beer?"

"No, thanks." I held up my Coke. "Sorry I'm late. Had

a few last things to take care of down at the museum." I deliberately avoided Evangeline's smiling face, afraid I'd give away my silly and presumptuous escapade with her quilt.

"You've done a great job with the festival," Jillian said, patting my hand. "I honestly don't see how you pulled this all together."

"Thanks," I said. "But I didn't do it alone. Believe me, it would not have been possible without all of you. We've collectively done a good job and now we can hopefully enjoy the fruits of our labor. So tonight, even though we still have a few strands of barbed wire to repair, I want us just to have fun and prepare ourselves psychologically for tomorrow."

"Here, here," Roy said, turning from the pinball machine and lifting up his mug of beer. "Let's just all have a good time. That's what storytelling is all about."

"As well as teaching truth," Peter said, speaking up for the first time. "And for passing on the survival wisdom the next generation is going to need to keep from having to live in a totally concrete, strip-mall world."

"Ah, put a lid on it, Greenpeep," Roy said. "The only reason you guys want to save the environment is so you rich kids will have something to play in while the rest of us poor working slobs who can't even afford one of your expensive yuppie climbing ropes are working to pay the taxes that buy those greenbelts and open space you all want."

Peter glared at him. "That's not true. The greenbelts and open-space lands bought by the conservancy are for everyone—"

Roy interrupted. "Sure, everyone who isn't working fifteen hours a day to make ends meet and can't even afford to buy a condo in Santa Maria."

"The pizzas are here," I said brightly. "C'mon, eat up, everyone, before they get cold." I gritted my teeth and wondered if there was anyplace in this town I could go where someone wasn't fighting.

Roy and Peter glared at each other, then sat down at opposite ends of the long table. Grace gave me an apologetic look, turned and whispered sharply to Roy.

''Nice save,'' Ash said, sitting down next to me. ''Pepperoni?'' He picked up my paper plate.

''Sure,'' I said absently. He pulled off two slices and slipped them on my plate. I stared down at it, my appetite suddenly gone.

''Don't worry, darlin',' Ash said. ''Those two aren't going to ruin the festival. They're just snappin' at each other for the pure fun of it.''

I picked up a piece of pizza and bit off the tip. ''It's not fun to me. I've got enough to worry about without them sniping at each other.''

''Like finding Nora's killer?''

I finished chewing my small bite, studying his face warily. ''What do you mean by that?''

He shrugged. ''Just that being the police chief's wife, I figured you have the inside track on information.''

''You're wrong there. Gabe and I agreed from the beginning of our marriage that his work life and home life are completely separate.'' I looked back at my pizza, hoping my face wouldn't give away that blatant lie. Composing my features into what I hoped was a neutral expression, I looked back to him and answered, ''You probably know more about it than I do.''

His eyes blinked rapidly, though his slick smile never lost a kilowatt. ''I doubt that.''

I took another bite of pizza and didn't reply.

''You became pretty good friends with her, didn't you?'' he asked.

''We weren't best friends or anything, but I liked her.'' At least I liked who I thought she was.

''Did you know she was the Tattler?''

"Oh sure, Ash. I even helped her write the columns."

His eyes widened slightly.

"For cryin' out loud," I said when I realized he was taking me seriously. "I'm kidding, Ash. I was as much in the dark as anyone else. Why are you so nervous? Did she have something on you, too?"

His hand froze on the handle of his beer mug. My stomach flip-flopped when I realized that I hit the fence post square on the head. I laughed, trying to cover up that I'd noticed his reaction. "Ash, she probably made up something about all of us. Don't forget, she was a storyteller."

He gave me a long look, rubbing his thumb absently on his chin. "Yes, but her stories hurt people. That's not what storytelling is about."

"I agree. Stories should build people up, not tear them down."

"It would be well for more people to remember that."

"Yes, I guess it would."

His gaze remained steady. "Seems to me anyone who could write the stuff the Tattler did . . . was a completely cruel and heartless person."

"I'm not sure I agree with you there. All the facts aren't in. The whole story of her life and motivations isn't known yet."

"But you're going to make sure it is."

"I didn't say that."

"Your face did." He drained his mug of beer. "I'm going to get another one. Want anything from the bar?"

"No, thanks." I pointed to my half-empty glass of Coke.

"Just remember one thing, Benni. It was something that Nora obviously had a problem with. 'A prudent man keeps his knowledge to himself, but the heart of fools blurts out folly.' "

"Sounds an awfully lot like a proverb."

"Chapter 12, verse 23. I'm not as decadent as I look."

"Even the devil quoted Scripture," I replied flippantly.

He grinned. "Touché, darlin'. You'd best remember that."

I stared after him as he walked toward the bar.

"What was that about the devil and Scripture?" Evangeline said, scooting closer to me. She offered me the vegetarian pizza. I declined, pointing at my still-uneaten slices. "You and Ash looked like you were debating the world's problems. Was he trying to put the make on you? That man sure has the nerve."

I picked up my cooling piece of pizza and took another bite, trying not to look Evangeline in the eye. If what everyone said about me was true, she'd be able to tell in one glance that I'd ripped apart her quilt looking for a clue. I needed to get a handle on myself. My mind was beginning to work like one of those characters in a mystery novel, looking for clues in everything people said and did.

"No," I replied. "He was just shooting off his mouth, like usual. He's gotten it in his head that I know more about Nora's case than I do."

She looked at me thoughtfully. In the background, Bonnie Raitt sang from the jukebox: "Let's give them something to talk about. . . ." She listened for a moment. "I've always loved that song." She drank from her glass of iced tea. "It could be about my life."

"Why?"

She shook her head and gave her musical laugh. "You know, life, love, men. I always seem to pick the ones like Ash. The smooth talkers. They're like irresistible honey to me."

I looked at her curiously and asked, "Did you and Ash ever have anything going?"

"No. At least I was smart enough not to fall for that one. Not that I wasn't tempted. He does have a certain charm." She swirled the ice around in her tall plastic cup. "But that man is definitely a *serpent d'eau*."

"A what?"

"Water moccasin. They bite without warning, and next thing you know you're floating in the water facedown."

Before I could answer, Ash walked up, Dolores glued to his side. They sat down across from us.

"What are you fine ladies whispering about?" he asked. Dolores gazed up at him with what could only be described as adoration. She definitely needed to have a long talk with Evangeline.

"Nothing important," Evangeline said.

Amusement crinkled his eyes. "I thought maybe Benni was tellin' you all the inside scoop about Nora's murder that she wouldn't share with me." He said it loud enough for everyone to stop chattering and stare at me.

"I don't know any more than anyone else," I said, glaring at Ash. I crumbled my paper napkin and threw it on my plate. "Let's start this meeting and get any problems solved so we can begin with a fresh slate tomorrow."

"I agree," Grace said.

I pulled my notebook out of my purse and quickly ran through the list of things that still needed to be done. After everyone had their assignments, had voiced their complaints and problems, and I made note of them, I closed my notebook and stood up.

"I'll see all of you tomorrow night at Farmers' Market. Remember, our storytelling booth opens promptly at six. The first story is at six-fifteen. Everyone is clear on their time, right? We want to attract people to the festival and show how storytelling is a means to promote peace and brotherhood. Let's keep it civil." I looked pointedly at Roy and Peter. Peter stiffened his bottom lip. Roy grinned and saluted me.

"Okay, then, good luck and knock 'em—" I stopped and rephrased my thought. "Uh, break a leg." A nervous laugh rippled through the group.

"Leaving us so soon?" Ash said, his arm still draped

over Dolores's shoulder. She rested her dark, shiny hair on his shoulder, her eyes glowing.

I glanced down at Jillian, who'd been unusually quiet during the evening, picking at her pizza and casting an occasional furtive glance at Ash. Had Ash officially dumped her? Was he with Dolores now? Or was he playing them against each other in a bid to . . . what? Jillian had financially helped both Ash and Dolores. Did seeing them hang all over each other like this make her regret it? I glanced around at all the people at the table and felt a dull headache start to smolder behind my eyes. Secrets. This group was full of them. Secrets they were afraid would get out. Secrets that apparently Nora knew. Secrets, or at least one secret, worth killing for.

I slipped out of the pizza parlor as everyone said their good-byes. I was opening the truck door when Grace caught my arm.

"Benni, have you got a minute?" Her red hair appeared an odd clownish orange under the parking-lot lights.

I shut the truck door and leaned back against it. "Sure, what's up?"

"It's about Roy."

She fiddled with her hair, and I waited silently for her to go on. In the distance the sound of raucous laughter came from the weight-lifting gym that occupied the second floor above Angelo's. I glanced up at the thick-necked guy in black bicycle shorts and a yellow tank top standing in front of an open window. He gave a Tarzan yell and beat apelike on his rippled chest.

"He was questioned by the police again today," she said, her clear green eyes darting up at the sound then back at me.

"He was?"

"You didn't know?"

I felt my jaw tighten. "Grace, how many times do I have

to tell people? Gabe doesn't confide in me about his work. You know that better than anyone."

"You said he was getting better."

"He is, but he's deliberately keeping me out of this particular investigation because I'm working with all of you." I paused for a moment, then compulsively asked, "What exactly did the detectives ask Roy?"

She shifted from one boot to the other. "They found out some stuff, and it . . . it doesn't look good."

I touched a hand to my forehead, not certain now if I really wanted to hear this. But I was involved with these people. They were my friends and also major players in the storytelling festival. It would be easier to put out fires if I had some idea about what started the flames, and of course, I was a bit curious. . . . "What stuff?"

"There was something he didn't tell the police. He saw Nora that night . . . the night she was killed. But he didn't do it! I swear, he was with me the whole night. And he'd never kill anyone. I know him."

"He saw her?" I repeated. "Where . . . what . . . ?"

"He went to the library after it was closed, and they got into this big fight. She was going to back out on the deal they'd made about Zar unless he signed away his part of the insurance money for their son. She'd been drinking, he said, and she was always irrational when she drank. I guess she'd seen us earlier in the day. Saw him give me a kiss or something, and that set her off again. We'd been careful, but sometimes you forget and . . ." Her voice broke. "The police." She looked at me accusingly. "*Your husband* thinks Roy did it, case closed. They're not even trying to look for anyone else. They've confiscated all his ropes to see if any fibers match. Can they do that? Should I get him a lawyer? Benni, can you talk to Gabe? Talk some sense into him? Roy didn't do it. He didn't."

"How did the police find out about the fight?" I asked.

"Someone saw it all and called the police. He said he

parked on the other side of the park so no one could see his truck at the library and start up a bunch of gossip again. I guess it could have been anyone, but it was late, past ten o'clock. The library had been closed for an hour. They argued outside, next to the employees' entrance."

"Why was she there?" I asked, though I knew, having heard Nick's story.

"She told Roy she'd borrowed Nick's keys and was using the computer room in the children's department because it had a color printer. He called her on her cellular phone, and they agreed to meet at the library." She gave a bitter laugh. "We're barely able to buy oats for the horses, and she's carrying a cellular phone. Guess she had to be available at all times for that final offer from the developer."

"Who did you say reported their argument?" I asked, trying to steer the conversation back to Roy and Nora's last encounter. Was it Nick? Jillian? I didn't want to scare Grace, but if I were her, I'd certainly be thinking about finding a lawyer. Fast.

She shrugged. "The proverbial anonymous caller. They apparently were convincing enough to make the cops question him again, and this time he broke down and confessed." Her nails bit into my forearm. "Benni, you have to do something. Everyone's more than happy to let the blame fall on Roy, but it wasn't him, and that means the real killer is out there and getting away with murder."

I didn't know how to answer her. What I really wished right at that moment was that I'd never started riding at Grace's stable, never become friends with her. My life was complicated enough without being torn between helping a friend and being loyal to my new husband. With my long ties in this town and his position, it seemed this situation was one that was destined to crop up between Gabe and me time after time. "I'll ask Gabe what's going on, but you know I can't guarantee any answers."

"Thank you," she said, loosening her grip on my arm.

I glanced at my watch, trying to tactfully hint that I had someplace to go. "I'll get back to you. I don't know when, but as soon as I can."

"You're a good friend," she said, her voice embarrassingly grateful and humble. "Sometimes I feel like you're my only friend." Her words made me feel like a real jerk after my own thoughts about our friendship.

I touched her hand briefly. "I'll do the best I can."

She nodded mutely and went back across the street, where Roy leaned against his truck, waiting.

It was past nine o'clock when I arrived at the museum. All I wanted to do was repair Evangeline's quilt and go home as quickly as possible. I informed the young security guard we'd hired that I'd be about a half hour and would lock up after myself. Inside the museum, I turned on only one set of track lighting in the main hall. I took down her quilt and carried it to the co-op studios, where there were quilting supplies and a place to sit. As I carefully tried to match Evangeline's neat, even stitches, I lambasted myself for seeing clues where there weren't any and for being so nosy. *Let the police find Nora's killer,* I told myself. *You have other fish to fry.* It was so quiet in the co-op, I could hear our ancient refrigerator cycle and buzz. Under the building's eaves, birds rustled and chirped, settling in for the night. I'd clipped off the last thread and was studying my stitches when I heard the noise. An unmistakable crunch outside the curtainless window. My blood froze in my veins as I stared up at the window, expecting a grotesque face à la Jack Nicholson to fill the window.

A tree branch, I told myself, when I heard it again. Or the security guard making his rounds. I moved away from the window, trying to decide if it would be better to attempt a dash across the courtyard and around the museum to the parking lot or creep over to my office and call the police. I hugged the quilt to my chest, my mind racing, wondering how solid the studio door's lock was and whether I was overreacting. If it was a tree branch or the security guard, I'd look like a fool calling the police. That was another irritating thing about being the police chief's wife—if I reported it, everyone and his brother would hear about it immediately and it would be the talk of the station. *You're imagining things,* I thought when everything became quiet again. I calmly folded the quilt and started for the door. When I passed the dark window, like a shotgun blast it shattered.

I screamed and instinctively hit the floor, the quilt cushioning my fall. I lay there for a moment, dazed. Then, crouching low, I scrambled toward the light switch next to the front door and flipped it off. I wouldn't be such an obvious target now. I sat with my back against the door, staring out at the broken window. I'd have to go past it to get to my office. Faint moonlight glinted off the broken glass covering the floor. Behind me, a fist pounded hard on the door.

"Mrs. Ortiz!" the security guard yelled. "Are you okay?"

I jumped up and unlocked the door. The guard stood there, his hand holding his cellular phone as if it were a gun he was going to draw.

"Are you okay?" he repeated. "I heard you scream and then I saw someone hop the fence and I couldn't decide if I should run after him or come see about you and I called my dispatcher and he said to go see if you were okay to let the guy go and I called the police and are you okay? This is my first assignment . . . and you the police chief's wife . . . oh, shit . . . I really screwed up—" I held up my hand for him to stop talking. He obeyed instantly, like a well-trained hunting dog. He hooked his thumbs in his thick black police issue utility belt in an attempt to hide their trembling. I flipped on the light and surveyed the damage.

I turned to the security guard. "What did he look like?" I asked.

His round blue eyes widened, making him appear about sixteen. He reached up and started picking nervously at a pimple on his cheek. ''He was dressed in black. I was at the back of the pasture, checking the perimeter. I couldn't see his face. He took off over the back fence and ran through the field and toward the feed store.'' Next door to the museum was an acre of open pasture, then the parking lot of the San Celina Feed and Grain Co-op.

''He probably had a car waiting,'' I said, more to myself than the guard, who was now shaking like a scared puppy. I looked back to the broken glass on the floor. A large rock sat in the middle of it, a piece of paper wrapped around it with a rubber band just like in an old ''Spin & Marty'' episode from the Disney channel.

I picked up the rock and read the message.

*Cruel death is always near; so frail a thing a woman.*

''What does it say?'' the guard asked, his voice a close imitation of Barney Fife. Before I could answer, a deep voice called out, ''Police.'' I stuffed the note in my back pocket and whispered, ''Forget this.'' I scowled to make my point. He nodded dumbly.

Two officers stepped through the doorway. Neither of them looked familiar to me. Gabe had just hired five new officers in the last few months, and these were obviously two of them.

''What's the problem?'' the male officer said. He was short and bull-necked and had that glossy, grooming-brush haircut that seemed to be popular among male patrol officers. His partner was a young, snub-nosed woman with a neat, blond braid and serious gray eyes. Both walked in holding on to the top of their unsnapped holsters in the same way the guard had his phone. The female officer's expression flickered with recognition when she saw me.

''Better call the watch commander,'' she started to say to her partner. ''That's the—''

"We can handle this," he interrupted her irritably. "Who called 911?"

She shrugged and fell silent, obviously the junior partner in this duo. At that particular moment, I blessed his arrogance. I'd prefer to tell Gabe about this myself.

"I did." The guard's voice quivered.

"So what's the problem?" His face held a slight sneer, telegraphing his feelings about security guards with a turn of a lip.

I jumped in, suddenly tired of all the fuss. "Someone vandalized the co-op," I said, holding out the rock. "I was in here working on a quilt, and someone threw this through the window. It caught me by surprise, and I screamed. Whoever it was apparently hopped the fence and took off toward the feed store."

The male officer nodded and pulled out a notebook. "Did you get a look at him?"

"No, when I heard the window shatter, I hit the floor. Then I crawled over and turned off the light so I wasn't an obvious target. Then the guard knocked on the door and identified himself. I recognized his voice and let him in. He'd already phoned the incident in to his dispatcher."

His eyebrows lifted. "Quick thinking . . . for a woman."

Behind him, his partner blurted out, "Lowry, don't be such an ass."

Ignoring her, he turned to the fidgety guard. "What did you see?"

As the guard told his version I went over to the maintenance closet and pulled out a broom and dustpan and started sweeping up the glass.

"Need any help?" the female officer asked. Her name badge said B. Girard. I idly wondered what the *B* stood for—Beatrice, Barbara, Bertha?

"No, thanks, Officer Girard." I dumped the glass into the trash can.

She watched me silently for a moment, then asked, "You're the chief's wife, aren't you?"

I looked up at her and smiled slightly. "Guilty as charged."

"This is kinda awkward," she said, shifting from one foot to the other. In the quiet, the leather of her black gun belt squeaked like a new saddle.

"Not really," I said. "Just treat me like you would anyone else. Make your report and go on with your watch. No one was hurt. It was probably just a kid screwing around."

She looked at me doubtfully.

"Don't worry," I said. "I'm going home right after this and I'll tell the chief myself. Don't treat me different, Officer. Really, this is no big deal."

"Want us to stick around while you lock up?" she asked, still not convinced that something special shouldn't be done.

"That would be great," I said. "I'm all right, but I think the security guard might be a bit skittish." We glanced over at him talking rapidly to the male officer, his face flushed in agitation as he pointed and explained. The macho police officer looked as if he were listening to a mosquito buzz.

"Men," she said, shaking her head.

"Enough said," I agreed, and laughed.

She gave me a curious look. "Are you sure everything's okay?"

"Absolutely," I said. She followed me into the wood shop, where I found a square piece of plywood, a hammer, and some nails, and fashioned a serviceable covering for the broken window.

The male officer came over when I'd pounded the last nail in place and inspected my work. "Looks like we got all we need for our report here." He turned and asked me "Why didn't you tell me you were the chief's wife?" He made an unsuccessful attempt to keep the irritation off his face.

I put on my most innocent expression. "Is that relevant? Would you have come quicker if you'd known my identity? I'm assuming that all the citizens of San Celina get the same high-quality police protection. At least, that's what my husband assures the city council and the mayor." I smiled sweetly at him. Behind him, B. Girard grinned and gave me the thumbs-up.

"Uh, yeah, sure we do," he said, snapping his holster shut. "You sure there isn't anything else you saw?"

"I'm sure."

"So, you ready to lock up now?"

"I just need to hang this quilt in the museum and I'll be through." I turned to the security guard and said, "Would you help me with this?"

In the main exhibit room, he helped me clip the wooden hanger onto the top of the quilt and hang it in place. I stood back, making sure it was even, and then asked in a low voice, "Did you tell them about the note?"

He shook his head no.

"Good, just forget you saw it. I'll take care of it." I used my most authoritative tone.

He nodded, his face sober and slightly green.

"You said this was your first job with the security company?" I asked, feeling sorry for him.

He nodded again, looking as if he were ready to burst into tears.

"I'm going to tell your boss how well you handled everything. Calling 911 before you checked on things was smart. You did the right thing."

"Thanks," he said, his cheeks starting to return to a more normal color.

"Are you going to be all right for the rest of the night?"

He blinked rapidly and held the front door open for me. "No problem." He started for his truck. "I'd better report to the dispatcher."

The two officers were still outside, sitting in their blue-

and-white patrol car. Officer Girard was on the passenger side filling out paperwork while Officer Lowry checked his hair in the rearview mirror.

"I'm leaving now," I called to the officers. "Thanks." Officer Girard looked up from her writing and gave me a half smile.

"You be careful now," she said.

"You bet," I replied.

It was past ten o'clock when I got home. Gabe was waiting for me on the front porch, his arms crossed. Apparently the officers weren't taking any chances on getting in trouble and had immediately reported the incident to their watch commander.

"Ten minutes," I said, walking up the steps. "That must be a record, even in this town."

"What happened?" he said, his voice just this side of spittin'-fire angry.

"Excuse me, but I thought we'd come to a mutual agreement about you talking to me like I'm your wife and not a marine recruit."

He unfolded his arms and tried again in a slightly less accusatory tone. "Are you okay?"

"The answer to that is obvious, seeing as I'm standing right in front of you. Next question?"

"Why didn't you call me?" he demanded, then taking a deep breath, added, "Sweetheart."

"I figured it would be just as easy to come home and tell you."

"Were you going to tell me?"

"Of course I was." I looked up at him and smiled. "Have I ever kept anything from you?"

"Benni, this isn't something to joke about. You could have been hurt."

"What did those officers tell you?" I asked, trying to keep my voice airy. He was right, but I didn't want to think about that until I was safely inside with the door locked.

"It was just a rock that some kid tossed through a lighted window. It startled me. That's all."

His blue eyes never blinked. A cricket chirped in a front bush.

I stood on tiptoe and kissed his unyielding lips lightly. "Everything's fine. It was a simple case of vandalism. Don't blow it all out of proportion."

"Was it?" His voice was sarcastic in the dark. "Somehow with you, things are never a simple case of anything." He took my chin and lifted it, looking intently into my face. "No more games. What did the note say?"

I jerked away. "That bigmouthed security guard—"

"The security guard knew about it?"

I looked up at him guiltily. "Uh, didn't he tell you?"

"No. Officer Girard did."

"What?" Well, so much for sisterhood. "But I didn't tell her—"

"She was my first pick from the academy," Gabe said smugly. "Her powers of observation were legendary, but what I especially liked about her was her understanding of the importance of following procedure and respect for the chain of command."

"How—"

He smiled at me, enjoying his moment of triumph. "She watched you sweep up the broken glass. There was a rubber band mixed in with it. She said she guessed by the way you were acting that you knew more than you were saying and that perhaps something was attached to the rock." He held out his hand. "Hand it over, Ms. Harper."

I gave him a dirty look.

"When are you going to learn not to try to pull things over on me?" Gabe said, his voice dramatically weary. "I *always* find out."

"Arrogance is such an obnoxious trait."

He leaned down and kissed me. "There are times when my arrogance melts you."

"Trust me, Friday, this isn't one of them."

"The note, please."

I pulled it out of my back pocket and handed it to him. His expression turned cold.

"Who have you been talking to?"

"No one!"

He held up the note and wiggled it.

"I swear, I've hardly talked to anyone about Nora's death. I've done practically everything but wear a sandwich sign saying 'I don't know anything about this case.' I've maybe said a few things in passing to people, but honestly, I haven't gone out of my way to investigate this."

He looked at me silently for a moment, contemplating and processing the information I'd just given him. "You're telling the truth," he concluded.

I moaned in exasperation. "Of course I am. I hid the note because I just didn't want everyone to know about it. It would've somehow gotten in the papers, and that would give the person who did it even more power. I was going to show it to you, really I was."

He gave me a dubious look and looked down at the small piece of paper, rubbing his thumb across it. "You know, this time you might be right. If what you say is true—"

I growled deep in my throat.

"Okay, okay, sorry. As I was saying, since you haven't really been asking questions about Nora's death, this might be intended for me."

"You?"

"What better way to divert my attention from investigating the Cooper homicide than giving me something more important to worry about—the safety of my wife."

"It sounds like something one of the storytellers might say, don't you think?"

He read the note again. "It's from *The New England Primer*. But it's been changed. The actual quote is, 'Our days begin with trouble here, Our life is but a span, And cruel death is always near, so frail a thing a man.' "

"How do you know that?" I said.

He smiled slightly. "My mother's a teacher, remember? She made us memorize poetry. It's from the same book as 'Now I lay me down to sleep. . . .' "

"That was the first prayer I ever learned."

He peeked out into the dark street, his face sober. "Let's go inside."

"You two done squabbling?" Dove said from her place on the couch.

"We weren't fighting," I said.

"And my peas are coming up purple this year," she said.

"We'll finish our discussion later, *querida,*" Gabe said, kissing the top of my head. "*Buenas noches, abuelita,*" he called to Dove.

"Good night, sweetie," she said.

I flopped down next to her on the couch. "Speaking of fights, how's the Battle of the Bible Verses doing? Who's ahead, the Bruins or the Razorbacks?"

"Hmmph," she said, sitting back. "You know what she did today? She called me an old woman. Said an old woman like me shouldn't be wearing pigtails." Dove grabbed her long white braid and shook it at me. "Does this look like pigtails to you? And who's that old woman calling an old woman?"

"Has she heard anything from Uncle W.W.?" I asked, knowing Dove's questions were purely rhetorical.

"No, and I think the woman has gone completely batty. You know, he was the only thing all these years that kept her from going over the edge. Ben called today and said she's rearranged all the living-room furniture. Twice. He's afraid to get up and pee at night, fearing he'll break his neck 'cause she's changed the coffee table while he was sleeping."

"And you're letting her get away with it?" I asked. "In *your* house? Boy, I sure wouldn't if she were my sister."

She gave me a dark, raptorlike look.

*Whoops, overkill,* I thought as I tried to smile innocently.

"Some things are more important than material possessions," she said disdainfully. "I told you, I'm not going home until she apologizes. Now, get on to bed and finish your fight with your husband. I've got work to do." She looked back down at her Bible. "I'm looking up the verses havin' to do with pride. There's more than a few that will apply to you-know-who."

"Yeah, I sure do," I said under my breath.

"You know, young lady," she said, not looking up, "you harangue that boy way too much. If you keep givin' him so much grief, someday he's likely to think you aren't worth it."

I walked toward the bedroom, thinking, *Nyah, nyah, nyah. Some advice from the haranguing queen herself.*

"Don't you make light of me, Albenia Louise Harper," she said. "The Lord can hear your thoughts."

I turned and looked at her, incredulous. Apparently He wasn't the only one.

She narrowed one eye at me. "Get on with you now. Breakfast is at seven sharp. You're going to need a good one tomorrow. I'm making chocolate-cinnamon pancakes and Louisiana hot sausage."

My favorite breakfast. Geez, how can you love someone to pieces and still want to throttle her?

*Easy,* I thought when I walked into the bedroom and saw Gabe sitting in bed waiting for me.

I undressed and crawled next to him.

"What's the news from the battlefront?" he asked.

"It appears to be a standoff, though I think the Razorback has got the Bruin on the run. Possession is still nine tenths of the law, right? And right now Aunt Garnet has captured Dove's home. I don't think that's quite sunk in yet to Dove. Once it does, I don't want to be around."

"I'll just be glad when our house is back to being *our* house."

I snuggled next to him. "So, what now, Chief Ortiz?"

"What do you mean?"

"The note. What should I do?"

"Nothing. I'm going to beef up security for the festival. Just promise me you will absolutely stay away from discussing this with anyone."

I thought about my talk with Grace tonight. "That's not as easy as it seems."

"Benni—" His voice was reproving.

I sat up and shook my fist at him. "Gabe." I mocked his tone. "I can't help what people tell me. I repeat, I have not asked any questions. But people do tell me things. They assume I know more than I do because I'm your wife. What am I supposed to do about that?"

He didn't answer, but pulled off his glasses and squeezed the bridge of his nose. I leaned over and ran my hand across his bare chest. "Don't worry, *papacito,*" I said. "I'm going to be fine. You're overreacting."

He pulled me to him, wrapping his arms around me. "I'd never forgive myself if you were ever hurt because of my job." He rubbed his lips across the top of my head. I felt my hair catch in his mustache.

"I won't," I said firmly. "You'll find who did this. I have complete confidence in you."

He sighed. "I'm glad somebody does."

"The city council hassling you again?"

"The city council, the city manager, the mayor, citizen's groups, the newspapers. So many people are roasting me right now, I feel like one of your dad's steers on the Fourth of July."

"Is that why you're trying to pin it on Roy Hudson?" The minute the words were out, I knew they hadn't sounded the way I'd intended.

"What?" He loosened his hold. "Who told you that?"

I scooted across the bed from him and cradled my pillow in front of me. "Grace caught me as I was leaving the pizza parlor tonight. She asked me if I thought she should get a lawyer for him. She said you were convinced he'd done it since they'd fought only hours before she was killed."

His lips tightened under his mustache. "What else did she tell you?"

"That you'd confiscated all his ropes. That it was an anonymous tip that told you about the fight. Is it true?"

He frowned. "What?"

"About the ropes. The tip."

"Yes, and that's all you need to know." I flinched at the sharpness in his voice.

I hugged the pillow tighter. "Gabe, why are you so angry?"

His face softened, and he reached over and pushed the pillow away, pulling me to him. "I'm not mad at you, sweetheart. I'm angry at people getting you involved when you shouldn't be. Mostly, I'm afraid for you. As much as I'd like to, I can't be with you every minute. Just try to stay around large groups of people for the time being, okay?"

At that moment we heard the front door open and Sam and Rita's loud, laughing voices fill the living room. Dove's voice soon joined the talking. Sam started telling a story about some kooky guy he'd just waited on at Eudora's, with Rita interrupting every so often with a comment about her short-lived career as a cocktail waitress and Dove's gruff voice telling them they don't know crazy people, listen to what Garnet just did—

"Somehow," I said, "I have a feeling that's not going to be a problem."

# 10

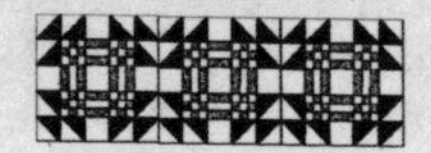

As I suspected, the last thing Gabe had to worry about the next day was me being alone. For the first time since all our company had landed like a flock of crows in a cornfield, everyone was present at the same meal. At breakfast Gabe and Sam didn't speak, but at least they didn't fight; Dove was in high spirits because Aunt Garnet hadn't left a message . . . yet. Even Rita seemed a little more cheerful. At least everyone's day was beginning on a pleasant tone. I walked Gabe out to his car, taking that time to tell him what Jillian had said about Nick and Nora's argument the night she was killed.

"I'm not surprised," Gabe said. "Detective Weber said he thought Nick was nervous about something." He opened the Corvette's door and stuck his briefcase behind the driver's seat. "I meant what I said last night. I want you to make certain you stay around groups of people."

"Should I leave the door open when I take a leak?" I teased.

He looked down at me, his face serious in the pale morning sunlight. "I'm not joking, Benni. I have half a mind to make you stay at the ranch for a week or so."

"Excuse me, Friday, but you can't *make* me do anything. Would you just let it go?"

"I'll increase patrols by the museum," he said. "What

are your plans for today? What time are you coming home tonight?''

I poked him hard in the chest with my forefinger. ''You don't listen to a word I say, do you?''

He grabbed my finger and shook it. ''I listen. I'm just ignoring it since you don't seem to grasp your precarious position.''

''I understand perfectly, but believe me, today of all days you won't have to worry about me being alone.'' I slipped my arms around his neck and kissed him hard. ''I'll meet you at Farmers' tonight. Next to the storyteller's booth at six o'clock. If you're real nice to me, I'll buy you dinner.''

''Call me if anything out of the ordinary happens,'' he said, his eyes still worried.

My prediction about not being alone was more true than I could have ever imagined. At the museum there must have been a hundred people working on booths and setting up camp. By midafternoon, we'd checked in almost every storyteller who'd reserved a camping spot, and most of the booths were finished. Between helping the campers get settled and giving them their festival packets, telling them the rules of the campground and their storytelling times, I helped out the unexpectedly overburdened docents by giving tours of the storytelling quilt and Pueblo storytelling doll exhibit. At five, just as I was getting ready to leave and drive downtown to grab a parking space before they were all taken, Constance Sinclair herself showed up with a group of friends who'd flown up from L.A. at her invitation. Naturally she wanted the museum curator herself to give a private after-hours tour, so it was past six-thirty before I made it downtown. The parking structure was already full, as were all the downtown parking lots, so I was forced to park the pickup four blocks away on a side street. I hurried down the dark street because I knew Gabe would be worried when I didn't show up on time. He'd already called me three times today to make sure I was still in one piece.

It took me about ten minutes to walk to Lopez Street, barricaded now at both ends for the three long blocks that made up downtown San Celina. The scents of Farmers' Market swirled around me as I stepped into the crowded throng of people—smoky tri-tip beef, huge turkey legs, Chinese shish kebabs, and peppery Portuguese linguica sausage barbecuing over thick chunks of white-hot oakwood; the toasty smell of homemade tamales and cooking pinquito beans; the sweet scent of fresh flowers from the commercial fields in Lompoc down south; and the sharp, bitter smell of cigarette smoke hovering over chattering groups of college students. Everything that made San Celina County special was represented at Thursday-night Farmers' Market—the rainbow displays of bright orange carrots, Kentucky Wonder beans, winter banana apples, lipstick peppers, sage honey, raw almonds, local wines, and fresh brown ranch eggs (happy chickens on the ground!), and the best caramel apples in the universe; the independent entrepreneurs hawking bead jewelry, balloon animals, hand puppets, velveteen hats reminiscent of Dr. Seuss characters, incense, face painting, and five-minute caricatures guaranteed to make you smile or your money back; the political and social booths of the humane society ("Adopt a Pet Today"), the always active Central Coast NOW chapter, Campus Crusade for Christ, Hemp for Life (Our ropes will never leave you hanging), Republicans, Democrats, Independents all trying to garner support, and the GreenLand Conservancy's "Save Our Mountain" T-shirt and bumper stickers table next to the Ranch and Farm Producers' Coalition table that hawked sweatshirts stating, "OUT OF WORK? EAT AN ENVIRONMENTALIST."

"Meet you at Farmers'" had been a mating call among Cal Poly students for as long as I could remember. Walking through the crowded streets, feeling the familiar sensation of being a spawning salmon caught in a mindless migration, I thought briefly of Jack. We were only eighteen when he'd asked me to marry him one night as we sat on the curb, the only table accommodations at Farmers', eating corn-on-the-cob drenched in sweet butter and sprinkled with Tabasco sauce.

Gabe, his face hard with anxiety, waited beside the small stage we'd set up for the storytellers. A Native American storyteller wearing a tall Stetson with a snakeskin hatband was spinning a tale about Coyote the Trickster. Gabe's tense expression changed to an irritated scowl when he finally spotted me pushing through the crowd. He glanced at his watch.

"I know, I know," I said, holding up my hands. "Constance showed up at the last minute with a bunch of friends and wanted a personal tour. I didn't think it would take as long as it did."

His face relaxed slightly, and he slipped a warm hand on the back of my neck. "I know you think I'm being overly protective, but I got an advance copy of tomorrow's *Freedom Press*. I'm worried about the repercussions."

"That stupid Will Henry. Is he trashing your department? I swear I'm going to buy one of those hemp ropes he's always singing the praises of and wrap it around his scrawny—"

The crowd laughed at the storyteller's imitation of a coyote's yip-yip. Gabe steered me a few feet away from the noisy crowd. "It's not about the department. The article's about you . . . us."

"Me? Us? What did we do?"

"It's actually just a couple of paragraphs on the Tattler page. It mentions your propensity for stumbling upon dead bodies. The writer questions my ability to control my wife and wonders whether that incompetency carries over to my running of the department. He suggests that it's the reason crime is increasing here in San Celina."

"Control me!" I sputtered. "I'm not a trained seal, for cryin' out loud. I bet Will Henry wrote that just 'cause I argued with him the other night. To imply you aren't running the department right is absolutely ludicrous. They can't blame you just because there's more crime. That's *why* they hired you. The crime came before you did. I am so pissed."

Gabe touched a large finger to my mouth. "That's not what has me worried. It's not the first time I've been trashed by a newspaper reporter, and it won't be the last. He also implies that I tell you too much, that you're too involved in my work. He called you the Hillary Clinton of the San Celina Police Department."

"Oh, great. I'm never going to hear the end of that from Elvia."

"Whoever did this might think you know more than you do, and that puts you in a dangerous position."

I looked up at his tense face, and guilt flowed through me like a river. "I honestly did try to stay out of it this time. I really don't want to cause you any trouble with your job."

Before we could continue, someone called Gabe's name. Michael Haynes, current president of the city council, strode across the street. Dressed in expensive slacks, a white Izod golf shirt, and tasseled loafers, he gripped a folded newspaper under his arm. His tanned face was very unhappy.

"Ortiz," he said. "We need to talk."

Gabe turned back to me, his face weary. "Where are you going to be?"

"Right here in the middle of this crowd. I'll be fine."

He hesitated a moment. "Don't be alone for a minute. Promise me."

"I *promise,*" I said, giving the councilman a hard look.

He kissed me on the top of my head and turned to Michael Haynes. "Let's go across the street to the Sundance,"

Gabe said in his all-business voice, pointing at the small pub down the street. "It'll be a bit more private than the street."

Haynes shot me an irritated look and started talking before they'd moved a few feet. "This just won't do, Ortiz. That wife of yours—"

I walked back to the storytellers' stage, a combination of annoyance and dismay filling me. I hated being a liability to Gabe's job, though I knew it wasn't really my fault I was so deeply involved in this investigation. And it hurt me to see his reputation publicly maligned. When I saw Will Henry again, I was really going to let him have it with both barrels. *Then again,* a voice inside me pointed out, *think of all the times you've read the Tattler and laughed. It's different when the boot's on the other foot, isn't it?*

On stage, the Native American had been replaced by a Jewish storyteller from Bakersfield. He was tall and thin, with alabaster skin and a long untrimmed red beard that he stroked as he talked. He sat on a low stool and drew his audience close with his pleasant, rumbling voice.

"Once, a long time ago, in a small village in Eastern Europe, there was a very important businessman in the community who took a disliking to the new rabbi. Every chance he could, he'd talk about the rabbi behind his back.

" 'Did you see his beard this morning?' he'd whisper to another man in the town square. 'Tangled as a rat's nest. Did his mother never teach him to clean himself? Tsk, tsk.' He'd shake his head and roll his eyes. 'Did you hear what he taught in the temple this morning?' he'd murmur to another man. 'Where did he learn the Torah, from a goat herder?'

"Finally, after weeks of slandering the new rabbi, who patiently ignored the whispers swirling about him, the businessman was confronted by a respected friend and reprimanded for his cruel words. He repented and, feeling guilty for his behavior, presented himself to the rabbi and begged his forgiveness, asking to make restitution. The rabbi, being a kind and thoughtful man, considered the businessman's request carefully and finally stated, 'Take your finest feather pillow and climb to the top of the highest hill outside the village. When you reach the top, cut it open and scatter the contents to the winds. After you have done that, return to me.'

"The businessman went up to the highest hill with his fattest, most expensive down-filled pillow, tore it open, and watched the feathers skip across the sky in the brisk wind. He returned to the rabbi and said, 'I've done as you asked. Am I now forgiven?'

" 'Almost,' replied the rabbi. 'There is still one more task before you. Go and gather all the feathers up again and put them back in the pillow.'

'But that's impossible,' cried the businessman. 'The wind has blown them away!'

" 'Yes,' said the rabbi, who besides being kind and thoughtful, was also very wise. 'And so it is also impossible to undo the damage your have done with your words, which can never be retrieved.'

"The businessman walked away, saddened by his behavior, but wiser from the lesson the rabbi had taught him.

"*Lashon hora,*" the storyteller told the crowd. "That's Hebrew for hurtful speech. In the Jewish tradition, malicious gossip is not regarded lightly. The Hebrew term for words is *devarim,* which also means 'things.' And, my dear friends, words are indeed things, capable of doing the greatest good, but also the greatest evil. Whenever you are tempted to speak ill of another, remember the slanderous businessman and his empty feather pillow."

"Quite a story," Ash's smooth voice said behind me. "Makes one think."

I looked up at him. "That's the whole point of storytelling, isn't it?"

He shrugged and stuck his hands into the pockets of his

slacks. He wore a tan cashmere sweater with no shirt underneath. "What's the deal with Mike Haynes and your husband? Saw them over at the Sundance, and Gabe didn't look like he cared for what Mike was saying."

I returned his shrug and didn't answer. The Bakersfield man stepped off the stage, and Peter took his place. He was dressed in a Johnny Appleseed costume complete with a basket of apples he was handing out to the children in the crowd. "Trees," he was saying. "When we destroy trees, we destroy ourselves."

"Have you performed yet?" I asked, wanting to stay away from the subject of Gabe. There'd be enough people talking about him and me both tomorrow when the *Freedom Press* hit the stands.

"I go on after Peter. How's ticket sales looking?"

"Advance sales were really good. We should have a big crowd tomorrow." I yawned. "I think I'll head on home. Looks like everything's under control here, and we all have a full day tomorrow."

He slipped his arm around my shoulders. "Where are you parked? I'll walk you to your car."

I ducked down and moved away from him, irritated by his familiarity. "No, that's okay. You might miss your session." Before he could protest, I waved a cheerful goodbye and melted into the crowd. I glanced back and caught him staring after me, an undecipherable look on his handsome face. I kept walking, wondering how I could get back to the truck and still keep the promise I made Gabe not to be alone. When I came to Blind Harry's Bookstore, I decided to go in and see if Elvia was around. Though I'd called yesterday morning and left a message with one of her clerks about the Datebook Bum's death, I'd been so busy for the last two days, I hadn't even told her about Gabe giving me the homeless man's diary. On the way to her office, I spotted Nick in the travel section of the bookstore.

"Planning a vacation?" I asked, walking up next to him. He cradled his motorcycle helmet under one arm as he flipped through a book with a glossy photograph of a long winding road on the front. His longish hair lay clean and shiny on the collar of his blue Arrow shirt. He turned green eyes on me, and I was relieved to see the whites clear and rested.

"Nah," he said, sticking the book back in the shelf. "Just dreaming."

"How are things going?"

"Maybe I should ask you that."

I gave him a puzzled look. "What do you mean by that?"

He pulled a copy of the *Freedom Press* from under his arm. "According to this, you have your finger on the pulse of the police department. Be nice if you could let a friend in on what's going on."

I leaned against the bookshelf. "Nick, you know Will Henry as well as I do. That paper twists the truth like uncooked pretzel dough. I swear that I don't know any more about this case than what we all read in the paper. How did you get a copy of the paper so soon anyway?"

"A bunch were dropped off early at all the stands in town here. I guess Will Henry couldn't wait to get this one out."

"He seems awfully intent on pointing fingers at everyone else," I said. "Makes me wonder if he's trying to divert attention from himself. Maybe he had something to do with Nora's death." Once the words were out of my mouth, I instantly regretted them, remembering the story of the Jewish man and his feather pillow.

"That's certainly occurred to me," Nick said. "And I'd spend more time looking into it if I wasn't so worried about my own butt."

"Why's that?"

"As if you didn't know."

"Nick, what are you talking about?"

"If the police were spending half as much time investigating the people she'd talked about in her column or her stinking ex-husband and his girlfriend as they are coming out and requestioning me, they'd probably have caught her murderer by now."

"They've questioned you again?" I asked.

"Don't pull that innocent game on me. I realize your first allegiance belongs to your husband, the police chief, so let's not pretend anything else."

"You've got it all wrong—" I started, trying not to give in to the anger rising up in me, telling myself he was just acting this way because of grief.

His voice swelled in volume. "Just give Gabe a message for me. Tell him I wouldn't kill my sister for any amount of money or land in the world. And tell him the next officer that shows up at my door will have to speak to my attorney." He threw the book he was holding back on the shelf.

"Nick, wait—" He whipped around and walked away before I could finish. I ran up the stairs to Elvia's office, bursting in without knocking. She was sitting in front of her computer, her chin in her hand.

"I am so sick of people," I said, flopping down in one of her peach-colored office chairs.

She continued staring at the brightly lit screen, then punched a couple of keys. "Tell me," she said, her eyes never leaving the screen. I ranted and raved about the Tattler column, about my encounter with Nick, about being blamed for something I hadn't done and indeed had spent an incredible amount of time trying *not* to do, and about the general jerkiness of the male sex altogether. She continued to work as I complained.

Finally she made an irritated sound, turned the computer screen off, and turned her chair to face me. "Speaking of the male sex, this new word-processing program has me ready to send a truckload of your best steer manure to Bill

Gates.'' She folded her hands in front of her, studied me with steady, black eyes, and said, ''So, what are you going to do about it?''

I slumped in the chair, suddenly so tired all I wanted to do was go home and crawl under the covers. ''I don't know. The most irritating thing is it's really no one's fault. I can't help it if I found Nora's body or that I'm so intimately involved with most of the suspects. Gabe can't help it that he's the chief of police. We can't help it that we happen to be married. You know, I've tried not to poke my nose into this one. I've just been in the wrong place at the wrong time, and now Gabe's reputation is paying for it. I'm so worried about him. With everything that's happened in his life the last few months, I'm afraid that this might be the one thing that'll cause him to snap.''

''Is he mad?''

''No, he's actually being pretty understanding about it. But Michael Haynes is probably chewing his ear off as we speak. Who knows what he's going to be like after that?''

''So, I repeat, what are you going to do about it?''

I shrugged and picked at a piece of lint on the chair arm. ''I'm tempted to actually start asking a few questions since I've got the name anyway. Maybe I can find out something that Gabe and his detectives can't and get this thing resolved and everything back to normal.''

She shook her head, her shiny black hair making a swishing sound on her silk collar. ''I knew you'd end up getting involved. I just hope you know what you're getting yourself into.''

I stood up and tugged my jeans down over the tops of my boots. ''You and me both. See you at the opening ceremonies tomorrow? My speech is at six o'clock.''

''If you're not in jail or the hospital,'' she said.

''Thanks for the vote of confidence, my beautiful and skeptical friend,'' I replied. ''Oh, by the way . . .'' I went on to tell her about the Datebook Bum's maroon diary.

"I feel so bad about him," she said. "I called Shaker's Mortuary and made some arrangements. I'd like to read it when you're through."

Outside, I walked through the crowd, trying to decide if I should try to find Gabe or just make a dash to the truck on my own despite his request. I stood on the street corner next to the Rocky Mountain Candy cart and looked out over the milling crowd. Surely there would be other people leaving at the same time. The side streets of San Celina weren't *that* deserted or dangerous.

"Whatcha looking for?" a familiar voice said behind me. I jumped, causing Sam to laugh at my skittishness.

"Nothing," I said. "Aren't you supposed to be working?"

"I'm on dinner break." He held up a foil-wrapped tri-tip steak sandwich and a caramel apple.

"Looks like the perfect dinner to me. How long do you have?"

"An hour." He unwrapped the sandwich and bit into it. Salsa dripped down his chin. I pulled a napkin from the candy cart's holder and handed it to him.

"Thanks. What're you doing?" he asked.

"To be truthful, I'm beat and want to go home."

He gave me a curious look. "So, what's stopping you?"

I sighed. "Your dad made me promise I wouldn't be alone, and the truck is parked four blocks away. He's all tied up with a city-council member, and I was standing here contemplating whether I should keep my promise or just not tell him I walked to my car unassisted."

"Hey, no problem. I'll walk you there."

"I don't want to take up your whole dinner hour," I protested.

"Not a big deal. We don't want to upset *mi padre,* now, do we?"

I laughed. "No, we certainly don't."

As we walked toward the car I told him about the newspaper column that would be officially hitting the streets tomorrow.

''Man, that's tweaked,'' he said sympathetically, finishing up his sandwich as we slipped around the barricades at the end of Lopez Street and walked through the shadowy streets toward the truck. ''Bet Dad's pissed.''

''Actually, he's handling it pretty well. But I have no idea what he's going to be like once that city-council member gets through with him.'' I reached up and batted a low-hanging maple branch. Leaves, bright red and gold from last week's early frost, fluttered down around us.

We crossed the Morro Street bridge, cooled briefly by the damp air rising from San Celina Creek. The tangy smell of rotting vegetation and damp earth surrounded us. Down on the dark banks of the creek that twisted through the city like a wine-drunk snake, we could hear the sounds of teenage laughter and the splashing of water. The streets were more deserted than I expected, and I was grateful for Sam's large, very noticeable presence.

We were about a block away from the truck when Sam said, ''Look at that.'' He pointed to the streetlight I'd cautiously parked under. It was burned out, and a small pool of darkness shadowed the truck. Out of the darkness a figure emerged. We watched, stunned for a moment, as the figure turned and raised a baseball bat, bringing it crashing down on the truck's windshield.

''Cut it out!'' Sam yelled, and sprinted toward the figure. ''That's my dad's truck!''

In a split second, from behind the truck another figure appeared. In the short time it took for Sam to reach the truck, the second figure had done his work. The back of the truck sank from two punctured tires. The first figure swung the bat and shattered the driver's window. Sam grabbed the man's arm.

The other figure started toward Sam, an arm raised. The knife in his hand flashed in the pale moonlight.

"Sam," I screamed, running toward them. "Watch out!" I reached the man holding the knife and threw my arms around his waist.

"Lemme go," the man said, twisting and turning to release my pit-bull grip. "Shit, leggo, lady."

All I could think was *I can't let Sam get stabbed.*

"Run," I screamed at Sam. He tried to wrestle the bat away from the man. Their grunts and cursing were muted in the dense air. My stomach lurched in relief when I heard the bat hit the street with a hollow clatter. Loosening my grip slightly, I twisted around and used my only weapon. I clamped my teeth down on the man's arm, biting down on the thin cotton covering his forearm. He yelped and jerked away. The knife hit the ground.

With an angry roar, the man threw me off him. I hit the sidewalk backward. Pain shot up my tailbone. Ignoring it, I jumped up and ran toward Sam. The baseball-bat man swung a huge fist at Sam's face, connecting with a sickening thud. Sam collapsed in front of the truck, blood spewing from his nose. The man swung his leg back to kick Sam in the crotch, and I sprang at him, catching the edge of his jean jacket with my fingers. He shoved me away, backhanding me in the face. I flew back with the force of his blow and hit the pavement again. Pain exploded across my cheekbone, blinding me for a moment in one eye. Out of the blurred vision of my good eye, I saw Sam roll to his side. The man's kick landed on Sam's thigh. The man yelled at his friend that they weren't paid to do anything but wreck a truck. Then they were gone.

"Sam," I croaked, forcing myself to crawl to him. "Are you okay?"

He wiped his bloody nose with the back of his hand, attempting a smile. Even in the dark I could see the blood staining his white teeth. "Are you?" he asked.

I tentatively touched my already swelling eye, my stomach churning from the sizzling pain. "Mostly." Before I could say more, two girls ran up.

"Hey, are you guys all right?" a girl wearing a white beret asked. "We saw those guys beating up on you. My friend went to get the cops." She looked at our ravaged faces and the smashed windows of the truck. "Man, why didn't you just let them take the truck?"

Sam and I caught each other's eye. For some reason, we found her perfectly sane and sensible remark hilarious, and we started giggling. We were sitting on the street with our backs against the bumper of the truck laughing like a couple of drunks when B. Girard and another cop ran up.

"Crap," she said. "It's the chief's wife." She squatted down and peered into my face. "Are you all right?"

I stared into her concerned face. "What's the *B* stand for?" I asked inanely, trying to think about something other than the blowtorch blasting my eye.

She gave me an odd look. "Bliss," she said. "I have a twin sister named Joy."

Only Sam seemed to understand how incredibly funny that was. We burst into another round of hysterical laugher. Officer Bliss Girard shook her head in bewilderment and stood up. "Call dispatch and have them get a hold of the chief," she told her partner, a thin Asian man who stared at us like we were a couple of three-headed cows. "Have them tell him his wife and—" She looked at Sam, a question in her steady eyes.

"His son," I said, in between gulps of laughter.

She was struck silent for a moment, then regained her composure. "His wife and son were mugged on the two-hundred block of Morro Street. And call the paramedics."

The paramedics were working on us when Gabe arrived. Gabe's head towered over the cute EMT who was cleaning around my eye with alcohol. "Ouch," I complained when the paramedic probed too deeply. I gripped the curb to keep from passing out from the pain.

"Sorry," he said. "Just want to make sure it's clean. You'd better keep ice on this for a couple of hours. But you're going to have a real shiner there, Mrs. Ortiz."

In my hazy vision, Gabe's face appeared as villainous and unforgiving as a hit man's.

"How's Sam?" I asked, trying to peer around the paramedic's body.

"He's fine," Gabe said. "Just a broken nose and some sore ribs. What happened?" His eyes were gray and hard.

The paramedic handed me a cold pack, and I placed it against my eye. "We were mugged."

He stared at me a long time without answering. Then he said, "We'll talk about it at the station." He helped me stand, keeping his arm tight around me while leading me toward a patrol car. Sam was already in the backseat, holding a cold pack to his swollen bottom lip. Gabe helped me into the seat next to Sam. "I'll be back shortly." He slammed the door.

I turned to Sam. His sun-reddened nose was twice its normal size. "How are you feeling?"

He shrugged and attempted a grin. Pain turned it to a grimace. "Okay. He's pissed, isn't he?" He sounded like he was talking through a mouthful of wet oatmeal.

"Without a doubt," I said, resting my head on the slippery vinyl seat. "What did you tell him?"

"That we were mugged. But it was pretty obvious that the truck was involved." He pointed past me. The truck was illuminated by the flashing lights of the emergency vehicles. The completely flat rear tires gave it a comical nose-in-the-air tilt.

I adjusted the ice pack on my eye and groaned. "How much longer is this going to take? I gotta go to the bathroom."

Officer Girard opened the driver's door and slipped in. "Chief Ortiz told me to drive you both to the station. He's going to meet us there."

"Please, just don't take any fast corners," I said.

When we pulled into the station's back lot, the Corvette's presence informed us Gabe beat us there.

"I'm sorry for laughing at your name," I told Officer Girard as she helped me out of the backseat.

"No problem," she said. "Happens all the time. My parents were hippies." She nodded toward the building. "He's waiting for you inside."

"Go ahead," I said to Sam when we walked through the station. "I need to hit the john before our interrogation or I'll explode."

"Thanks a lot," he said, giving Gabe's closed office door a baleful look. "Let me face the lion alone."

"I'll just be a minute," I said, giving him a small push. "Besides, haven't you heard that male lions are all roar? It's the lioness you really need to fear." I pinched one of his biceps and giggled, regretting it when pain shot through the side of my face with tiny lightning bolts.

He turned dark, soulful eyes on me. "I see my mom's reputation precedes her."

When I returned I could hear Gabe's deep voice shouting through the heavy oak door. His voice rose and fell in that mixture of Spanish and English he slipped into whenever he was feeling very angry or very romantic. Sam's slightly higher-pitched tenor yelled an answer. I pushed open the door.

Gabe and Sam faced each other, noses only inches apart, wearing expressions of rage so similar I fought the urge to chuckle. If I ever wanted to know what Gabe had looked like when he was a rebellious and cocky eighteen-year-old, here it was in living color. The tendons on Gabe's neck stood out as thick as ropes. "Of all the stupid, idiotic—" he was saying.

He stopped midsentence when he noticed my presence.

"They can hear you two clear to Santa Barbara," I said, keeping my voice light and calm.

"Am I under arrest?" Sam spit out, his voice thick with sarcasm.

Gabe looked at him with flint-colored eyes. "Don't be ridiculous."

"Then I don't have to listen to any more of your bullshit. All I was trying to do was prevent a crime, and you treat *me* like the criminal. So why don't you just shove it?" Sam stormed out the door, slamming it behind him. On the tan wall, a picture rattled.

Gabe walked out to the hallway and calmly told a nearby officer, "Go take a statement from him while the incident is still fresh in his mind."

"Don't you think you might have been a little rough on him?" I said when he walked back into his office.

Gabe turned still-angry eyes on me. "You think so? What you two did could have gotten yourselves killed. And for what? A stupid vehicle. You know, I can see where in his youth and stupidity Sam might be that foolishly impetuous, but you should have known better." He picked up a large plastic bag that held the knife the man had used to slash the truck tires. The blade was narrow, evil-looking; its sharp tip had punctured a hole in the thin plastic bag.

"Do you know what it feels like to be cut, Benni? With one thrust, you could have been dead." He tossed the bag back down on his desk.

"He was going after Sam," I said in my defense. "Gabe, I didn't even think. If I had stopped and thought and ran for help, Sam could be dead."

He turned away from me, inhaling deeply. "I could have lost both of you," he said hoarsely.

I went over, put my arms around his waist, and laid my head against his warm back. "But you didn't. We're okay."

"Whoever did this is trying to get me to back off on the Cooper investigation."

I walked around and faced him. "That's ludicrous. They

have to know you won't give in to this kind of threat."

His face hardened. "You should go out to the ranch for a few days."

"No way. The festival starts tomorrow. I have a speech to give and a billion other things to do. I refuse to let this person intimidate me."

He touched my cheek, his face softening slightly. "Very brave sounding, sweetheart. But foolish."

I put my hand over his. "Gabe, about you and Sam. Maybe you should try to mend some fences."

The softness went out of his face. "What I said to him still goes. It was stupid and thoughtless to confront those men. He put his life as well as yours in danger just because he wanted to play Rambo."

"He only did what any eighteen-year-old boy who was raised by a macho-cop father would do."

"Are you implying his behavior is my fault?"

"All I'm saying is I suspect at eighteen you would have reacted in a very similar way."

"I don't want to talk about this anymore," he snapped, walking around and sitting down at his desk. I perched on the edge of his desk, facing him.

"Fine," I said. "But think about it."

He leaned back in his tall executive chair and rested his chin on his hand. "What I need to think about is who among our many suspects in this case could have arranged to have this done."

"Where's the truck?" I asked.

"I had it towed to Bill's Auto Body over on Broadway. He's done some good work for the department. He'll give me an estimate tomorrow."

"Guess I'll have to find some other wheels for the time being."

"Get your truck back from Sam."

I didn't answer, but made a mental note to call about

renting a car tomorrow. "So, who *is* tops on your suspect list?"

He gazed at me silently for a moment.

"You might as well let me in on what's going on. Everyone thinks I know everything anyway, so keeping me in the dark is no protection."

He nodded, a look of reluctance still coloring his face. "I suppose you're right. Especially when the *Freedom Press* hits the county tomorrow."

"I forgot, how was your meeting with Michael Haynes?"

"I let him rant and rave and threaten and then I made all the comforting sounds a police chief is supposed to make. What I wanted to do is tell him that if he didn't like the way I was running the department to just shove it."

I smiled at him. "Very grown up."

He gave me a weak smile back. "Yeah, I know, it's just that I'm just so friggin' tired." He ran a hand over his face. "And this case has got me baffled. When I was working homicide, I always hated cases like this."

"Like what?"

"So many suspects. No witnesses. Sex, money, and jealousy. All the biggies when it comes to motive. It's messy and disjointed, and I feel like every time we make progress on one little point, a hundred others come up." He pulled a small tape recorder out of the top drawer of his desk. "Tell me what happened from the beginning. I want to get a statement before you forget anything." He punched the recorder on.

I told him everything I could remember, though like most highly charged emotional incidents, your memories are selective and somewhat convoluted. My voice shook a little when I told him about the man backhanding me. He reached up and gently touched my swollen eye, the skin around his eyes taut.

"I'd like to kill him," he said softly.

"I'll heal," I said. "Who do you think might be involved in this?"

"Those two guys were probably just hired thugs. You and Sam need to look through some pictures and see if you can pick out anyone, but I'm willing to bet that they were paid a couple of hundred bucks to vandalize my truck. There's enough unemployment in San Celina County these days that finding people to do this sort of thing is getting easier and easier."

"So, if you find these guys you'll know who the killer is."

"Not necessarily. They probably don't even know who hired them. There's a lot of ways to pay people to do illegal things without the employee ever knowing who employed them."

I slipped down off the desk. "There's not much you can do about it right now, is there?"

"Not unless you feel like looking through some pictures tonight."

"Would it make any difference if I wait until tomorrow?"

"Not really."

"Let's go home, then. I've got an incredibly packed day tomorrow." I glanced at my watch. "It's past eleven already. Did you call Dove?"

"Yes, and she's all primed to chew your tail when you walk through the door."

I shook my fist at him. "That's why you didn't yell at me."

He ruffled my hair and gave a halfhearted laugh. "I figured I may as well leave it to the expert."

And I did get a tongue lashing when I got home.

"Albenia Louise Harper, I'm surprised at you," she scolded. "No, I take that back, I'm not surprised at all. You were full of the dickens when you were a child, and it's only getting worse as you get older." As she inspected the now purple-and-green bruise under my right eye, she continued to scold me. I countered with the fact that my impetuousness was obviously genetic (Let's not forget that incident in Bakersfield four years ago, I reminded her. That was different, she said, that little punk was trying to take my *purse*. I'd have caught him, too, if I'd been wearing my sneakers). Gabe sat on the sofa drinking a grape soda, enjoying every minute of Dove's lecture. She only stopped when Sam walked in. After an uncomfortable silence, Gabe went into the bedroom. Sam stared after him, his face angry.

"Let it go," I told Sam. "He'll get over it."

"Who cares?" Sam said. "As soon as I've saved enough money, I'm gone."

Dove gathered up her study books. "Honeybun, you'd best get some sleep now. You have a big day tomorrow. You, too, Sam."

During the night something woke me. Not a sound exactly, more of a feeling that things weren't right. I turned over and touched Gabe's side of the bed. The quilt was thrown back, the sheets empty and cool. Over at the window there was a movement, and in the pale light filtering through our sheer curtains, I could see Gabe watching the shadowy front lawn. Navy sweatpants rode low on his hips, and he hugged his bare chest as though he were cold. I could see his body rock back and forth slightly in a self-comforting way that reminded me of a child. I wanted to go to him, hold him, and murmur words that would make the hurt of losing Aaron disappear. But I didn't. I knew at this particular moment this was a road he needed to walk alone.

For weeks after Jack's death, I rode my horse over miles of cow trails, ranting and railing against God, my head lifted up and shouting at the pale gray sky. Agitated blue jays flitted from tree to tree, screaming back at my violent words. My anger and blasphemy was so venomous, I expected to be struck down, a lightning bolt straight from the God I'd trusted since I was a child. And I wanted to be struck, to feel an electrified physical sensation of such mind-numbing proportions it would blot out the pain eating my insides like the maggots I pictured devouring my husband's body.

God's only answer was a piercing silence.

Eventually, when my torrent of words had been expelled, in the forgiving quiet, healing began. A still, small voice, like the gentlest wind, reminded me that death was as much a part of life as love. That with death, life doesn't end, love doesn't end. I started letting Jack go that day, and though there were still times when I longed to hear his laugh, moments when it seemed the sound of his voice would be the only thing that would ease the hurt deep in my chest, I was able to turn back to life and appreciate again the wet delicate nose of a newborn calf, the sweet, hopeful taste of an early strawberry, the solid feel of another man's chest.

I watched my husband's broad shoulders slump in the dim light, and my heart swelled with grief for him. I could not share this lonely journey with him or make it any less difficult. All I could do was stand at the end of the rugged, rock-strewn path and wait.

# 11

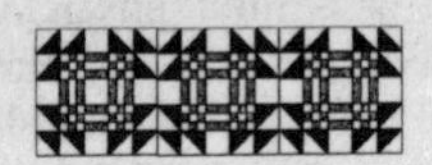

"DON'T FORGET TO come down and look at some pic-tures," Gabe said the next morning. "It's probably a wast of time, but you never know."

I stuck a slice of sourdough bread in the toaster. "Befor I do anything I need to rent a car."

He turned his head away from his glass of orange juic to look at me. His face held his autocratic-ruler expression "I told you to get your truck back from Sam."

"He has to get to work."

"His problem."

I turned my back to him and concentrated on my toastin bread. This morning there was no way I was getting pulle into an argument about Sam, who had wisely left befor Gabe woke up. The air vibrated as we nonverbally strug-gled for control. His fatigue was deeper than I realized; h conceded much quicker than usual.

"I have to get down to the office," he said, tossing hi plastic glass into the sink with a clatter. "Let me see wha I can do about a car."

"I need to leave by ten o'clock." I smiled sweetly a him.

"I'm only doing this because I'm too tired to argue."

"You are a wonderful husband," I said, not flauntin my win.

With his forefinger, he carefully traced the area underneath my swollen black eye. "People are going to think I beat you," he said softly.

"Especially after they read the Tattler."

He drew his hand back, his eyes full of pain.

I grabbed his hand, regretting my flippant teasing. "I was just kidding. No one would ever think that about you."

The look on his face said he didn't believe me.

"Friday, anyone who even suggests you wailed the tar outta me gets this." I brandished a fist at him.

That made him laugh. He kissed my clenched fist.

"Don't forget my speech at six o'clock," I said, handing him his briefcase.

I was spreading blackberry jam on my toast when Rita walked in.

"What happened to you?" she exclaimed. Before I could open my mouth, she promptly started telling me about her date with Ash. "Ash is so much fun. He *always* has money and is not afraid to spend it. It's nice to be treated like a lady for a change." She grabbed the jam-covered toast I'd just put on a plate and poured herself a cup of coffee. "Good kisser, too."

"All that practice," I muttered, taking another slice of bread out of the bag and dropping it in the toaster.

"I know he's a runaround, Benni," she said, sipping her coffee, "but at least he's up-front about it. I really respect that."

There was no way I would even attempt to explain to her that a man being honest about the fact that he cheats on you is not exactly a virtue. I pulled my bread out of the toaster, catching a glimpse of my face in the appliance's shiny exterior. My purple, green, and yellow eye looked like a $1.99 Mardi Gras mask. I let out a soft groan.

"I've got some makeup that would cover that right up," Rita said.

I sighed. "Bring it on, then. I've got a speech to make

tonight and I don't want to scare the little kids.''

''Where's Dove?'' I asked when she returned with her tackle box of cosmetics. She pulled out a tube of beige goop and started smearing it on my face.

Rita shrugged, unconcerned. ''She gets up so dang early. Gramma Garnet left a message this morning after Dove left. I erased it.''

''Smart move,'' I replied, impressed with her cunning. I flinched when she blended the goop over my face with a cosmetic sponge ''Ow, watch it.''

''Hush, you know what they say. Sometimes looking beautiful hurts,'' she said. ''So, what door did you run into?''

I told her the story as she finished with my skin, and we wrangled over whether iridescent pink eye shadow would or wouldn't draw people's eyes away from my injury (it would, but I'd rather have people gossiping about my black eye than my lack of makeup sense).

''Heavens,'' she said, her eyes wide. ''What a close call.''

''You're telling me.'' I inspected her work in the plastic makeup mirror she handed me. I had to give Rita credit for expertise in one area. Except for the swelling, the rainbow bruises were almost hidden.

''Oh, my, he could of slashed your face,'' she said. ''You would of had a scar!'' Her round little mouth gaped in horror.

''Rita, I could have been dead.''

She blinked. ''Oh, well, that, too.''

While dressing, I contemplated who might have been involved in the attack on me and Sam last night. Gabe was right; anyone could have arranged it. At any time. Still, I couldn't help but wonder what Ash was doing last night around the time Sam, Gabe's truck, and I were being bashed around. I quickly changed into new black jeans, a maroon silk cowboy shirt, and maroon Justin boots.

In the living room, Rita was lounging on the sofa painting her nails with a gruesome shade of reddish black.

"Vampire night at McClintock's Saloon?" I inquired.

She held out her hand and studied it. "It's the latest color. I had to wait three weeks before I could get a bottle."

I paused, trying to make up my mind about whether I should do this, then ignoring the reprimanding voice inside me, asked, "So, where exactly did you and Ash go last night?"

I listened to her ramble about this bar and that bar, glancing at my watch impatiently. "Rita, where were you all around eight o'clock?"

She flipped her hair out of her face and looked bemused. "Heavens, I didn't keep track of the time. We ate right after he did his story, then we went to a couple more places to listen to music." She carefully painted a thumbnail. "Why?"

"No reason." It was a pointless question. If Ash had arranged it, he'd done it before his date with Rita. I grabbed my leather backpack from the coffee table and started out the door before it occurred to me that I had no vehicle. I was picking up the phone to call Avis when a police car pulled up in our driveway. It was followed by a bright red Ford Taurus. Elvia's brother Miguel climbed out of the Taurus just as I stepped out on the front porch.

"Chief sent this over." He handed me the rental-car keys. "Heard you and Sam took a beating last night. You don't look too bad."

"My cousin Rita did the beauty bit on me this morning so I wouldn't scare too many people. Has anyone heard anything about the people who attacked us?"

Miguel crossed his arms over his wide chest, his muscular legs spread wide. "We'll probably never find them. Scumbags like that are a dime a dozen."

"That's what Gabe said. He wants me to come down to the station and look through some pictures anyway."

"Sam already dropped by this morning, and he didn't find squat."

"Then I doubt I will either."

"The chief's got extra patrols going by the folk-art museum today, and we'll be cruising by your house a lot. He's real jumpy."

"I know." I glanced over at the bright red Taurus. "Is that why he rented such a bright car so you all couldn't lose me?"

Miguel just grinned. "You keep your eyes open, Benni."

"I will. At least the good one anyway."

After a few minutes of getting used to the bells and whistles of an unfamiliar car, I drove to the museum. D-Daddy's commanding voice could be heard the minute I stepped out of the car. I waved at him across the parking lot and headed straight for our small kitchen. Someone had been astute enough to bring another coffeemaker, and there were two full pots. I poured a cup and hightailed it to my office. There was no doubt that people would be taking numbers today and waiting in line for me to deal with some horrible catastrophe. Before that line started forming, I needed to inhale a few more ounces of caffeine.

On top of my desk lay a copy of the *Freedom Press*. I wondered if it was friend or foe who left it. I'd checked the *Tribune* on my way in, and the attack on me and Sam wasn't in it. Apparently we'd been mugged too late to make the Friday-morning edition. Maybe, I thought optimistically, they'll forget about it by Saturday. Yeah, right. I compulsively turned to the Tattler page, cringing inwardly when I read the sarcastic words about Gabe and me. Hearing about it was bad enough, but to actually see it in print gave it a potent reality that tasted like a mouthful of sour milk. I thumbed through the rest of the paper, which also carried a flattering article about the storytelling festival and praise for the number of community-oriented activities the museum had sponsored in the last year.

But my thoughts kept compulsively returning to the Tattler column. Where *was* that last column written by Nora? What was in it? I agreed with Will Henry about one thing. It had to be about the storytellers, and so that narrowed down, in my mind, the suspects in her murder. But there was still Roy to consider. I couldn't imagine what it must have felt like to be killed by someone with whom you'd once made love. I shivered and threw the paper in my trash can. This whole thing reminded me of something a minister once said that always stuck in my mind—that the line between hate and love is as thin as a strand of baby's hair. That the people who profess to hate the most are the ones peering the most furtively over their shoulder, the ones desiring love in the most basic way. Hatred, he contended, was much easier to change to love than indifference was.

Was that the true story of Roy and Nora? Was their hate just one step away from turning back into love? Had it been on the verge of doing just that? If that was true, I knew one person who would have been devastated. But would Grace be crushed enough to kill? To kill the object of love in hopes of killing the love? I didn't want to think that about my new friend, but she was a passionate woman, a woman who never did things halfway. I leaned back in my chair and pressed my warm mug of coffee against my temple.

"Headache?" Evangeline asked as she walked through my open door. She was dressed in a long, gauzy dress the color of celery. Tiny silver stars embossed in the fabric caught the light when she moved. Her black hair was piled high in a chignon with curly tendrils trailing down. Her only jewelry was a large silver pendant depicting a Pueblo storyteller doll.

I set the mug down and smiled. "Not yet, but I'm sure I'll have one before the night is over."

"Let's at least make an attempt to be optimistic, *'tite amie.*" She bent close to look at my shiner. "I heard you saved your stepson single-handedly last night. A real Clint Eastwood rescue."

"It was probably more along the lines of Lucy Ricardo. Some punks were vandalizing Gabe's truck, Sam rushed in, and one of them went at him with a knife. All I did was grab the guy around the waist and hang on." I watched her face as I told the story, a small part of me wondering if she could have hired those guys. I remembered that she'd once worked at Trigger's, a local cowboy and oil-field workers' bar on the rough side of town and probably knew guys who would do anything for the right price. Yes, she could have, but why? I shook my head in disgust at my growing cynical nature. Next thing I knew I'd be suspecting Aunt Garnet of being involved.

Her face remained sympathetic. "Scary. How did Gabe take it?"

"Take a guess. He's absolutely furious. What's worse is it caused another argument between him and Sam. One I'm not sure is going to be easily mended. He lost his temper and really let Sam have it, and Sam responded predictably. I can't picture either one giving in this time."

*"Bon chien retient de race,"* she said, holding a palm up.

I raised my eyebrows in question.

Her musical voice was low with amusement. "Like father, like son."

"I'll drink to that." I held up my coffee mug. "I'd like to say you oughta see the other guy, but unless my teeth managed to break through his cotton sleeve, Sam and I got the worse of it."

"You bit him?" She gave a delighted laugh. "Good goin', girl."

"Are you all ready for your first session tonight?"

"All set. I'll be taking the stage right after your welcoming speech."

"My very short welcoming speech. Just the thought of

people staring at me makes me want to hide under the bed. I just hope my cousin Rita's makeup job holds up."

"You know, there's this great makeup that covers bruises like a dream. It's called Dermablend. It'll cover anything."

"I'll look for it. I have no idea how long this shiner will last."

"About a—" She stopped abruptly. I waited for her to continue. She pulled at a loose strand of hair and gave a glittery laugh. "You can get Dermablend in any department store. I use it for stage makeup. Kind of an old thespian's trick. Like Vaseline on the teeth. Well, gotta go. I promised Dolores I'd hear her story one more time. She's as nervous as a wild turkey about her solo appearance tonight. Wait'll you see her costume. It's out of this world."

"I'm looking forward to it."

I watched her walk out, mulling over our conversation. Especially the point where she paused—something Gabe said he always looked for when interrogating someone—that moment of hesitation. Something she'd said triggered a memory. I closed my eyes and willed the thought to form. After a few minutes it came to me. A segment on a television-magazine show about abused women disappearing into the underground. Some had children they were protecting, some were just trying to start a new life. All had the experience of being battered, some almost to death. They were sitting in a circle discussing with a frightening dispassion the different methods they used to cover up the marks left from their beatings.

"Dermablend's great," one had said. "They got a leg makeup that almost makes the marks disappear." Was that why Evangeline and her father were here in San Celina? Was she hiding from an abusive husband? If Nora was mean enough to reveal that, it might be reason enough for Evangeline . . . or D-Daddy to kill her.

I unlocked the file cabinet that held the co-op members'

applications for admittance. Our criteria weren't strict, but since we did have people on the premises working with dangerous equipment, we were required to carry liability insurance as well as a next of kin to notify in case of emergency. That meant we had to keep some kind of records. I pulled out her file, closing my office door before settling down to read.

In her large, curvy handwriting was her name, address, next of kin, doctor's name and address, the type of art she worked on, and a paragraph telling her artistic goals and intentions. We really didn't ask much information of our prospective co-op members. What we cared about most was their dedication to their art, their ability to work within the boundaries of the co-op, and willingness to lend a hand in our mostly volunteer organization.

I looked for her former address, something that was more a formality than anything, and Evangeline had simply written Louisiana.

There was only one way I could get any information about the southeast part of our United States. I picked up the phone and dialed Sugartree, Arkansas.

"Sweetcakes," my cousin Emory said. "Y'all haven't paid me for the last little bit of detective work I performed for you." One year my junior, Emory Delano Littleton is somehow, in that complex Southern way, distantly related to me on both sides of my family tree. His grandfather and Dove's father were first cousins by marriage, and his father, Boone Littleton, married my mother's third cousin, Ervalean, who played the organ at my parents' wedding, which is where she met Boone.

The job Emory was referring to was some investigating he'd done for me on my trip to Kansas a few months back. He was sort of a private detective/investigative reporter for the *Bozwell Courier Tribune*. Bozwell was a town just south of Sugartree, just north of Little Rock. It was a job his father finagled for him when Boone's chicken business took a downturn ten years ago and Emory had to drop out of law school. Emory was actually pretty good at his unplanned-for journalism-detective career, being the sort of man who loves gossip and was almost as nosy as me.

I'd promised him a date with Elvia, whom he'd had a crush on since the summer of his eleventh year. He stayed with us at the ranch because his mother had just died and his father didn't know what to do with him. Elvia didn't know about my bargain with him yet. And for a very good reason. He had annoyed her from the very first minute she heard his molasses-tinged Arkansas drawl. Since Emory was terrified of flying, I'd been hoping he had forgotten all about my rash promise. No such luck.

"I'm waiting for your explanation, sweetcakes. When is Elvia, queen of my adolescent dreams, expecting me?"

I bit my lip, trying to think of a way to answer without actually lying.

"Albenia Louise! I know what that silence means. You haven't even arranged it. Ingrate. Why should I help you again?"

"I'll tell her the minute you make your plane reservation," I promised.

He paused for a moment. "It might be even wiser to wait until I'm actually there," he said, proving he was no dummy.

"I was thinking the same thing." I leaned back in my chair and prayed his fear of flight would continue to overshadow his lovestruck libido.

"Okay, you're off the hook," he said. "For now. But I'll be showing up on your doorstep someday, and you'd better be ready to pay up."

"I will," I said, trying not to think about all the horrible torture techniques I knew Elvia had acquired from growing up in a family of six brothers. "But now I need you to use your contacts to search for information on someone." I told him about Evangeline and what I thought.

"If she's in hiding she may not be using her real name."

"It's worth a shot. Do you have any contacts in Louisiana?"

"Sweetcakes, I've got contacts in places that would curl your toes."

"All female, I bet." Though I'd never tell him to his face, Emory was an extremely handsome, articulate, and amusing man with oh-so-polite Southern manners that could charm the . . . well, I'll just say that even Aunt Garnet has trouble saying no when he wants something. Now, if I could convince Elvia—

"She works for the New Orleans Police Department. A lieutenant, I think now. Brightest red hair and the cutest little ole—"

"I don't want to hear any more," I interrupted. "Just get me the information." Then an idea occurred to me. "Hold on a minute, Emory. I have someone else I need checked out." I dug through the filing cabinet and pulled out Ash's file. "Do you have any contacts in Mississippi?"

"Never dated a Mississippi woman, though I've heard they are as sweet as the magnolia of their state flower. But I do know a guy there who works for the *Jackson Clarion-Ledger*. Neil McGaughey. He reviews mystery books for them. Knows everyone who's anyone in Mississippi. Comes from one of those old monied families. Has a rare-book collection that's worth millions."

"See if he knows or can find out anything about an Ashley Stanhill. Says on his file here his last address was Natchez."

"Will do. Now, about my fee."

"I told you I'd tell her as soon as you buy your ticket."

"I mean for this little foray."

"What do you want?"

"Elvia's fair hand in marriage."

"Emory, try something that is possible in this millennium."

"Okay, fine. Pay for our date. And I don't mean dinner at Carl's Junior and a matinee at the Fremont."

I considered his request. "Fifty dollars."

"Oh, please, that wouldn't get me to first base. Two hundred."

"Emory, it'd take the Crown Jewels and a tank of nitrous oxide to get you to first base with Elvia. Seventy-five."

"Hundred fifty. You've never seen me when I really want something."

"One hundred, and that's my final offer."

"Sold. It'll at least pay for the limousine. I'll get back to you."

"Hurry, Emory. I need this information yesterday."

"Dear cousin, dare I ask? Does your hunka, hunka Latino love know about this?"

"Call me here at the museum. Otherwise, I'll call you."

"That answers my question. A bucketful of luck, sweetcakes. Sounds like you're going to need it."

After I hung up with Emory, I started to put away Evangeline and Ash's files when the sound of angry male voices echoed from the main studio. I rushed out of my office and found Peter and Roy rolling on the floor while a bunch of quilters were backed up against the wall, clutching the quilt they'd been free stitching.

"You guys stop it," a woman yelled. "Take it somewhere else."

"For crying out loud," I said. I ran into the kitchen, grabbed a pitcher of ice water out of the refrigerator, and dodging their rolling bodies, dumped it on them. The shock stopped them momentarily. They sat with legs intertwined, panting like dogs, water dripping down their faces.

"Get up," I said, grabbing Roy's wiry arm. They both struggled up, glared at each other, and started swinging again. I threw myself in front of Roy as he strained to reach for Peter, wondering if my other eye was going to be blackened in the process, when D-Daddy, Evangeline, and a couple of college kids rushed into the room. D-Daddy pushed me firmly aside and grabbed Roy.

"*À ça oui!* That's enough." He jerked his head at Peter. "Hold that one back," he told the college kids who'd come in with him. He pulled Roy across the room. Roy struggled briefly, then gave in to D-Daddy's steel grip.

The kids hesitantly approached Peter. He held up his hands and growled at them, "Don't touch me."

"Both of you, in my office," I snapped. "Now." I turned and told the crowd, "The fun's over. I'll take care of this."

"I be waitin' outside," D-Daddy said.

"That's not necessary," I said.

"I be there." His determined face dared an argument.

"Okay, thanks, D-Daddy."

Inside my office, both the men had claimed an office chair, scooting them as far apart as they could in the small room.

I sat down at my desk, picked up a pencil, and didn't say anything for a minute or two. They shifted in their seats, avoiding my gaze like guilty schoolboys.

"I should toss both of you out of the festival right now," I finally said, running the pencil through my fingers.

An infinitesimal grunt came from both of them. Then Roy leaned forward in his seat and said, "I didn't start it. Peter—"

Peter broke in. "Me? He's full of crap. I—"

I slammed my fist down on my desk. "Both of you shut up. I don't care who started it and I don't care what it's about. All I care about is this festival going off without a hitch. Now, you both are already on the schedule, and people are counting on hearing you, but one more incident like this and you're both going to be escorted off the premises by a police officer and not allowed back on. And I've got the power to do that. Got it?"

They both started to talk.

I held up my hand for silence. "Got it?"

They nodded.

"Then get out of here and get ready for your performances. And stay away from each other. That's an order."

After giving each other a fierce look, they left. Once he saw I was okay, D-Daddy nodded and followed them outside.

"Is it safe to enter?" Evangeline poked her head around the corner of my doorjamb, her wide-cheeked face worried. "Are you all right?"

"Just another fun-filled day in paradise. Though Eden would certainly be a lot more pleasant without Cain and Abel."

She made a sympathetic clucking noise. "What did you tell them?"

I lifted up my hands in exasperation. "What could I say? They are both featured storytellers. People are expecting to hear them, and it would really hurt the festival if I kicked them out. Not to mention it looking to Constance like I can't handle my job. On the other hand, I can't have them throwing punches at every turn of the hat."

"Don't worry, D-Daddy will be keeping a close eye on them now."

"Easier said than done." I took my purse out of my drawer. "I have to go down to the police station and see if I can identify anyone from the pictures they've pulled. Is there something you needed?"

"I just needed to use your phone, if that's all right," she said. "I know we're supposed to use the public phone in the kitchen, but it's to my doctor and I need a little privacy."

"Sure, help yourself. If anyone asks, I'll be back in about an hour."

"I'll pass it on."

I was halfway to the police station when I remembered that, distracted by the fight, I'd left Evangeline and Ash's files sitting on my desk in full view of anyone who walked into my office. I hit the steering wheel in frustration at my carelessness. Unless Evangeline was blind, it was going to be obvious I was looking into her and Ash's backgrounds. I sat in the Taurus for a moment in the police station parking lot, rolling my shoulders, trying to get the tenseness out. If I was lucky, Gabe would be busy and I wouldn't have to see him while I looked through the pictures. He'd sense my tension immediately and, before I knew it, extract out of me the reason why. Up till now I'd kept my promise to stay out of the investigation—the call to Emory changed that.

Luck was with me when I walked through the busy office and parked myself in front of Maggie's desk.

"He's up to his ears in meetings," Maggie said. "He left orders for you to look through the pictures sent over from the sheriff's computer."

She sent me over to the detectives' department, where a young man in an olive tweed jacket and new Levi's sat with me while I studied the pictures. Like Sam, I couldn't make a solid ID.

"They *all* sort of look like them," I said.

"That's the whole idea," the young detective said. "We use your description and run it through the sheriff's computer and see if we get a match. You sure none of them are the guys?"

"Pretty sure," I said.

He sighed in frustration. "It's always a long shot, but we have to try."

I was on my way out when Maggie called to me.

"I forgot," she said. "Gabe also said to tell you that if you wanted to look through the stuff found with the John Doe body, it's in the evidence locker. We'll be tossing it out at the end of the month."

I glanced at my watch. It was getting close to one o'clock. I didn't want to stay away from the museum much longer and still I needed to get something to eat. "I'll look through it real fast, and then you can toss it.''

She handed me a pair of thin rubber gloves. ''Better use these,'' she said. ''You never know.''

The large navy gym bag was full of worthless junk as Gabe had told me. A strong smell of mediciny-mint assaulted me when I unzipped it. A small bottle of Listerine mint-flavored mouthwash had leaked all over the contents. I felt an incredible sadness as I picked through the Datebook Bum's meager legacy—plastic cups from McDonald's and Burger King, a few paperback books with the covers ripped off, dozens of pens and stubs of pencils, a worn toothbrush with DR. GARDINER SAYS SMILE on it, a couple of old copies of the *Freedom Press,* a bar of soap in a plastic holder, two old shirts, and a pair of socks with a hole in one heel. The only thing that really intrigued me was a large Tupperware container of keys. Something in me told me to save those. I set them aside and zipped the gym bag back up. I stripped the rubber gloves off my hands and tossed them in a nearby trash can.

''You can dump it now,'' I told Maggie. ''It was just junk.''

Maggie shook her head and turned back to her typing. ''We have a lot to be thankful for, don't we?''

I drove through McDonald's on my way back to the museum. The first thing I did in my office was check for Evangeline and Ash's files. There they were, right in plain sight where I'd left them. I stuck them quickly back into the file cabinet and locked it, the barn-door analogy not lost on me.

After eating my All-American Big Three lunch of grease, carbohydrates, and sugar, I felt equipped to face the world again. A final, compulsive walk-through the exhibit assured me that everything was ready for the five o'clock opening. I became the first official visitor when a ticket seller attached a green plastic band to my wrist, an easy and inexpensive way to identify who'd paid admission for the three-day festival.

I found D-Daddy under an oak tree at the back of the pasture, sipping a lemonade from one of the concessionaires.

"Looks delicious," I said.

"I'm their test taster, me," he said, giving me a wide smile. "I taste the sausage and beignets after this. Make sure they all right for folks."

"Sounds like a pretty clever scam to me," I said, laughing. "But a good way to get a free dinner." I leaned against the tree and gazed out over the field dotted with purple alyssum. "Did anything exciting happen while I was gone?"

"No, *ange*. Those boys, I'm keeping an eye on them. Don't you worry, no. D-Daddy make sure they stay far, far apart."

"Thanks. I'll keep an eye out, too, and I'll let Gabe know about it. He's supposed to be here when I give my opening speech at six. By the way, have you seen Evangeline?" I made my voice light and casual.

"She left an hour or so ago. Had a doctor's appointment or something. Then some errands. Don't worry, she'll be back in time."

"I'm not worried," I assured him. "I'd better get back to my office and read my speech over a couple more times. With all these professional storytellers performing, I'm a bit nervous about giving it."

"You be fine. How can they not love a *jolie blonde* like you?"

"D-Daddy, if you were a few years younger and I wasn't married, we'd be in real trouble."

"Trouble?" He grinned. "You wouldn't be no trouble at all, *chère*. No trouble at all."

I squeezed his arm affectionately and laughed.

Evangeline, if she'd seen the file on my desk, had obviously not discussed it with her father yet. I knew D-Daddy would not be that friendly if he thought I was in any way threatening his daughter. I couldn't imagine Evangeline having anything to do with Nora's murder, but there was something in her background she was trying to hide, something I was sure had to do with an abusive husband or boyfriend. I couldn't imagine the Nora I'd known publicly revealing something so cruel and possibly life threatening. But then, the Nora I thought I'd known would never have written the Tattler column. It all came back to that old question—can we ever really know another person?

Back in my office, I scanned my speech once more, checked the clock, and noting I still had an hour before I went on, told myself I needed to quit worrying and turn my mind to something else. I dug through my purse, searching for the paperback I usually carried, and came across the homeless man's diary. It was the only thing I had to read and I really needed something to take my mind off my pretalk jitters, so I settled back in my chair and read through the almost yearlong record of his life. It ended on the day before he was found dead. His routine was the same as the first four months I'd read the other day—Blind Harry's, the Mission Food Bank, the YMCA, various other businesses in San Celina, the library, and the stone bear fountain outside St. Celine's Catholic Church, where many homeless sat and warmed themselves in the sun on the concrete benches.

On September 1 he wrote with a precise dignity that brought a lump to my throat, "Happy Birthday to me." I set the book down on my desk and stared at the Noah's Ark picture hanging on my plain white wall. It was a Grandma Moses primitive-style painting by one of our artists in the co-op. The animals all had hopeful smiles on their faces as they marched up the long ramp. I had fallen in love with the whimsical picture as I watched the artist create it, and somehow, though I never mentioned it to Gabe, he'd found out and bought it for me for my birthday.

"I want to keep the concept of pairs firmly affixed in

your mind,'' he'd said, his eyes sparkling with humor.

I looked back down at the datebook and wondered if the homeless man had ever been a part of a pair. Was there someone, somewhere, who still missed him every day, would always wonder where he'd gone? I thought about the compulsiveness of his routine and how even the homeless, people we think of living as footloose and free a life as we can imagine, develop routines to bring order in their life. Again I wondered what he'd thought of all of us, what he saw as he went about his rounds.

*What he saw.* I flipped through the book to the days before and after Nora's murder. Nothing. He'd made his circuit, which seemed to have a three-day pattern, and recorded nothing that would give any hint that he'd seen anything to do with Nora's murder. But, if what Gabe estimated was right, she'd been killed at a time when the Datebook Bum most likely hadn't been around. On the other hand, I had no idea where he'd slept. I couldn't help but wonder if his death was truly an accident. I stuck the business diary back in my purse and made a note to ask Gabe what the John Doe's autopsy had finally shown as the cause of death.

At ten minutes to six I went out to the field, where a large green-braceleted crowd had already gathered around the main stage. All of the hay-bale seats were occupied, and D-Daddy and one of his young helpers were fooling with a portable microphone. I felt a small flutter in the pit of my stomach. Though I'd grown more accustomed to speaking in public since I'd become museum curator, it was not my favorite part of the job. As D-Daddy fiddled with the sound equipment, I laughed along with the rest of the audience at the antics of a mime who stood at the side and mimicked D-Daddy's irritable expression. The scent of roasting beef, chicken, and sausage from the steel barbecues set up hours earlier gave the evening air a pungent, homey smell.

A warm hand slipped underneath my hair and gently squeezed my neck. "Nervous?" Gabe whispered in my ear.

I smiled up at him. "You made it! Yeah, my stomach is like a snow dome someone just shook. I'll be glad when my part is done and I can turn it over to the professionals."

"You're going to do fine," he said. "How can they not love you?"

"You sound like D-Daddy," I said, leaning into his comforting bulk. He couldn't have looked less like a police chief tonight in his washed-out Levi's, black T-shirt, and black leather jacket.

"I think I'm going to have to keep an eye on that old coot," he said.

"He's a charmer, all right," I replied. "But you don't have to worry. Charming guys have never been my type."

"What?" he said, his hand dropping down to my waist and tickling me. "What's that supposed to mean?"

"Hey, Chief, don't get the curator too riled up before her big speech," Jim Cleary said behind us. He carefully pushed the wheelchair holding his wife, Oneeda, and settled her on a solid, level piece of ground.

I stooped down and took her thin brown hand in mine. She gently squeezed back. "Oneeda, I'm glad you could make it. I'm sorry I missed our weekly tea, but like I told you over the phone, this week's been a disaster."

Her black eyes twinkled. In spite of the multiple sclerosis that had twisted her body to the point of being unable to dress herself, her mind was sharp as a twenty-year-old's, something most people didn't realize when she talked with her slow, garbled words. Four months ago Gabe had asked me if I knew of anyone who'd be willing to quilt a wall hanging that Oneeda had pieced before the MS had made it impossible for her to sew. When no one in the co-op could work it into their schedule, I'd agreed to do it, as a favor to Jim and Gabe, and started going over there every Friday to stitch the small quilt, a New York Beauty pattern she'd pieced years ago in honor of her home state.

I'd gradually learned to understand her speech, and though we were as different as two people could be—twenty years apart in age, my rural background, her New York Harlem background, and our obvious racial difference—she and I had formed an unexpected friendship that continued after I finished the quilt. We discussed everything from people's distorted views of the handicapped to what it was like to grow up black in the fifties to how I felt about never knowing my mother and growing up in an environment almost exclusively male. And she was brutally honest in telling me what to expect now that I was a cop's wife.

"So," I said, "you finally talked Jim into unlocking your cage?"

"Mr. Big Stuff letting me kick up my heels." She laughed and pointed down at her feet with a gnarled hand. "New shoes."

"Cool," I said, admiring her silver tennis shoes. "How's the Ohio Star coming along?" We'd been piecing together a baby quilt she intended for her youngest daughter's first child. She'd arrange the pieces, and I'd sew them.

"Good," she said, nodding her head. Her sparkly silver earrings swung jauntily. "Have it just how I want it now." She gave me a bright smile.

"Good, 'cause I ain't gonna rip it out one more time," I said.

"Unless the general commands you to," Jim said mildly.

We all laughed at his accurate assessment of his wife. Somehow, when Oneeda wanted something done, it always got done. Her way. And remarkably, she made you feel wonderful about it.

Gabe tapped his watch. "Looks like you're on, sweetheart."

"Okay." I stood up and kissed Oneeda's cheek. She patted my shoulder comfortingly.

"You'll do fine, sweetie," she said, winking at me. "I'll

send up a quick one for you.'' She pointed to the soot-colored sky.

''Thanks. I'll see you all afterward in the food court.''

My speech went smoothly, with only a few screeches in the PA system. Luckily most of the storytellers were trained in projecting their voices and wouldn't need it, though with the crowds that were gathering, it might come in handy. I made a quick announcement about Nora Cooper and why she wouldn't be performing and told the crowd of her love for children and her desire to serve them through her personal life and her work. I saw more than a few skeptical faces in the audience, but refused to let that sway me. No matter what she did as the Tattler, it still didn't negate the good things she had done in her life.

''Magical mysteries, fabulous fables, soulful songs, and terrifying tales. You'll hear it all in the next two and a half days. So set your imaginations free, hold on to your hats, and let the stories begin.'' I ended my speech with an Olympic-like flourish. Evangeline took the stage after me, pulling up a stool and calling the children to come close to the stage to hear the story of Gabriel and Evangeline and their porcine adventures.

''You're missing your story,'' I told Gabe when I joined him and the Clearys at a redwood picnic table near the food court.

''I'll survive,'' Gabe said. ''What do you want to eat? Jim and I were just going to check it out.''

''What story?'' Jim asked. I explained about Evangeline's swine-filled rendition of the traditional Cajun poem.

''Sounds interesting,'' he said, nudging Gabe. ''Too bad we're missing it, Oneeda.''

''She's repeating it tomorrow,'' I said. ''Check your program. I just wanted something special to get the ball rolling.''

''Let's see it, Jimmy,'' Oneeda said.

''Whatever you want,'' he replied, his hand stroking her

thick black hair. His actions with her were always so easy and caring. I knew from Oneeda that her illness, first diagnosed when she was in her late thirties, had been difficult on both of them, but the deep and steadfast love of thirty-five years had seen them through the days when they both wanted to walk out. I glanced over at Gabe, who watched their actions with an odd look on his face. Was he wondering the same thing I was? We hadn't even known each other a year. If that were him and me in that position, would our love be that strong?

Jim gave Oneeda's hair one last stroke. "Now, what is it you ladies are craving? Me and the boy here will see if we can use our hunter skills to capture it." His teasing words told me that Jim had moved into his civilian mode. At work he was entirely professional in his relationship with Gabe, but whenever we saw them socially, he instantly took advantage of the twelve-year difference in their ages and treated him like a younger brother.

"Go, go," Oneeda said, waving her hand at him. "You choose."

"I want beef," I told Gabe. "None of those barbecued vegetable kabobs. And a Coke."

"Help, I can't breathe," he said in a squeaky cartoon voice. It was a joke he'd started in an effort to get me to eat better. Supposedly it was the voice of my arteries screaming for mercy.

"Chief Ortiz, you're going to be screaming you can't breathe if you don't go get my dinner without any back-talk."

"Tell 'em, honey," Oneeda said, hitting her hand lightly on the handle of her wheelchair and letting out a delighted chuckle.

"Better do as she says," Jim advised. "She's been in training with a pro. The things I could tell you Oneeda's done to me—"

"Hit the road, Officer," she commanded.

"Yes, ma'am," he said, saluting her. He and Gabe laughed easily as they melted into the crowd moving toward the snack booths.

"Okay, girlfriend." Oneeda reached up and gestured her knuckle toward my swollen eye. "Doorknob?" Her expression was a mixture of affection and the look a mother gets when you've done something you shouldn't have. After raising four children, Oneeda was especially proficient with that second look.

I gently swatted at her hand. "Now, don't try and mother me. I know Jim told you the whole story. And you would have done the same, so don't go throwing any sharp stones at my little glass bungalow."

She smiled slowly. "Yes, but I still worry. How much did Gabe yell about this one?"

"Not much," I admitted. "Frankly, I think poor Sam took the brunt of it. I'm really worried about him and Gabe. It doesn't look like they're ever going to be on decent speaking terms."

"Jimmy and Martin didn't talk for two years once." Martin was their only son. He was thirty-two and an assistant DA in Fresno.

"Jim and Martin? No way! They get along so well."

"Now. Sam and Gabe will, too. When they both grow up a little."

"Well, I hope they do it soon. It's gettin' real old, you know?"

She nodded sympathetically. "Any leads yet on your case?"

I gave a guilty laugh. "Now, Oneeda, you *know* I'm not supposed to be involved in any of Gabe's cases."

"That wasn't what I asked."

Before I had to make any excuses, the guys came back with more food than we could possibly consume at one sitting. Between bites of corn-on-the-cob, tri-tip beef sandwiches, fried zucchini, shrimp-on-a-stick, and slices of thick vegetarian pizza, we talked about the festival and read our programs.

"We can't miss this," I said, pointing to Dolores's name. It was a ten o'clock performance, what we called our Late-Night Cabaret. It consisted of stories that might be a bit too mature or scary for children. Dolores was first up. "I'm so curious about her story. She's been working on it for a long time and won't tell anyone what it is."

"We must see it, then," Oneeda said. "I wonder why she's keeping it a secret? I can't wait to see."

"For exactly that reason," Jim said laconically.

After we'd finished eating, we agreed to part company since we had different storytellers we wanted to hear.

"I've got extra patrol officers covering the festival," Gabe told Jim. "So you're off duty, okay? Just relax and enjoy yourself. Show your wife a good time."

"Likewise," Jim replied.

Oneeda and I looked at each other and burst out laughing. "Pot telling the kettle it's got too much water in it," she said.

"Tell it to me, Sister Oneeda," I said, holding up my hands, fingers spread. She giggled like a young girl.

"Quick, let's split them up before they start to unionize," Jim said, pushing Oneeda's wheelchair toward the craft booths.

Gabe and I strolled through the crowd, holding hands, stopping briefly at each storytelling area. He patiently followed me as I surveyed each craft booth and checked on the museum and the storytelling classes going on in the studios. After taking care of my official duties and seeing that the festival seemed well on its way to settling down, for the first time in a week I felt myself begin to relax. By ten o'clock the crowds had started to thin out. The festival was open until midnight, and though I was exhausted I was determined to stay until it closed. Gabe and I walked over to the main stage and grabbed an empty hay bale in the back. Most of the seats were already taken as people waited for Dolores's performance.

"Thirsty?" Gabe asked.

"Get me a Coke. I'll save a place for you."

I was looking over the crowd, trying to see who was attending tonight, when I felt the hay bale shift.

"How's it going?" Jillian asked. She was dressed in off-white jeans, a golden-brown cashmere sweater, and chamois-colored flat heel boots.

"So far, so good." I held up crossed fingers. "What do you think of the festival so far? Has Constance been here? I haven't seen her."

"She was here earlier," Jillian said, lacing her fingers around one knee. "She's having a party tonight with some friends from L.A. She'll be around tomorrow. She seemed happy enough with everything." She gave me an encouraging smile. "Everything's going great, Benni. Don't worry. You've done a marvelous job."

"Thanks," I said. "That's exactly the response I was fishing for. I can't tell you how often these last few weeks I've wondered if we'd bitten off more than we could chew with this festival."

She nodded knowingly. "I felt the same watching the new library go up. I thought I'd pass out from anxiety until the last flower was planted in the patron's garden."

Then the lights went out. An excited murmur rippled through the crowd. The moon, as if on cue, moved behind a plum-colored smattering of clouds, giving the atmosphere an even spookier tinge.

"Dolores must have higher connections than any of us," Jillian said, her tone slightly sarcastic.

A rattle of chains against metal sounded in the grove of pepper trees on the edge of the pasture, and the crowd instinctively swiveled toward the sound. "Beware the weeping woman!" a deep male voice called. *"La Llorona!"*

A puff of smoke snapped our attention back to the stage,

and through the smoke an apparition in white appeared. I gasped along with the rest of the audience. Her dress was long, silvery, and appeared to be made of layers and layers of cobwebs. Straight black hair streaked with white flowed down past her waist. Her face, a pale green white, seemed to pulsate in the flickering light of the single candle she held. Her nails were as red as fresh blood. Dolores had really started out our Late-Night Cabaret with a bang.

"Have you seen her perform this yet?" I whispered to Jillian.

"No," she whispered back. "I've never even heard this folktale."

Dolores lifted her hands, nails flashing in the candlelight, and began her story.

"Once in a small village in Mexico there was a very beautiful peasant woman. Her hair was as black as the sky's darkest night and her lips as red and inviting as the finest wine. All the young *hombres* were in love with her. She was her parents' only child, born in their old age, a gift from the blessed *Madre de Dios*. She was loved and cherished by all who came in contact with her. She worked for the richest lady in town, washing her fine linens in the clean, clear river. One day, when she was at the river washing her mistress's fine lace she was spotted by a passing *hidalgo,* a Spanish nobleman of great riches who had come to town to court her mistress. But he fell instantly in love with the beautiful and innocent peasant girl. Being a man of dashing looks and flattering words, he seduced her there by the flowing green river. They met there day after day for weeks. When it became apparent she was with child, the nobleman's visits ceased, and she was left brokenhearted to bear the child in shame. He married her mistress and took her to live with him in the beautiful hacienda that he had described to the peasant girl each day after they made love. The peasant girl returned to her parents' small cottage and lived her life weaving brilliantly colored rugs each with a strand of green river flowing through them. When her son was three, the *hidalgo* returned to the village. The peasant girl was very happy, for she had believed in her heart of hearts that he would someday return. But she soon realized he only returned to claim his son, telling her she could never be his wife, that she was not of the right class, and that because her former mistress, his new wife, was unable to bear a child, she had given him permission to bring his son to live with them so his family name would continue. He would give the peasant girl two goats and a pearl rosary in exchange for her son.

" 'Let me stay with my child one more night,' she begged him. He agreed and made plans to come back the next day. Late that night she took the child down to the river and drowned him. Laying his small body out on the bank where she and the nobleman had made love, she took a wood-handled knife and plunged it deep into her chest, the last words on her lips curses on the man who had betrayed her not once, but twice. And because of those curses, the nobleman was never able to make love to another woman, and his wife shriveled up and died from a disease that turned her skin the texture of a snake's, her punishment for trying to steal another woman's child."

Dolores pointed a long red fingernail into the audience. "La Llarona still lives among us today. At midnight you can see her walking among the reeds in the marshes wailing for her lost child, weeping for the love betrayed her. You men!" She flicked her hand, and a spark of fire flew from it, causing the audience to jump then titter in nervous laughter. "Do not stay out all night drinking and seduce a woman only to leave her to cry alone as you stagger back to the woman you have left at home. La Llarona will find you, and when she does, you may lose more than the *cerveza* and tequila you have consumed. And you women who steal the hopes and dreams of your sisters, La Llarona will find you, too, and your dreams will turn to ashes in your hand, and your lying lips will taste the blood that drips from La Larona's knife.'' She held up her hand, and we watched mesmerized as blood seemed to appear and drip down her fingers. Behind us a voice screamed, and we all jumped. Another puff of smoke and the stage was empty.

I turned to Jillian. ''What did you think—'' But she'd disappeared.

''Boy, that brings back memories,'' Gabe said behind me.

I turned, surprised to see him standing there. ''I didn't hear you come up. Wasn't that amazing? Dolores certainly raised our collective blood pressure a notch or two.''

''My grandma Ortiz used to tell about La Llarona. She'd wait until my parents had gone out with my aunts and uncles and she'd tell us kids scary stories. Her version was different, though. It was more along the lines of we'd better obey our parents, or the weeping woman would get us. Hers had seaweed hair and was betrayed by a sea captain. She'd scare the pants off us kids, then warn us not to tell our parents what she'd said. My mother, for the life of her, couldn't figure out why we'd be too afraid to go to sleep without a light for weeks after visiting California. I think my dad knew, but he never said anything.''

''That's terrible,'' I said. ''He just let you go on being scared?''

Gabe laughed. ''He grew up hearing those stories and he survived. I guess he figured that our fear was nothing compared to the fear he had of being in a fight between his mother and his wife.''

I laughed in agreement. ''Smart man.'' I looked back at the empty hay bale, wondering about Jillian.

''What's wrong?'' Gabe asked, his senses instantly alert to the perplexed look on my face.

''Jillian was sitting next to me, then she was gone. I guess she must have left during Dolores's performance. Or right after.''

"So?"

"I don't know, it bothers me. She and Dolores haven't been getting along that well, kinda arguing over Ash Stanhill, and then Dolores told this story. Maybe it was a subtle threat to Jillian."

"I think you're letting all this spookiness get to you. Reality check, *mi corazón*." He tapped my head with his knuckles.

"And what reality might that be, Friday?"

"Two women catfighting over some man that neither will probably want next week."

I slugged his arm. "Catfighting? That remark is going in your permanent file under sexist remarks. Which, I might add, is getting quite extensive."

"Oh, no," he said, feigning horror. "Not my permanent file."

It was after midnight when Gabe and I got home. Dove had long since gone to bed, though her evening's activities were still apparent, with three different versions of the Bible and a Bible dictionary spread out on the kitchen table. Rita had, of course, still not come in. Neither had Sam. I'd glimpsed Rita a few times tonight with Ash and a group of people and I'd assumed they'd gone barhopping. That made me think of Jillian again. Just how involved were she and Ash? And how did Dolores fit into the equation? How were they all involved with this? Or were they? Maybe Gabe was right and the spooky stories really were affecting my imagination.

"What time should I set the alarm?" Gabe asked.

"I should be there before ten. Make it eight." I yawned and crawled under the covers. "I don't know if I can stay up this late again tomorrow night and still function. I don't see how Sam and Rita do it."

"Youth," Gabe answered, catching my yawn.

Sometime during the early-morning hours, I woke up and with the insomnia brought on by anxiety, couldn't get back to sleep. The bedside clock read four-fifteen. Next to me, Gabe lay deep in sleep. I eased out of bed and pulled my thick terry robe over my T-shirt. Slinking through the living room where Sam was sleeping, I slipped into the kitchen, closing the door behind me. As I heated a mug of almond milk I sat at the kitchen table and looked over Dove's books. She and Garnet were apparently heavy into Proverbs now. I glanced at the page in the Bible subject index that Dove had marked lightly with a pencil. She'd made it as far as the *K*'s. The line she'd copied on notebook paper was under the word *Keeps*: "Proverbs 17:28—Even a fool is thought wise if *she*"—(Dove underlined *she* three times)—"*keeps* silent, and discerning if *she* holds *her* tongue."

"Garnet's gonna love that one," I muttered. I wondered if it occurred to Dove that the quote could easily be thrown back at her. My eyes traveled down the page, perusing the subject headings. One intrigued me, and I read the four listings under the word.

*Key (Keys)*: "Isaiah 33:6—The fear of the Lord is the *key*/Revelation 20:1—having the *key* to the Abyss/Matthew 16:19—I will give you the *keys* to the kingdom/Revelation 1:18—And I hold the *keys* of death."

*Keys,* I thought, pouring my milk in a mug. I looked down into it, staring at the light reflections in the whiteness. Why did that strike something in me? *Keys.* What do they do? They unlock things. Actually, they unlock places where people keep things. Things they think are important. Things they want to hide. Things they want to save.

*Keys.* Then it occurred to me. The Tupperware container of keys I found in the homeless man's duffel bag. His daily routine. A routine that made me think before that maybe he'd seen something. Or found something. Something he kept. I went outside to the truck and brought the container of keys into the kitchen. There seemed to be at least fifty, maybe more—all shapes and sizes. Staring at them, I drank my milk and wondered if they opened anything of significance. When I crawled back in bed, Gabe stirred.

"Everything all right?" he muttered, curling himself around me.

"Fine," I whispered. "Go back to sleep."

*Keys,* I thought drowsily as the warm milk started working. Just before I fell asleep, the last line of the Bible index, the one from Revelation, floated back to me. "I hold the keys of death."

For one foreboding moment, a tiny icicle of fear pierced my heart.

# 12

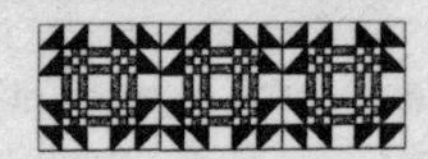

THE NEXT MORNING Dove handed me the Saturday *Tribune*. "You and Sam made front page."

I glanced at the article in the lower right hand side. POLICE CHIEF'S WIFE AND SON ATTACKED AT THURSDAY NIGHT FARMERS' MARKET. Fortunately there was yet another budget crisis going in Washington, so we didn't make the bold, black headline.

"Has Gabe seen it?" I asked apprehensively.

"Yes, he has," he answered, walking into the kitchen. "Don't worry about it." He opened the refrigerator and took out a pitcher of grapefruit juice. His casual acceptance of the probably negative article made me suspicious, but I didn't press it. Maybe he was learning to accept the fact that he and I were destined to be one of San Celina's more colorful and controversial couples.

"Are you coming to the festival with me?" I asked.

"No, I'm going to work on the thesis-with-no-end," he said, pouring a glass of juice. "I'll drop by later on this afternoon. I don't want you alone after dark."

On Saturday everything went by without a major hitch. I nervously attended both Peter and Roy's performances. They kept their word to me and didn't cause any trouble. Ash and Dolores's San Celina historical stories were naturally a big hit. They were a wonderful storytelling team with an instinctive ability to read each other's cues and follow each other's rhythms. I was glad that Jillian was at the horse show in Santa Barbara today so she couldn't see how attractive they looked together. Dolores's scary story about La Llarona came back to me, and I couldn't help but wonder if sooner or later that little triangle was going to explode. The fact that my cousin Rita was smack dab in the middle of it didn't make my heart sing. Maybe I should try to hunt Skeeter down and let him know what was going on here.

*Maybe you ought to just mind your own business,* a little voice said as I walked into my office. *Let these people work out their own problems. You've got a festival to get through, a household of people to get rid of, and a husband who is teetering on the edge of an emotional abyss. Rita and Skeeter's love life should be the least of your worries.*

Gabe showed up promptly at dusk and tagged after me like a trained guard dog. We left at nine that evening when I found my head lolling toward his shoulder during Roy's cowboy poetry reading, something I normally would have enjoyed.

I was so tired when we got home I just crawled into bed, gave Gabe a distracted kiss, and went to sleep. I remembered the homeless man's keys Sunday morning when I was brushing my teeth. I went into the kitchen all primed to tell Gabe about my theory—until I saw the look on his face.

"What's wrong?" I asked.

He stared stonily out the kitchen window. "Nothing."

"So what are you going to do today? Work on your thesis again?"

He shrugged and continued to stare and sip his coffee.

"So, if you aren't going to work on your thesis, do you want to come to the festival with me?"

"I don't think so," he said. "You'll be home before dark tonight, right?"

''Sure, don't worry about me. I'll be careful.''

''Maybe I'll take a drive up the coast, then.'' He stood up and started toward our bedroom.

''Wish I could go with you,'' I called after him. He didn't answer. Something had to have happened this morning because he'd been fine last night when he'd come to the festival, even cheerful because he'd written five whole pages on his thesis.

Dove came in dressed for church and started closing her Bibles and reference books, stacking them neatly on the kitchen counter.

''Giving up?'' I asked hopefully.

''Not by a long shot,'' she said. ''I'm taking Mac to lunch after church today so I can pick his brain.'' MacKenzie Reid, or Mac as he'd always been called, was our minister at First Baptist. A local boy who'd gone away to play football at Baylor and live in Los Angeles for a while, he was now back shepherding the local Baptist flock. In his early forties, he was big as a grizzly bear, widowed, and so handsome that attendance among single women had tripled since he'd arrived.

''Don't you think that getting a professional involved is cheating?'' I asked. ''Sort of like using a ringer?''

''Garnet's been calling Brother Connors back in Sugartree,'' Dove protested. ''I can tell.''

''You don't know that.'' By the peeved tone of Dove's voice, I was safely guessing that Garnet was coming up with some zingers. ''Maybe she's just using all your reference books. Heaven knows, you have enough of them, and they're all at *her* disposal.''

Dove's face blanched. I guess she hadn't thought of that.

''That settles it, then,'' she declared. ''Going to Mac will even things out. He's got a computer program. You just punch in a word, and presto, there's a verse.''

''Then good luck, I guess.'' I picked up the Tupperware container of keys I'd left on the counter last night and contemplated them again. Were they significant? I stuck the container in a drawer. No time to think about it today. The time for that was *after* this festival was over.

"By the way, did something happen with Sam and Gabe before I got up? Gabe's in a foul mood, and he won't give me a clue why."

Dove's white eyebrows arched. "Could be that *Tribune* article from yesterday."

"He was fine with it yesterday. That's old news now."

"Apparently someone left him another copy on the kitchen table this morning—parts about Gabe's incompetence underlined. He saw it before I could throw it out."

"Someone who is royally pissed at his dad maybe? Next time I see Sam, he's really going to get it."

"Stay out of it, honeybun," Dove said.

"Why should I?"

"Do you remember that bull we had back in the late eighties, the speckled-face one?"

"Sure, King Arthur."

"Remember his son? The one with the crooked tail?"

"Lancelot. He was a good bull. Kinda wild, but good."

"Don't you remember, though, that we always had to keep three pastures between those two? Never saw two bulls so willing to hurt themselves just to get at each other. It's 'cause their hormones came from the same pot. They both wanted to rule the roost."

"I think you're mixing your animal similes, but I get your drift. But the way we solved it was by selling King Arthur to that guy from Kern County. What am I supposed to do here?"

"Wait. Eventually they'll work out a pecking order they're comfortable with. Just takes time."

In this case I knew I should bow to her expertise. "Okay, I'll back off, but if it's not resolved soon, it's the Templeton stock auction for them."

"They appear to have good bloodlines," Dove said,

winking at me. "Bring a fair price, I imagine."

Sunday's storytelling sessions went by without incident. At three o'clock I finally found the time to grab a barbecued chicken dinner and hide in my office for a few minutes. I was chewing a mouthful of coleslaw when the phone rang.

I paused for a moment, swallowing, then said, "Hello. I mean, Josiah Sinclair Folk Art Museum. Benni Harper speaking."

"Sounds like you got a mouthful of mush," Emory said.

"You should talk," I said, taking a drink of Coke to clear the mayonnaise taste out of my mouth. "Did you find out anything?"

"I'm just fine, sweetcakes, and how are you?"

"Oh, for pete's sake, Emory, just tell me what you found out."

"My, my, we're sounding premenopausal today."

"Emory—" I warned.

"Just ribbin' you, cousin. Actually, I couldn't wait to call. Just talked to Neil and have I got some dirt." His voice was gleeful over the phone. Part of me was feeling the same kind of surreptitious curiosity that compelled me to read the Tattler every week, but a part of me felt sick, knowing now how much public discussion of a person's private problems hurts. But if something in Evangeline's or Ash's background helped solve these murders, that was the important thing. Nora might have had some truly despicable traits, but that didn't give someone the right to take her life.

"What did you find out?"

"First, Mr. Ashley Stanhill. Our Mr. Stanhill has been a very, very bad boy. He has quite a few people in Mississippi mighty peeved at him."

"Why?"

"Apparently our boy is one platinum-tongued devil. He's convinced more than one group of investors into putting money into a business he has proposed. Then he does very well for the first year, paying them their dividends and a year-end bonus. Then the second year the business takes a dive and the investors lose all their money. I don't know the particulars—you know the only thing I know about money is how to spend it—but apparently Mr. Stanhill always comes out of it with a pocketful of change and smelling like a truckful of magnolia blossoms heading to a cotillion."

"How many times has he pulled this scam?"

"About four times in Mississippi that Neil knew about. Mr. Stanhill's been involved with an ice-cream parlor, an arts-and-entertainment magazine, a fried-chicken restaurant, and an art gallery. Every one of them made tremendous profits the first year and bombed the second."

"So you're saying he embezzles money?"

"That's such an ugly word, sweetcakes, and so inflammatory. Don't forget, nothing was ever proven in any of the cases. His paperwork was meticulous. The man is Teflon-coated down to his Calvin Klein boxers."

"It certainly sounds like he wore out his welcome in Mississippi."

"Truer words. California was probably looking very good to him. He missed being indicted on the last one by the hairs of his chinny-chin-chin."

"And if Nora found out about it, and I'm assuming she did, that could ruin his new image here in San Celina. Quite a few important people have invested in Eudora's. The question is, would he kill to keep it quiet?" I wrapped the phone cord around my finger. "Okay, what about Evangeline?"

"All I have to say is y'all are sitting in a real sweet little nest of water moccasins there."

"What?"

"Just a minute, let me decipher my notes here." I heard a shuffling of papers. "Evangeline Yvette Boudreaux Savoy. She has quite the dramatic history, little Evangeline Yvette does. Got this from a stringer for the *New Orleans*

*Picayune*. Met her at a newspaper convention five years ago. Gorgeous little Cajun girl. Man, that girl could dance, not to mention—''

''Twenty-five words or less, Emory.''

''All right, keep your britches on. It appears Evangeline is very fond of target shooting—''

''Emory—'' I whined loudly, and slumped down in my chair.

''Using her husband as the target.''

I bolted up. ''What?''

''In shorthand, cuz, she blew her husband away.''

I switched the phone to the other ear, not quite certain what I was hearing. ''Are you sure?''

''Absolutely. Your little quilter killed her hubby in cold blood with one gunshot wound to the chest. Then again, with a shotgun I guess one's all you'd need.''

''But . . . what . . . how . . .'' I stuttered, trying to connect this with the gentle, peace-loving woman I thought I knew.

''Here it is in jingle length, as you requested. Husband drank. When he drank, he beat her. She didn't leave, heaven knows why. She had a baby. Baby cried one night and irritated drunk husband. He backhands baby. Baby dies. Your friend gets a shotgun and pumps him full of buckshot. She gets off with temporary insanity. Case closed.''

''And apparently she and D-Daddy moved as far away as they could to start a new life.''

''Appears so. She and Mr. Stanhill both had very valid reasons to leave their respective homes and head west.''

''And reasons to kill someone who might reveal their secrets.''

''Like I said, a nest of water moccasins. But tell me, wouldn't your dear husband be privy to this sort of sordid background history?''

That was a very good question. ''Thanks, Emory. Can't wait to get together. Hugs and kisses to you and Uncle Boone.''

"Don't forget our agreement," he was saying as I hung up the phone. "Tell Elvia my lips are anxiously awaiting hers."

I hung up. "Over my dead body," I said to the phone, knowing that's exactly what it would take for him to get a kiss from Elvia.

I leaned back in my chair and pondered the information Emory had given me. A soft knock sounded at the door. "Benni?" Evangeline's soft voice called through the door.

"Come on in," I said, feeling a spasm in my stomach.

"I need to talk to you."

"Sure, have a seat." I started shifting things around on my desk, picking up my stapler and setting it neatly next to the tape dispenser. Then I started fiddling with the pencils in my pencil cup, hoping my face didn't reveal the shock I was feeling.

Her gaze was cool and level. "I saw my file open on your desk the other day. You know, don't you?"

I nodded, not knowing what to say.

"I didn't kill Nora," she said, lifting her heavy black hair and laying a hand on the back of her neck. "Let me try and explain. She and I became pretty close, as you probably guessed. We were drinking wine one night at her place, and she started telling me about how she felt when her son was dying. After a couple of glasses, I don't know, my guard came down and I hadn't talked to anyone about it for so long. And with her losing a child, too, I just thought—" Her eyes darkened. "I told her about Antoine. He was my little boy. I had no idea she wrote that column. And I had no idea what sort of person she was."

"Was she going to put it in her column?" The thought of it shocked me as much as the discovery about Evangeline. "How could she do that to you when you both had lost a child?"

Her laugh came out harsh. "Because after she heard my story, she became furious. She said that, unlike her, at least

I had some control of the situation. I could have saved my child. That I could have left or shot Joe before he killed Antoine.'' Her chin dropped to her chest, and her voice became a whisper. ''Didn't she think I'd thought of that so many times myself? Those same thoughts keep me up night after night until sometimes I feel like I'll go crazy. That's why D-Daddy brought me here. Everything in Louisiana reminded me of Antoine and how I failed him as a mother. But I guess Nora felt I hadn't been punished enough. She was going to make sure people knew just what sort of mother I'd been.''

The barbecued chicken rose up sour in the back of my throat.

Evangeline looked up, her cheeks wet, and said, ''Gabe knows.''

''He does?''

''He didn't tell you? I thought you were looking in my file for him.''

I just shook my head no.

She stood up, wiping her cheeks with the back of her hand. ''I have an alibi for that night. D-Daddy and I were at home.''

I nodded, but even she had to realize it wasn't an airtight alibi. D-Daddy was an old man whose hearing wasn't necessarily that good. She could have left and come back with him none the wiser. He could also lie to protect her. Knowing D-Daddy's fierce loyalty, he probably would.

''They'll find the real killer,'' I said, with more confidence than I felt. ''I'm sorry.'' I lifted my hands in helplessness. ''About . . . everything.''

''Me, too,'' she said sadly, walking toward the door. ''I liked it here. It was almost beginning to feel like home.''

I went over to her. The scent of her fear was sharp as a lemon. ''There's no reason why you should leave. That column hasn't been found yet. There's a good chance no one will ever know.''

"The one thing I've learned is that nothing is predictable. And once one or two people know, it doesn't take long. Look what happened with Nora."

After she left I sat in my chair for a long time. The first thing I should do when I got home was tell Gabe I knew about Evangeline and Ash and how I found out. With his irritable mood, it wasn't something I was looking forward to. Most likely we'd end up in a fight about me getting involved after promising I wouldn't. So I procrastinated around my office, cleaning my desk and picking dead leaves off plants, avoiding the inevitable. It was past six o'clock when I finally emerged into the parking lot. The last of the storytellers had spun their tales at five, and the vendors were busy packing up their unsold wares. Most of the campground was empty and the campers on their way home. By tomorrow all traces of the festival would be gone.

"You look beat," Burl, one of the co-op board members, offered. "Go on home and get some rest. I'll lock up here."

I thanked him and headed for my rental car. On the way home, I fervently hoped that the drive along the coast had mellowed Gabe's mood. I was too tired and sad after hearing Evangeline's story to be very supportive and upbeat tonight.

He and Dove were in the kitchen, where the comforting scent of frying chicken greeted me. Gabe was laughing at something Dove had said to Rita while handing her a paring knife and a potato. My tense neck muscles started to relax. Maybe I'd wait until tomorrow to tell him what I'd learned about Evangeline and Ash. It would be nice to have one calm, quiet evening.

"What's so funny?" I asked, setting my purse on the counter.

Before they could answer, Sam walked in behind me.

"Hey, what's for dinner?" he asked, peering over Dove's shoulder. "Some poor chicken gave up its life for us. Watch out, Dove, I'll sic the chicken-rights people on you."

"I'll chicken rights you," she said, reaching back and smacking his shoulder. He continued to tease Dove until she pushed him toward the table and said, "If you want to eat anytime soon you'd best start peeling those potatoes with Rita so I can fry them up. There's a bowl in the top cupboard."

"We're having the heart-attack special tonight, huh?" Sam pulled off his sweatshirt and threw it over a kitchen chair. He wore a sleeveless denim shirt. A tanned biceps flashed when he reached for the bowl.

"Sam, what's that?" Gabe said, his voice sharp.

Sam turned around and faced his father. "What?"

Gabe crossed the room and grabbed Sam's upper arm, lifting it slightly. "That." He pointed at the inside of his biceps.

Sam's expression lost its animation. "A tattoo."

Dove turned and watched them, her metal spatula dripping grease on the floor. Rita stopped peeling mid-potato. I walked over to get a closer look. The tattoo was of a grayish-green Polynesian-style sun with jagged flames. The words TRIBAL SUN were tattooed underneath.

"When did you get it?" Gabe asked flatly.

Sam shrugged. "Me and some buddies did it a few months ago."

"What does Tribal Sun mean?" Gabe asked.

"Just a surfer thing. You wouldn't understand. We were kinda ripped when we did it. Someplace in Long Beach, near the docks, gave us a deal—two for one, I think."

A muscle in Gabe's cheek jumped. I put a hand on his arm. "Gabe, it's just a tattoo," I said, trying to head off the explosion.

He ignored me and said in a dangerously low voice, "A lot of those tattoo parlors have sanitary procedures that aren't worth shit. You could have gotten hepatitis. Or worse. And what have I told you about drinking? Was there anyone in your group sober enough to drive?''

''What do you care?''

''I care because you're underage, and it's against the law. Besides, someone who is too immature to drink responsibly is certainly too young to get a tattoo.''

Sam's dark eyes flashed. ''Aaron told me you were drunk when you got your tattoo in Saigon. And you were eighteen, just like me.''

Gabe inhaled deeply and answered, ''It was different circumstances. I was a man.''

Sam laughed bitterly. ''Oh, yeah, that's right. You were in a *war*. I forgot.'' He turned and looked at the rest of us, his lip curled in a sneer. ''In my dad's eyes you don't really grow *cojones* until you kill someone.''

We all froze. Gabe's face turned pale with rage. Sam's brown eyes widened when he realized he'd gone too far this time. Gabe jerked his arm out of my grasp and slammed through the kitchen door. I ran after him and stood on the front porch watching as he jumped into the Corvette and backed out of the driveway, wheels screeching. In seconds, the car disappeared around the corner.

Inside, Rita and Dove had gone back to preparing dinner, and Sam leaned against the counter, his arms folded, staring at the floor.

''Dinner will be ready in about fifteen minutes,'' Dove said, her voice serene. ''Sam, you get those plates and glasses out and start setting the table.'' After raising four sons and spending countless summers watching passels of grandsons, the pawing and snorting of the male sex didn't faze her in the least.

''Benni, you get over here and watch these potatoes,'' she said, wiping her hands on her apron. ''I'm fixin' to die if I don't have a glass of iced tea.''

We ate the meal in silence. We were almost finished when the phone rang. I jumped up and answered it, disappointed when it was for Sam. He had a quick conversation, then hung up.

"Gotta go in to work," he said, crumpling his napkin and throwing it on his half-eaten dinner. "Two people called in sick. I'll probably close."

"Be careful," Dove said automatically, picking up her plate and his. She and I cleared off the table while Rita retired to her bedroom to call her mother and various girlfriends in Little Rock.

Dove and I did the dishes and cleaned the kitchen without talking about what just happened. Then we went into the living room and turned on the television. She gave me a skein of red yarn and told me to starting rolling. Three quarters of the way through a boring disease-of-the-week movie, I finally said, "This can't go on."

Dove gave me another skein of yarn. "It'll go on as long as it takes. These things always work out, just never in the time we'd like."

"I hate seeing Gabe torn up like this. I want to do something."

"Sometimes, honeybun, the only thing you can do for someone is just be there when they're ready for someone to be there."

I set my half-rolled ball of yarn down and grabbed my purse. "It's ten-thirty. If I have to sit here and wait any longer, I'll go crazy. I'm going to find Gabe."

She picked up the yarn and continued where I left off. "Have any idea where he might have run to? Gabe's not one for bars and such."

"I have a pretty good idea."

# 13

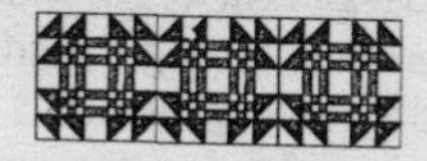

I WAS RIGHT. At Gabe's old house, the Corvette was parked in the driveway at a crooked angle as if the driver was in a hurry to see someone inside. I pulled in behind it. The night air was quiet and cool; dampness from the salty ocean breezes sidled over the hills and settled on my skin like a thin layer of spicy cologne. I walked through the opaque shadows cast by the towering pine and ash trees, glancing at the empty home to the left of Gabe's and at the dark Cal Poly pasture to the right. Gabe had rented the house because of its large garage and its privacy. When we were dating, it was one of the places we'd come when we truly wanted to be alone. I'd often wondered if we'd been better off moving here when we married rather than into my house.

One of the miniature horses from Cal Poly's animal-husbandry department lifted its shaggy head and gave an anxious whinny as if sensing the same emotion in me. The tiny horses liked to scratch their haunches on his backyard fence and beg for the sugar cubes Gabe always kept next to the back door. When I accused him of breaking some kind of dietary control-type rule and ruining someone's weight statistics by feeding them, he just laughed and asked when had I all of a sudden become such a law-abiding citizen.

When I reached the front porch, I could hear music vibrating through the solid core door—a sad Spanish song that throbbed like a fresh bruise. I stood for a moment with my hand on the doorknob, letting the cold metal soothe my sweating palm. Taking a deep breath, I opened the door.

Inside, the music was louder, the sweet, clear voice of Tish Hinojosa, the only country-western musician Gabe liked. Her music, an unusual fusion of Texas roadhouse honky-tonk, sad Spanish love ballads, and high-energy Mexican folk music, had struck a kindred chord in him. The room was darker than outside; through the six-pane windows the thin light of the moon and the flickering streetlight cast squares of gold across the carpeted floor. Blue light from the stereo glowed across the room as she sang in Spanish about being alone and the pain deep in her chest.

"Gabe?" I called out softly.

"Why are you here?" Gabe's cold, husky voice asked from a dark corner. My eyes slowly started adjusting, and the outline of his white T-shirt emerged. He sat on the floor, his back against one side of the corner fireplace. He'd left so quickly he hadn't put on shoes. For some reason the sight of his bare, vulnerable feet tightened my throat. His face was in shadows, but a flicker of moonlight caught a glint of liquid when he lifted the bottle and drank.

I froze, shocked.

His voice came from the shadows again. "Answer me."

I spoke through the dry cotton feel in my mouth. "I was worried."

"No reason." He stood up and came toward me. His face moved in and out of the murky light until he stood close enough for me to smell the sharp, sweet whiskey on his breath. He brought the Jack Daniel's bottle up and drank again.

I stared up into his face, crisscrossed with shadow stripes from the windowpanes, his expression rigid and unassailable with that macho Latin bravado he did so well. An electric-quick memory jolted through me—Jack's young face in his polished mahogany coffin, the lips I'd kissed so often as cold and lifeless as the wooden casket he was buried in.

"Gabe—"

"Go home," he said, his voice as unyielding as his expression. "You shouldn't be here."

"You're wrong. This is exactly where I should be."

His eyes never left my face as he lifted the bottle and drank.

"You don't have to go through this alone," I said quietly. "You can't keep it all inside." When he didn't acknowledge me, I said, "Maybe you should take some time off—"

"Stop it!" he snapped, his translucent eyes alcohol-bright and wild. "You're just like everyone else. You think I can't handle this? Well, you're wrong. I'm handling it fine, but I'd certainly get a lot more done if everyone would just leave me alone and let me do my job."

"I didn't mean—"

He held his finger and thumb an inch apart. "I'm this far from charging someone, but if everyone doesn't get off my back—"

"Who?" I asked before I could stop myself.

He narrowed his eyes. "I told you to go home."

I held back the urge to ask more. Right now Nora's killer took second place to my husband's precarious mental state. "No, I won't." I stretched up and kissed him gently on the mouth.

He hesitated, then set the bottle on the floor. He put a cold palm against my cheek. "Poor little *niña*," he whispered. "You had no idea what you were getting into when you married me."

"I'm not a little girl." I kissed him again, not as gently this time, and he responded. The whiskey taste of him was startling and unfamiliar, like kissing a stranger.

He started unbuttoning my chambray shirt. "You shouldn't have come here," he murmured against my throat, then groaned softly. *"Querida, querida, estas una frego en mi alma."*

I felt myself tremble slightly. Something in him echoed the feeling, and a shudder ran the length of his body. He pulled us to the floor, and moments later we were frantically tearing clothes away, trying to find skin for our lips and tongues to touch. We made love quickly and silently, desperate to connect in the only way we never seemed to get wrong.

As our breathing slowed back to normal I lay with my cheek pressed against his neck, feeling the hard pulse of his heart. After a few minutes he pushed me away, standing up to slip on his Levi's. He immediately reached for the bottle, drinking long, without taking a breath, his throat a small moving animal in the moonlight.

Anger and humiliation rose up in me, bright and hot as a fever. Anger at his stubbornness, his stupid pride, and for turning to the one thing that held such horrible memories for me. And humiliation for thinking I had any kind of power to keep him from it. "That won't solve anything," I said bitterly, buttoning my shirt.

He shrugged. "My business."

"As long as we're married, it's my business, too."

He turned away and lifted the bottle again. I stared at the tattoo on his bare upper back of the snarling marine-corps bulldog. The tattoo I'd traced so many times with my fingers and my lips. He turned back to me.

"The only business I'm interested in is how quickly I can finish this bottle. So unless you want to stay and watch, I suggest you run along home."

I grabbed my purse and walked over to him, so angry I could barely say the words. "Give me your car keys."

Surprise, then disbelief darkened his face. "What?"

"You heard me." I held out my hand.

"You're kidding."

I gritted my back teeth and spoke very slowly. "Listen up good, Chief Ortiz, 'cause I'm only going to say this once. I am not *ever* going to bury another husband because of that." I pointed to the bottle in his hand. "Not if I can help it."

His harsh laugh reverberated across the empty room. "Believe me, sweetheart, I've seen more than my share of bodies scraped up off the asphalt. Unlike your dear, departed Jack, *I'm* not that stupid."

I flinched as if physically struck, but continued to hold out my hand, hoping he was too drunk to notice its trembling.

He let out an angry breath, dug into his pocket, and tossed the keys at me.

"One more thing."

He waited.

"Give me your gun. I know you keep one in your car."

His voice was cold. "No one takes my gun."

"Give me your gun."

"No."

I took a deep breath. "If you don't give it to me, I will call Jim Cleary and tell him you are drunk and—"

"You wouldn't."

"Try me."

He let out a long string of Spanish words, most of them too garbled for me to understand. I stood with my arms at my side, refusing to budge. He stared at me a long moment, then went over to the fireplace, his bare feet making a slurring sound across the carpet. He took his 9mm from where it lay on the floor and shoved it into my hands.

"Now get out," he said.

"With pleasure. Enjoy your whiskey."

Clutching the heavy pistol to my chest, I opened the front door, feeling like someone had sliced my heart in half with a razor blade. But a faint surge of hope blossomed when the last thing I heard before the oak door slammed behind me was the unmistakable sound of glass shattering against brick.

# 14

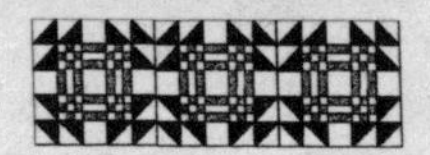

IT WAS PAST midnight when I finally stopped driving and ended up where I always ran when I had nowhere else to go.

The comforting thing about Liddie's Café was that it never changed. At least not for the thirty some-odd years I can remember. It had the same red leatherette six-person booths, the same black-and-white photographs of lambs and steers from the Junior Livestock Auction, the same speckled commercial-grade carpeting, the same cigarette-scarred Formica tables, and the same glass case in front containing faded packages of Juicy Fruit gum, Red Man chewing tobacco, rum Life Savers, and ratty old postcards showing Liddie's famous neon coffee-cup sign: OPEN 25 HOURS—GOOD FOOD.

I grew up having breakfast there every Saturday morning. Daddy and the other local ranchers always commandeered the back tables, pushing them into two long ones. While me and the other ranch kids carved pictures in our butter-soaked pancakes and shot straw-wrapper bullets at each other, our fathers would discuss for hours the price of calves, the price of feed, the price of gasoline, stopping every so often to drawl at us kids to quit our tomfoolery or next time they'd be leavin' us home.

But now, at midnight, the back room was full of students.

They always took over after the nine o'clock dinner crowd. Their high, excited chatter struck a familiar chord. I experienced a few all-night study marathons here myself when I was preparing for finals at Cal Poly. Even Gabe held a place in my memories of Liddie's. The first time we kissed was in the parking lot on a cold moonless night last November.

I slipped into an unoccupied booth, ordered coffee, leaned my head back, and closed my eyes. My mind whirled with thoughts about what had just taken place between me and Gabe. How close to the edge was he? Should I go back? Should I call someone? Who? His grief was so deep and unreachable I felt powerless. I remembered how three days before Aaron died, he had tried to prepare me for this.

"Benni, come sit over here," he'd said, patting his hospital bed with a weak hand. He'd sent his wife, Rachel, and Gabe on a manufactured errand so he could talk to me alone. His red hair was sparse and pale from the chemotherapy treatments, but his smile was as warm as always. I'd never known Aaron until he was sick, and could only imagine the huge, deep-chested man who, according to his delighted telling, could pin Gabe to the ground no matter how much Gabe worked out at the gym.

"I'm going to get right to the point," Aaron said. "When I go, Gabe's going to be in tough shape. You're going to have to be strong."

"I know," I replied, taking his hand in mine.

"I'm not sure you do. Gabe's had a lot of hurt in his life. He keeps things inside too much and then explodes in unpredictable ways. You have to be ready for that. But he's a good man. A man I've been honored to call my friend." A coughing spell interrupted his words.

"Aaron, he's going to be all right. I'll make sure of it."

He studied me with sad brown eyes. Eyes that had seen

a lot of the same pain as Gabe. "You're the best thing that's ever happened to him."

I smiled and rubbed his icy hand, trying to massage some of my own warmth into it. "We'd have never gotten married if it hadn't been for you. You're the one who convinced us that waiting is crazy in this unpredictable world. I'm glad we listened."

He chuckled softly. "I knew if you and Gabe didn't get hitched fast, he'd pussyfoot around until someone else snatched you up. I wasn't about to let that happen."

"Our own personal Tevye," I teased. "We didn't have a chance."

We sat for a moment without talking. He squeezed my hand gently. "My little shiksa cowgirl," he said. "Don't give up on my buddy, okay? Promise me. No matter how hard it gets?"

I leaned over and kissed his dry, rough cheek. "I promise, Tevye."

"He said you'd be here." A voice interrupted the scene in my head.

I lifted my head and blinked my eyes under the golden glare of the overhead light. Jim Cleary slid into the seat across from me. The waitress was there in seconds with a steaming pot of coffee. He poured cream into the thick white mug and stirred it, his black eyes watching me with a quiet scrutiny I was growing used to since being married to a cop.

"What are you doing here?" I finally asked, reaching for my coffee. It had gotten cold, but I took a deep drink anyway.

"Gabe called me."

"He did?" I wondered how much he told him.

"He said he was in no shape to drive, that he'd been drinking, that you'd had a fight, and you'd taken his car keys and his gun."

I nodded silently, surprised at Gabe's honesty.

"Good girl," Jim said, and sipped his coffee.

"Is he all right?"

"Yes, he said he's just going to sleep it off now. Gabe's not a foolish man, Benni. He handled it exactly how I would have."

"Not exactly," I said, tearing my paper napkin into strips. Jim was a man with a deep faith in God who, according to Gabe, never lost his temper even when he'd been called names that would have caused other men to draw their guns.

Jim laughed softly. "Obviously Oneeda hasn't filled you in about my misspent youth yet. I know you think I've never done anything stupid, but I have. We all have. No one's perfect, Benni. We all need grace. Need it more than water and air. God gives it to us first, and then we give it to others. I know you've heard a few sermons on that in your lifetime."

I stopped tearing the napkin and looked up at him, knowing he was right, but wanting to stay mad. "He won't let me help him, Jim. Tough macho cop going to handle it all on his own." Remembering who I was talking to, I gave a sheepish half smile. "Sorry."

His answering smile smoothed out the two deep lines next to his mouth. "That's the grace part, honey. Just give him some time. When the hurt gets bad enough, he'll come to you."

"And if he doesn't?"

Jim patted my hand. His palm was big and warm, and I fought the urge to hold on to it. "Then there's nothing you can do. He had to swallow a huge chunk of pride to call me and ask me to look for you. That right there should tell you something."

A deep fatigue flooded through me. "I should go home."

"I think that would be a good idea," Jim agreed.

He walked me out to my rented Taurus. I pulled Gabe's

gun from under the front seat and handed it to him. "Maybe you should take this."

He took the pistol and stuck it in the pocket of his leather jacket. "If you want, I'll go by tomorrow and give him his car keys, too."

"That would be great," I said, handing him the keys. "Thanks, Jim. For coming by tonight and, well . . . just thanks."

He looked at me silently for a moment. "Don't give up on him, Benni. He's a good man and a good leader, no matter what the press says. He really cares about his officers and about the people in this town. All the people, not just the ones with money. Aaron was right to recommend him."

"I know," I said. "Tell Oneeda I'll call her this week."

"Will do. You take care now."

It was past one A.M. when I arrived home. Sam was asleep on the sofa, and I managed to sneak into bed without waking anyone. Exhausted, I fell into a deep sleep.

The house was silent when I woke the next morning. The day was cloudy, so I was disoriented, thinking it was early, until I looked at the bedside clock—ten o'clock. I threw back the covers. Because of what happened last night I hadn't told Gabe what I'd learned about Evangeline and Ash. Though I didn't relish the idea of talking to him this morning, I really did want to keep our relationship above-board. That meant not hiding anything else from him. If we fought again, so be it.

When I turned my head I saw them sitting on the dresser. A bouquet of red roses and white daisies in a crystal vase. An odd combination of flowers that somehow didn't surprise me. I must have been sleeping like the dead because I never heard him come into the room. The small white card on the plastic holder read: *I'm sorry. I love you.*

Short and to the point. So enigmatic in some ways. So completely straightforward in others. Worry, anger, and sadness all intermingled when I thought about what happened between us. But I temporarily shelved those feelings while I took a hot shower and dressed. After inspecting my now green-purple-yellow eye, I decided to forgo makeup. At this point I couldn't care less what people thought.

As I gulped a glass of orange juice I peered through the kitchen curtains. The darkening sky threatened rain. Perfect weather for my somber mood.

At the museum, D-Daddy was busy overseeing the final dismantling of the booths. The curt nod he gave me revealed that Evangeline had told him I knew about her background. I hid in my office drinking coffee and shuffling through paperwork rather than actually doing any. Finally, knowing I shouldn't put it off any longer, I headed for the police station.

I was on the way downtown when I remembered the homeless man's keys. I swung by the house and picked up the Tupperware container. I still wondered if the Datebook Bum saw something and had a record of it somewhere and that maybe these keys were involved somehow. Where would the homeless lock something up? All I could think of was school lockers, lockers at the roller-skating rink, lockers at the gym where Gabe exercises. In front of me, a school bus belched exhaust that was immediately picked up by my vent. I gagged, closed the vent, and then it occurred to me.

The bus station. It was as plain as that yellow school bus in front of me. I must be tired, I thought. That's a clue Nancy Drew would never have missed. I fought the urge to run by the bus station and check myself and decided, for once, I'd tell Gabe immediately and let him decide what to do.

It was almost one o'clock when I reached downtown. The spots in front of the police station were blocked because the city was working on the streets . . . again, and all the spaces in the parking garages were full . . . again. I was forced to park five blocks away and walk to the station. I was a block away when I saw Gabe come through the glass doors and start walking up the street with a determined stride. I started to call out to him, but something held me back. Instead, feeling slightly ridiculous, I followed him at a discreet distance. With his hands in his pockets and his head slightly bent so he wouldn't catch anyone's eye, he walked until he reached St. Celine's Catholic Church. He walked up the steps, stopped for a moment to read something on the door, then went inside.

In front of the church a table was set up where a group of citizens were collecting signatures to try to get a proposal on the next ballot to change San Celina's grammatically improper adulterated name back to its original Santa Celine in celebration of the mission's upcoming two hundred-and-twenty-year anniversary. I told them I'd catch them later and followed my husband up the stairs. When I reached the top and read the small sign underneath the times for masses, I felt really embarrassed and more than a little pathetic.

CONFESSIONS HEARD—MONDAY AND THURSDAY—1:00 P.M. TO 3:00 P.M.

I turned to leave when the heavy wooden door of the church flew open and a person barreled out, almost knocking me down. I found myself staring into the stricken face of Dolores Ayala. Her dark eyes were full of tears. A look of panic contorted her face when she recognized me.

"Are you all right?" I said, putting out a hand to steady her.

She gave a small cry and shoved me away, running down the steps.

I watched her hurry through the square and disappear around the corner. Questions swirled in my head as thick as the flocks of seagulls circling the mission's bell tower. Had Dolores just been at confession? What had she confessed that made her so upset? Could she be involved somehow with Nora's death?

The door of the church opened behind me, and an older

woman wearing a white lace covering over her gray hair came out. It occurred to me that Gabe could come back out anytime, so I started walking back toward downtown. The murder of Nora Cooper had so many loose ends that I could imagine how crazy Gabe and his detectives felt. Between that and the pain of grieving for Aaron, I was truly afraid for him. I'd definitely have to tell him about Dolores, too, but this was not the right time. I glanced at my watch. What I could do was go down to the bus station and check my theory about the keys. Maybe I'd be able to hand some evidence over to him that would help solve this case. Then he'd at least have one monkey off his back.

If San Celina had a bad side of town, the area around the bus station would definitely qualify. I was right about one thing. It was the place for the homeless to hang around without being harassed too much. Inside, the smell of Lysol, exhaust, and fried food made my stomach churn. I walked past a group of teenagers sitting on huge duffel bags and smoking cigarettes. Their conversation was in German, and one bare-chested boy sported pierced earrings on both nipples plus one on his upper lip in the shape of a black bat. When Gabe regained his sense of humor, I'd have to point out to him that there were definitely worse things than a small tattoo of a sun.

I checked out the locker situation. They were the type where you put four quarters in and removed the key. The kind we used as kids at the roller-skating rink. There were approximately thirty of them. The price was one dollar for the first twenty-four hours and two dollars each additional twenty-four hours with a ten-dollar lost-key charge. I read the notice on the front. ARTICLES LEFT WITHOUT PAYMENT AFTER TWENTY-FOUR HOURS SUBJECT TO IMPOUNDMENT. Then I carefully studied the key. I had a feeling with those sort of prices I was barking up a wrong tree, but I sat down on one of the blue plastic chairs and dug through the Tupperware container. The attendant behind the counter must have seen stranger things because he didn't even look twice at me. None of the keys matched.

Disappointed, I put the lid back on the container and thought for a moment. Where else could the homeless store things? I got up and went to the phone and dialed an acquaintance, Sister Clare, down at the Mission Food Bank. A nun who was also a social worker and ombudsman for the homeless, she probably knew their world better than anyone else. I'd met her when the co-op had donated a quilt for a benefit auction to raise money for the food bank's new commercial-size freezer.

"Sister Clare, this is Benni Harper. I'm not sure you remember me—"

"Sure do," she said, her slight Scottish accent denoting her birthplace. "Run that museum, you do. What's up? Got a pretty penny for that quilt. We do thank you."

"Anytime, really. Our artists have a real commitment to helping the community. I have a question about the homeless."

"Shoot."

"Where do they keep their possessions?"

"What they don't keep with them, they usually keep down at their camps. But they sometimes split their stuff up and store it in different places around the city. Lots of times they even forget where, poor souls. A lot of them just are singing their own tune, you know? Why? You looking for something specific?"

"Not really. It was just a question."

"Doing a little investigating, are you?"

"Well . . ." I hedged, not wanting to lie to a nun.

"You don't have to answer to me. I think a wife should be involved in her husband's life. And I think the journalists in this town are doing a real injustice to Chief Ortiz. He's a fine man. Since he's been chief, his officers have treated the homeless with real dignity. He concentrates on the real criminals, not the poor disenfranchised souls the rich folks think muck up our pretty streets. The only other thing I can tell you is that the shelter down by the bus station keeps lockers for the homeless. They have to be looking for a job, though, and they're inspected regularly. First sign of drugs or booze, they kick 'em out.''

''Thanks,'' I said. ''I'll give them a try.''

''Tell Frank I said you were okay. He's a little distrustful sometimes.''

The shelter was only two blocks away. Frank's suspicious demeanor disappeared when I dropped Sister Clare's name.

''Sister Clare's good people. There's about fifty lockers. We provide the locks, but we keep a copy of their key. We do spot inspections, but usually everyone follows the rules. They use them mostly to keep clothes in.''

I described the Datebook Bum to him.

''Oh, you mean, Mr. Iacocca.''

''What?''

He laughed and brushed some invisible dust off the sleeve of his green double-knit shirt. ''That's what we call him. Sure, he kept some stuff here. Haven't seen him for a few days, though.'' He leaned close and said in a confidential voice. ''Technically I shouldn't keep his stuff. Guy's never going to get a job, but he's a nice old coot and doesn't bother nobody. I made an exception.''

I told him about the police finding the man's body and the futile search for any family.

''That's real pissant,'' he said, his voice genuinely sympathetic. ''I always wondered about him. Figured a guy like him musta been somebody at one time.''

''About his stuff—''

''Ain't much, but you're welcome to look at it. Long as Sister C says you're okay, you're okay.''

He brought back a small stained duffel bag. ''You may as well keep this junk,'' he said, sliding it across the counter to me. "Nobody else is going to claim it, and we'll just throw it out."

"Thanks," I said, grabbing the bag.

In the car I unzipped it. There was a pair of clean khaki pants, a bunch of pens, and wrapped in a threadbare towel about fifty rainbow-colored computer disks with all the labels torn off. Deep in my gut I had a strong suspicion, or hope, that they were Nora's missing disks. Would her last column be on one of them? And the question remained, where did the Datebook Bum find these and who threw them out?

Now *you should go to Gabe.* I glanced at my watch. But if he'd just got back from confession, the last thing I wanted to do was start another fight. At least give him time to do penance before I forced him to sin again.

One more hour or so wouldn't matter, I convinced myself while heading for Elvia's store, the only place there was a computer at my disposal. She wasn't working tonight, but her clerks knew me and let me into her office. I switched on her IBM and pulled out the disks, my heart sinking just a little. It was going to be a tedious business. I glanced at her expensive desk clock. Five-forty. I could work until about six-thirty or so without anyone wondering where I was. Then I'd have to call home and make some excuse as to why I was late.

Not being an expert on the computer by any means, it didn't take me long to realize that Elvia's software program was different from the one Nora used. No matter what I tried, I couldn't get the disks to read. I'd have to take these somewhere else, someplace that had a large variety of software programs on the hard drive. A computer store? I wasn't sure that they'd let me use a computer for hours. If I walked in carrying fifty some-odd disks, it would be pretty obvious I wasn't there to buy a computer. The only other place I knew with that sort of equipment was the library. I hesitated for a moment, then shook off my uncertainty. It was a public place, and no one would have a clue as to what I was doing.

I glanced at the clock again, then picked up Elvia's phone. Rita was the only one home, and I quickly told her to leave a note telling Dove and Gabe I'd be at the library for a few hours. I shoved all the disks in my backpack and headed for the library.

I was disappointed to find all six computers in the computer lab full, with no time slots open until the next day.

"Is it always this crowded?" I asked the clerk.

"Sorry, school's back in session. You know how that goes."

My desperate look must have touched him.

"Say, you could always use one in the children's department," he suggested, "if you don't mind sharing the room with kids. The computers are a little older, but they still work okay."

"Do they have a variety of software programs in them?" I asked.

"Not if you're looking for the absolute latest, but they have the old standards."

"I'll give it a try. Thanks."

I only had to wait a half hour in the children's department.

"Monday nights aren't as popular," the library clerk told me when I paid my two dollars. "Parents are still recuperating from the weekend. Wednesdays are another story. You'd have to sign up a week ahead of time for Wednesday."

The computer room was in the corner of the children's department, with a small glass window and a cooling system that obviously needed work. The air in the room was freezing. There were four computers, but only one was occupied. The young girl and her mother were using Print Shop to make invitations for her upcoming birthday party.

I switched on the old IBM, pulled out the stack of disks, and stuck the first one in.

My prayers were answered when I saw that one of the software programs matched Nora's. I opened the first file and scanned the table of contents. It was a list of stories based on African animals and folklore. I opened each file and read the first few lines to make sure that's really what the file contained, then opened the next file. When I finished one disk, I popped it out and opened another one. It was a tedious search. Nora had accumulated a vast library of stories and storytelling reference materials, and she was a meticulous recorder. I finished scanning the twenty-third disk and leaned back in my chair, rubbing my neck, almost ready to toss in the towel and take these to Gabe. Let his detectives perform this excruciatingly boring work.

Number twenty-seven changed my mind.

# 15

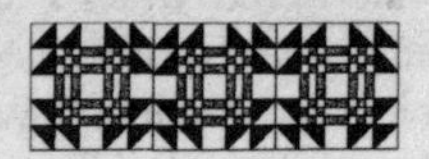

IT WAS NORA'S last column. The one that should have run this week instead of the one about me and Gabe. And would have if she hadn't been killed.

I scanned down the page looking for a clue as to who might have killed her. As with all the other Tattler columns, she didn't name names, but there were a few people I didn't have trouble picking out. She hinted at a deadly secret in the past of a storyteller known for her animal tales with a touch of Tabasco: "Believe me, this storyteller's secret will give y'all more bang than a sawed-off shotgun," Nora had written. I flinched inwardly at her cruel remark. Nobody who knew Evangeline would miss that one.

Nora also wrote about the financial background of another storyteller who was "mired so deep in Mississippi mud it'd take a semi to pull them out." I knew that was Ash, and so would anyone else with half a brain. Then she wrote about a library employee involved with the storytelling festival who had quite an exciting story involving lust, revenge, and murder. That maybe it was time the tale was told. She was deliberately obtuse with this one. A library employee? The three employees affiliated with the storytelling festival were Dolores, Jillian, and Nick. What secrets could each of them be hiding? Lust, revenge, murder? Certainly secrets many people had killed for. But I couldn't imagine her deliberately revealing something that could hurt her brother. They'd always been so close, but Nora, even according to Nick, had changed after her son's accident. And then there was the disagreement they had over the land she inherited, that last argument in the library—

I rubbed my temples. Three library employees. A body that would have been literally deadweight. I couldn't see how either Jillian or Dolores could physically manage to move the body out to a car and down to the lake. That left Nick. No, I protested mentally. No way. Not Nick.

The only thing to do was give Gabe the disk and let him and his investigators decide what to do. Maybe information on it would correspond with something said in one of their suspect interviews.

I started closing the program when a voice behind me said, "All through now?"

I jumped at the sound of Jillian's voice and fumbled for the off switch on the computer. "Uh, sure—" I stammered. "Just doing some research for Dove. Historical Society stuff." I looked down, cursing my expressive face.

"Well, the library's been closed for half an hour. I was making the last rounds and saw you in here."

I looked through the small window of the computer room. The library was completely dark. Apparently the children's librarians had forgotten I was in here. I looked back at her, realizing something else. Something I hadn't noticed when I sat down. The screen of the computer I'd been using was visible to anyone standing at the window. Anything on it was completely readable to someone with halfway decent eyes.

Anything.

The palm-sized handgun Jillian pulled from the pocket

of her Armani suit was as elegant as she was. At least I'd die with class.

"You really never know when to stop, do you, Benni?" she asked.

"You?" I said. "But why?"

"You know why," she snapped.

I started to protest, then stopped. Though I can be very stupid sometimes, I wasn't stupid enough to argue with a crazy woman pointing a gun at me. Especially when she'd obviously killed once already. She must think that I'd found something that incriminated her on the disks. That means she couldn't have read them from the window.

"Walk ahead of me," she said, gesturing with the gun. I contemplated one of those quick, clever moves you see on TV—karate-chopping her hand, then kicking the gun across the floor. Then I pictured it failing and imagined what a bullet tearing into the soft skin of my stomach would feel like. Better rethink that plan.

As I walked past her into the dark library I thought, *Use what's around you to your advantage.*

The next thing I knew a trainload of firecrackers went off in my head, and everything went black.

It was still black when I regained consciousness. Black and dusty and cold. The floor I was curled up on was concrete. A generator vibrated the air around me. My hands and feet were tied, and my head throbbed like an abscessed tooth.

I tried to struggle loose, but whoever had trussed me up knew something about knots. I had no idea how long I'd been out, but my extremities were already numb. Lying there on the icy floor, I worried about permanent damage. A hysterical laugh fluttered deep in my chest. Permanent damage? The woman had already killed once. Damage to the nerves of my feet and hands was the least of my worries.

I lay my head back down on the concrete and tried to assess my situation. *Keep calm,* I said, feeling an uncontrollable trembling start. I blinked my eyes over and over, trying to force them to adjust to the darkness. My skull felt as fragile as an egg, and I would have given anything at that moment for a handful of aspirin and a soft pillow. *Think,* I commanded my brain. *Where could you be that would be this dark and cold?* But my brain wouldn't function, and all I could do was swallow the sob starting in my chest. *Please, God,* I begged. That's all I could think to pray. *Please, God.*

I drifted in and out of consciousness, so it seemed like hours later when I heard a door open and the click of footsteps coming down stairs. A single fluorescent light came on, and I looked up into Jillian's face. Then I realized where I was. The library's basement. Used to store bulk office supplies, old weeded books waiting for the Friends of the Library's yearly sale, holiday decorations, and custodial supplies, it was a standing joke among the employees.

"Going down in the Pit," I'd heard them say to each other. "Send the search and rescue if I'm not back in an hour." Was this where she killed Nora and hid her body until taking it over to the lake? It would have been the perfect place. My stomach churned. Were the ropes I was bound with the ones used to strangle Nora? I closed my eyes and contemplated whether screaming would help.

"She's awake now," she said. Even in the fuzziness of my confused brain, I wondered about her pronoun. Who was she talking to?

"What are we going to do?" a woman's voice answered her. "*Madre de Dios,* what are we going to do?"

"Dolores, would you shut up," Jillian snapped. "I need to think."

I opened my eyes and looked up into Dolores's frightened face. Jillian and Dolores? They were in this together? Boy, was Gabe going to be surprised. A wave of pain zigzagged through my head. Unfortunately I wasn't going to be around to see it.

"Sit up," Jillian said, reaching over and pulling me up by the upper arm. I leaned against some pasteboard boxes and finally found my voice.

"You two killed Nora?" I stuttered, my words tangling around a tongue that felt thick, like someone had shot it full of novocaine. "Why?"

"You know why," Jillian said. "I had a feeling you found the missing Tattler columns. Where did you find them?"

"The Datebook Bum," I said. "I think he found them in the library trash . . . but they don't incriminate you. Not really."

"They say enough," she snapped. "Enough to get me"—her eyes trailed over to Dolores—"*us,* questioned again, and I can't afford to let that happen."

Dolores's dark eyes looked as wild and frightened as a trapped animal's. I realized what Jillian was worried about now. If the police questioned Dolores again, there was a good chance that this time they could probably break her down.

Through the basement's open door I heard a buzzer. Apparently someone was at the employees' back entrance upstairs.

Jillian frowned, then turned to Dolores and said, "Watch her." She walked up the stairs and pulled the heavy door behind her.

I opened my eyes and stared at Dolores. She stared back, rubbing her hands over and over. High-school Shakespeare flashed through my mind. A picture of Lady Macbeth trying to rub the imaginary blood from her hands.

"Dolores, how did you get involved with this?" I whispered.

"I can't talk to you," she said, her face lightly sheened with perspiration.

*Think about how you can use her. Remember the things you've seen on TV. Go for the weaker partner. She's alone and frightened. Use that. It's what Gabe would do.*

Gabe. I couldn't let these people kill me. He'd never forgive himself. The guilt would eat him alive.

Guilt. My disoriented brain floated back to a good-natured argument he and I had recently had about that subject. I pictured his smiling face.

"Catholic guilt is worse," he'd declared while scrambling us some eggs a few weeks ago. Except for his wonderful Mexican hot chocolate and spaghetti, they were the only thing he knew how to cook.

"Ha!" I'd said. "That's because you've never felt Baptist guilt. You all at least get to have fun and then go to confession afterward. We feel guilty the whole time we're sinning." I watched him put jalapeño peppers, fresh onions, cheddar cheese, and a dash of Tabasco in the eggs.

"But we have to worry about dying before we get to confession. Most of you Protestants believe that once saved, always saved, no matter what you do afterwards. You can die in the middle of adultery and still squeeze through those pearly gates."

I laughed and stuck my fork into the finished eggs. "That may be technically true, but I'm sure it's not something that Mac would want touted as a major selling point for the Baptist faith." I took a big bite, savoring the taste. "You know, Friday, if nothing else, I would have married you for your *huevos*."

"Is that right?" He grinned at my unintended double entendre.

I smacked him in the chest. "You know what I mean."

"Well, I can tell you one thing about guilt, whether it's Baptist, Catholic or whatever. Except for the sickest sociopaths, everyone feels it at some time. And I've often even wondered about them. There's no doubt, though, that without it we'd definitely have a lot fewer criminals behind bars."

I opened my eyes and looked at Dolores's agitated face. She'd come out of the confessional just after Gabe went in. Had she confessed to her part in concealing Nora's murder? If she had, that meant she probably felt guilty about it. I could use that. Right now it was the only weapon I had.

"I saw you at St. Celine's today," I said softly.

She widened her dark eyes and didn't speak.

"What happened?" I asked again. "How did you get mixed up with this?"

I didn't think she'd answer, but after a few seconds she started talking in a low monotone.

"I didn't want to help her. I just happened to be there that night. I was coming downstairs to get some construction paper. She didn't know I was here."

"Jillian?"

She nodded.

"She killed Nora," I prompted, wanting to keep her talking.

Dolores nodded again.

"But why?"

"Her husband," Dolores whispered, then glanced furtively up the concrete stairs. We could hear low voices from behind the closed doors. I contemplated screaming, but I remembered the pistol. Where did Jillian hide it? I couldn't imagine her talking casually to a library employee while brandishing a handgun. And I didn't want to put anyone else in danger.

I shook my head slightly, trying to get it to stop feeling so fuzzy. It only made it worse. "Because of Roy?"

"No." Dolores shook her head furiously. "Not Nora's husband. Jillian's. She poisoned him 'cause he cheated on her all the time. He's buried under the patio off her office. Before they poured it."

"The patio?" I repeated. This was getting more bizarre by the moment. I flashed back to the party she'd given when the patio and patrons' garden were finished. Jillian had been drinking champagne and eating shrimp puffs while standing on her husband's grave.

Dolores nodded dumbly. "I heard Nora tell Jillian that she'd found out and that she was going to print it in the Tattler column. They started fighting, and somehow Jillian got a rope that we'd used in a ranching display and choked Nora. I saw it all from the stairs. I was too scared to move or do anything. I thought they'd stop. I didn't think anyone would get killed."

"Why didn't you go to the police?"

Tears streamed down her face. "Jillian took me to her office and kept talking to me. I was crying so hard I couldn't breathe. She kept saying that Nora deserved it, that she was an evil woman. And she said that Nora was going to write things about my parents' restaurant that would close it down—about how we buy black-market beef and how my oldest brother, Felipe, was dealing cocaine to keep the restaurant going. I don't know how she found out about that stuff. My parents didn't even know. My father was still getting over his kidney operation, and there was no money and—" She broke down and started sobbing. "Benni, she said if I helped her she'd make sure that my family was taken care of, and she kept her promise. I didn't kill Nora. All I did was help take her to the lake."

*Guilt,* a little voice reminded me. *You don't have much time. Think.* "Dolores, you can't help her kill me. That would be . . ." I thought hard for a moment, trying to remember what little Catholic doctrine I knew—venial sin? No, that was for the ones that weren't so bad. The ones you could be forgiven for. Death—mortality—mortal. That was it. "A mortal sin," I finished. "You'll go to hell. Murder is a mortal sin."

She looked up, her tears halted, her black eyes wide with shock. "No . . . I . . ."

"Yes," I insisted. "Helping her after she killed Nora was one thing. But you know God could never, ever forgive you helping her kill someone else. You *know* that."

*Lord,* I prayed, *I don't believe that's true, and forgive me for messing with Your theology, but I'm in real trouble here.*

"You'll be a murderer. You'll go to hell," I repeated, and hoped that the Catholic guilt that Gabe and I talked about would kick in.

"No," she moaned. "I'm not a murderer. I'm *not.*" She started praying softly in Spanish—*Santa Maria, Llena de gracia. . . .*

"You're not yet," I said. "Please help me, Dolores. Don't let Jillian make you be a murderer."

She opened her eyes. "What should I do?"

"I don't know yet, but I have to know I can count on you. If I tell you to do something, then do it, no questions. Can you manage that?"

"Yes," she said, her voice determined. "I can do that."

The door to the basement opened, and in the dim light Jillian started down the stairs. I concentrated on trying to think of a way to get the ropes untied.

"What do you think we should do?" Jillian asked. "Her being the police chief's wife makes it more difficult—"

I peered up at her through the pale light. Was she asking

me? I couldn't believe she'd be consulting Dolores; it was obvious Jillian was the ringleader here.

"Get rid of her," a man said bluntly, and my heart jumped into my throat.

"Ash?" I stammered, shaking my head. This all had to be a bad dream. Three of them? Geez, it was like one of those tiny Volkswagens at the circus where clowns keep tumbling out. Would the whole storytelling committee be showing up eventually? Would they have to take a vote on how to get rid of me? I felt a hysterical giggle rumble in my chest. Then my hopes plummeted. Me and Dolores against Jillian was one thing. Ash in the picture made my prognosis look very grim.

"Just makes it more of a challenge, darlin'," Ash answered Jillian. "We'll put our clever heads together and think of something."

"You were in on Nora's murder, too?" I asked. "Why?"

"I imagine you can guess," he said. "She knew a little too much about my background and was a little too willing to use it. I didn't kill her, but I'd gladly have held one end of the rope."

I glanced over at Jillian. "How did he find out about . . . what you did?"

She shrugged. "I accidentally told him one night after we'd drank too much. No big deal. I'm worth more to him out of prison than in."

He gave me a cocky grin. "And the side benefits aren't bad either. Breaking the law and getting away with it can be quite the aphrodisiac."

No wonder Gabe and his detectives had a hard time figuring this one out. It seemed too fantastic that three of the suspects would be in on it together and that one of them hadn't broken under questioning. Then again, I thought about what Gabe said last night—that he was close to charging someone. Which one? That certainly seemed irrelevant to me right now. There was one last puzzle piece, though. If I was going to die, I wanted to know the whole story.

"How did Nora find out?" I asked Jillian. I couldn't imagine her murdering her philandering husband being something she would casually talk about over drinks.

Her carmine-red mouth pulled back in an irritated scowl. "It's so ridiculous I hate admitting it. Then again, you'll never tell anyone, will you? Plain and simple, she saw me. Apparently she liked wandering Central Park late at night. I'd timed it so that I'd avoid the regular police patrol, but I didn't count on our little Nora skulking through the woods that late at night like a crazy woman. She didn't even tell me at first. I guess knowing people's secrets made her feel powerful. She told me she was just waiting for the right time and she decided the storyteller festival was it. Now, enough of this. We have to get this taken care of so I can go home. I'm exhausted."

I glanced over at Dolores. Her face was frozen in fear. *Please,* I communicated to her mentally, *don't let me down.*

"Untie her legs, Dolores," Ash said. "I'm not carrying her deadweight up those stairs. I pulled my back out playing squash last week and I don't plan on aggravating it more."

Dolores stooped down and undid my legs. An idea started to form. "Go ahead of me," I whispered. She gave an almost imperceptible nod.

"Quit talking," Jillian snapped. "Now get up."

I struggled up, my knees popping, barely able to stand because of the numbness in my feet. "I don't know if I can make it up the stairs," I said.

"Shut up and start walking," Ash said.

Dolores scooted ahead of me. "I have to use the bathroom," she said. "I'm going to be sick."

*Good going,* I thought.

I saw Ash give Jillian a significant glance that told me

something I had guessed in the last few minutes. Dolores wasn't going to come out of this alive either. I would bet they'd try to make it look like she had killed Nora, then me, and then committed suicide. It was a plot straight out of a soap opera. And it was corny enough to work. I hoped Dolores realized it was her life she was fighting for, too.

Ash pushed me ahead of him, and Jillian followed behind us, still holding the gun. My opportunity came when I reached the top step. I dragged my toe across the top of the step and purposely stumbled. Ash grabbed my upper arm, squeezing it painfully. "Watch it," he snapped.

"Sorry," I said, catching onto the wall with my bound hands. "Numb feet."

Then, taking a deep breath, I turned and with the flat of my foot shoved him in the crotch. Thrown off balance, he yelped in surprise and, arms flailing, fell backward against Jillian. Her scream merged with his as they tumbled down the long, concrete stairs. I reached over, flipped off the light, and slammed the basement door shut.

"What should I do?" Dolores cried.

"Does this door lock?"

"Only from the inside."

I glanced quickly around and spotted a tall file cabinet next to the door.

"Help me," I told her. We rocked the full cabinet until it fell in front of the door. It would keep them down there temporarily anyway.

"What now?" she asked.

I pointed to the bright red fire alarm on the wall. "Pull it," I said. After she did, I said with a deep sigh, "Now we go outside and wait."

With her helping me, we stumbled our way around to the front of the building. By the time we got to the front of the library, and she had managed to untie my wrists, the first fire truck arrived. The siren cut through my aching head like a freshly sharpened knife, but it was the sweetest sound I'd ever heard.

"What's going on?" a firefighter, looking about the age of Sam, asked as he jumped off the truck. A nonsensical thought passed through the smoke rapidly clouding my head. Why are firemen always so darn good-looking? Is it, like, a rule or something? In the background, a police siren screamed, and I felt an overwhelming sense of gratitude and relief. I looked up into the endless universe and whispered, "Thanks."

"Tell him," I said to Dolores.

Then I passed out.

# 16

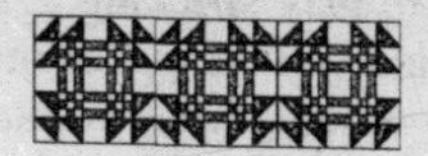

"YOUR WIFE MAY experience some memory loss, Chief Ortiz," the doctor said, studying my chart. He had spiky black hair and wore ostrich cowboy boots. "Dizziness, nausea, headache, confusion. What she's got is a plain old concussion, if a concussion can be called plain. It appears pretty minor, but she'll need to rest a bit. And someone should keep an eye on her for the next few weeks, for any lingering symptoms."

"No problem," Gabe said. "I'm going to handcuff her to our bed."

The doctor looked over his round steel-colored glasses and smiled. "Lucky for you I'm not a gossip. The Tattler would probably pay me a mint for that little gem."

Gabe and I looked at each other soberly. The doctor had no idea how ironic his statement was.

"Did you call Dove?" I asked when we were alone. I struggled up in the hard hospital bed. My head spun with vertigo, and I carefully eased back against the pillows.

"Yes," Gabe said, sitting on the edge of the bed. "Lie still. You heard the doctor. You need to stay quiet."

"What did she say? She's going to kill me."

"She was ready to come down and storm the barricades, but we talked her out of it. Told her you were fine and that I'd bring you home tomorrow."

"We?"

"Me, Ben, and Garnet."

"Aunt Garnet? Are they speaking again?"

He brushed a strand of hair out of my black eye. "Apparently the library wasn't the only place that saw some action tonight."

I gave a weak laugh. "Who gave in first?"

"According to Dove, it was a mutual decision brought about, believe it or not, by your infamous cousin Skeeter."

"Skeeter's here?"

"He showed up on our doorstep earlier this evening, lovesick as an old hound. Dove's words. He was telling her his side of the story when Rita sashayed in and started getting ready for a date with Ash. She made certain Skeeter knew exactly who she was putting the leather miniskirt on for and why. To make an extremely long story short, Skeeter threatened to find Ash and relieve him of some of his more important personal body parts, and Rita naturally protested. Actually what Dove said was she pitched a hissy fit. Then Rita locked herself in our guest bedroom and threatened to kill herself by eating a box of Dexatrim."

I gave him a doubtful look. "Is that possible?"

He scratched his dark cheek stubble and grinned. "I have no idea, but it scared Dove enough to call Garnet and tell her to get over there and talk some sense into *her* loony granddaughter. Oh, and just a warning. Dove's a bit upset at you."

"I wasn't even there!"

"She apparently really rubbed Garnet's nose in the fact that all the nutty genes had leached down the family stream into *her* granddaughter's pool. That was before she heard what crazy thing you were doing at the time."

"Don't you dare compare me to Rita. What she did was crazy, what I did was—"

"Crazy," he finished. "Irresponsible. Impetuous. Immature." He paused.

"You can stop there," I said, slapping his hand. "Before I get mad."

He raised his eyebrows. "We won't talk mad until your concussion is completely healed. Anyway, to continue with the story, Ben drove Garnet down from the ranch, and they all eventually talked Rita out of the bedroom. By this time I'd called Dove to tell her about you. I told her to tell Skeeter that Ash wasn't going to be a problem for a very long time."

"What about Dove and Garnet?"

"Ben says the whole Bible verse/domino incident appears to have run its course. They were talking a mile a minute about how irresponsible young people are today, how we don't know what we want, how all we think about is having a good time. They were packing up Dove's things as they talked."

"Hallelujah," I said. "But what about Uncle W.W.?"

"That problem hasn't been resolved yet, but with Dove and Garnet playing on the same team now, I'd safely bet that poor man doesn't have a snowball's chance."

"I'd say you called that one right, Friday." I gave him a big smile. "That means we're two down, one to go."

"Make that three down," Sam said from the doorway of the hospital room. He was followed by Dove, Garnet, and Daddy. I should have known she wouldn't be able to sleep until she saw me with her own two eyes. We went through the obligatory hugs, exclamations, and explanations before I could ask Sam what he meant.

"He means he's found somewhere else to crash," Dove said.

"Oh, for heaven's sake, Dove," Garnet said, her thin lips pursed in disapproval. Her short, bubble-teased hair was tinted the same Band-Aid beige as her prim linen dress. A matching handbag hung off her milky arm. "Must you insist on talking like a hooligan?"

Dove's blue eyes gave a vexed roll. "Hooligan? Sister,

no one's used that word for fifty years. Get with it and watch a little MTV."

"I will not!" Garnet said, pulling her leather purse closer to her body, her eyes blinking rapidly. "Dove Ramsey, I swear California's turned you into a heathen." I looked at Gabe in dismay. The reconciliation between Garnet and Uncle W.W. better happen soon, or we'd all be back at square one.

"So where are you staying?" I asked Sam.

"With my new gramma," he said, slipping an arm around Dove. "Out at the ranch." Dove's face glowed with a loving but devious expression. I almost laughed out loud. Sam had no idea what his future held.

"I'm letting him stay in the bunkhouse," she said. "It's empty now that all our hands are day workers. We're going to be castrating and tagging next month. We'll see if we can teach this young man a thing or two."

"I'm keeping my job in town, though, or I'll find another one if Eudora's closes down," he said, still looking at me and avoiding his father's eyes. "I might even sign up at Cal Poly next semester."

Dove beamed. "We'll make a rancher out of this boy yet."

I glanced at Gabe. His expression was as emotionless as a brick wall.

"It's so cool," Sam said. "The bunkhouse has a TV and stereo and six beds. I could sleep in a different one every night."

"Not with me doing the laundry you won't," Dove said.

"What happened to Rita and Skeeter?" I couldn't resist asking.

Dove cackled. Garnet set her lips in a straight line. Daddy just looked bemused as he did most of the time when Dove and Garnet were together.

"They're down at the Best Western motel," Dove said

with a big wink. "Gonna work on their problems, Skeeter said."

I laughed. "Yeah, and they might eventually talk, too."

A nurse walked in and clapped her hands sharply as if we were a bunch of rowdy children. "Except for Chief Ortiz, you'll all have to leave. It's late, and Ms. Harper needs her rest."

Dove shook a finger at me, her face stern. "I'll save my lecture for when you're feeling better, missy. You could've been killed. Why, I still get chicken skin just thinking about it. You'd best be thanking the Good Lord tonight before you go to sleep."

"Believe me, I already have," I said.

She leaned close and gave me one last hug. "Don't you be worrying about Constance now," she whispered.

I looked at her, tears stinging my eyes. How did she always know exactly what I was thinking? "I'm sorry it had to be Jillian. I'd give anything for it not to have been."

"I know, honeybun. No one could have ever known Jillian was such a troubled girl. It's not your fault. Constance knows that, and if she doesn't, I'll tell her. She's not going to blame you." Dove and Constance were old friends. If anyone could talk to her, it would be Dove. "Constance is a bit snooty at times, but I've never known her to refuse to look truth in the face."

"It must be very hard for her right now."

"Jillian will have the best lawyers, no doubt about that. All we can do for her and Constance and the Ayalas at this point is pray for them." She patted my cheek, her wrinkled face sad.

They hadn't been gone more than a minute when the phone rang. Gabe picked it up and, after hearing who it was, handed it to me.

"Hey, kid," Nick said. "Heard you had a rough night." In the background, I heard a burst of laughter, the tinny sound of a jukebox, and the clack of pool balls.

"How'd you hear so fast?"

"First Peter called me. Then Evangeline called and then five other people. I finally left because I couldn't stand talking about it anymore. I'm down in Pismo at Harry's Bar. I'll feel more like dealing with it tomorrow. I'll have to, I guess. It'll be in all the papers. How are you feeling?"

"Well, as Dove would say, I'm still suckin' air. My head feels like a cracked walnut, but they say I'll be okay."

"Really?"

"I'll get there." I paused for a moment. "You will, too, Nick. It'll just take time."

"I just can't believe it," he said. "Jillian, of all people. I thought we were friends. And Ash and Dolores. And that part about burying her husband under the library's patio. The next thing you know, they'll be making a movie-of-the-week about it. This sounds crazy, but I feel responsible, like I should have seen it, somehow saved Nora."

"There's no way you could have, Nick," I said. We listened to the static on the phone for a few seconds.

"I'm leaving San Celina," he said abruptly.

"I can understand why. What about the land?"

"Maybe I'll sell it, maybe I won't. Right now I just want to go somewhere quiet and think about it. The lawyers say I've got a month or so to make the decision, so I'm going to take it. Maybe there's a way I can figure out a compromise. Just sell part of it or something."

"Giving the decision some time is a good idea," I said.

I heard him take a deep breath. "Benni, I'm sorry you got hurt and that in a roundabout way, Nora caused it. Please understand, she wasn't an evil person, just hurt. Just real, real hurt."

I didn't know what to say. There was so much I didn't understand about how people handled the pain in their lives, how some, like Nora and Jillian, wanted to hurt others as they'd been hurt, and some, like Evangeline, took their hurt and became someone who wanted to help others. All

I knew was I never wanted to be like Nora or Jillian.

"Are you going to be able to get home all right?" I asked.

"Don't worry, Peter came with me. He'll make sure I get home in one piece."

"Call me if you need to talk. Promise?"

"Sure," he said, and hung up.

"What's going to happen to Dolores?" I asked Gabe.

"She's an accessory, but if she'll agree to testify against Jillian, they'll probably make a deal with her for less prison time. Ash's case is a little more complicated. He's an accessory, too, but he didn't actually see Jillian commit the crime. This is the part where the attorneys take over. We suspected Ash and Evangeline from the beginning simply because of their backgrounds. But Jillian? That came out of the blue." He shook his head and stared at the wall behind me. I knew he'd think about this one for a long time—try to go back and piece together where they'd missed the boat. I knew, as he did, that there was nothing anyone could have done until Jillian showed herself. He and his investigators did their best—sometimes that's all there is to say.

"It's all so sad," I said, pulling my thin hospital blanket closer. "Gabe, I need to tell you something. I found out about Evangeline and Ash's background on Sunday. I was going to tell you, I swear. But then we fought, and the next day—" I stopped, not wanting him to know I followed him to St. Celine's.

He sat on the edge of my bed, his face sober. "*Querida,* when you're feeling better we've got some things we need to discuss. Things like boundaries."

"I agree."

"Boundaries in my work you shouldn't cross over."

"And boundaries in your life you need to stretch a little."

He sighed. "We're going to be fighting about this on our fiftieth wedding anniversary, aren't we?"

I smiled and took his hand in mine. "If we're lucky."

We stared at each other for a moment. He spoke first, studying my hand as he talked. "When the dispatcher called me and told me what had happened to you, I called myself every name in the book. I'm sorry for what happened the other night between us. I never wanted you to see that side of me."

"What night?" I interrupted. "I have no idea what you're talking about. The doctor *did* say there was going to be some memory loss—" I brought his hand to my cheek. "All I remember is that I love you, Friday, and that your wonderful Catholic guilt is the reason I'm still alive."

"What?" he said, confused.

"I'll explain later."

"How's your head?" he asked.

"It only hurts if I turn it too fast."

"They're going to be waking you every hour for the next twelve hours, but while you're sleeping you can relax. I'm going to be right here."

"That sure brings back old memories. A hospital bed was the first time we technically slept together. Remember?"

"Believe me, I remember." He gave me a lingering kiss, slipping a hand underneath the covers and caressing me through my thin hospital gown. "Well, woman, now that we're finally going to be living *alone* again, I will actually get to make love to you without my hand over your mouth."

"Like you're so quiet." Laughing, I wiggled away from his hand. "Watch it, Chief. I still have a concussion."

"My hand isn't anywhere near your head," he murmured, bending to kiss me again. We were interrupted by the loud sound of a clearing throat. Gabe's hand flew out from under the covers.

"Sorry to disturb your *rest,*" Sam said, grinning at his father's red face. His hair and clothes were dark with water.

"Is it raining?" I asked.

"Yeah, just started," he said. "I wanted to give you these before driving out to the ranch." He unzipped his damp sweatshirt and pulled out a white bundle and a long envelope. He handed me the envelope. "It's only half what I owe you. I'll pay the rest back on my next payday." He glanced at Gabe, who had walked over to the window, his back to us.

"Sam," I said, "I told you that money was a gift."

"Thanks, but I'm paying it back." His voice held a familiar trace of Ortiz stubbornness I knew better than to argue with. At least when I was feeling this weak, anyway.

"Hey, Dad, this is for you." Gabe turned around, and Sam tossed the white bundle at him. "Saw it a couple of days ago and thought you might get a kick out of it." His light tone contradicted the tense set of his shoulders.

Gabe unfolded the white T-shirt and held it up. Sam and I watched his face as he read the shirt's message. Slowly, like the sun peeking out from behind black storm clouds, he smiled. Sam let out a relieved breath.

"What does it say?" I asked.

Gabe turned the shirt around for me to read.

In jagged bright letters, underneath a bearded old man leaning against a long surfboard, the No Fear brand T-shirt said, THE OLDER I GET, THE BETTER I WAS."

I laughed. "Boy, he sure has your number."

Gabe smiled at Sam. "He always did."

Sam zipped up his sweatshirt and said, "Dad, about what I said the other night—"

"Forget it," Gabe said, looking first at me, then back at Sam. "We all do things we regret sometimes. Believe me, it wasn't any worse than some of the things I said to my dad."

"Then you must have been a real jerk," Sam said.

Gabe gave a low chuckle. "Yes, I guess I was."

"I'll leave you two old folks alone now. I gotta get out to the ranch."

"One more thing, son," Gabe said.

Sam's face grew instantly wary. "What?"

Gabe cleared his throat. "Since you're going to be staying around San Celina, I was thinking . . . well, maybe sometime I could buy you dinner. When you're not working. If you have time." He watched his son with unblinking eyes, the muscle in his jaw fluttering like a captured moth.

Sam fiddled with his gold stud earring. "That sounds great. I'll call you when I get settled, but the first dinner's on me, okay?"

Gabe nodded, his face solemn. "I'll make sure and skip lunch that day so I'll be good and hungry."

Sam looked over at me, jerking his thumb at Gabe. "A joke. The man actually made a joke. You'd better take care of yourself, *madrastra*. Otherwise, I'm going to be stuck with the old fart here. And I don't think he or I would survive that for long."

"It's a deal," I said.

After Sam left, Gabe went over to the window and stared down into the brightly lit parking lot. I carefully climbed out of bed and slipped on the heavy cotton robe Dove had brought me. From the second-story room we watched Sam step into my Chevy pickup, fiddle with the radio, and drive away. The rain was coming down heavy now, causing a golden mist to swirl around the parking-lot lights.

"He's a good kid," Gabe finally said.

"Yes, though not much of a kid anymore."

Gabe gave a half smile. The tightness around his eyes that had been there since Aaron died seemed to soften. "I guess he isn't. You know, Aaron always told me Sam was going to turn out okay. Even when he was so irritating I'd have gladly paid someone a thousand dollars to take him off my hands, Aaron assured me that he would turn out fine. He said he could tell by the way Sam looked at me when I wasn't watching."

I laid my hand on Gabe's arm. "Aaron was a wise man."

Gabe swallowed hard and nodded. A minute passed. I stroked his forearm, the hair like fine wire under my hand. He cleared his throat, choking slightly as he did. "I miss him," he said.

"I know." I slipped my arm through his and rested my head against his shoulder. I could feel his body give a small tremble. We continued to stare out the dark window, listening to the hissing of the wind. The rain flowed down the glass in tiny light-filled rivers, and in the blurry reflection, if you squinted just slightly, it almost appeared as if we were crying.

20x